CW01648649

THE DEVIL'S BAIRN

Meg Woodward

Copyright © 2023 Meg Woodward

All rights reserved. No part of this publication may be reproduced or transmitted in any form or by any means, electronic or mechanical including photocopying recording or any information storage or retrieval systems, without prior permission in writing from the publisher.

ISBN 978-1-9997592-1-6

Published by Tulloch Books

Contents

A Riddle:-

Nine mills were built on the River Lossie as it flowed past the mediaeval royal burgh of Elgin. One belonged to the Valliscaulian monks at Pluscarden Priory and by royal decree they were allowed to build it on the east bank because of the way the current flowed. The river marked the boundary between Priory land on the west and Elgin Town Lands on the east, so this mill stood on the town's land although it belonged to the monks. To complicate matters the monks hired a miller who was a bondsman of the Bishop. When the tithes and taxes were collected as usual at New Year (25th March) - who would get the money?

It is this conundrum which provides the grit for this story.

Chapter 1 - The Call of the Cuckoo

A young merchant was piddling on the Priory pear trees when his fate caught up with him. Above him on the hill which sent the monks to bed early in its shadow, trees were drowning in a thousand greens. On this last Wednesday in May, the air was heavy with the sickly scent of hawthorn and Will Forbys grinned to himself as he remembered his first visit to the orchard the previous Sunday afternoon.

'We waste nothing here.' Brother Justin had been nudged by the Prior into escorting the guest outside. The young lay novitiate was not bound by the vow of silence. If they had an interdict against folly, he appeared unbound by that too, although at first his face had remained bone straight while he watched for the shock which would surely greet the indecent hitching up of his heavy white habit. Only when his steaming stream hit the bark did the lad grin, if a little sheepishly, his alert, triangular face lighting up

'We move around according to which part of the garden needs nourishment most. They put pavers down below the fruit tree roots. To stop the goodness seeping away, I suppose.'

A cuckoo had called during that first excursion to the gardens, mocking Will's discomfiture. The gowk was there again now, three frustrating days later, echoing down from the Heldon Hill above Pluscardyn Abbey. By the bee-bole, its slate-coloured mate hovered to snatch at incoming bees, sweet-laden, while leaving the outgoing foragers alone.

Suddenly, in mid-stream once again, Will's laughter froze. A single bright eye was gleaming at him. He had assumed privacy behind the high sandstone wall which divided the orchard from the neat kitchen plots to the east; unusually, the bee-bole had been driven all the way through the stonework and the straw skip jammed into the gap had left a small space at the top corners. The owner of the eye peering through could have been hiding there for some time.

Fighting annoyance, Will had no option but to complete what he was doing but then he strode towards the end of the wall to cut off the voyeur's escape.

Seeing the game was up the brat scrambled out of the berry bushes, making a play at nonchalance. A wide, gleeful mouth dangled from his ears in defiance.

'Yours is bigger than any o' theirs.'

'So'll my thrashing be, ye wee...'

'If ye catch me. They never can,' the child smirked, dancing around to keep himself just out of reach, thinking the merchant's threat was idle. 'They canna run in thay gowns anyway. Are you takin' their glass tae sell in Flanders?'

The frankness of that question set the merchant back on his heels. Before he could reply, the child assumed it was positive and asked another. 'What's yer name?'

'William Forbys. What's yours?'

Again the brat smirked, this time with a sly cock of his head. 'I was born on the feast of St Stephen.'

Will narrowed his eyes. He was being invited to believe that the brat carried his saint's name but the mischief sparkling in the elfin face filled him with misgiving. 'Never mind. I'll ask your faither.'

'You dinna know my faither.' Uncertainty made the words wobble, though the grin remained in place. When

Will let his eyes wander eastwards to the meal mill the little face turned a shade paler.

'I see somebody catches ye noo and then,' Will said dryly, thinking maybe he wouldn't administer the thrashing after all. For an instant he had glimpsed real fear in the child's eyes - but the wicked joy was soon back.

'Ye dinna sound German.'

Will's mouth opened. 'Who said I was German?'

The child shrugged, nodding sideways at the towering buildings whose sandstone walls glowed creamy white in the sunshine. 'Them.'

'Who's them?'

'Them in there.' He nodded again towards the Priory. How the child heard silent monks discussing private business Will had no idea, and said so.

'Och, the gairdeners blether. And them up at the kiln. And they never stop speaking ower in the quarry.' The kiln-house and its adjacent workshops for making both coloured glass and pottery ware stood next to the meal mill which was built by the bridge over the Black Burn. It was there that Will fancied he had seen this wee rascal before, along with another, a sibling by the looks of him. Bonnie bairns they were, very bonnie, if thin and dirty.

The scamp's last comment caused Will sufficient anxiety not to pursue the matter. Evidently much of what went on inside the Priory became everybody's business, but he sincerely hoped that not everything had got out. Thinking to deflect the child, he demanded, 'Does William Forbys sound German to you?'

'No.'

'Well then. You've already said I dinna sound German. Now, get oot o' here and dinna come back. This place is nae for you.'

'They dinna mind really.' The child gave an elaborate shrug, with the faintest touch of appeasement included. 'As long as I dinna go right inside. Sometimes they'll gie me wee jobs and pay me wi' stuff to take home for our denner. I've been weeding, so I'll just wait a whilie longer.' Somehow he managed to keep any triumph hidden beneath the reasonable tone, but Will would roast in hell before believing it wasn't there inside the brat ready to be taken out and gloated over once he was alone. Breathing noisily through his nostrils the merchant turned on his heel and headed for the Chapterhouse. It was time to tell his hosts that he could spare no more time. Let them make up their minds by ten for that was when he intended to leave. His Bethoc had waited long enough for him already.

After announcing his plans to the Prior, he left the monks to finalise their business while he made a last visit to the kiln by the stream. It had produced the stained glass he was to transport to Lille and Brother Michael, the man in charge, had promised him a bag of coloured samples which might tempt more European buyers.

When the two men emerged into the rising heat of the day, their ears picked up a torrent of shrill words floating over the wall from next door. Brother Michael's face grew rigid, for the voice was ringing with emotion - and vocabulary very different from that Will had heard half an hour earlier. The words came from the meal mill, an untidy run-down affair with bags stacked here, there and everywhere awaiting attention, a puzzling situation for late spring.

Observing the monk's pitying disapproval shade into sudden deep anxiety, Will wheeled and headed smartly for the yard. Again the brat from the orchard was dancing in defiance. This time he flitted between the miller and a cowering, terrified younger child on the ground behind him and his shrieking insults were so foul that Will blinked. The considerable skill the lad showed at both evasive movements and swearing showed ample experience at both. This time, however, as well as fury and pain, the shouting must have been prompted by an urgent need to attract attention, for the old man had a flail in his hand and was swinging it crazily at the children. The miller was in a frenzy and the boy was ducking and prancing around to avoid a direct hit. He must have caught the movement of Will's arrival from the corner of his eye for he suddenly cleansed his language, although the volley of fury continued.

It took Will a few seconds to realise that it was the younger child, perhaps eight years old and seemingly incapable of protecting himself, which the miller was trying to strike. The older lad was intervening at considerable personal danger.

'You leave Nicol alone, ye rotten auld sinner! He canna help it. I'll get the monks on ye, I will. I'll tell them ye're a whoremonger. I will! I'll tell them ye've been spying for the Bishop an' all, and they'll believe me! They will!' The miller took another almighty swing with the flail. The leather thong which attached the head to the stock gave a loud crack, but still the lad screamed on. 'I'll tell them ye've been beating Nicol again and they'll have you oot o' here. They tell't ye last time they would and the time afore that. I heard them. And then what'll ye... Ooh-uh!'

The miller finally got in a glancing blow to the side of the lad's head. As he slithered to the ground Will strode forward, drawing his sword and sticking it out to intercept the next enraged swipe. Had it arrived, the flail-head would have driven into the small skull like a hammer into an eggshell, for the blow was coming with the full force of the big man's body behind it.

Only when the stock split in two on the sharp edge of the sword did the miller realise they had company but even that did not bring him to his senses. Beyond all control he raised the stump in his two fists, grasping until the knuckles shone like fleshless bones. With all his might he made to jab at the boy at his feet with the sharp, splintered end. Again Will's sword went into action. Twisting the stock out of the man's grasp he sent it twirling off to one side. Then he brought the point of his blade to the miller's throat. Only when a prick of blood was drawn did the man at last become still. His face swelled, purpling with frustration, and the bleary eyes blinked in time to strange snuffling, jerking breaths.

'Hector, Hector!' At last Brother Michael stepped forward, clutching the miller's upper arm. 'Calm down, Hector! You mustn't let your troubles take you over like this. You know you mustn't. This really isn't good for you.'

Will stared at the monk's unlikely reaction, - and wondered why none of the workmen inside the glass-making shed had come out to help the children. Leaving Michael to steer the slavering miller into the mill and calm him down as best he could, Will bent to attend to the fallen lad, running gentle fingers over the skull where the flail had struck.

'I'm fine,' the boy muttered, struggling to sit up. 'There's been a lot worse than that, I can tell ye.'

'It's a wonder you havena been killed, then. That last blow would have done for you if I hadna stopped it.'

'Na. He'll never do that. He never loses his wits that far.' He seemed very sure, almost casual about it, but Will was not. The child had been on the ground with his eyes shut, possibly even unconscious for a few moments. Perhaps he had not seen the true depth of the miller's rage this time. Will had no doubt that the swingeing blow he had intercepted could indeed have killed, and the second vicious stab might well have done so too. It was not until he had helped the victim to his feet that he gave the younger child his attention. Nicol was quiet now, still sitting on the ground gazing at Will with enormous blue eyes.

Will caught his breath. Under the dirt and smears of tears and snot, Nicol was the most exquisite child Will had ever seen, like a golden angel come to earth. As he gazed, two more details struck Will with chilling force. The eyes, beautiful as they were, held no comprehension whatever of what had just occurred; if Nicol had been afraid two minutes earlier, that fear was now utterly forgotten. And Will's nose confirmed that the child had soiled himself. Was that the result of the fear? Or was it the event which had tipped the miller into his terrible rage? The child seemed unaware of his incontinence too. Will glanced at the brother, who shrugged uncomfortably, as if to acknowledge that Will had picked up the correct signals.

'He canna help it. It's just the way he is. The way he's aye been. But... other folk think he's, well, a Devil's bairn. They say he spells ill for anybody he looks on. They winna come here unless he's out o' sight...' The boy's eyes filled with tears and Will put a hand on his shoulder to stop the stumbling explanations. The folk around here were plainly superstitious. He had to admit that the folk in most villages were fools of much the same stamp, and a good many folk in more sophisticated city or burgh circles as well.

'And you canna explain to Nicol?' he asked sadly.

'The monks are okay,' the lad added. 'Since my grandfaither is fee'd to them he has to obey when they tell him not to beat Nicol. Only, sometimes... If he's had too much to cope wi' and then Nicol does something that undoes it... Och, I don't know why God did this to us!'

To that Will had no answer.

'And be quick, Brother Alexander. Captain Forbys is anxious to be on his way.' The Prior of Pluscardyn returned to the document lying before him. Not large but of the finest, most durable new parchment, it was no more than fourteen inches wide by ten high. The writing covering it from edge to edge was small, elegant, concise in every sense, with around thirty words in each line, and each line following closely after the one before.

On the table a tall candle guttered for a moment in the draught caused by the Cellarer's curt departure from the Chapterhouse. By its light the Prior read the contents once more. The firm hands on his lap were clasped lightly, not quite reminiscent of prayer, and the heavily incised ring glittered blood red. The Prior bowed his head. Minutes passed. Several more were spent in thought, then he raised his dark eyes to look at each of the cowled men standing around him. Each one held his gaze, unmoving, unprotesting.

Only then did the Prior lift the quill, dip it into the heavy glass decanter of ink and sign his name. Thomasus Fullonis, Prior of Pluscardyn. The document was then passed around to be scrutinised and returned to the table where, one by one, the silent Brothers added their names. Lastly, the sole guest stepped from the far side of the Chapterhouse. He did not try to read the paper. He was not required to, probably would not have been allowed to. He merely testified to the other signatures by adding his own, as independent witness to the signing alone. A name, however, leapt out and caught his eye, probably because he recognised it. Robert de Chisholm.

In stark contrast to the clipped tonsures of the severe Valliscaulians around him, Will's hair flopped in a wild silver-blond mop over his brow as he wrote; it merged at the ears with vibrant carrot-coloured whiskers and beard.

Villem Vorbus. Since everybody was watching the pen, none would have seen the flare of the Prior's patrician nostrils. It was the writer who sensed doubt and looked up suddenly.

'The form I use in Danzig,' he explained as he straightened. 'It's best that folk ken it's me. There are too many other Willie Forbyses in Scotland.'

The Prior nodded. It made sense. Let there be no doubt. Then he added the date. 'On the feast of St Brendan, MCCCLXX.' Pulling the candle closer he held a stick of red wax in the flame before folding and sealing the document, stamping it with the monstrous ring on his finger and letting it harden before handing the missive over to the merchant. By the time the Cellarer returned with a package of food and a skin of watered wine, Prior Thomas had risen to escort his guest to the door.

'You are under oath, Captain Forbys,' he murmured when the others had withdrawn out of earshot. 'This must not leave your hands until it reaches His Holiness.'

'But that was not the agreement! I said I would ensure it reached Avignon in the shortest possible time. If I take it myself, the journey will take three times as long as a relay of couriers.'

The Prior looked alarmed. 'No, no! You must go yourself! Otherwise, how can you possibly ensure its security?'

'Trade letters and bills of promise pass all over Europe all the time, Father. Do you think the German merchants or the bankers of the Italian houses would entrust their business secrets to their courier services if they did not believe them to be completely reliable? You said it was imperative that you have the Pope's answer by the feast of St Bartholomew. If I go and return myself, that is simply not possible. No man can ride twenty hours a day for weeks on end.'

His sideways glance confirmed that the Prior realised, if rather late, that a relay of couriers might indeed deliver such speed. He knew, of course, that the couriers Will was suggesting were those committed to the enigmatic Hanseatic League, which demanded as much honesty, commitment, and honour of themselves as they did of others. Unlike his monks who never left the precincts, the Prior was not unworldly, but he still took a deal of persuading that the risk of tampering was low. Will did not know what had been written, but he had become increasingly suspicious during his stay that the content was dangerous. The searing anxiety in the Prior's thin face served to confirm that, sending prickles of apprehension down his spine.

'Very well,' the Prior agreed at last, nostrils flaring and lips pinched tight. 'Against my instincts, I shall accept your assurances. But I shall hold you to account if this lands in the wrong hands.'

Will was turning away when the Prior spoke again, this time with hesitation. 'Captain, on another matter, I - enjoyed our discussion on Sunday afternoon. It is not often that I have the opportunity to talk so freely and, mm, with such exhilarating range and depth. Thank you for permitting me to indulge myself.'

'The pleasure was mine, Father.' Will's answer was spontaneous. Then he grinned. 'The chance might come more often if you talked the other six days of the week! You and the others.' But instantly he saw he had spoken too freely. The Prior was Father of the house, after all, the master, the governor, the disciplinarian and the fount of all orders. His prime task would be to maintain the Rule of the Order, whatever that entailed. Obviously he felt he could do his job only if he held himself apart from those he governed. As he bade farewell Will realised that Prior Thomas was a lonely man, a highly intelligent scholar starved of intellectual stimulation except from his books.

Before he left, Will came across another boy in trouble. Brother James, a year or so younger than Justin, was in charge of the draft animals and had been detailed to look after Will's horse. Almost as tall as Will with shoulders likely to broaden more, he was desperately thin. His arms were skeletal and the structure of his big, open face was almost skull-like. When he brought the horse, beautifully groomed but skittish and eager to get moving, the lad had some difficulty in controlling him. When Will noticed his eyes wander towards the pack of food he was about to put in the saddlebag, his offer of a large chunk of the oaten bread was instinctive.

James looked startled, then guilty, and shook his head. But he looked back at the bread with such longing that Will pushed it into his hand and turned away to finish his packing. He had seen the lad in the refectory during the two meals he had eaten there. On each occasion James had been on his knees before the Prior's table. He had not been given anything to eat on either occasion and Will had assumed he had fed later with the cantor and the cooks, or earlier with the servitors, perhaps. Now he wondered. Deliberately he kept his back turned. From the voracious chewing sounds the lad was gulping down the dry bread, occasionally coughing as it made its way down.

'Take some water, laddie, or you'll choke.' He was taken aback at how his words were taken literally. James dipped a trembling hand into the oxen's water trough by his elbow, scooping up handfuls and slurping greedily.

'You won't tell, will you?'

That made Will swing round, his eyes widening.

'Why should I?'

In the doorway appeared a figure gobbling with rage. 'What do you think you're doing? Who gave you permission to flout the Prior's orders, Captain Forbys?' It was the Cellarer, Brother Alexander.

Will blinked. 'What orders?'

'What's the good of punishing the boy if you come along and undermine his willpower with your surreptitious high-handedness? How will he ever learn to accept the disciplines of this Order if people like you come along and offer temptation every hour of the day?'

Will's first instinct was to defend himself, but knowing he was a guest in this place he managed to stay calm. 'I apologise, Brother Alexander. I was not aware...'

'He was not to eat for three days. You must have seen him on his knees during the repasts. Well, didn't you?'

Biting even harder on his tongue, he nodded. 'I did not know what it meant.' The monk was scowling with a fury that was near to malevolence, or so it seemed. 'What sin has he committed that he should be starved? He is still a growing boy.'

'He's a thief,' the Cellarer snapped, the scorn in his voice making James cringe, near to tears. It hurt Will to see the lad reduced to such humiliation. Hardly Christian, he thought. Brother Alexander ranted on. 'Can you imagine that? A thief. He stole. Stole! In a monastery. I'm sure that's not advocated by your precious St Thomas of Aquinas.' This barb stung, aimed as it was against Will, not the boy. Angry enough to fear making a reply which could spill beyond courtesy, he turned away and busied himself with finishing his packing. Was the man jealous that Prior Thomas had chosen to converse with Will and not one of his own monks? Could that be it?

Stamping alongside the horse, it was the Cellarer who saw him away in stony silence, looking as if he had swallowed one of the Priory bees. He escorted him to the main gate and no farther. Today was not one of the man's days for bringing in supplies; he was the only member of the community allowed to leave the Priory, apart from the Prior himself and, occasionally, the sub-prior. His farewell was another barb.

'Why Father Thomas chose you to deliver his message I can't imagine. If it lands in the wrong hands it will be the end of all of us.' When the gate clanged behind Will and the cuckoo mocked yet again with its clear yodel from the woods, he felt a further icicle of disquiet chill his back. What was he carrying? He should have insisted on some indication. At the very least he should have enquired who it was who should not be afforded an opportunity to see the missive. Against whom should it be protected?

He threw a glance over his shoulder as he rode off, reluctant to admit the strange draw of the place. Others had warned him that the peace of Pluscardyn had a bewitching quality. Had it not drawn the first Valliscaulians all the way from their Burgundian home? Will had scoffed, knowing himself to be a free spirit, eager to travel the open roads and sail the wild oceans. His mind was always open; questioning and reasoning, untrammelled by the superstitions which cluttered the lives of so many of his fellow men. Yet, there was no denying that this beautiful, austere settlement in the Vale of St Andrew was dragging at his spirit, urging him back inside its high, confining walls.

Was it, after all, so unlikely a valley in which to find a crazed miller sheltering his grandchildren, one a forever witless innocent?

Chapter 2 – The Trap

Suspecting that he was being watched, Will turned his horse westwards. A couple of miles on, however, where gorse and thorn trees hugged thickly on a double curve of the road, he veered suddenly, driving his doubtful mount off among the bushes while hidden from travellers before or after him. Turning south he sped up the narrow cutting into the hills. Behind him the valley widened northwards on to the fertile Laich of Murray which lay along the Firth. There, as the Prior knew, Will's fleet lay at anchor in the busy little trading port of Finderyn. Certainly the monks had expected Will to head for there.

Fine, fashionable seamen's boots were not the best gear for fast riding on a hot day, but with his good animal beneath him Will reached his first destination in less than an hour.

'Took your time, didn't ye?' Geordie Buchan clapped his tankard on the board table and wiped his high bald pate with a clout already damp with sweat. His fluffy ginger-grey hair stood out in an unlikely tonsure. 'They think I'm trying to pickle mysel'.' The alehouse hung in a drunken slouch against the ruined wall of Dallas Castle. 'Anither day and I'd have done it.' Will snorted. No man in the entire Baltic had drunk his fleet captain under the table. Besides, while waiting for Will to turn up, Geordie had been visiting his sister Jean, whose husband was the innkeeper here, and Will knew she would have had him working in the fields for his keep. 'And the wind is right. If we're to catch the night's tide we'll hae to move. We've a full cargo then?'

'We have. Three cart loads o' top quality stained glass pieces packed in linen. They set off at dawn.' Will waved for a drink of his own. 'And another five wi' casks of salt salmon. Should be loading right now. Who's in charge?'

'Aonghus the Heilander. Och, I ken he hasn't much Scots in among his Erse, but he's got the best eye for a balanced cargo that ever I came across. He'll hae the wits to pack the Carmelites' wool round the glass. - Man, but the price they're charging! And yon Kinloss Abbey o' theirs is bonnier than Elgin Cathedral itself. Little wonder Bishop Barr is green.'

'Got inside the Abbey, did ye?' Will said sarcastically. 'It's a wonder they let ye oot again, them being a closed order.'

'They let you oot o' Pluscardyn, I see, though it took them lang enough.' Geordie cast a curious glance at the younger man, knowing he would have spent as much time as he could get away with in the Priory's famed library. At twenty three Will had moved smartly on from his boyhood during which, as Geordie's summer pupil aboard ship, he had learned all he could of the craft of seamanship under the master mariner; Willie could sail as well as any captain now, although he was just young enough to escape involvement in the ten year war the Hanseatic cities had been waging with Waldemar of Denmark. One day Geordie expected the lad might even be better than him, given the chance of experience to build up his confidence and knock the knobs off the cocky insecurity of youth. Will was just coming into that realisation himself. Yet an air of unexpected polish hung about him. In spite of the wild disarray in which he left his hair and beard, he moved with a reserved self-control, and he had a courteous way with him which left folk wondering about his background. Not the sea, that was certain.

A ponderous approach to obstacles gave the initial impression of a lack of attention, even a shortage of wits - although that impression did not last for long for those with wits of their own. In fact the slowness was a preference for thinking things through before making his first move. It masked a ferocious intelligence which, if discovered, was then treated with extremely careful respect by everybody - except by Geordie who had skelped him often enough as an adventurous lad. Proximity had long ago doused any awe of the boy who at fourteen had become heir to one of the richest Hansa trading businesses in the Baltic.

For Willie had not been entirely truthful in answering the Priory brat's curiosity. His mother was Dolinda, the only daughter of the late owner of the House of Bromse based in Danzig. If not wholly so, Will was indeed half German. Otherwise he would never have been accepted as a full member of the Danzig City Council, which he was; or as an accredited Hanseatic trader, for which he required German blood and outright ownership of property in a German city belonging to the League; and he had to make sure he spent a sufficient number of days each year living in Danzig, attending council meetings and dealing with city business along with the other burghers, in order to retain his citizenship rights and status.

Now he downed the Dallas heather ale with ill satisfaction. It was nothing like as good as the barley brew the monks had produced but the hot ride had made him thirsty and he called for a refill.

'There was a gowk on the hill the day.' He licked his lips and sucked the froth from his beard. 'And I'm wondering...' Gowk meant more than cuckoo in the local parlance.

Geordie waited a bare half minute. '...if you're the fool and nae the bird?' He sighed. 'So what have ye let us in for? I knew there had to be something or ye'd have been here twa days ago.'

Will thought for a minute longer before standing up and nodding sideways to bring Geordie outside into the sunshine away from long ears. 'O'er here.' He headed for a couple of trees and made to relieve himself, taking a good look around to ensure they were alone. Then he grinned to himself, tickled by the repetition of the orchard act. 'I've taken a missive from the monks,' he murmured, 'to be delivered to the Pope. I've to bring them an answer by St Bartholomew's day.'

'What!' Geordie looked alarmed, but still had the sense to keep his voice down. 'I suppose the Pope's still in Avignon, but even so, it's tight for time. A bare three months, for Guid's sake! Besides, ye've other things tae do, ye daft...'

'Not me personally. I've just to see it gets there and back without anybody, well, knowing it exists. If possible.'

'And ye've been trailed?'

'Not that I've noticed, but I've a notion the Priory is being watched all the time. Maybe even from inside.'

'Who's interested?'

'Yon Bishop o' Murray for one. Nothing was said, but I fancy there's nae love lost between him and the Prior.'

'Why?'

Will shrugged. 'The usual, I suppose. Taxes and revenues that the Bishop thinks he's entitled to and the Prior thinks he's nae.'

'Is there the same ill will at the Carmelites at Kinloss Abbey? I didna get that notion.'

'Ah, but the Carmelites are powerful. Everybody knows they're answerable to their own chapter heads in France as well. Besides, they were the first Abbey to go up hereabouts, and by royal charter before the cathedral was even thought about. Pluscardyn is a royal benefit too, mind, half a dozen kings ago. No, I think the real problem is that the Valiscaulians' are even more reclusive. Their head house is in Burgundy and they've only three places in Scotland. I fancy the Bishop is trying it on because they're so small and weak here.'

'Claiming visiting rights, ye mean? Fetching his taxes by riding in with all his retinue and eating the monks out of house and home until he decides to ride back to Elgin?'

'Or Spynie. That's where the Bishop has his palace.'

'A rich wee borough, that,' Geordie nodded. 'Wi' a harbour. Ye can smell the money. And it's some palace.'

'A fancy pile of stone that. Built for defence. I rode over two days ago from the Priory and it opened my eyes.'

'And Elgin?'

'Aye, I rode through Elgin on the way back. Seems every chaplain has his ain stone manse and all. Seventeen, would ye believe? Aye, there's a lot o' wealth in Murray, and most o' it is sticking to the Bishop's fingers.'

'Well, that's just fine then,' grumbled Geordie, 'for it'll be kept oot o' other hands. Look, I've peed enough so get on wi' your story.' Then he turned to Will, screwing up his top lip as an unwelcome idea struck him. 'So if you're being followed, you'll be wanting me to tak the letter. Is that it? For delivery by sea, you'll be thinking.'

'It's much faster. There are plenty safe, fast, trading ships heading down the German Sea for Bordeaux and then it just needs a courier across Gascony.' Will took his time about tidying himself. Reaching into the high flap of his riding boot, he kept his body between any eyes in the inn and what he produced. 'Shove this out o' sight.' The swift exchange took no more than a second as Geordie stowed the flat package against his heart.

'Or?' This was very dry. Will shrugged.

'Try Aonghus. For all his pagan fancies he's still in awe o' the Church. If you tell him this is for the Pope and has to get to him in a hurry...' He held Geordie's eye for a moment.

'I didna swear I'd use the Hansa riders, just that I'd get it there as fast as possible.'

'And that's by using Black Donald's birlinns,' was Geordie's glum response. 'Given the right weather.'

He knew the geography of the west coast of Europe even better than Will. Given the right weather, the Irish Sea route was faster and much less likely to be plagued by privateers, being under the thumb of the Norse, mostly. But they both knew how fickle Donald of the Isles was, what with his wife's close kinship with the King and his eye on the throne for himself. 'My, ye dinna tak' on one risk at a time. Ye ken there's been trouble atween him and Robert Stewart, I suppose. First thing I heard aboot when we got back from Bergen last month.'

Ah yes. Robert the Steward, Earl of Fife. Nephew to the King of Scotland, although at the age of fifty four he was eight years older. He was also the putative heir to the throne, since David had no legitimate offspring from two wives, nor even rumour of any irregular children.

'Aye, well,' muttered Will. He knew even more of the quarrel than Geordie, for his own father had been in the thick of it at Court. 'It'll be a while yet afore either Donald or Robert gets his eye on any crown. The King's fit and fettlesome and like to be wi' us for mony a year yet. But if you're to catch the tide ye'd better be moving.'

'And you? Ye'll be for Druminnor?' That was Will's family home in Aberdeenshire. 'My respects to your mither. And yer faither, of course,' the seaman added hastily. It was with Dolinda that Geordie did business, not her bluff husband. 'Ye'll be for collecting at Aberdeen as planned, given the lady Bethoc's leave?'

'Provided you've got the message on its way, aye. If not, I'll be obliged to take it back and try another route.'

Geordie ducked inside the inn to bid his farewells while Will, who had noticed some activity inside the old Dallas castle itself, headed for the broken-down gateway.

He entered without hindrance and eventually found a small group of men scowling at the great holes in the walls. They had been smashed by Edward of England's catapults over sixty years earlier. The leader of the group, distinguished by his finer dress, left the others and came to greet Will in court French, a habit invigorated to please Euphemia Ross, Robert Stewart's wise and gentle second wife.

'Well, what do you think, Guillaume? Is it worth rebuilding?' Will knew that George de Leslie had another, less battered stronghold at Rothes and wondered why he needed this one repaired.

'Show me round.' Used to Will's brevity, de Leslie led him all over the castle, right up to the top of the shambolic surviving bastion, explaining all the way how he would do what, and where he would find the materials, the men and the expertise. Not the money, though. The only other question he did not address was the one Will put to him, finally breaking his silence.

'Why?'

'To protect the route from Badenoch through to Elgin and the Laich.'

'Against whom?'

'An attacker.'

'What attacker?'

De Leslie puffed frustrated indignation through his broad nose. 'Any attacker. You never know... It's not that long since there was war here and who knows when it might return. When the king dies, for instance.' Here, at last, he stopped speaking and threw a wary glance over his shoulder at the rest of his party, now kicking their heels far below in the ruined court. 'I wouldn't want you to repeat that, of course,' he muttered uneasily.

'I won't.' After a moment Will grinned, knowing full well that George thought he had uttered treason, which he would never have done if he had not trusted Will completely. 'But there are even more ways into Murray than there are gaps in your walls here to let in the wind. One small castle slap in the middle of the broad Lossie Valley is not going to stop anybody from getting through, now, is it?'

De Leslie was most unwilling to grant that, but could think of no argument to put up against it. Hadn't Edward of England demonstrated just how easily Dallas Castle could be swatted? Willie's next inevitable question discomfited de Leslie even more.

'Who's paying for it all?' Could it be Robert Stewart? Will did not dare put that into words, but his wondering increased when no answer came. 'No, I don't see the point, George. Look for yourself.' He gestured at the flattish land all around, much of it marsh or peat moss rutted with workings, and at the hilly undulations just a bit too close to permit a good view of an enemy approaching from any direction. The little village crouching at the castle base was run down and poorly maintained and the farming, what there was of it, would be hard put to support a garrison. 'Why don't you use the best stones from here to repair Rothes and live there. At least that's a good defensive position at the head of the Lower Spey Valley.'

'It's not for living in that I want it,' grumbled George. Then he shrugged. 'But you're right. Why prepare for a war that may never come?'

'Especially when there's no real sign of one in the offing,' Will grinned again. '*Delusions de grandeur*, that's what you have, *mon ami*!'

'Aye, weel,' George finally gave way to good Scots. 'I canna afford it anyway. Not with another tranche of money being demanded by John of Gaunt for the King's ransom arrears. My taxes are spoken for at least for anither five years. Yours and all, I shouldna wonder.' That was blatant fishing. Knowing of Will's wealth he shot him a sharp glance at this point, hoping for some enlightenment about the Danziger Scot's financial situation with regard to the ransom. Rumour had it that Will paid nothing, while his father was being hard pressed to pay the Forbys's share. It did not give a good impression of any son's attitude to his father's problems. 'Will ye be at Court this summer?'

'Other commitments, I'm afraid.' He knew full well what was being asked. Everybody knew John Forbys was land rich but cash poor like a great many other Scots courtiers. His son was also taking good care to keep himself out of the King's way. And Robert Stewart's. 'Still, I wish ye well with this, if ye tak it on. But I wouldna.' He had a feeling de Leslie wouldn't either. Not now. He also had a feeling George was rather glad to get the opinion he had.

Leaving de Leslie to his companions, Will headed off southwards using the summer drove road, which was merely the most pronounced of the network of paths criss-crossing the moors. Passing Knockando when the afternoon sun was at its hottest, he began to wonder if Jean's ale might have been stronger than he realised for he was growing drowsy and careless in the management of his horse. It was a strong stallion with plenty of energy left to expel and had become skittish. Eventually he drew off the road into a clump of trees by the edge of a burn, leaving his horse on a long lead to drink and graze on the sward while he pulled off his boots. Ten minutes later, after a paddle and drink, he tightened the rein to bring the beast into the shade and limit its food intake, for there was a long way to go yet. Then he leaned back against a burly oak and closed his eyes for a few minutes, thinking of the King and his nephew.

Aye, Robert the Steward. He was the one to watch. Son of Marjorie Bruce and grandson of Robert the Great, this Robert Stewart, as he styled himself, had also inherited the Stewardship of the realm from his father, Walter. Together these made his claim to the throne strong, especially as he had acted as Regent during the two long spells which David had spent out of Scotland. The first was when David was a growing youth in France, along with his child bride, Joanna, who was sister of Edward III of England; the second, even more significant absence was during David's recent eleven years of imprisonment, however comfortable, by the English.

Back in Scotland, despite generations of profound Norman influence which now dictated primogeniture as the means of succession, there was still a hankering among the Scots nobles, especially those of Celtic heritage, for the older method of electing the best king for the job from within an accepted spread of families with royal blood. Robert worked hard against that angle too, because there were other contenders, good men at that.

It was Robert who, some thirteen years ago now, had been the main instigator of the ruinous ransom agreement which brought his uncle out of England in 1357. By that time the Regent had managed to marry his own distant cousin by whom he already had a clutch of bairns. - He had brought the union off just a year after David's capture at Neville's Cross. - A good many more Stewart progeny had been delivered indiscriminately by the ladies of the land, if rumour held good. Initially the Pope had jibbed at the Steward's marriage because of the closeness of blood with his wife; they shared a great grandparent. Only by a grudging Papal decree in 1347 had the security of the marriage been established, along with many other royal and noble, unions, but there were still many Scots who might reject the legitimacy of the bairns in question. Not a point in favour of his succession.

It was with surprise that Scotland's nobles had greeted Robert's efforts to fetch his uncle back home when he was having such a fine time acting in his stead, and him with less blue blood in his veins than most of them. For his father, Walter the Steward, had been a commoner, and of English descent at that. Many believed that David was redeemed only when it became obvious that the King could father no bairns, having tried and failed with a second wife after Joanna's death, leaving the way open for Robert and his rapidly expanding brood.

King David, then, was brought home in order to observe his nephew's loyalty and, possibly, the efficiency with which he had ruled while the king was absent. And, of course, to confirm Robert as the future ruler. Without the king's sanction there would be challenges, among them a few who could claim through earlier Celtic royal lines as well as through one or other of the twelve claimants of whom the Bruce's' had been but the dominant. If nothing else Robert Stewart was a clever background operator, a manipulator of the political scene. All of his allies, mostly relatives, direct or by marriage, by now sat securely in good stone edifices, brooding eyries strategically positioned and well garrisoned and scattered all over Scotland, particularly in the south and west. Daughters were married off to men whose claims to succession would be rendered more tender by the tie.

Robert's hold on the North, however, was slight. Could that be why he had suggested de Leslie rebuild his castle with Stewart money? Could that also be why he had chosen Euphemia, Countess of Ross in her own right, as his second wife? Will prayed that nobody was after his own Bethoc, for he had little chance of winning her against the determination of the Steward's mighty clan of henchmen. She carried no blue blood, but as heiress to Francis Gordon she was rich enough to tempt a noble husband needing money for castle building.

On his return King David had set his stamp on Scotland with unexpected success. However his citizens kicked against the trebling of the taxes on their trading goods, (which they did) so that David could send the ransom money (years in arrears) to England to pay for the annual instalments of the hundred thousand merks which had redeemed him. But also, however much his squabbling nobles resented their king's wish to see Scotland and England brought closer which was implicit in the marriage made for him as a child, the Scots could not deny that the David had achieved a clever balance between Scotland's political commitments to both England and France, even while those were warring enemies. In doing so, he had established a thriving trading base far sounder and more lucrative than the country had had for generations. He had also gained some international respect for the little nation. Willie Forbys was only one of many merchants making the best of it.

No, it was not with David that folk had disagreements. Not even the Lords of the Isles, or not openly. Good George of Isla, the father, was perhaps kept quiet because of his second 'May to November' marriage to Margaret, the daughter of Robert Stewart and *his* second wife. She was that Euphemia, heritor of the Earldom of Ross. In time this premier earldom would pass to Margaret; it was Donald, their son, as heir to both parents, who was highly ambitious. He certainly saw himself, in spite of older half-siblings, as future master of his own kingdom in the west. This alone would comprise nearly half of all Scotland, being all the Western Islands and a huge slab of the mainland in the West and North. The Lords of the Isles already ruled there in reality, their obeisance to David perfunctory. As long as they made no overt challenge against David, the King was content for the time being to leave them to control the area; it was extremely difficult for any Lowland ruler to do, given the constant conflicts whisked up among virtually ungovernable clans.

Donald regarded himself even more highly, believing his own claim to the throne of all Scotland as good as any. He was furious when he found Robert nipping away at some of his western strongholds, seeing the creeping annexation as a threat not just to his claim to the throne, which was speculative at best, but also to the sub-kingdom his father did rule *ipso facto*. In an effort to counteract Robert's deliberate undermining, Donald, undoubtedly with his father's agreement, had built up a formidable sea-going force, retaining a fleet of clinker-built longships long after they had been abandoned elsewhere.

Unlike trading cobs, these birlinns, splendidly built and maintained, were rowed by freemen who vied with each other for the pride of serving in them. These oarsmen were no slaves or serfs. Nor were they criminals serving out their sentences. Their skills were awesome. The crews trained and regularly competed against each other, striking fear and wonder in their enemies at the speed and agility with which they manoeuvred their sleek craft. Such birlinns were ideal for the narrow, stormy seas around the west coast skerries and inlets. In addition they were equipped with a removable mast and heavy sail which could double as a cover in violent weather. With the capability of dropping covers over the oar-holes when not rowing, they were also well able to sail the open ocean.

It was in this role that the Lords used them to maintained regular contact with the courts, colleges and markets of Europe, especially Scandinavia, France and Iberia. Long ago such craft had taken the old Vikings to almost every corner of the known world and beyond, sometimes with astonishing speed. Why abandon them in favour of clumsier, more expensive cogs and caravels when they suited Donald's purpose so well? They could transport goods too, if in small quantities. More ominously they could carry men at arms, even animals, horses for instance, at great speed given the right weather conditions - which sent a shiver down Will's back. No doubt down Robert Stewart's too.

Chapter 3 – The Follower

A shudder of apprehension jerked Will out of his dozing. Vaguely he remembered hearing a horse go by heading south. Clickety-clump, clickety-clump. A recalcitrant hill pony with a stone in its shoe? A little later a group of market folk followed, arguing over prices. Then another troop headed north in the other direction, probably gypsies, for down through the trees which hid Will tinkled the faint, regular clank of metalware and tools jingling in unison. And were there a few notes of music from a tin flute? He was no musician himself, but he liked to listen to Bethoc on her small harp. She had a wee flute too which made his toes dance.

Minutes later a single horse cantered south, its urgent hooves striking on intermittent stone. His guess at this was a messenger on a decent animal. Rousing himself he stretched then, alarmed at the position of the sun, he realised that somehow he had mislaid several hours. Kneeling he plunged his head into the sharp chill of the burn waters. It was time he was gone.

Within five miles he caught up with the first traveller to disturb his dreams. Sure enough, the grey pony was limping, favouring its left foreleg, while the careless bundle hunched on its back bobbed about like a slovenly, precarious sack. A poor pace they were making between them. The courier would have taken no time to overtake them, and the folk trudging home from market must also have passed them or turned off. As Will came abreast he glanced at the rider to see if help might be sought, then gasped and reined back in surprise.

'What are you doing here?'

'Followin' you.'

'No, you're not. I've just caught up with you.'

The brat glowered at him, unwilling to quibble. A second look at him shocked Will. The child was shivering and his eyes were swollen and over bright, popping out of his head. Although his clothes were filthy, much worse than they had been in the miller's yard, his face was cleaner than before, but where Will had earlier glimpsed a golden skin beneath the dirt, it now looked grey.

'Are you ill?'

The boy shook his head. 'I fell in the river, that's all.'

'So why did you want to follow me?'

'I'm comin' wi' you.' The pert defiance sat ill with his bedraggled discomfort.

'No, you're not. So just you turn around, now, and go home. - But I'll see to the pony's hoof first,' he offered. From the way the lad rode, Will doubted if he had ever been on a horse before. He slithered off fast enough now and stepped back in an odd despairing relief, accepting Will's offer with a low, wide-open hands gesture.

'Where do you want to go?'

The boy shrugged then, spitting in his vehemence, he burst out, 'Anywhere! Wherever you're going. Just away from yon horrible place. I hate it.' The fury silenced Will. What had happened? Earlier in the day, shocked by the close encounter with death, the young merchant had left the grandfather in no doubt that he was not to beat the children again. Having been driven by his own apprehension to interfere where he had no real sway, Will had specifically warned that he would tell the Prior what had already happened, while promising to ask for leniency this one time.

As further protection for the children, he had also declared that he himself was returning to Murray and would check again on the situation. If there had been any ill-treatment in the meantime, he would hold the grandfather to account, - though he was not entirely sure how. What else could he have done? What more? He was still convinced that the miller had come within a hair's breadth of killing this child beside him and possibly the idiot bairn too.

The pony stood quietly under his hands, allowing him to check her withers and fetlocks. She was in fact in very good condition and used to being handled, barely flinching when Will began to work on the injured foot, his brain as busy as his fingers. A sharp stone had worked in under the iron shoe and was tightly wedged between the inner rim and the tender part by the hoof. In addition, a thorn had entered where the stone had made a gap and it was this which had caused the limp. The poor beast had been driving it further into the quick with ever step she took.

'You've cared badly for your beast, my lad.' Will bent his head over his hoof. 'There's no excuse for this. She'll give you good service but only if you serve her well first. Did your grandfather not teach you that?'

'No. An' your horse is off.' With the briefest touch of rebellious satisfaction, the brat pointed at Will's animal nudging his way among the trees, perhaps looking for another patch of sward by a stream. Only its rump was in sight. Will stretched out to hitch the reins with his boot before it went too far, then tucked his head down against the pony's haunch to concentrate on the tricky job of removing the thorn from its foot without breaking it and leaving the tip in the wound to fester. As he worked he again heard fast hoof beats, this time heading north, but by the time he was able to look up, all he saw was a departing cloak billowing behind a figure on a handsome dark horse.

'Yon's the Bishop's messenger.' Thc boy scowled after them, looking very scared. Will raised an eyebrow. 'I ken the picture on his chest.' It was only after several seconds of anxious chewing of his cheek that he slewed his eyes towards Will, a new thought joining the old. 'Is he looking for you?'

'Not as far as I know. - Hold still, lass! Uh, there we are. Now, look at that sharp devil. Do you wonder the poor beast was hirpling?' The lad had the grace to look ashamed as he squinted at the long thorn under his nose. 'This your grandfather's pony?'

After the barest of hesitations the boy said, 'No.'

Will's voice sharpened. 'You know you can be hung for stealing a horse, don't you?'

'I didna steal her.' He was too calm in his answer. 'She's mine.' When he made to mount again, Will stopped him and went searching for healing herbs with which to pack the space between shoe and hoof until they found a smith to reshod her.

'I have a long way to go yet. Too far for this little lass.' Will was prepared to be patient, suspecting a flat order would be disobeyed, directly or indirectly.

'I'll just follow on, then.'

'But by the time you get to where I'm going, I'll be long gone. You'll have to go home in the end. Look, it's well on in the day already. By the look of the sky there'll be a thunderstorm before night. You might as well accept reality and go home now rather than later.'

'I won't. I'm not *going* back. I'm *never* going back there. *Not ever*.' The vivacity of the Priory orchard had been lacking since Will had caught up with him, but now a fierceness took its place which contained a touch of hysteria which Will did not like.

'What about Nicol? Won't he need you?'

The child's eyes were suddenly magnified with tears, which he fought against spilling until his face seemed to swell. It was alarmingly like the effect of the old miller's rage, but Will was sure this was not anger. Not this time.

'He's nae there. He's... He's gone back to our mither.' The words slithered out of the tightly pinched mouth like sad, painful darts. Then, as if daring Will to challenge him, the lad added more calmly, 'He'll be fine noo. And... And my grandfaither'll be better without me. I'm tellin' ye, he will. He aye said so.'

Suddenly the boy shuddered, then shuddered again and tried to mount the pony, making a mess of it because he did not even know to gather the reins and settle her first. 'Ye needna try makin' me go back for I'm nae going.' With difficulty he finally managed to get up on to the pony's back, coming near to heading off the other side by tugging too quickly on the reins to turn her head south.

'Why me?' asked Will, fetching his own horse and heading in the same direction. With a good pacer beside her, the pony immediately picked up her speed. By now Will was profoundly alarmed by the unstable tension in the child. What now? The bairn was a bundle of nerves, his emotions swooping from one extreme to another. If Will took him as far as Balvenie, would he be able to calm him down by then? Once there, he could surely find somebody going down Strathspey who could take him back to Pluscardyn via Elgin.

'Ye're the only one that's ever stood up for me.' They rode on in silence for a good mile. 'I'll be your squire if you like.' The offer came out of the blue. When the young merchant gave a bark of surprised laughter, far from being put out the lad from the orchard suddenly reappeared, or a lack-lustre shadow of him at least. 'I'd be better than ye know,' he promised, his eyes lighting up a little more, which told Will that he had only just thought of this idea, was beginning to consider it seriously and liked it. He was seeing a means of persuading Will to take him along after all.

'Squires start off as pageboys.'

'I'll be your page-boy, then. What do I do?' Will could hardly believe the transformation. The sullen, sick, scared child of a minute before had been fading away as they rode south widening the distance between them and Pluscardyn. Now it was snuffed out by the perky scamp once more willing to tackle the world.

'One, learn to ride properly and take care of your mount. Mine too.' The brilliance wavered. Aye, he was not familiar with horses. 'They need grooming and feeding every single day of their lives. If there's no stable boy around, you clean and polish the harness brasses, taking it all apart, washing it and putting it all together again. Then you fetch me my food. You polish my boots and clean my clothes, make sure my knives and sword are kept properly sharpened, run any errands needed, write my letters, draw my maps, take readings from stars when we are at sea, scrub the decks, clean out the latrines... Gone off the idea, have you?'

It was not fair to tease the lad, especially when there really was no chance of him ever being given such a job. He was the wrong class for a start, as was Will. 'Och laddie, I'm not a knight. I'm a merchant. - And I do like to have a name when I'm speaking to somebody.' For an instant the scared, sullen look flashed across the boy's face again. 'I don't think yours is Stephen, is it?'

'Francis, if you must know,' he muttered after a pause. A moment later he had switched back to pretending there was nothing amiss by peering with exaggerated interest down the valley at the cluster of houses below them.

'Right then, Francis. I'm in a hurry. You can come as far as Balvenie with me if your pony doesna go lame again. Then we'll need to have a serious talk.'

The storm hit them half way up the Fiddich valley. Already delayed by waiting an hour for the ferryman to take them across the Spey, they now had to tackle the quagmire the driving rain created. By the time they arrived at Balvenie Castle, which was a former Commyn holding given into Forbys care, Will was as wet and filthy as the boy and his temper was shortening by the minute. For the last couple of miles, as well as managing his own horse he had also had to lead the pony, for guiding it had been beyond Francis. At least the brat had the sense to keep silent.

'Hoy there!' Will battered on the closed gate and glared up at the stone walls towering like cliffs above him, fearsome, dark and dripping. The hefty moat around them stank as if still filled with ancient Viking bodies. 'A Forbys! A Forbys! Open up!' It took an eternity to knock up a response and the welcome, when it came, was grudging at best.

'How was I to know you were coming?'

'Ye didna,' snapped Will. 'But I've no doubt your chief would expect ye to provide for travellers, especially his ain family. You're James Forbys from Echt, are ye no?'

'Yer ain faither being?'

'John, Maister o' Forbys, Standardbearer o' the Realm and your ain clan chief.' Will kept his voice flat. His father held Scotland's most ancient office, its origins stretching far back into Celtic times long before the Norman-Flemish influence clamped its dominance on the land.

James Forbys was not overawed. 'And which son are you? The heir or one o' the German wife's droppings?' The slur was fully intended but when Will pulled himself upright, feet apart and well balanced, James recognised the stance of a schooled fighting man and began to change his tune. 'Weel, weel. The meal is past lang since but I'll cry up some bread and cheese for ye. The lad can fetch it from the kitchen.'

'The lad stays wi' me.' Will ducked his head under the gateway into the courtyard, letting James and any watchers inside see just how tall and powerful a man he was. He had not indicated whether or not he was the Forbys heir. 'Stick by me, Francis,' he muttered.

'Ye'll hae other men wi' ye?' James probed

'They're seeing to themselves.' Disliking himself for letting the lie slip out, Will wondered if perhaps he should have given the castle forewarning. This antagonism he had not expected. 'And we'll be on our way in the morning,' he continued very quietly, his voice deepening. 'All we need is a corner where we can dry out and sleep. And the bread and cheese will be welcome. My thanks to ye.'

Balvenie Castle was a man's abode. On behalf of his chief, James held it and the surrounding land with the help of a small group of fencibles under his command, about thirty in all. Most were young and unmarried. A handful of older men had families who were quartered in the adjoining village where the husbands went out to visit them. The women and children never came inside the castle walls. In other words, this was a garrison without the civilising restraint of wives and family. Without strict discipline the customary hard drinking and wild talk in the great hall could lead to all manner of trouble. Petty squabbles were common among the men inside and small offences could blow up when least expected. Worse still, infringements by neighbouring clans could become exaggerated by drunken talk until they festered into causes of minor warfare.

Even before James left them to their own devices, instinct told Will that the discipline here was lax. 'Bide close to me,' he murmured again to Francis, who needed no warning. He, too, sensed animosity and was never more than two inches from the merchant's heels. Misliking the covetous look the stableman gave his fine animal, Will spoke more loudly. 'We'll see to the beasts ourselves,' and began to unbuckle the harness.

The man shrugged, on the edge of impertinence, then took himself off.

'Bring a couple of buckets of water, Francis. Then wash yourself while I rub down the animals.' Will pointed to the well in the corner of the empty, silent yard. He noticed the boy shudder as he stepped into the last of the daylight, which barely reached down into the cavernous pit created by the sheer walls on all sides. No other animals were quartered inside but fresh dung lay around and nothing had been cleared out for days. Out of the corner of his eye he watched the boy, wondering how far to push for information. There was no doubt that the brat was still strung up, tight as a bowstring ready for release. He kept chewing his bottom lip and, every now and then, would jerk in nervous reaction to any noise outside. He must have guessed at Will's decision to send him home because several times he said, in increasing despair, 'I'm nae going back.'

Will worked on in silence, drying his horse with twists of straw. 'You're nae going into the Hall in that state either,' he said mildly. 'Have you anything cleaner in your pack?' When he unbuckled it to groom the pony, however, it was so light that it could have held no more than a few bites of food. No water. How the lad had expected to survive he had no idea. Francis stood and glowered at him until the job was finished. When Will had washed himself he saw the lad's hands were still filthy. He took them in his own and tutted, 'Wash them again.'

The reaction to this simple act shocked him. The child flew into a paroxysm of fright, dragging his hands out of Will's and hiding them behind his back. When a shout, nothing to do with them, came from outside, he nearly jumped out of his skin and, just for a moment, his eyes began to fleer upwards as if he were going to faint.

Will grasped him by the shoulders to keep him upright. By the time the boy was steady again, Will knew his own eyes were reflecting his own distress. At times of deep emotion, his pupils would enlarge abnormally so that the colour was no more than a brilliant blue rim round a great black hole. He had no control over it whatever. Normally he would have looked down at his boots to mask the revealing reaction, or even turned away. However, the boy was so deeply disturbed that he did not dare to break eye contact, although the weird phenomenon made the child stare in even greater terror and try to pull away in a shuddering, superstitious frenzy. To make matters worse, Will's ears caught the sound of approaching horses and men's voices outside the castle gate.

'It's all right, laddie,' Will soothed with a desperate calm, gripping him too firmly to let him away, but still gently enough to offer no threat. 'It's all right. Are ye sure you're not ill?' Francis gave a headshake. After a minute or so, when the tumult was beginning to abate, Will withdrew his hands but, remembering the boy's agility, he positioned himself near the stable doorway ready to grab him if he tried to escape. 'Look at my hands. These are what I call clean.' He held them out, first palm upwards then downwards. Well-manicured while still retaining the roughness acquired through his sailing and riding, they were clean as a result of the bucket of water he had been using along with the currying brushes. 'Now let me see yours. I want them fit to dip into any bowl of stew I'm eating from.'

He waited for another full minute before the boy complied, most unwilling. His hands were cleaner than before, but under and around the nails was a crusting of dirt he had not removed. Mud... Will sucked in a gasp. Or blood? The boy held his eye again, this time grinding his teeth and holding his breath and again his stare grew wide and terrified. Will looked down at the filthy yard smock now wet from the well. It had become distinctly pink. For the first time he realised the boy was wearing another garment underneath. On lifting the smock Will saw the lighter linen shirt the boy had worn that morning, but it was now caked heavily in reddish brown stains. Will's breath came near to choking him.

'Is that your blood?' Face pinched with intense dread, Francis shook his head, and shook it again when asked if he was injured. Forcing himself to be calm Will muttered, 'Well, you definitely can't go into the hall wearing that.'

'I've nothing else.'

'I'll give ye my spare shirt. But ye'll have to get more of that stuff off your hands or there could be questions asked. The men inside here will know blood when they see it. When you take these off, roll them up and put them into your pack. We'll be taking our things with us into the hall.'

Sure at last that Will was still on his side, Francis took the horse brush offered and began scrubbing with a pathetic desperation at his nails over the water pail. Outside the troopers were clattering into the yard. When footsteps sounded approaching the stable, Will ducked outside to find the rain had stopped.

'Are ye not coming in?' The newcomer was not James Forbys but a younger man Will had a vague memory of meeting somewhere before. Nor, apparently, was he one of the returned men for he was clean and neat.

'The laddie's changing. He'll be out in a minute. I'm Will Forbys.'

It brought the response he hoped for. 'Camus Forbys o' Duthil. You're Maister John's son, aren't you? Mistress

Dolinda's?' Camus must have heard James's insult for he looked apologetic and dropped his voice. 'He's like a man with a boil on his backside today, surly blighter. Never heed.'

'He's still captain of the garrison?'

Camus's smooth speech indicated that he had some Court connections, which could put him well above James in status. 'Aye.' That was rueful. 'I'm to be around for another month before going to France so I have no say here. I think I can last it out.' His pleasant smile twisted a little.

'Ah, yes. You're to study for the priesthood. Am I right? Paris, is it?'

'Aye. But come away in.' He glanced over his shoulder at the stable then began to grin, drawing Will's attention to the dejected apparition in the doorway. The shirt came to the boy's knees and the sleeves almost brushed the cobbles. Before Will could offer help the lad thought of a solution for himself.

'I need a belt. A bit aff the pony's harness maybe?' Wrapped round him twice, it did the trick, and with the sleeves rolled up into gargantuan cuffs Francis did look a little like the pageboy he wanted to become. Again his behaviour made an unpredictable switch. He pulled himself straight and marched into the Great Hall with enough of a swagger to make Camus and Will exchange amused glances. Some of the troopers made comments which Will did not catch, but presumed were ribald. Perhaps because James of Echt saw the familiarity between the two younger men, he did not ask to disarm Will who neither offered his sword nor flaunted it, merely placed it beside their travel bags under the fireside bench to which they were escorted. His dagger remained hidden in his boot.

Will's suspicions proved right. The drinking continued throughout the evening. He was glad that they had entered the Great Hall before the troopers because they were able to obtain a comfortable corner by the hefty fire where they were not entirely surrounded by the soldiers. With little solid food to mop up their liquor, the main meal having been in the afternoon before the troopers went out, the arguments increased and grew more fractious. To Will's surprise, however, the majority of the fencibles were Gaelic-speaking Highlanders, Mackintoshes Camus told him, and he wondered if his father knew about that. The Mackintoshes were more often raiding enemies than friends. He hoped none of those could speak Scots either, for some of the Forbys contingent, who were in a different corner and were by far the more quarrelsome among themselves, were mouthing sly, complicated insults about the 'Erse savages'. These were going unanswered, for the moment. Camus watched Will take all this in before murmuring, 'James speaks both languages.'

In other words, James should have been reining in his Forbys men to head off trouble. Instead he was ignoring them, sitting alone but drinking as hard as the rest, on a stool across the fireside from the visitors but making no effort to converse. Eventually, he rose and left without a word to anybody. With an apology Camus, too, left to follow him and Will made himself comfortable, stretching his long legs on a bench and leaning against the wall by the fireside. The rest of the company was leaving the visitors alone but something warned him not to let his guard down.

With the benefit of an afternoon snooze behind him, - well, a good two hours of sound and trouble free sleep, - he could doze sitting up, glancing occasionally to where Francis was curled up in a borrowed blanket on the floor beside him. The child had fallen asleep so swiftly, so suddenly and deeply, that Will now realised he was suffering from shock. It had been a struggle to persuade him to eat even the meagre rations they were offered. In the end Will had to insist. Between them his sword lay just below his dangling fingertips. He eased the knife in his boot, so that it, too, was readily available if needed.

As darkness blackened the high fleche windows, Camus came in and snuffed most of the lamps. By then some of the men were already asleep, either slumped over the trestles or curled up on the thick straw along one wall on the floor. In the far corner one group of MacIntoshes murmured on, occasionally breaking into song. The music was soft, out of drowsiness rather than consideration, Will thought, but it was enough to keep anyone unused to it half awake. The most fortunate event of the evening was when one of the clansmen, almost the last to settle, knocked his drinking jug off the table with his elbow so that it bounced on to a wooden bench. The thump echoed round the walls, unnaturally loud in the quietness, then bounced off hitting a bare patch of the paved floor even more loudly.

It wakened Frances.

Chapter 4 – A Revelation

The noise also wakened another MacIntosh and the two clansmen swore at each other in Gaelic, their whispers sibilant and carrying in the snuffling, snoring quietness. Soon Will sensed a clandestine earnestness enter their talk. Minutes later a small hand tugged his own. Before he could respond, the main door from the yard swung open and two men entered, Camus and a man in a heavy, black cloak which glistened with raindrops in the dim firelight. Camus went straight to the fire and threw on another log, brightening the gloom and disturbing a few more sleepers. He looked around towards Will then indicated him to the newcomer before leaving again with a nod.

Will heaved himself up out of the slouch into which he had slipped. Leaning upright against the wall, he lowered his right leg to the floor, making space for the man to sit down. At the same time he raised his left knee, sliding the sole of his boot along the bench surface until his heel met his haunch. It made his plaid sag between the stranger and the child, leaving him tucked out of sight between the bench and the fire. Will kept his knee raised, prompting the stranger to choose the darker side of the bench if he wanted a seat. Francis could not see the newcomer, but as soon as the man spoke the small hand still in his under the plaid gave a faint but distinct jerk before being removed.

'Maister Forbys?' The visitor loomed above Will and murmured, mindful of the sleepers.

'Aye.'

'You're a slippery man to catch up with.' Will said nothing. The man did not sound unduly testy, just weary. 'I gather that I've twice travelled on the road you were taking today and saw you neither time.'

'What road?'

'Pluscardyn to Balvenie.' The man narrowed his eyes at Will. 'I had news of you at Dallas. It was only on my second trip south that the Carron ferryman told me you had crossed the Spey. It's strange that our paths did not cross.'

'Hm.' Will took his time about answering. 'And you are?' He eyed the badge emblazoned on the man's chest.

'The Bishop's Messenger.' There could be many of them, and he had not specified which Bishop. Will watched as the man shrugged off his cape, shaking it gently before setting it before the fire to dry on a couple of logs from the pile by the far side. Not once did his eyes turn to the bundle beneath Will's plaid. By now several men were awake and eyeing the courier's insignia. It stirred further unease within the castle, or perhaps the animosity was being transferred to a different and more feared quarry. Whether the niggle of ill will among the fencibles was against Will himself or between the two clan factions making up the garrison he was uncertain.

'Your name?' Will prompted.

‘You may assume the Bishop we are talking about is Alexander Barr of Murray.' This time the courier's lips did thin. 'My name is Hugo de May. Why were you hiding from me?'

'I'd no idea you were looking for me.' When Will smiled, however mildly, people forgot that he was ugly. 'Did you try the Dallas ale?' He pouted his amused distaste, and de May was tempted into copying him. He was probably no more than five years older than Will himself and by any measure much better looking. 'I, um, found myself in need of a sleep after it so I found a shady spot off the road, down by the Ballintomb Burn. Come to think of it, a fast horse did disturb me. As for your return journey, was that you cantering north when I was head down mending the shoe of a hill garron.'

Again, the courier's full lips pulled down, this time in resignation. Reasonable explanations, both. He stood gazing at the silent merchant hoping for more, gave a sigh and then sat himself on the bench at last.

Several minutes passed before Will murmured, 'Are you staying overnight here?'

'No, I'll continue to Mortlach.' It was what Will expected in spite of the late hour, after midnight he guessed. Who would sleep among dirty straw on a crude castle hall floor when the Dominicans would provide a fellow churchman with a comfortable bed. Will was regretting that he had not made the same choice himself.

'Then please ask your questions. I'll answer as well as I can.'

De May shuffled his buttocks on the bench and frowned. 'You, uh, have been residing at Pluscardyn Priory, yes? Can you tell me why?'

'Business.' After a hesitation Will added quietly, 'My business, but I do not believe it is yours.'

'I have been charged with finding out.'

'By whom? The Bishop?' De May nodded. 'Why?'

'I - cannot explain.' Because he did not know? Or had the courier been forbidden to pass on information which he did possess? Will could see the man was uncomfortable. By nature Will was inclined to be silent and good sense told him that in this situation he kept the upper hand by remaining so. After another pause de May went on, 'I know you spent five nights as a guest of the Prior and that while you were there you visited Spynie Palace. Also Kinloss where you spoke with Abbot Richard, the master of the Cistercians there.'

'I also spoke with the Bishop's Chamberlain at Spynie,' Will offered, since de May probably knew that already. 'I explained my business and gained all the permissions I needed.' The courier nodded. He must have guessed what Will was wondering. Why had the Bishop not had the appropriate questions asked then which he now needed answering.

'You are a merchant. You buy and sell any goods which bring you a profit. May I ask what brought you to Murray?'

'I fancy you know.' Will rubbed the sleep out of his eyes, beginning to realise he ought to concentrate. 'The stained glass made at Pluscardyn is gaining a reputation on the Continent for its clarity and brightness of purple colour. Lille Cathedral ordered new glass two years ago for windows being donated by the Duke of Burgundy. I merely came to collect it.'

'Did you bring the original order?'

'No. That was negotiated by a group from Lille, I imagine including a master glazier and some members of the Cathedral Chapter. Whether they visited in person or merely sent the details by independent messenger I don't know.'

'And the purpose of your other visits while here?'

Will saw no reason why he should answer, but he did, while raising a disapproving eyebrow. He had nothing to hide. 'Business again. Buying wool from the Cistercians at Kinloss, and delivering five books for the Bishop from the Beguines in Bruges. As a lover of books myself, I asked to visit the libraries at both Spynie and Kinloss. In fact,' he added, 'tomorrow I shall be calling at Mortlach to deliver one of the books I brought to the Sub-Prior of the Diocese there.' He saw the news was fresh to de May, but Will's frankness served to appease any doubts the man might have about his honesty. 'He governs the community there, doesn't he?'

'Father Ranulf... Yes.' De May fiddled with the cuff of his riding glove as if wondering how to continue. 'You're a

Hansa merchant, aren't you? I've heard that your courier service rivals those of the Italian bankers.'

'It doesn't.' De May looked up in surprise. 'It's better. Perhaps not faster but it's certainly more secure. Perhaps because it carries routine business letters rather than promissory notes. Dull stuff rarely of value to any bandit.' A courier would certainly understand that. 'Why? Do you wish to send something? Or does the Bishop?'

'Er, no. Are you carrying any missives now?'

'No. Nothing but a bag of glass samples.' De May looked up and held Will's eye. Since he was speaking the truth, Will had no need to feel evasive. 'But if I were,' he made a gentle admission, 'would I not be breaking my trust if I admitted it, even to a Bishop's messenger?'

Since they were speaking very softly, in consideration of the sleepers around them as well as keeping their business private, the weight of Will's words sounded more critical than he fully intended; but De May's flush of embarrassment made him think he had made another wise move. It had underscored the demand for trust upon which the Hanseatics insisted.

'What if the missive were subversive?' That made Will himself frown.

'Subversive? Against the crown, you mean?'

'Who knows? Or against the Bishop, perhaps?'

'I would never accept a missive of that nature.' But had he? He did not know the contents of the document now on its way to Avignon. One is inclined to trust a Prior, and the letter concerned was addressed to the Pope, publicly written, signed and witnessed. Witnessed by himself. He stroked his beard a couple of times, then made an offer. 'I am carrying no documents at all on this journey. If you wish to search me and check my baggage you may do so.'

'That will not be necessary, Maister Forbys.' De May was taking a risk. They both knew Will could be bluffing. On the other hand, he was a fully accredited Hansa merchant, and the Hanseatic League relied on their merited reputation for honesty throughout Europe to bring them business. In any case, he had no need to lie. If he had still been carrying the missive he might have admitted it but would not have handed it over. He would not even have revealed either its origin or its destination. It was highly unlikely that de May would have dared to try taking it from him, or not while he was still inside a Forbys stronghold. But later in his journey perhaps? Was it possible that the Bishop was anxious enough to have him apprehended and searched in some lonely place? The Church, or some elements of it, was none too nice about having its own way on occasion. He had no idea if Barr was one of those.

Suddenly the courier wiped the weariness from his eyes. 'Forgive me. You've been frank when you might not have been. I shall leave you to your sleep.'

Will offered even more. Tomorrow I'll be travelling by way of the Kirktown of Insch to my father's house at...'

'Druminnor, I know.' The courier heaved himself up to his feet, ignoring another of Will's frowns. 'If you like, I could take the book to Father Ranulf. It would save you a detour tomorrow. I wonder the Bishop did not suggest that in the first place.'

The note of pique in that comment had Will wide awake. After a moment's thought he too got up, and found himself barely taller than de May, a rare thing. He gazed at him intently. 'Do you mean, since you would be following me anyway? How long ago did you receive your order to do so?'

'Ah - midday. No, I was told to find you, that was all. I didn't know I'd be following you to this area, and nor would the Bishop have expected it but... ' He looked down, at last realising there was someone sleeping nearby, although he could not see the face beneath the blanket. In a sudden flash of annoyance he let his suave gentility slip. 'If there is anything to be delivered to the Dominicans, I usually do the job,' he snapped, then added stiffly, 'that's all I meant. When did your page join you? He wasn't at the Priory.'

'Along the route by Knockando. By prior arrangement.' It was true, if in a contorted fashion. 'How did you know I'd taken this road?'

The courier collected his cape and turned towards the door, nodding sideways to Will to accompany him out of earshot of the child. Will, still courteous in spite of the other's sudden stiffness, escorted him out of the hall, carrying a cruisie lamp to light their way. They reached the courtyard before de May spoke again. 'I went to Finderyn first, then back to the Priory. When you weren't at either I retraced my steps until I found where you'd left the road. Since your horse has three shoes of one pattern and one of another it was easy enough to track you from there on.' The dry amusement in his voice did not help Will's chagrin.

'Ah! I suppose the alewife at Dallas told you my route anyway. Well, you found me in the end and I hope you've had your answer.' But the man was not listening.

'A bit of advice, Captain Forbys,' the messenger said at last, his voice still cool and low. 'Don't return to Murray.'

Will's eyebrows shot up. 'Of course I'll return! The monks are hoping I'll bring further orders for their glasswork. And the Kinloss wool is the best in Scotland. The Scots Staple in Bruges will be crying out for it.'

'You're sure?' The man seemed to make up his mind about something. 'Look. I'll be as frank with you as you've been with me. You might find yourself in trouble if you return. I know you left the Priory at ten. I also know that an hour earlier you were involved in some trouble at the mill.

Weren't you? Before witnesses, too. Well, later that day, between the time you left and the time I returned from Finderyn, the body of a child was found in the river and another child is missing. So is the miller who is their grandfather. - I see from your face that this is news to you. You may find yourself being made a scapegoat. From what little I heard, you were already being implicated, so have a care. A stranger invites danger in events like this.'

'But I never went back to the mill!'

'It - might depend on what happened when you were there the first time. As I say, there were witnesses.'

'Including you?' Will demanded, by now both angry and scared. 'Are you trying to blackmail me? I can assure you that I am not carrying any messages, for or against the Bishop or anybody else. If that is your suspicion, I demand that you search me and my...' Suddenly he had a vision of the blood soaked yard smock in Francis's pack.

'How dare you accuse me of such a thing!' The two men glared at each other in the lamplight, then both came to their senses. Both were worldly men. 'Maister Forbys, I am merely warning you so that you do not ride into danger unwarned. Do you wish me to take that book to Ranulf?'

'I - I'll take it myself.' To ameliorate the abruptness of this he added, 'I'd like to meet a fellow booklover. But thank you. - I think you're a fool to try and get there in this wild darkness. You'd be better to bed down here and come on with me in the morning.'

'No thank you. My presence will be needed there.' His horse was inside the stable but had not been unharnessed, had not even been rubbed down. Poor beast, thought Will.

Inside again, he had no sooner settled on his bench when the brat tugged his arm. Will leaned over to listen to his whisper.

'They're aifter yer horse.'

'Who? The heilanders?'

'Aye. Them by the door. I heard them planning it afore the messenger cam' in.' One of the men he indicated was the stableman whose help Will had refused. He straightened and leaned against the wall once more and thought for several minutes. Then he leaned down again.

'So you understand the Gaelic. Do you speak it as well?'

'Aye. Sort of.'

'How brave do you feel?' The child stirred and sat up properly. The cruisie was snuffed again but in the firelight his head was held high with a pride which conflicted somewhat with the look in his eye. 'Brave enough to go over and deliver a message from me?'

'Now? Aye.'

'Then go and tell those two that the horse in the stable belongs to the Chief of the Clan Forbys, the very man they have taken service with. And that Chief would take it badly if his horse went missing. Will ye do that?'

Francis thought about it, perhaps searching for the right words, then slowly stood up.

'Quietly now. Dinna cause more disturbance than ye must.'

His sword was already free of its scabbard and he was now grasping the haft, though it was still out of sight as the boy set off across the hall, stepping like an elf over the sleeping forms. His flickering shadow loomed black on the far wall, gliding with a distorted feline grace which scratched at something in Will's brain. It chimed well with the coquettish manner of the brat in the orchard and the sinuous agility with which he had dodged the miller's flail. And, for that matter, with the flair he had used to kirtle the over-large shirt wished on him. Something did not fit.

Another thought kindled. Born on St Stephen's day he had said, the day after Christmas. A winter bairn, then.

Certainly the name Stephen did not suit him, a rugged, solid name. Instead they had called him Francis, a gentler appellation to live up to - and suddenly Will gasped. That Saint Frances was a female saint. At the same moment as the truth hit him, the child herself let out a squawk, startled when one of the prone figures on the straw grabbed her ankle.

Next moment the grasp was released and the owner's hand spread wide under a heavy boot as the point of a sword pricked the back of his neck. Will did not know how he got there so quickly but a bellow behind him came from one trampled body, catapulting the whole chamber into uproar. Mercifully, his was the only fighting weapon, but a number of dirks appeared. Had those been used against him there was no way that Will could have survived, one man against so many. As it was, the men were startled so suddenly out of sleep that they hesitated, trying to assess what was happening before they took action and instinctively expecting to divide into two factions, Forbyses and MacIntoshes. When they saw just one red-bearded stranger bending over a Heilander but not, in fact, raising his arm to do damage, everyone froze. His strange, pale hair shimmered in the firelight as he waited for the panic to settle, then he nodded to Frances.

The child's clear Gaelic came soft and hesitant. If any of the Forbys men understood they gave no indication, but the others, the majority, listened then stirred uneasily, glancing at several of their fellows, which helped Will to identify those he needed to keep an eye on during the rest of the night.

'Back to the fire, Frances.' Once the child had returned, wide-eyed and nervous, slowly Will removed his sword from the harasser and wagged an angry finger at him before returning to his bench to slap his back against the wall once more. He let them all see that he had left his sword lying snug against his leg with his fingers still hugging the haft. Silence thickened around them for many minutes before the soldiers began to settle themselves, many still puzzled about what had happened; others, he hoped, were rethinking their plans. Everybody else would sleep more lightly now, keeping half an ear open for other folk on the move. Anyone trying to leave would be observed and identified by plenty of witnesses. He smiled to himself. Now he could safely close his own eyes and sleep soundly.

It did not happen that way, of course. Beside him Frances wriggled and fretted until Will had to reach out and stroke the hot head. Immediately the child lay still. Then, 'Please,' she whispered, barely making a sound but shuddering with the intensity of it. 'Please take me with you. Don't send me back. Oh, please!'

'Yes, I'll take you with me,' Will promised. 'I'll take you to my mother's house. She will care for you. Now go to sleep.' He continued to stroke the moist brow, gently smoothing the hair again and again until he heard the child's breathing settle into the rhythm of sleep. He refused to speculate on his mother's reaction. Or Bethoc's.

Again he tried to settle himself but as soon as his determined blanking out of the events of the day drifted towards slumber his mind filled with pictures. Beautiful blond children playing with water which sucked them into itself; horses bearing terrible secrets being waylaid in lonely valleys; riders left drowning in blood; himself, hanging from a great oak at a crossroads, choking...

In the end Will gave up trying to rest. Instead, whenever Frances began to stir he gentled the child back to sleep by stroking her brow, all the time watching the high arrow-shot windows in the east wall for the first signs of dawn. Since his mind was already a churning maelstrom he let it get to work on notions of crimes and deceptions and the growing evidence suggesting both. He had decisions to make and he wanted them to be correct.

Chapter 5 – New Relationships

As soon as it was light enough for horses to see where to put their feet, he wakened Frances and chivvied her, still heavy-eyed, out and on their way. Nobody tried to stop them. After a handful of oats their horses, rested and willing, set off with their tails whisking.

The storms of Wednesday night had gone and the sky arched above them a clear, unblemished bowl of blue. They found themselves alone in the world, free but insignificant among the raucous cacophony of birds calling their joy in life. Their chorus was at its loudest as they turned their horses out of the new-leaved trees and up towards the short gap leading over the hills to the east. The whin thickets and verges were scuttling with animal industriousness which they sensed rather than saw. It took time for the mud underfoot to dry out but despite its hindering they would still reach Mortlach before the second offices of the day were sung.

This ancient house of St Moluag had long ago been transferred to the See of Aberdeen, which meant that the writ of Bishop Barr of Spynie, the primate of Moray, should not have operated here. That Father Ranulf was one of his sub-priors and was ruled from Elgin Cathedral was an anomaly which puzzled Will. Nor was it clear why this was a Dominican community, whose friars preferred bustling places where they could minister to the folk within towns and boroughs. Mortlach was, quite literally, at the back of beyond; to reach it they had to branch off from the hardened surface of the drove road, to which they would return later, and plowter along a boggy stretch in a more southerly direction. At one point it had been churned into something resembling black porridge, much to the dislike of their horses.

Once through that mire Will reined in his horse, fetching out some bread and cheese he had held over from the evening before, and a skin of water.

‘I should have thankit ye for keeping your ears open last night, Francis. If you hadna heard those caterans we'd be in a pickle now.' Francis shrugged, then shook her head when offered the food. 'Come on, now. We're not going another step until you've put something into your stomach. Ye'll feel the better o' it, I promise.'

A little of the food eventually disappeared, but it was plainly an effort, which made Will decide to leave until later the suspicion which had struck him during the night. It would be enough for the child to deal with something far more urgent.

'We must see to yon bloodied clothes in your pack.' Instantly Francis became rigid. 'Are ye ready yet to tell me what happened?' Will's probing met with a glare, but the attempt at anger was feeble, defeated by wide eyes glazing with terror and lips pinched until they grew pale. 'Ye'll hae to tell me sometime,' Will tried again gently. But the child shrank away from him, turning to stare back the way they had come, struggling to breathe. 'Well,' Will heaved a worried sigh, 'we'll leave that for now. But what about the clothes?'

'I'll wash them in the next burn,' the bairn muttered. Will said nothing. Dried blood was more difficult to get rid of than folk expected. In any case, he doubted if the lad would ever want to wear the garments again; it was obvious that the associations were hideous.

'Then let's get on. We've twa days’ journey from here. I'd rather it didna become three.'

As it turned out, there was no stream before Mortlach, which was barely half a mile beyond. The setting for the little, ancient, rectangular church was exquisite. High above the Dullan river overlooking a wooded valley it smiled towards the rolling, cattle-rearing hills of Aberdeenshire which provided its living. There had been a religious foundation here for centuries, established some said by St Moluag from the time of the good St Columba before the Roman church had come to Scotland. The river was far too easily overseen from the hamlet beside the kirk for secret washing to be done.

Will led the way towards the church door, skirting the turf cottages and nodding acknowledgement as the villagers greeted them. Francis hung back near a small, penned flock of goats and sheep.

'I'll bide here till ye've finished.'

Will opened his mouth then closed it again. It was not something to make an issue of. He found Father Ranulf at work on his own toft, setting out rows of colewort and radishes behind hazelwood hurdles erected to keep animals off the patch, and watering them carefully. Well into his thirties, a good decade older than Will, he was vigorous and welcoming.

'We're always glad of visitors here.' Within his curling tonsure, the freckled dome of his head, more bald than shaven, glistened in the sunlight as he bustled Will indoors and immediately began to prepare a breakfast, brushing aside the merchant's objections. 'Especially when they bring such a treasure as this book. My thanks to you, *sieur*. I shall spend this afternoon in the garden with Juvenal here, - if the Dear Lord keeps the day as fine as it is now.' So much for maintaining monastic rigidity here. It turned out the Dominican was the only priest at Mortlach, helped in his parish and gardening duties by several young novices who were also learning from him the rudiments of church life and letters. 'Mind, we rarely get around to the letters unless the weather's too bad for work to be done in the fields,' Father Ranulf admitted frankly, chattering on, 'and between my forty duty days in Elgin. The lads get on much faster during the winter - then forget everything in summer so we have to start all over again after the harvest is in!'

Will grinned, warming to the man. 'A good excuse for letting the lads remain here another year, maybe?' The priest chuckled. 'So you've been well provided with visitors today. I know I'm the second.' At that the man's smile faded into surprise, then alarm as Will continued, 'The Bishop's messenger? Did Hugo de May not arrive in the night? He left Balvenie soon after midnight.'

Abandoning the meal, Ranulf hurried to the door, tucking his scapular up out of the way as he called to his acolytes. 'Fetch in the horses from the far field. Harness them, lads, and hurry!' Then he turned back to demand, 'You're sure he meant to come here? He said so?'

Galvanised by the anxiety, Will unfolded his long legs and headed out to his own mount. 'Stay here!' he commanded as he passed Francis, still by the goats, and cantered off the way they had come until he reached the mud patch half a mile back. Within minutes, Father Ranulf and three lads in working smocks had come up behind him, but they obeyed Will's raised palm and stopped short to watch as he examined the mess as closely as he could without leaving further footprints. The three-and-one shoes of his own horse were shamefully easy to identify. Little wonder Hugo de May had been able to follow him so easily, and Francis. The pony's prints were also visible, fresh like his own but filling up more rapidly with glaur because they were smaller.

'These,' he pointed to other marks, more faint but still clear around the edges, 'these are earlier.' He followed their tracks with his finger, tracing into the oily quagmire and out again, then round one way and back to try the other, showing where the rider had sought a better way through. These were already flattening out.

'But there's evidence of other traffic,' he murmured, pointing again. 'Father Ranulf, have you had other visitors in the last day or so?'

'Nobody. As far as I know nobody has come through the village in either direction for more than a week.' Father Ranulf was clicking his teeth but was otherwise in control. 'I would have known. We all would. There's no way in or out except by this route.'

The sound of lightly trotting hooves approaching from the village made them both turn round. Francis had disobeyed.

'What in the name of...' The friar checked himself, eyes widening as he straightened up. 'Mary Mother of God, whatever are you doing here, Francie?'

The child did not answer, merely swallowed hard then looked at the various prints which they had been examining, curiosity and dread fighting for the upper hand.

'Francis came with me.'

'Why?' Ranulf swung back to Will, his bonhomie dispelled by indignation. 'By what right have you taken her from her home?'

Will's mouth opened, and then closed. 'Well, that answers one of my questions.' He scowled over his shoulder at the brat who had the grace to blush. A girl. Born on the Feast of St Stephen. 'She followed me,' he explained to Ranulf. 'I don't know why but she was adamant that she would not return. I shall place her in my mother's care.'

'That I won't allow!' Ranulf turned full face to him, this time very angry indeed. 'You shall not abduct this child. Not while I have the power to stop you.'

'I'm not abducting her! All I want to do is to place her somewhere safe while I find out what in the...' He caught his breath on the oath. '...what's happening back there in Pluscardyn. I can think of nowhere safer that my own home - along with my mother and five younger sisters. Will that not suffice as protection?'

'What has happened?' Bewildered, Ranulf turned to Frances. 'What *has* happened, Francie? What's going on?' But he took the hint when Will reached to grasp his arm, shaking his head fiercely and frowning.

'It's more urgent to find... to attend to this job. - Frances, go back to the village.'

'No. I won't.' He was at a loss to know what to do in the face of her defiance. 'It's Hugo, isn't it? Has he got lost? Or...'

'Or what?' Will gulped his annoyance, forced himself to speak quietly. 'Dinna let your fancies run wild, Frances. It'll help us most if you go back and tell the villagers to bring ropes. It looks as if the messenger has stumbled off the road and hasna found his way back on it again. Or not yet. Will you do that for us?'

It was Will's elaborate gentleness which alerted Ranulf to the depth of the trouble, diverting the priest's rage which probably arose out of protectiveness. But she had asked a good question. What had happened to Hugo? The men had all seen the evidence that there had been several horses in the mud patch during the last few hours. At least two of them they could not account for. Their hooves were a little smaller than those of either Hugo's animal or Will's but larger than Francie's pony. In addition, those two, with Hugo's mount in the middle, led off the path and on to the scrubby moor.

'What's in that direction?' he murmured to Ranulf, hoping Francie would not hear.

'The peat workings,' the friar replied, but he wiped his muddy sleeve across sudden beads of sweat which had sprouted on his upper lip. 'And bog,' he breathed. 'Francie, off you go now! We need more people for the search party. And tell them to bring those ropes.'

But her hearing was sharper than they wished and one of the novices had to be sent instead. She had also learned horse management fast. Her face a picture of fright, she kicked the pony viciously which drove the animal off the road between two twisted hazels and out over the moor towards the peat drills. The men were obliged to race after her for fear she ended up in the bog herself. Will spared Ranulf just one glance, seeing on his face a similar distress to hers.

'Francie, stop!' This time Will bellowed. 'You're ruining the tracks we need tae follow!' His voice would have carried above the wildest storm at sea. It echoed round the hills and made the child jerk suddenly, then drag at the pony's bridle as she tried to turn it aside. It was too much for the puzzled animal and she veered, dumping the child neatly in a sump of stinking glaur where cattle had been puddling. The squelching splash drowned out most of what she swore after she went sailing through the air.

Nobody laughed. Nobody paid attention, which at first enraged her as she struggled to her feet, dripping, raging and filthy. But even she, while fighting her tears, became diverted by the two strange patches on the ooze stretching before her.

Everywhere was a maze of brilliant verdure, tufts of spring weed glowing over-bright in their greenery, mounds of many-coloured mosses speckled with tiny iridescent flowers; the complex patterns were intercut with the deep, dark mouldering of old peat runs filling with amber water after the storm. It was the apparent solidity of these which had tempted Francie into thinking it was safe to ride across the moor. Only where the top growth had been skimmed off, or perhaps been dragged under, was the danger beneath revealed. Two expanses held their eyes, dark, glistening sheets of oily liquid the colour of bad black beer. The scum on top was being disturbed by occasional belches of gas bubbling from far below, a flutter of insects trawled for food, and the lightest of breezes stirred the surface, making it roil like living watered silk. Lazy, tainted rainbow colours mocked the watchers, enticing them onwards into the sunlit mire.

Silence held them motionless. Then Francie began to weep in earnest and Ranulf crossed himself in horror and began to pray. 'May the Lord receive his soul in peace.' The novices copied him, their young faces reflecting the friar's distress but with a puzzled incomprehension.

'We can't be sure,' muttered Will. 'We must go on looking.'

'Rubbish, man!' Ranulf threw up an arm in despair, pointing over the bog. 'How can any man possibly...?'

'Then why two patches? Why not one? Or three for that matter? Three animals came along here. Just look!'

The tracks were plain, right up to the edge of the last worked peat drill. There they became mussed as if a struggle had ensued. 'Look, there's been plenty coming and going here. They must have realised the danger and...' Francie limped to within earshot leaving one of the lads to catch her pony. Will glanced at Ranulf, seeing in his face the same sudden questions he was asking himself. Had there been some effort to save somebody? Or to throw somebody in? If Hugo had been waylaid by caterans, it was highly unlikely that they would have let his fine horse drown; it was worth far too much to them, but the messenger's fate would mean little. And yet, two disturbed patches in the bog? Will clambered forward, stepping gingerly from tussock to tussock, approaching the bog pools as near as he dared, and peered at them, searching for further signs of a struggle, for anything which might confirm that somebody or something had indeed been sucked beneath the treacherous ooze.

Defeated he returned to the others, now grouped together near the peat stacks with a dozen villagers already arrived and shaking their heads, fearing the inevitable. If anybody had ridden into that muck, he wasn't ever going to ride out again.

'How well did the messenger know this road?'

'Very well.' Ranulf now had his arm around Francie's shoulders and she was leaning against the priest, having no hesitation about seeking comfort there. The little face was dirtier and more pathetic than Will had yet seen, clarted as it was with grey-black mud as well as tears. 'He comes up and down at least six times a year.'

'On Cathedral business? Were his visits pre-arranged?'

'Not always. At least... I didn't know he intended to come around now. In fact I would not have expected any message before Whitsun. Not for another fortnight. Something must be amiss.'

'Even more amiss now,' Will muttered. 'I'm going to have a look around the edges of that bog.' Then he eyed the sodden linen Francie was pulling away from her skin in disgust. 'That's my last clean shirt. My best one and all. Ye'd best beg something in the village and clean yourself up before I get back.'

'I'm coming with you.'

'No you're not. If you disobey this time I'll send you back to Pluscardyn.' The irritable threat was thoughtless and immediately regretted when the child blanched and trembled. Then he realised he had found the stick with which to make her oblige him, loth though he would be to use it again. 'I don't want you struck down with a fever, Francie. Now, be a good girl and do as I ask. I promise I won't be long. - And yes, Father, you can rest assured,' he added grimly, 'I'll be very careful indeed.'

Will did find one thing as he scoured the moorland around the swamp that Thursday morning, which itself must have covered half a ploughshare of land. He found time to think. By the time he had returned to the hamlet he had his questions ready.

'How did you come to know Francie?'

'I haven't spent all my life here in Mortlach, Captain Forbys.' The Dominican's answer was subdued. He was stunned by Hugo de May's disappearance. Like all the villagers, he was assuming that the Bishop's messenger had ended up in the bog. 'Most of my ministry has been in and around Elgin. I know the miller's family well. The miller used to work the Bishop's Mill on the River Lossie, you know. Two years ago he exchanged places with the man at the Prior's Mill who is now in Elgin. I have watched Francie grow up.'

'And Nicol?'

Ranulf grew still, then crossed himself. 'And Nicol. Poor child.'

'Is that why the miller was sent out to Pluscardyn? Because the Elgin folk would not accept Nicol's... his lack of wits? Wouldn't they leave the family alone?'

'Nicol's mind never grew, that's all. In every other respect he was a normal child. Everyone knows that. - They were told often enough.'

Will drew a deep breath. 'But preferred to believe that a damaged child belongs to the Devil and not God?' It was brutal but he was sure the friar had heard it often before. Again Ranulf answered patiently.

'Those who do so are as children themselves, children in danger of losing their way, too. At least within the precincts of the Priory the poor child is less open to torment. The rest of the family as well.'

They had entered the church by then and Will was facing away from the light. He had positioned himself deliberately that way, hiding his eyes, before asking his question, for he expected the answer just received. From what Hugo had told him, he now feared a horror far worse than the friar believed, and he knew the strange widening of his own pupils would betray his intense distress. He did not yet want to reveal that the family might have brought the clown child's greatest danger with them. For surely the killer had been the grandfather and he might be following them now, if he knew he had been observed. But that knowledge might interfere with Ranulf's direct answering of the next questions.

'Francie knew the messenger too. She seems especially concerned about him.'

'She thinks Hugo might be her father,' Ranulf snorted. That took the wind out of Will's sails. Before he had recovered, the child herself turned up in the doorway, cleaned up - sort of - and clad in a girl's raggedy tunic which made her look more of a waif than ever. The joyous brat in the orchard had evaporated. Perhaps Will had imagined him.

Her presence now stifled his curiosity, but he wondered if there was more Ranulf could tell him. 'Father, I've been thinking. Is there any way in which you can have the child taken to my mother's home from here? I feel I ought to...'

'No!' Francie wailed. 'I want to stay with you! You take me. I dinna want to go with anybody else!'

'Then go back with him to Pluscardyn,' Ranulf put in tartly, guessing what had not yet been voiced. Again

Francie's terror reared - or could she be acting? For the first time Will wondered, then dismissed it. The two men were judging from her physical reaction alone since she was now the one outlined against the bright doorway with her face hidden. But no, he could never explain away the blood on her yard tunic, - and he was not ready to mention that to Ranulf .

Francie crept towards Will. 'You're not going back, are ye?' she whispered.

'I'll have to eventually,' he said cautiously, readjusting his plans for her benefit. 'But not yet. I think I ought to follow the tracks of those horses, just in case Hugo de May has taken a tumble and is lying injured somewhere.' The sudden hope in her face twisted his guts.

'You think so? You really think he might be alive?'

'I don't know either way. That's why I must check. - But you're not coming with me.' He forestalled her firmly. 'I might need to travel farther and faster than you could possibly manage. If I had you to look after as well it would slow me down, and that just might cost Hugo his life. You wouldn't want that, would you?'

This time she swallowed her disappointment and shook her head.

'Then you can either go on to Druminnor, if Father Ranulf can find you a guide, or stay here until I come back. It could be days, you know.'

'I'll stay here,' she insisted.

'Druminnor did you say? - You're surely never the Maister o' Forbys, are you?' He meant the heir to the clan chief.

'No, that's Jock, my older brother. Half-brother.'

'Ah, so you're the German lad.' Out of the corner of his eye he saw Francie blink, then rear her head in indignation, at last showing a spurt of spirit.

'My mother's German, yes. Are you willing to look after Francie until I get back.'

'Of course, of course! I'll - find a place for her with one of the wives of the parish.'

'Then I'll be off.' He fished a silver merk out of his pouch for the poor box and headed for his horse. Perhaps Ranulf would have better luck in winkling out Francie's story without him. They obviously knew each other well. Maybe better than had yet been admitted. He had a feeling the priest had not told him all there was to know. Not by any means.

Chapter 6 – Searches

When Will returned to Mortlach he was hot, weary and frustrated. He fumed at his horse, wishing it were a ship; he swore at the deep, dusty heather rugging and tugging at him, hindering his progress and hiding whatever clues there might have been of the passage of other folk, whatever their business, for there were no paths at all here; most of all he cursed at the solid, soaring hills, in reality not that high, but they had none of the undulation of crests and troughs which waves would have created, allowing him regular revealing glimpses into the neighbouring valleys. Worst of all was the wicked little breeze which, instead of the cool refreshing of an ocean wind, delivered a hot, harsh dryness to scour his skin already a permanent sailor's brick-bronze; and a bushy beard was the last adornment he needed on a day like this. In other words, he wished with all his heart that he was safely back at sea away from the sinister troubles now threatening to embroil him. Questions were plentiful, most of them unpleasant. Answers were not forthcoming.

'Found anything?' Father Ranulf looked up as his visitor trudged back towards the end of the broiling afternoon. Will handed his animal over to the care of the blacksmith who promised four matching shoes, and now he brought his anxieties to the church, his bare feet thankful for the coolness of grass and his thigh boots slung over his arm. The priest had set a small table just outside the church door to take the weight of the Juvenal, for the parchment pages were heavily protected by finely tooled kidskin. Will took note of the sunburnt nose and skull, and the straw hat lying forgotten by the side of the priest's stool. Ranulf grimaced. 'Yes, I've been losing myself in reading. It's - one way of shutting out pain.'

'I don't blame you,' Will assured him, adding wearily. 'I'm sorry. I saw no point in searching further.' While reading, Ranulf was having his tonsure tidied up by one of the novice lads. 'He's good with the shears,' he offered. 'You would feel cooler without that fleece on your head.'

Hoping he was not in for a tonsure as well, Will let the boy have his way and was given an enthusiastic beard trim as an extra. When they were alone again he turned to the priest.

'Have you got anything out of the bairn yet?' Ranulf shook his head, his glance drawing Will's attention to Francie sleeping like an angel in the shade of the hazel hurdles. These sported two drying shirts, both Will's. Francie must have gone into his saddle pack and found the other dirty discard there and washed it along with the one she had worn. There was no sign of her own bloodied sark.

In the dappled shade she slept on. An angel... Nicol's body fetched from the river, had been Hugo de May's description. Gone back to his mother, she had told him. Fell in the river, was the explanation for the state of her clothes. But not for the blood. A fallen angel? Caught unawares by these unbidden memories slotting together, Will's eyes filled with tears. Ranulf turned back to him just in time to see these and the damnable widening of his pupils but Will was past caring. 'Then I think I should go back. Find out more.'

'Will you take her with you?'

'No! That would be - unwise, I think. Will you care for her here? Or send her on to my parents' house? Please? But only if you can find somebody you can trust.'

Ranulf nibbled at his thumb knuckle. 'I'll take her there myself,' he offered. 'But I ought to know what to tell your mother. More than you have told me so far, eh?'

'I don't know much more. Just that the child followed me and won't go back. You've seen the fair fright she flies into when we suggest she returns home.'

'But what about Nicol? You should know that she's really a little mother to him. She - protects him. Perhaps I shouldn't put it that way but that's what it... Dear God! What has happened?'

Will wiped his hands down over his face. 'I am not sure if I should be telling you this.' He wiped again before deciding. 'Hugo de May told me that, uh, Nicol's body has been fished out of the river.' That was enough. He would admit no more. That was all that the messenger had said to him, after all, and it may yet be the whole truth. The poor innocent might indeed have stumbled in when nobody was looking. Except, 'And the grandfather's missing. They think Francie is missing as well, but of course we know otherwise. At the moment I know no more about what actually happened. Neither did the messenger.'

'That man!' the priest whispered. 'That wicked, deluded old man!' They both knew he was referring to the grandfather.

'If it was him,' Will muttered, throwing himself down on the grass between the table and Francie in the hedge. 'Maybe he'd just reached breaking point. It's busy enough for any man, running a mill. Hard physical work, and he isn't young.'

'Add in two children,' Ranulf sighed, 'one of them a lively brat and the other forever to be an idiot, a totally dependent baby in the body of a growing boy getting too big to control. Add the superstitious fantasies of silly folk who believe more in the Divvil and the old gods than in a good Lord in Heaven, folk too scared to do business with him.'

'Life must have been grinding him into a despair as hellish as...' Suddenly Will demanded, 'Where's the mother? I should have asked sooner.'

Something about the silence made him raise his face from the grass. Ranulf had frozen, his eyes on Francie. She was still sound asleep, making up, no doubt, for the stress and restlessness of the day and night before, but the pity and anxiety Ranulf exhibited also held shock. 'Dead.' It was no more than breathed.

Will jerked himself up on one arm. That answer stripped bare his own fears.

Seeing that, the priest added more, as if forced unwillingly from deep within the priest's soul. 'She - drowned.' Dear God. Will hated asking the next question, and hated the answer even more, harsh even in its harrowed softness. 'No, Amelia is not buried at the Priory, nor yet in Elgin. The Bishop persuaded himself that she entered the water deliberately and therefore they would not inter her body in consecrated ground.' Several breaths hissed in and out between Ranulf's teeth. So she's buried where, Will wanted to ask, but did not dare. The answer came anyway, laced with a vicious anger. 'They dug her a pit in the forest, like a diseased pig or some such. Without even a coffin. And certainly without any prayers.'

For her corpse to be unearthed and consumed by the wild creatures, he meant, unshriven and unforgiven. Will hid his horror in his arms. Poor Amelia; forever damned to the hideous tortures of the Hell so vividly depicted in the countless pictures before the populace whenever they entered any of the holy places with which the land was peppered; forever to suffer, without any hope of restitution on the Day of Judgment since there would no longer be bodily remains to be reunited with her deranged spirit. The messages had been especially bright and hypnotic in the glorious glass windows in the Bishop's great Cathedral of Elgin. That magnificent, monstrous Lantern of the North could be seen from far across the Firth, forty miles or more away, when all the candles were lit for Mass. Will had glimpsed those windows from the outside and even then had marvelled. They were as stupendous as anything he had come across in all the Baltic's rich, bustling city states.

To Will's mind - he was part Celt, after all - Amelia's was not such a terrible fate. She had been taken back by the spirit of nature and surely God, if there were a God, would as her Creator look kindly on her soul. But he knew there were very few who would not be scandalised if they knew what he thought. He would be seen as a worse sinner, a heretic, and condemned to the same everlasting torment as hers. High and low, rich and poor, old and young, oh, especially the vulnerable young, everybody was taught to read in those pictures almost all they would ever know of the Bible, of the Gospels and their promises and threats.

Will had been more fortunate, provided with knowledge from his early childhood through books and treatises, a rare and wonderful privilege. With it had come understanding of the arcane, protected Latin texts in which the Holy message was poured upon the congregations from the mouths of the priests, who harnessed for themselves power through the ignorance of others. The common folk had to rely on these pictures alone for their religious instruction. From their first toddling steps worshipers had been told what to believe, too often by lesser priests with little more learning or Latin than themselves but possessing wonderfully dramatic and evil imaginations and determined talents for fantasy. These limited men had had their own superstitious minds bludgeoned with deliberation by the prelates building their own towers to both ecclesiastical and temporal superiority.

'Sick,' he growled, then looked up in anxiety. He had no wish to be charged with heresy by this kindly, distressed man. Yet the priest would not have spoken if he had not had at least some sympathy with his own view. Perhaps not too much. Ranulf was crossing himself with his eyes closed, his face muscles tense and his throat swallowing hard on unpalatable truths.

Under the hedge Francie stirred, silencing the men. 'Stay till morning,' Ranulf invited, his voice distant. He closed Juvenal with a clap. 'I have another book which might catch your interest. And you should write a letter about Francie to be taken to your parents.' They left it at that. Ranulf disappeared and Will laid his head on his arm again. In spite of everything he had learned, which ought to have kept him awake and suffering, he immediately fell asleep in the late afternoon sun, as exhausted as the child nearby.

'Twa good days then back to winter,' muttered Ranulf late that evening. This time the rain was much colder and Will feared a dismal journey next morning. 'At least you have two clean shirts out of it. I was hoping...' He stopped short as Francie appeared in the doorway. The Bishop's chaplain obviously did for himself while at Mortlach and had produced a rich stew which would feed all of them, with some left over for beggars if there were any in this isolated, self-sufficient community. 'Come to me after the last prayers,' he finished abruptly.

And so it was not until Compline was over and everybody else in bed that Will and Ranulf managed to talk openly, each at last prepared to say things otherwise unmentionable.

'Grapples. That's what we need. Would there be any at Balvenie, do you think?' Will promised he would ask. He would also seek human help, for soldiers were much better at handling such tools than religious men. Ranulf wanted to fetch up whatever had gone into the bog, and neither of them had much doubt that there was something there to find.

'Should I stay and help?'

'N-no. We need to know what's going on at Pluscardyn. But I was thinking while you were out.' The priest hesitated.

'So was I. Perhaps Hugo was not the intended victim. But if it was meant to be me, I don't know why.'

'Your horse?'

'It's possible, but I doubt it. Francie did hear a couple of Heilanders talking about stealing it, but we challenged them, which makes it unlikely they would have carried it out. Besides, none of them left the castle.'

'You're sure? How?'

Will explained, described Francie's little dance over the sleeping bodies in the firelight, which had left them all watching each other. 'I saw Hugo de May to the door. - I told him he was mad to go out into such a night, but he wouldn't stay. He seemed anxious to get here as soon as possible.'

'To tell me about the tragedy,' Ranulf nodded. 'I see that now.'

'To you? Why should that matter so much to you?'

'Nicol is my godchild.'

'Father Thomas will want you to wait here for him, Captain Forbys.' The Cellarer was insistent, frantic even, ushering him in through the Priory gates and closing them against the three riders he had brought with him. As the solid wooden barrier began to swing between them, Camus held Will's gaze, telling him silently that he would keep the bargain they had made on the journey from Balvenie. On his hunt for Hugo de May, Will had ended up at the castle just after dawn, seeking the use of grappling irons and men to use them in a search of the bog pools. At the same time he had managed to talk privately for a few moments with

Camus, asking which two Hielanders would be the best fighters in a tight corner and who could also speak enough of either English or French to enable communication. When he then asked for three men from an unwilling James Forbys, Camus was ready with his selection. The journey today through driving rain had been swift and anxious, and it was mid- afternoon before they reached the Priory.

Now the Cellarer summoned the horse boy with a shout. It was Brother James who appeared, ashen faced but pitifully anxious to please, although he looked taken aback when he saw Will had returned. 'Come along, boy! This animal needs a good rub down. Can't you see how he has been sweating? Now Captain, the Sub-prior is in the Chapter House. I am sure he will wish to see you.'

'Very well. But let me reassure you, Brother Alexander, these men are not brought to intimidate. They came for my safety on the road.'

Alexander's eyes widened with fright. 'You mean... You've lost it, haven't you?' He meant the document.

'No, no. It is long gone on its way. I assure you it is safe. No, I returned to find out about the tragedy. The miller's grandson? I heard he was drowned the day before yesterday. On Wednesday, the day I left.'

The Cellarer's glance towards the riders was shifty. Drawing Will out of earshot, he hissed, 'I can't imagine how that news reached you.'

'Hugo de May told me.' When Alexander began to panic again, Will shook off his arm and turned his horse towards the stables. 'He met in with me on his way to Mortlach, that's all.'

James reached up to stroke the stallion's neck. 'I'll take care o' him, sir!' The big horse was splattered with mud and foam, and sweating in a manner Will would never normally have driven any mount to. In the first ten years of his life he had lived almost entirely in Scotland and his father had drummed into him the connection between respect and care for animals and their overall value - although Will was kind to them instinctively, seeing them as friends and fellow creatures. He handed over his mount gladly to Brother James, sensing a kindred caring, but immediately began to frown. The big horse pulled itself towards the water trough, throwing its head upward, all but knocking the young monk on his back.

Will still had one hand on the bridle and jerked downwards. That was all it took to bring the mount under control again, yet James was still reeling. 'I'm sorry,' the lad muttered, half glancing over his shoulder lest the Cellarer was watching. 'I'm so sorry, sir.'

Seeing the Cellarer stamping his way towards the church, Will demanded, also quietly, 'When did you last eat Brother James?' James's eyes wandered sideways, then flickered towards Will's saddlebag then away again. 'I mustn't be tempted,' he mumbled. 'I mustn't give way. Not again.'

'Good heavens, lad, you're starving! How can you do God's work in the state you're in?'

James met his eyes at last. Then he stepped back in alarm at the growing blackness in them, for Will was struggling with a string of strong emotions. His initial anxiety slid into sharp anger. The blame must surely be Brother Alexander's. He was at the root of James's abjection. For the moment at least the lad believed that feeding himself was a sin. What fanned Will's fury was fear; James was so pale and bleak, so much weaker than two days earlier that his very life might be at risk.

'You're not denying yourself water as well, are you?' This time he did not bother to keep the sharpness out of his voice. 'Believe me, Prior Thomas would consider thirsting yourself to death as the greatest sin on God's earth.'

'I mustn't,' the boy moaned. 'I'm not to be tempted. I'm not to drink again till I'm told.'

'Well, I'm telling you now that you must.' He handed his waterskin to the boy. 'It's clean burn water. Nobody'll know.' But the boy stood shaking his head over and over again, staring at the half-filled skin as if it were his passport to Hell.

Seeing the boy had not the strength to handle his mount, Will did the job himself. By the time he had finished, Brother Justin had turned up. His eyes filled with glee as he took in the transformation in Will's coiffure, the same glee Camus had shown on his return to Balvenie.

'Aye, the barber was a touch ambitious,' Will snapped before Justin could open his mouth. 'Another minute and I'd have had a tonsure and all. Well?'

Justin knew when not to tease. 'Father Gregory will see you now.' He led the way into the church, its high plain interior cold after the afternoon sunshine which had driven the rain off. There were no colours in these windows, just plain, greenish glass with medallions in the middle. Against the lime-washed walls and the plain, varnished woodwork, they emphasised the cool simplicity akin to the Carthusian Rule, broken only by occasional tiny geometrical patterning on the glass.

'We put up tapestries, but only when the public come in to worship,' Justin murmured, bowing first to the nearest altar then to the high altar at the Eastern end, above which hung the sacred Host. Its gilded vessel was suspended from the soaring ceiling on a slender chain with a pulley which allowed the movement up and down to allow refilling with holy oil. Except when in use, it was veiled by a white kerchief. 'With Biblical pictures,' Justin added, aware that Will had seen the glory and splendour of Elgin Cathedral just five miles away and must be comparing the vividness with this reserved simplicity. 'That's only on feast days and festivals.'

When Will's grim nod indicated more pressing matters, the youngster headed diagonally to the right towards where a flight of narrow stone steps was built against the wall. These led to a doorway well above them and were just one person wide with no protective barrier and no handhold, making their negotiation precarious.

'This leads to the Brothers' Quarter,' explained James. 'And Scriptorium.'

It was there that they found Brother Gregory. Or was it Father Gregory? Will had heard him called so several times. No matter. The old man was bent very closely over a charter bearing a large blob of green wax, the colour of a bishop's seal. His broad tonsure was creased by three parallel dents which told Will that he had been struck on the head long ago, probably in a battle now forgotten. With a smile of genuine friendship he rose to greet the merchant. He appeared not to notice the state of Will's eyes in spite of the line of high windows on either side of the Scriptorium which filled the room with light. At the far end another monk was busy, bent over a parchment and surrounded by pots of inks and brushes.

The Sub-Prior, who also acted as Dean, did notice that Will had been barbered and the gentle smile broadened with humour. It pulled the papery skin of age tightly over a handsome bone structure which seemed very sparsely fleshed. 'A monk's efficiency, I would say?'

'A novice's. Up at Mortlach.' The priest's smile wavered. 'Please help me, father. I have four matters needing attention - no, five, and I think I should put the fifth first.

Father Gregory heard the sharp anxiety. When Will began 'Brother James...' the ushering hands froze in mid-air.

'He has become ill? - Well, has he?'

'You seem to expect it.' Will could not keep the dry anger out of his voice. 'I don't want to be rude, Father, but the lad's starving. And yes, I think he *is* near to collapsing. It's time to do...'

The old man raised a hand. 'Say no more, my son. I am only the Sub-Prior. I do the Prior's bidding while he is out of the house, but I do not stand in his shoes. That I must never do.'

'And if James does collapse?'

'Ah, that is different. That becomes an emergency.'

'Does it now!' Rage exploded the last of Will's courtesy. 'Well, tell me this, if he does collapse how do you get an unconscious boy to swallow the liquid his body is dying for the lack of?' The angry words made Father Gregory draw his breath in sharply.

The next few moments illustrated to Will just how effectively silent men could communicate. At the far end, the illustrator shoved back his stool and turned towards the speakers, his ugly, heavily boned face black with protective anger. As he made to cross towards them, plainly intending to throw Will out, Father Gregory raised a gentle hand and found a smile from somewhere, a weary resignation but within it an odd relief.

'This is Brother Daniel.' He touched Will's arm, urging him towards the work Daniel was doing. It was a colouring of the calligraphic letter T, showing the top bracket of the letter sheltering tiny figures being fed by tonsured men in cowls. Daniel's watchful glare must have registered Will's instant admiration - the work was exquisite - for his body sagged slightly as his tension eased. When Will's eyes had scanned the text already written in, he looked up, first at the old man and then at Daniel. Both looked back at him in solemn expectation and he knew, more clearly than any words could say, that it was up to him to take the matter forward. They were almost begging him to do so.

'When will Prior Thomas be back?'

Father Gregory shrugged unhappily. 'Not till Vespers.' Hours away. 'Shall I send a messenger?'

'N-no' Will said, thinking of Camus hanging around nearby. 'I could. But it would save no more than an hour. In the meantime, may I instruct the lad to drink.' Silence. But it was stony as well as embarrassed. No, then. The order could come only from the Prior. Enraged, Will turned to go, but again the priest laid a hand on his arm. Slowly the old man shook his head then gestured to the text again.

'Speak to the Prior as soon as he returns. Please, captain. God has sent you to do His will, I am sure. Do not subvert it.' In other words, do not head for the stable and tell James he had permission to drink when it was not yet so.

Will glared again, but nodded at last. Maybe God would be good enough to keep the lad conscious long enough for the Prior to return. 'I'll be waiting for him when he comes in the gate,' he growled, and the old man smiled and nodded.

The text on which Daniel was working was from The Beatitudes. And the sentence he had chosen to illustrate was not the first. It was, 'Those who hunger shall be fed and those who thirst shall be quenched.'

It was a long afternoon. Twice, Will fell foul of the Cellarer who shooed him away from the stables where Brother James was making heavy weather of cleaning his harness. Brother Alexander saw and removed the waterskin on the first occasion, earning a glare which told him everything. Will found his bags dumped at the Guest House door, with the waterskin but no indication that he would be offered a room. In the church, his next destination, the Sacrist was replenishing the host and preparing the two large candles which stood on the floor immediately before the altar. On ordinary days only one was lit, enough to enable the Cantor to read the manuscript in use. When Will prowled around, showing no sign of private contemplation or of entering any of the five side chapels to indulge in prayer, he found himself thrown out again with one imperious gesture. Since one of the chapels was curtained off, somebody else must have been praying. The adjoining library was locked, and would remain so without the Prior's permission to open it.

With the kitchens under the Cellarer's command, Will headed out to the gardens where the white-haired Infirmarian was busy among the herbs with Brother Justin. The former was under a vow of silence, but Justin could speak with Will, and did, but only after his master limped off to trim some rooted lavender cuttings. He was another old man, older than the Cellarer though not quite as old as the Sub-Prior.

'We didn't expect you back.' Will heard the hesitancy in the lad's voice.

'No?' When Justin remained silent Will threw out a lure. 'I'm getting bored here. Maybe I'll head down to the glass kiln and watch them at work.'

No!' Then Justin clamped his teeth. His usual sunny outlook had been doused today. Now he was sharp with anxiety. 'I mean - wait till Father Thomas comes back. You should stay inside the gates till then. Stay within the precincts, I mean.'

'You mean,' Will mocked, 'the kiln doesn't belong to the Priory?'

'Of course it does! And the mill, whatever the... What I mean is that the public road goes right by them,' he adjusted. So the mill's ownership was under challenge, was it? Was that relevant to the tragedy there? 'No, it's just that the miller was the Bishop's man.'

Will turned to look straight at the boy. This comment chased his thoughts along fresh channels - as if he did not already have too many speculations hovering. He opened his mouth to ask for clarification when he realised Justin was regretting his words. Instead he asked, 'Are you hungry?'

Justin blinked. Then he blushed as Will's eyes switched to the stables. 'No,' was all he said. No more.

'So they don't starve you?'

'Nobody's being starved.' That was firm enough. 'If it's Brother James you are thinking of, he'll be off his penance the day after tomorrow.'

'Why's he being punished?'

After a short pause Justin said, 'He stole.' Then he turned away and picked up his hoe. The message was clear. Whatever damage Justin had done, or thought he had done, through careless speech he had no wish to compound it. Neither had Will any desire to make him - but he wished with all his heart that he could ask straight questions of somebody, anybody, with some prospect of getting straight answers. And how he wished now that he had not been so canny about digging out answers from Father Ranulf either. Forcing back his frustration he found an old oak tree with straggly grass beneath and lay down to think after kicking off the shoes the Mortlach cobbler had unearthed for him. His boots would go home to Druminnor with Francie.

Immediately his mind returned to Mortlach. Would James Forbys do as Will had asked and use the grapples in the castle to dredge the bog? He had been far from willing and had succumbed only when Will had pulled rank (if only as the second son of the chief). Or was it when Will told him he had tracked two riders all over the moors beyond the bogs - and back to the road just two hundred yards from Balvenie Castle. There was nothing at all to indicate whether the riders had turned left towards the River Spey or right towards the castle, or even into it but it was enough to let the suspicion hang and it sent James into a mild panic of self-defence. And willingness to help, at last.

All the while Camus had stood to one side waiting for Will to make his next move. 'And James, I need three men as escort.'

'Can't afford them. The garrison's unbalanced as it is.'

'If I were to take Camus here, we could add a couple of MacIntoshes as well.' One Forbys to two Heilanders chosen by Camus, not James, was his preference.

'Why d'ye need them?'

'How are we to know the rogues who attached Hugo de May didn't think he was me?'

James stared. 'Why would anybody wish you ill?'

Will eyed the grumpy garrison captain, sure he was being obstructive for the sake of it. He mentioned his desirable horse, but he fought shy of indicating his even more desirable person as a ransom prize. Nor would he ever reveal that there might be those around who might want him dead in preference to allowing a letter to be delivered to the Pope.

Later on during the wait for the ferry, Camus did hint with his questions that he had thought of such threats. He was given no direct answers but they did discuss possible future actions before settling into fast riding again. Will's escort would hang around unobtrusively outside the Priory until told by Will, and Will alone, to do otherwise.

Then there was Francie. Will was sure Ranulf would keep his promise and take her to his parents in Druminnor, but not before he was sure that the bog had given up its secrets. Will feared the body of Hugo de May would be dredged up, and probably his horse. He guessed that had plunged too far for the miscreants to rescue it. Yes, they had left empty-handed - unless the courier's bag had gone with them along with whatever it contained. Presumably there had been a message for Ranulf in it. Ranulf thought there must have been.

Ranulf, now. Will had liked the man straight off, his reaction strengthened by the evident trust between him and the child. It had not taken long, however, for Will to realise that Ranulf was far more than the happy scholar he had first seemed. Any sub-prior of a great Cathedral was not likely to be a simpleton. This was a complex man, perhaps a man with secrets. It may have been Will's imagination but he sensed real distress in him over Hugo de May's demise. Probable demise. They did not yet know that for certain. It may have been his stay in a silent convent trying to read silent communications around him, but Will thought Ranulf's distress was much greater than that of just a fellow cleric. Come to that, he was not even sure Hugo was a cleric. He had just assumed it because of his trade and employer. A Bishop was unlikely to entrust his private business to any man without having complete trust in him - and power over him.

Did he have that? If Ranulf was right, - no, if Francie was right, - if Hugo was indeed her father, the relationship was not acknowledged, it seemed. But if the Bishop knew about it, and if Hugo cared enough for his child, that could be a very powerful lever indeed.

Chapter 7 - Challenging the Prior

Twenty minutes of idleness was all that Will could stand. He jerked himself to his feet and headed for the empty Chapter House where he walked round it ten times in one direction then three times in the other before the Sacristan, Brother Mark, turned up and ejected him again with another supercilious gesture. His imperious stand was seriously undermined by the silly little button nose in an otherwise distinguished face. Mark wouldn't let him use the Auditorium next door either. It was there where the men spent their blessed Sunday afternoons talking, their sole speech in the week. What on earth did they talk about, Will wondered, especially if the topics which mattered were too sensitive to raise for fear of offending the Prior? The condition of Brother James was at least one instance.

Despair and frustration battled within him as he trudged after Brother Mark into the sunshine, to find even that waning. All the doors were shut behind him. The Sacristan then headed towards the beehives and Will went to ask Justin for a job to stop himself from going mad. An hour later his hoeing brought him close to where Mark was working. With only three hives done, Will realised by the ginger handling of them that the Sacristan was afraid of the insects.

Late May was always the time when his mother checked her skeps with particular care. This was when a colony with a weak queen would try to raise a replacement. If successful, the danger was that at least one new queen would fly off with a caste including a large number of the original colony. A swarm which settled elsewhere would be lost to the monks, and the mother colony might also be weakened too much to survive, making another loss. It was to check for new queen cells that the Sacristan was examining each hive. Even Will's unmusical ears could hear the two colonies which buzzed on a higher note. They were the most likely to throw a caste soon. When he suggested checking them first, the Sacristan merely gave him a haughty stare, forcing him to turn away and get on with his hoeing.

Five minutes later, the Cantor, Brother Stephen, bustled out to help. He picked out the same two hives and without reference to Brother Mark he set about checking them. Will kept his head down but saw out of the corner of his eye that each of them did indeed have new queen cells. Brother Stephen used a long, slim knife to cut out all but one, the best and most advanced, of the long wax fingers before hunting for the old queen and killing her. A quick glance at Brother Mark's face told Will how relieved the Sacristan was that somebody else had done that job. Was that why Stephen had come out to do it? The Cantor went on to whip through the remaining hives in a fraction of the time it would have taken Mark at his pace. He crooned to the tiny creatures leaving them far less disturbed than Mark had left the three hives he had done on his own.

The two monks then joined the Infirmarian and Justin in the bean patch and Will was summoned to help raise netting over the entire area, a large one because beans were crucial to the diet of men who ate almost no meat. They had barely finished when a memory jogged Will. Out of the blue he asked, 'Who's inside the last chapel? The one that's curtained off?'

All four monks froze, then looked at each other. It was Justin who had to answer, just as the truth hit Will.

'Nicol.' The two young men said the name together.

The moment Will turned to go and see, however, Brother Mark had him by the wrist. There was both power and anger in his fingers but Will could have broken the grip with ease. Instead, although a surge of annoyance stiffened his own muscles for a moment, he forced himself to relax. Feeling this, Mark loosened his grip and let Will slip his hand free.

'Am I not allowed to pay my respects?'

Justin stood chewing his tongue as Will gazed at the Sacristan, the Cantor and finally the old Infirmarian. He did not know who was the most senior but all three had high status within the community. All, he suspected, were ordained priests. He tried again. 'Is there no-one sitting with him?' Brother Mark moved a hand towards Justin.

'He's never been left alone,' the boy said. 'Brother Infirmarian sat with him till None and Brother Alexander is with him now.'

Will grimaced. It would be the Cellarer. 'May I go?' He looked at the Sacristan, imperiously back in control now that he was free of the bees. 'Please?'

In the end, another gesture gave him leave. He was at the church door before he realised that all three senior men were on his heels. Justin in the distance was chewing at his tongue harder than ever.

Brother Alexander had heard the footsteps and risen from his knees before the curtain was pulled aside. The last person he had expected to face him was Will, but the presence of the others kept Alexander silent. After a second's personal debate, he stepped aside with reluctance and Will saw behind him a child lying on the stone floor, with the figure of St John the Baptist looking down from behind the small altar. The body was concealed by a linen cloth but the face had been left uncovered.

Oblivious of the monks behind him Will went forward and knelt on one knee by the little form, his whole being filling with a tumult of shuddering, tearing pain. Nicol's angelic face now looked waxen, or marble, frozen in its beauty and apparently unblemished. A moment later he brushed a tear from his cheek.

He had been on his knee for several minutes when he became aware of the arrival of Father Gregory, fetched by the Cantor. It was to the Sub-Prior that Will finally spoke.

'Father, forgive me. I know that maybe I shouldn't be here but - where was the child found?'

'In the river.'

'River? Not in the Black Burn here?' The tension in the tiny chapel tightened.

'No. Where the burn joins the River Lossie. Why, my son?' Father Gregory spoke quietly, while the other four kept a rigid silence.

'Do you know if that was where he went in? Or just that that was where he was found?'

'Please explain.'

Will stood up, now in control, if only just. 'Father, I came back here because I learned that Nicol was dead and that I had been implicated.'

'You were seen.' That snipe came from Brother Alexander. Before Will could challenge it, Father Gregory moved a hand to silence both men.

'Who told you, Captain?'

'Hugo de May.' That, too, sent their anxiety rocketing. 'He said Nicol's body had been fished out of the river. I assumed the child had merely fallen in until he warned me not to return. And why.'

The silence grew cold, and possibly confused. Will was not yet ready to tell them more while they were far from certain of his motives. It was news of the missive they wanted, he was sure, fearing it had got into Hugo's hands. 'What I do know is that Nicol did not die from drowning. I am a sailor, and I've seen drowned men. They don't look as

- as untouched as that. I would guess that he wasn't choked to death either.'

They allowed him to speculate. When the warning screech of a blackbird outside echoed round the cavern of the great church, every one of them shivered. 'Isn't it the case that such faces are blue and discoloured?' He looked at the Infirmarian who nodded slowly.

'May I remove the cloth?' This time his eyes went to Father Gregory. The old man hesitated. When he too nodded Will pulled the linen shroud gently aside. What he saw made his gorge rise.

Had there been blood he would have vomited, no doubt spectacularly, all over the chapel floor. The metallic smell was bad enough. As it was he had to gulp several draughts of cold air before he could open his eyes and look again. The stabbing had been fierce, most of the blows driven deep into the flesh. And yet, with the passage of two days since the killing and the body's immersion in flowing water, the wounds appeared almost artificial, like the stripes of a marble Christ.

Will gritted his teeth, struggling to impose control on himself. This was no place for ranting and raving. He stood up, raising one hand to comb back his hair with his fingers, only to find himself irritated by its new lack of abundance. Then he knelt again, this time on both knees, crossed himself and bent to examine the wounds more closely. The others watched and frowned.

'Eight wounds,' he murmured.

'There is a ninth,' the Infirmarian said, speaking at last. 'At the back, below the left shoulder-blade, straight into the heart. I believe that was the killing blow, possibly the first.'

Will frowned up at him. 'So why the rest?'

The Infirmarian's shrug was more an expression of despair than bewilderment. 'Frenzy? Fright? Not knowing whether the child was dead? Not knowing whether the attacker wanted him dead?' He was giving four separate suggestions, not four variations of one explanation.

'But - the killer turned him over,' Will mused. 'That's deliberate. Scarcely frenzied.'

'Unless the child rolled with the first blow?' That was the Cellarer. There was still antagonism in his voice, but a new uncertainty had crept in.

Will was bending over again, peering in the gloom at two marks on the small body, faded but not yet gone. 'Bruises?' The Infirmarian nodded. 'Done before death?'

'Not long before, but yes. Definitely before the child died.'

'Maybe...' This time Will's hand went to fondle his beard, and found little more than air. He bent to examine the bruises, one on the left shoulder and spreading in a lozenge shape towards the centre of his chest, the other similar in shape across the lower left abdomen. 'These could be marks of the flail head.' He looked up, settling on Father Gregory again. 'You know, don't you, that I intervened in a beating on Wednesday morning? The miller was trying to attack the older, uh, child. Both bairns were on the ground but this one was farther away. I'm wondering if he had been the first to be struck and then the other intervened. Does that sound plausible?'

'Highly likely.'

'And the miller was swinging right handed,' Will remembered.

'What? One handed?' Brother Alexander was sharp again.

'No. Both hands were on the shaft, but he was swinging the thing from right to left. That would tally with these bruises. Father Gregory, may I bring my sword and dirk in?' He had had to leave them in the repository on entering the precinct gates.

The Sub-Prior's surprise was not fearful, unlike the Cellarer's, who spluttered a shocked refusal before Father Gregory could speak.

'Fetch them, brother.' Father Gregory held Alexander's eye until he obeyed, rancour steaming out of his ears. When the weapons arrived, Will laid them on the chapel floor near Nicol's body. Immediately it was obvious that neither fitted any of the visible wounds. Something broader and fatter had been used, with a pommel considerably bigger than on either of Will's pieces, because around five of the entry points bore visible bruises indicating a protective shaft larger than the handles on most blades.

'Maybe not a fighting weapon at all? Too sharp for carrying around.' None of the monks interrupted his speculation. 'Nor a normal eating blade. So - a tool perhaps? Something with quite a short blade, unusually broad at the base where it joined the pommel but ending in a point.' A couple of stab wounds were shallow and revealed the sharp widening behind the tip. Will screwed up his face in puzzlement. 'Something more or less triangular? Could that be possible?' The expressions around him, when he looked up, were blank. Or closed, deliberately refraining from revealing anything.

'May I turn him over?'

'Oh, leave the child alone!' muttered Brother Alexander, but even he was not surprised when once more he was over-ruled. The Infirmarian knelt and helped, holding the face off the floor while the ninth wound was revealed. It was quite different. A narrow, slim blade had been slipped in leaving a small puncture with scarcely any puckering or bruising around it. Will looked at his own knife, along with everyone else.

'Something like that could have done it, I suppose.' There was no point in saying otherwise. Then he thought of the

Cantor's hive knife hanging on his belt. 'But so could dozens of others. - When was the body found?'

'Shortly after two.' It was again Father Gregory who answered.

'Who found him?'

'A serf repairing the river bank after winter floods. He recognised Nicol and brought him back to Pluscardyn. Carried him on his back. When he couldn't find the miller or Francie he brought Nicol here to us.' He moved his hand to encompass the chapel.

'How long had he been in the water?' He turned to the Infirmarian.

'You are right, Captain. Not long. Not long enough for the water to begin affecting the skin even. Say an hour? Quite possibly less but two hours at the very most.' Long enough to wash the blood away.

'So, after mid-day by the time he was, er, put in?' He sighed. 'By that time I had been in Dallas for nearly an hour.'

'Dallas!' Two of the men gasped, and Alexander exclaimed. Father Gregory merely waited for Will's explanation. 'Oh, don't worry. Your missive was safely on its way by then.'

'How?' The sharp enquiry was from Brother Mark, the first breaking of his silence. Will did not answer. When Mark pressed, he was told that couriers had their own ways and means and that success often depended on being circumspect about them.

'But I spent half an hour in the hostelry there, as I am sure the innkeeper will confirm. And his wife and customers. I also spent a while in the company of Sir George de Leslie who was busy looking at the holes in his castle then I left shortly after one.'

'To go where?' Brother Mark would not leave it alone, irking Will.

'Balvenie Castle, of course. It's a Forbys holding and my father will want news of it.' That shut the Sacristan up, a very sound and plausible explanation which only Will knew was just a convenient excuse. He was unwilling to add to it for the moment. 'So you see...'

'You had no motive for killing the child in any case,' Father Gregory cut him off. 'You did not even know the family. But I have to tell you that we are becoming increasingly worried about the other child. Both she and the grandfather have gone missing.'

'And my pony,' Brother Alexander added peevishly. Will's heart gave a jolt, not in the least offset by the way the Cellarer squirmed when the other monks looked at him in disapproval. The Valliscaulians were allowed no personal property.

'You mean the pony leased to the Priory for general use, brother.' Father Gregory rubbed his upper lips with a careful finger. 'Although I grant that your provisioning expeditions will be more difficult and tiring without it.'

'The pony was in the paddock at mid-day,' Brother Stephen said suddenly, the Cantor's first contribution. 'I remember seeing it as I crossed to the kitchens. I went to drink before taking the reading during dinner.'

After digesting this, Father Gregory asked, 'And after dinner? When you had finished reading, did you eat your own meal in the refectory or in the kitchen with the cooks?'

'In the kitchen, but - I am sorry. I can't remember whether the pony was in the field then or not. I probably assumed that its grazing had taken it out of sight behind the trees.'

By now Will's imagination was working furiously. 'A white pony? Was that the one?'

'That's the one,' the Cellarer confirmed, too glum to wonder at this question and turning his head towards a noise in the main church. The door from the Brothers' Quarter had opened and Daniel was rushing down the narrow steps, his white woollen gown flapping. Father Gregory interpreted the signs immediately.

'The Prior at last! He's coming over the bridge so he'll be at the gate in five minutes. But...' Daniel's agitation grew when Will got up to head for the gate. He held up two fingers then put both hands on his head. 'Oh dear. He is not alone. And I do believe his companion is a neighbour with whom we are having - a small difficulty. He might even wish to stay for the evening meal.' He held Will's eye. 'Discretion will be required. Brother Cellarer, please warn the cooks. Brother Cantor, perhaps we should alter the chosen text for this evening. Envy is not the most tactful of topics when Robert de Chisholm is present. And Brother Daniel, come with me. We must tidy away the papers before they arrive in case Sir Robert requests a private audience. We shall remove all the charters from Father Thomas's chamber and lock them in the library.'

The old man's voice never lost its courtesy, but the slight quirks at the corner of his mouth caused a wash of comprehension in Will. The Sub-Prior thought de Chisholm was highly unlikely to wish to look at books. It tallied with Will's knowledge of the man. He probably could read, but not much. Certainly he always used scribes or notaries for his business. Most landowners did. Will's father would have done the same but for his clever wife's skills; as an only child she had been as well trained as any son by her Hanseatic merchant father.

Will did meet the Prior at the gate but not, after all, to accost him instantly with Brother James.

'I - did not expect you back so soon!' Father Thomas struggled to cover his consternation.

'Neither did I.' Will had had five precious minutes in which to compose himself and plan his approach. 'I've sorted out my business,' he stated firmly to allay fears of the missive being the cause of his return, 'but four other matters have come up, - no five. Father, I'd like your advice on one of them, please. Soon, if ye can.' He nodded to Robert de Chisholm. They stood equal in height but, while Will was built like a sturdy prize ox, de Chisholm, who might have been four years his elder, had the slender elegance and bearing of a consummate courtier. Will switched to full court French instead of the Anglicised form the monks were used to. 'Do you mind, Robert? Let me have a couple of minutes.' He dredged up a smile, holding Robert's eye.

Robert laughed, setting his big velvet hat bobbing before replying in rich Scots. 'Ye aye were an impatient brat, Willie Forbys. I'm sure I'll find a pot o' good ale while I'm waiting.'

As Father Thomas led the way to his own chamber, they met Brother Daniel departing with a bundle of scrolls under his arm. The two monks nodded to each other in full understanding and the Prior handed over a key before the door was closed behind the scribe.

'Well, Captain Forbys? What are your problems.'

'My own good name is what brought me back. The others are Francie, the pony and Hugo de May.' Thomas's face registered a number of emotions. 'Then I came on Brother James. He's the one needing dealing with in a hurry.' Will was blunt. 'What good does it do anybody to starve the laddie to the danger o' his life?'

'He is not being starved! He is being - punished.'

'So what did he steal?'

Father Thomas took a moment to answer. 'Food.'

Will stared. He closed his eyes, took a deep breath and stared again. 'Food?' It was no good. This time he let his temper fly. 'Now why do you think a growing laddie was stealing food, eh? Because he was hungry. Starving, even, if the evidence of his fleshless arms and face tell me anything. In the name of... He could have at least two years growing to do yet and he's big. Very big. Of course he needs food. And if he doesna get it he'll grow crooked, you'll see! Maybe in mind as well as body.'

'But - he is *not* being starved!' Father Thomas insisted again.

'Aw, come on! The whole lot of you are starving and it shows.'

'We are not...'

'I've never seen such an ill-fed, listless bunch of skeletons. Ye're all stick thin and your daily rations would hardly feed a sparrow. What's more, just let anybody bring in illness and you'll all be down with it within days. Are you that poor?'

'Of course not. It is the Rule to which...' Father broke off and turned away abruptly. Facing the stark crucifix on the wall he crossed himself - and Will shut up at last, horrified that he had been so rude, and so cruel. He did not need to be told that the House of the Valliscaulians followed strict rules and that these were bound to include dietary restrictions. After a couple of minutes chewing his conscience, however, he remembered James's pathetic glance towards the waterskin, the desperate slurping of the lad's drinking from the horse trough.

'Surely he deserves to drink, at least,' he murmured. 'Without water he'll die within...'

'He has water!' Thomas swung round, his voice shrill with fear.

Will shook his head, sobering quickly. 'No water since I was last here, and no food since last Sunday, I'd guess, apart from a crust I gave him, not knowing he was under orders not to eat. I'm surprised he hasn't collapsed already.'

The Prior crossed himself again and panic flared in his eyes. 'It was never my intention...' He rushed to the door and called for the Cellarer. Alexander must have been hovering nearby, possibly on Father Gregory's advice. Seeing the Prior's distress he glowered at Will as he entered.

'Brother Alexander, what sustenance is Brother James receiving?'

'None, Father.' Then he hesitated, becoming distressed before adding, 'As you instructed.'

The silence lasted for a full minute. 'I did, didn't I,' the Prior agreed at last, his face gaunt with shock. ‘I did use the word starve.' Thomas bowed his head. When he continued his voice was trembling. 'Forgive me, my son, I have put you in an appalling situation. I intended to instruct a continuation of bread and water for three more days, not a complete withdrawal of everything.' By now his voice was a hoarse whisper. 'I hope I haven't killed the boy.'

The Cellarer's jaw clenched. He would have waited forever for his next orders and once more Will butted in.

'He'll need a careful start again. You can't just sit him down to a square meal straight off.'

'And what would you suggest?' Brother Alexander's voice scraped the Spartan walls of the room, bringing Will back to his senses. He was intruding disgracefully.

'I - think the Infirmarian would advise a beaker of water first. With a spoonful of honey in it and perhaps a good pinch of salt. If - when that has stayed down a while then a few spoonfuls of broth. Maybe?'

The Prior nodded to Alexander who left, throwing Will another glare. The next silence was long and painful.

'The other men must have realised what was happening.' Thomas's voice was thick with sadness. 'Yet none of them gave me any hint.' Will examined his boots. 'Perhaps they want me to fail here.'

'I shouldn't think that, Father. More like they're trying to protect you from the day to day running...'

'But that is my function, Captain. I am the father of this community. I have the overall responsibility for every detail here.'

'Well, maybe that's it. They took your word for it and trusted you to know what you are doing. - Were they presuming that James's punishment is laid down in whatever rule it is you are all following?'

'St Basil's.' The next pause was long enough for Will to begin to wonder why Robert de Chisholm had come to Pluscardyn. The same person must have invaded Thomas's thoughts for suddenly he snapped out of his distress. 'I must see to my other guest.'

'So I can stay here the night?'

'Oh, you must! Captain, you must not leave these precincts until - until I tell you it is safe for you to do so.' Then, 'We shall talk later, I promise you. As for the other matters you mentioned, tell me just this for the moment. Is Francie safe?'

'Yes.' It was enough. Relief galvanised the Prior into steps so quick that even Will's long legs found it hard to keep up. 'She has stolen your pony, I'm afraid.'

'Not stolen.' Thomas threw the reply over his shoulder. 'It was delivered for her two years ago by Hugo de May, but she was too small for it then and it was leased to us until such time as - ' He stopped suddenly and Will cannoned into him. 'Does she know about Nicol?'

'Oh aye! She certainly knows. But I could get no details from her. Maybe when her terror passes she'll tell...'

Thomas's brown eyes widened. 'Yes,' he said very softly, 'you are wise not to pester her. Later, my friend. We shall talk when the house is gone to bed and our guest has left. Meanwhile I'd - be glad of your assistance with him. Our

Rule does not hone our conversational skills.' Nevertheless, Will was not assuming the imposition of the Rule had damaged the Prior's wits. Not at all.

In the refectory he was relieved to see no sigh of Brother James. The Infirmarian was also absent. For every other meal Will had attended, James had been present too, but on his knees before the Cantor's lectern, remaining unfed through the meal. It must have been torture for the starving boy.

Chapter 8 – Sifting Evidence

Friday meant fish for supper, carp from the Priory pools. The Cantor joined the top of the table along with Father Gregory to keep the conversation flowing while the rest of the monks ate in silence. Will sensed that Brother Mark's patrician pride was offended that Brother Stephen had been selected rather than him. Mark's rare speech had held a smoothness suggesting an upper class background which could have bred ambition in the man.

The entire conversation was, of course, audible to everyone. At first it amounted to little but pleasantries, easily contrived and meaningless. When town gossip came up, Will noted a sharper edge, but not being acquainted with either the events or the burgesses of Elgin and their squabbles he was unable to interpret the hidden satirical fencing undoubtedly going on. Much of it involved contested ownership of something or other, mills and their multures, the odd acre here and there, hunting rights and whose serfs were entitled to purloin the odd rabbit or pigeon. Robert de Chisholm was doing ninety per cent of the talking, giving the monks - all of them - an entertaining and amusing picture of life in the vibrant borough just four miles away which they were unlikely ever to see for themselves.

The only members permitted to leave the precincts were the Prior and the Cellarer, and occasionally the Sub-Prior, usually in his other capacity as dean in order to deal with fiscal matters. Lay monks in charge of labouring had to attend to their duties, of course, which often took them to Priory lands or quarries beyond the immediate grounds, some tracts far away, but, like other serfs, they could not stray beyond their own community's defined limits unless travelling between its properties. The Prior ran its various businesses to a high standard, including the management of the royal forest at the back of the Priory itself. There were the many scattered farms and quarries, the saltpans and fishing rights on the shore, the freshwater fish-pools on the River Finderyn, on the Spey and Loch Ness, the kilns, of course. - Will saw Brother Michael down at the bottom of the gloomy table. - And the mills. The only exception to the norm seemed to be Hector's unhappy, unkempt mill attached to the Priory itself, which many must have queried.

'...a thorough mess it is. I wonder you put up with it.' Robert's frank words caused a chilled shock in the room and it was this rather than the comment itself which dragged Will's thoughts back to the conversation.

'There are reasons.' Father Gregory gave the mild answer, sensing Father Thomas's struggle with distress.

'L'Enfant du Diable, you mean?' Robert went on chewing, unaware of the waves of unease he was creating. Or did he intend to give the impression of oblivion? A muscle was jumping below his ear.

'Nicol is dead.' It burst from the Prior's lips. Robert went on chewing for a couple of seconds before slowing, stopping, swallowing then laying down his eating knife.

'Dead?'

'His body was found in the river on Wednesday.'

After half a minute of total stillness, Robert picked up his knife again. 'I suppose it was bound to happen. A daft bairn living beside water, I mean.' He speared a tender piece of carp from the large helping before him, transferred it to his mouth then spoke around it. 'How did Francie take it?' Everyone else froze anew.

'I don't know.' Thomas stared at the meagre meal before him almost untouched. 'She has disappeared. So has the grandfather.' This time alarm did jolt Robert although he tried to hide it.

'So has the pony I used for my provisioning expeditions,' Brother Alexander muttered from farther down the table. No reprimand came this time.

'What? The wee grey?' Robert's knife was back on the table. 'So they've run, have they?' He looked around. All eyes were on him and he knew it. Indentured servants had no right of removal without permission. 'In other words, Nicol was pushed? Aye, well, maybe it's for the best.'

'No.' Something in Robert's flat assumption drove Will to speak at last. 'Nicol was skewered.' Immediately he wondered if he had said too much, for Father Thomas stiffened where he sat between his guests. Robert's hand, which had reached for his dish knife again, stilled for a second then finished its movement; another piece of fish was cut and transferred to his mouth. Everybody watched him chew, then swallow. It took a long time.

'Then it’s no wonder they ran,' he said at last. 'Who d'ye think did it?' He was asking the Prior. 'The miller? Or Francie? Rage or pity?'

At the far end of the great table a figure jumped up, shattering the hostile silence by knocking a wooden mug over. 'It was him! It was him!' Brother Michael was pointing straight at Will, his eyes wild and his finger trembling. There was no vestige of doubt in his voice. 'I saw him in the yard just minutes before I found the blood.'

'And when was that, brother?' Father Gregory's voice brought a measure of calm. 'When did you see this man?'

'As I returned after the mid-day meal. I saw him in the yard.' The kiln-master recovered a little, aware that the eyes of some of his fellows held doubt.

'How far away were you?'

Brother Michael's eyes widened. 'I was - coming out of the North Gate on my way back to the kiln.'

'Are you sure it was Captain Forbys?'

'Absolutely! He'd been in the yard earlier that morning, in the kiln too. I could recognise him easily.'

'Yes, I know that.' The Prior made no attempt to interfere with Father Gregory's handling, which was masterly in its calmness. 'But brother, Captain Forbys left us over two hours earlier and...'

'It was him, I tell you! He must have come back. And see - he's changed his looks. Cut his hair and his beard and exchanged his boots for shoes. Isn't that a sign of guilt?'

A flash of irritation twitched the Sub-Prior's mouth. 'Brother Michael,' he broke into the illogical stream of accusations, 'let me prove to you why it could not have been Captain Forbys you saw.' Michael stared, appearing almost crazed in his conviction that he was right, and turned to the Prior for support.

Father Thomas shook his head. 'Listen to Father Gregory, my son. Let us all listen.' Michael collapsed on to his bench, silenced but still convinced by the evidence of his own eyes. 'Father Gregory?'

'Captain Forbys was in Dallas Castle at the time you claim to have seen him. I have no doubt that he can call a number of witnesses to testify to that. One of them is Sir George de Leslie.'

'The gentry always back each...' Michael ground to a halt, eyeing Robert de Chisholm. Neither of them would have been five years older than Will if that, but Will appeared the senior.

'As for the barbering,' Father Thomas intervened, 'I have no doubt he arranged that because he needed it.' He cleared his throat then threw a leavening of humour into the argument, 'We all saw that. The point, surely, is this. If he had murdered Nicol, and I cannot see any logical reason why he would want to, why should he return now demanding that his name be cleared? He could have been at sea within hours and far beyond the reach of the law.'

As they all waited for Michael to rethink his evidence, Robert dropped an adjustment into the silence. 'Scots Law maybe. Ecclesiastic law would follow him everywhere.'

'That's why the Bishop wants him tried at the Cathedral.' This was Brother Mark.

Will stood up in surprise. 'Does he?' he demanded of Father Thomas, who nodded. 'Then let him. I'm more than willing to...'

'Nicol was killed on Priory land. The investigation will take place under my jurisdiction here at Pluscardyn.' Prior Thomas's voice was very firm.

'How do you know where he was killed?' Will asked, glancing at Mark.

'Because when Brother Michael went to investigate he found a large pool of blood just outside the doorway of the mill, and a dragged trail leading across the yard towards the Black Burn.

'But,' Robert interjected again, 'Hector was the Bishop's miller.'

'On lease of exchange, which in effect makes him a Priory man.' Father Gregory's voice was becoming strained. 'The child was still killed on Priory land.'

'And now you've got your hands on the felon and that gives you the greater power!' Robert was enjoying the mockery.

'He is not the felon.' Father Gregory's irritation was growing, but still the Prior left him unchecked.

'Maybe no, but a trial would be handy, wouldn't it? Demonstrate a point?' Robert's taunting at last told Will about the relationship between the Bishop and the Prior. A standoff obviously existed which was familiar to the locality. Was it also the reason for the missive sent to the Pope? Was this why Father Gregory was ruining the last of his eyesight searching through old charters for evidence? The Priory would need to prove that it was an independent ecclesiastical foundation and not under the hegemony of the Bishop of Murray, already a powerful prelate. Maybe too powerful in some eyes. Will wondered if there were any proof to be found.

He looked at the Prior, and found himself being watched in return. His thought processes were being followed. Their eyes held for a moment.

'Who would you prefer to judge you, Captain?'

Will answered after a hesitation, 'Both together might suit.' A brief spark of mischief lit in the Prior's eyes. It was soon doused when Father Gregory murmured news of a third claim for Will's neck.

'I regret, Captain, that just before you arrived today, we also received a request from the borough of Elgin. I quote. The Court of Burgesses require that, in the event of the return of Captain William Forbys, merchant, to Pluscardyn, the said Captain William Forbys should be detained and presented to the Court Offices of the said borough of Elgin to answer a charge of murder, the said victim of the said murder being a child, Nicol, grandson of the miller of the Prior's Mill at Pluscardyn in the Vale of St Andrew, whose body was retrieved from the River Lossie on a town beat on the said river.'

'Bah!' Robert de Chisholm barked. His soft, sandy hair flopped over his brow as he whipped his head round to wiggle his eyebrows at Will. 'Well memorised, Father Gregory. They fairly mangle the King's Scots tongue, don't they, these toon lawyers.' Then he laughed outright. 'They're all out to truss ye, Willie!'

'So it seems.' Will sat down again, realising at last why the monks had been so anxious to keep him within their walls. Presumably Camus, still hanging about outside, had uncovered the same information. He was busy wondering what Camus would do with it when Robert turned to Father Gregory.

'Where was the body found, exactly?'

'At the junction of the Black Burn and the Lossie.' Something told Will that Robert did not like the answer.

'The Black Burn? The one other folk call the Lochty Burn? But my land butts there.'

Father Gregory made a firm point. 'Downstream of the burn yes, and on the west bank of the river only. The bank builder was working on the town beat on the east and pulled Nicol out on that side. It was natural. - But I do wonder who told the burgesses about Captain Forbys being accused. Our brothers and all the staff were told to say nothing outside the Priory.' The Sub-Prior had kept his eyes on Robert, but Brother Michael jumped up again anyway, this time in surprise.

'*I* didn't! It wasn't *me*!'

According to the silence, nobody else did the telling either. It was at this point that the Prior stopped all speculation, or at least all speech.

'My sons, and my honoured guests, we are destroying the enjoyment of our meal with such irregular talk. Let us continue according to our Rule, in silence apart from the Word of Our Lord. Brother Cantor?'

The reading no longer touched on envy, but whoever had replaced it with an analysis of the meaning of the Murder of the Innocents by St Augustine had been highly provocative.

Robert 's curiosity having uncovered that Nicol had been taken to the Priory, he stayed for Vespers, and announced that 'he would have a look at the body.' Will remained in the main church for the few seconds it took, then watched along with the monks as their awkward neighbour departed. It was then that Father Gregory passed him a small hourglass, murmuring, 'Go the Auditorium an hour after Compline.'

Will arrived first, knowing all the monks would - or should - be asleep, although even tucked into the east side of the hill the light would not leave the valley sky for another two hours this late in spring. There was certainly enough to enable Will to see that the front of the Prior's vestment was dusty.

'I've been praying,' was all he said. Face down on the chapel floor it must have been.

'You look exhausted, Father,' Will murmured, 'and I know you need to be up at two to lead Matins. Do you want to leave this till tomorrow?'

The Prior rubbed his eyes, then resisted the tempting offer. 'No. This may be the only privacy we shall find. But let us be quick. Ask your questions then I shall ask mine.'

'Suits me. So who's your traitor?'

Father Thomas looked shocked. 'Traitor?'

'The one who told Hugo de May that I was carrying something away for you?' Thomas's mouth opened. 'The one who told the town folk where Nicol was found - though that could have been the bank builder. But he wouldn't have known that I was seen, or supposed to have been seen, in the mill around noon. So who told the Town I was implicated? And who told the Bishop? And I noticed that you kept to yourself the fact that Francie is safe. Are you afraid she might not be any longer if her whereabouts become known?'

Thomas put a hand over his eyes. 'You are too swift! Too acute.'

'Is it Michael?'

'I - don't think so. He certainly believes he saw you but he is loyal to the Priory for many reasons. He may have told Hugo de May that you had left here, but how Hugo knew you were going south to Dallas I cannot imagine.'

'He didn't. Nobody did except the man I met there. And anyway Hugo went to Finderyn first. It was when he came back to look for a new trail that he learned that Nicol had been found. - But I'm inclined to agree. Whatever Michael did tell him was said maybe without tact but without malice or design either. So who else?'

'I don't know. Truly, my friend, I do not know. What suspicions I have are not sufficient to name any man here.'

'Brother Alexander? Or is he just crabbit with hunger and sore feet? He has enough loose skin about him to suggest that he was once fat. - Forgive me, father. That was uncalled for. - But Brother Alexander does seem loyal to you as well. Keen to stand by your decisions over Brother James anyway, even if he had doubts them.'

'Does he? Did he?'

'Uh, maybe. He - was a bit over-jittery for comfort.'

Will hated himself, seeing the words strike pain in the brown eyes fixed on his own. Thomas put all his fingertips to his brow, spread so that Will saw his eyes shut. The action made him seem younger. He seemed young to hold the position of Prior at any rate, younger than all four senior clerics. The position brought with it a seat in the Scottish Parliament. Nowhere near forty, he was pleasant looking rather than handsome, of medium height and dark-haired with deep-set eyes and thin clean-cut features with a long nose and wide mouth; unremarkable, until he looked at someone. Then the intelligence and compassion became magnetic. When he looked up suddenly, Will was the one transfixed.

'May I ask a favour?'

Will blinked. 'Ask away.'

'Please call me Thomas.' The voiced was charged with wistfulness. 'Only when we are alone, I mean. I have called you friend because you have done me a great service. You alone have confirmed a fear which has been growing within me for many months now. If any one of God's servitors here had as much as hinted that they had similar reservations about the severity of the demands of our Rule, I would have responded instantly.'

'James? - Sorry, but what else is a friend for?'

'You are right.' Thomas managed a faint smile. 'Yes. James. I am sad to say he became a victim because I had my eye on too many other things. - You're not surprised?' He smiled again, and the glint of mischief reappeared. 'Then tell me what you think those were,' he challenged.

'Humph. Trouble with the Bishop? Was he the subject of your message to the Pope, maybe? Your charters should clarify things but you can't find what you need. You're probably right to think a Papal writ would stop any more arguing. No. I didn't read it. Mind you, the name of Robert de Chisholm came out and hit me as I signed, so I fancy he's your second problem. Is he trying to nip at your boundaries? Looking for rents from tenants he thinks should be his, not yours?'

'God's. The rents are collected for delivery to the Papal court at Avignon.'

'I know Robert needs the money, like every other landowner in Scotland. My own father's another. John o' Gaunt has sent a new demand for the unpaid ransom moneys due to the English crown for King David's release. – Did you know? You'd think they'd let up after eleven years, wouldn't you?'

'Especially as they had no right to imprison him in the first place,' agreed Thomas, his face glum. 'But we must concede that there was a little matter of the battle of Neville's Cross, on English soil, Captain.'

'My friends call me Will. Or Willie, if they knew me as a bairn.'

Thomas grinned at last, his thin countenance lighting up for an instant, but he took the hint in the dry words. 'Then Will it shall be. - But you are uncomfortably accurate.'

'And there is trouble over the mill. Mine wasn't the first intervention between the miller and his grandchildren, was it?'

'No.'

'Michael? He was on guard? Maybe it's guilt at failing the bairns that is making him look for another to blame.'

'You don't think he could have done it?'

Will's mouth opened in surprise. 'Do you?'

'I - think it is doubtful. May I ask some questions now?'

Within twenty minutes Thomas had extracted almost every detail of Will's side of the story, and Francie's as far as he knew it.

'So the men hanging around the gate are yours. I did wonder when they refused to move on.'

'They pose no threat, Father... Sorry. Thomas, I mean.'

'Is it so hard?' Bleakness again lowered the Prior's voice. 'Forgive me if I ask too much. It is just that - I have no-one left in the world who may call me by my given name. None of my birth family now lives, and here... Here I am father to this enclosed family and have been cut off by my authority from familiar intercourse with those around me. I fear I'm a poor father too, if my sons are unable to confide in me when they are distressed. Not even during confession.'

He stood up abruptly and turned towards the last of the light in the west, presenting his back to Will rather than expose his distress to scrutiny. Will held his tongue for a good two minutes before becoming practical.

'Thomas, how long have you been Prior?'

'Two and a half years.'

'By election of the brothers? Unanimous? Well, you must have merited it then, so why not now?' Will's prosaic flatness brought the other man round. 'And did you have to go to Avignon to be confirmed?'

'To Burgundy, our mother community at Val des Choux. But once our Prior-General had confirmed my election he did send me on to Avignon for ratification by Pope Urban.'

'Did he now! Urban is a scholar in canonical law, isn't he? Sounds as if your Prior-General anticipated that the Bishop of Murray fancied confirming rights for himself.'

'He did because I told him so. The confusion arose out of an irregular arrangement made about twenty five years ago. Somehow a previous Bishop of Murray persuaded the Prior-General's emissary here on pastoral duties to sign a document giving the bishop visiting rights. It was under the guise of protection since we are so far from Burgundy. And at a time of plague. A number of local men of power also signed as witnesses, but significantly the king did not. Nor is there mention of the king making any recommendation.'

'And that matters?'

'Certainly it does. This is a royal foundation and has always remained in royal hands, not the bishop's. And yes, this rogue signing took place after the king was captured by the English, although he still had to sanction any rupture of his remit, even from England.'

An unwelcome thought poked its way into Will's head. Thomas was no doubt content with David Bruce as king and master, but would he be so happy if it became Robert the Steward? The Bishop might just become preferable. Uncannily Thomas picked up Will's speculation.

'As a royal foundation we are under the King's protection. But since the Scottish king is not a dignitary of Holy Church we remain under the supreme charge of the Pope himself. Whatever tithes we gather we pay to His Holiness alone.' So that was what the Bishop was after. He had his grand cathedral to maintain and embellish, to say nothing of his powerful palace at Spynie a mile to the west. Will had seen new building going on there turning it into a stronghold. No doubt he thought Robert Stewart would also cast a greedy eye on Pluscardyn's wealth as well as seeing Murray as a comfortable home for his boots.

'So why were you founded here in the first place?'

'Undoubtedly to act as a counterbalance between the See of Murray in the east and the Carmelite Abbey of Kinloss in the west.'

'Mm. And the king chose you as a different order so that you wouldn't join up with one and leave the other peeved, or overpowerful.'

'Exactly.' Thomas sat down again. 'But this was a hundred and forty years ago, when the church was being used to quell a rebellious land. At the same time the last of Macbeth's descendants were being wiped out. His followers were transported elsewhere and Flemish knights settled here as king's men, holding royal lands in equal proportions to the Church possessions. What made things awkward for everyone was the way the lands of almost every landowner, Church or crown, were chopped up and scattered far and wide in little parcels. The whole region became a patchwork of legal disputes. It was a mess.'

'Is it any better now?' Will raised an eyebrow.

'Not much,' Thomas sighed, 'and I seem to be in the middle of most of the trouble. Outside and in.'

'There you are then. Your monks will know this, I'll wager, and will be trying to keep the domestic troubles off your shoulders to leave you free to play politics.'

'But a prior should not be playing politics! His prime position is that of father to his community. - You make a tempting Devil's Advocate, Will.'

'I'm trying to talk sense. When are you burying Nicol?'

'I had hoped tomorrow, but the Bishop insists that his own Scrutineer sees the body first. I - thought it politic to comply.'

'Then ask an Elgin Court Officer to come too.'

Thomas exchanged a sudden grin with Will, each tickled by the thought of playing the rivals off against each other.

'I am enjoying your company, Will!'

'Who's sitting with the body now?'

'Justin. I know he's young, but he asked to do so. He has spent some time with both children over the last few months and was unusually patient with Nicol.'

'Sounds appropriate. - Thomas, have I done the right thing with Francie? Should I have left her with Father Ranulf?'

Thomas thought for a while before answering. 'I am sure she is safe with him,' he said at last. 'However, he may not take her to your mother.'

'Why not?'

'Because you would know she was there. And you might tell others. You have already told me, haven't you? Father Ranulf might reason that others could guess that your home is her destination, once they learn that she is safe. At the very least I must tell my family here that I know that she is, if only to ease their heartache.'

'So you think she might be in danger? Is that what you're saying?'

'Of course she is. You know that yourself, for you took her with you instead of sending her back. And you have told nobody but me where she is. - Or have you?' His voice sharpened.

'Nobody. Yes, I'm afraid for her too. And yes, one possibility is that she saw what happened and is able to tell. The killer - or killers - might wish to stop her speaking out. But there is another possibility.' He took a deep breath. 'Father Thomas, may I speak?'

He knelt before the Prior, that and the formal use of his title making it plain that this was a confession. The Prior hesitated.

'My son,' he warned, 'I am confessor for everyone within the Priory, but I too must have a confessor.'

'Father Gregory?' Father Gregory was the man Will would trust most with what he had to say. 'That's fine by me.' The Prior took Will's praying hands between his own.

'Then what is it that you wish to confess, my son?

Chapter 9 – A Confession

‘You won't like it. When Francie caught up with me she was wearing a tunic on top of her yard smock. I didn't realise that until she got soaked in the rain and - the tunic began to turn pink. Underneath, the smock was drenched with blood.' He cleared the lump of horror from his throat. 'She swore she had no injury herself, and I certainly didn't see any sign of her being in pain or slowed down in any way. She had made some effort to clean herself up as well, but once I knew to look I saw blood remnants under and all round her fingernails.' By now his hands were being squeezed tightly between Thomas's.

The Prior began to pray, very softly but fiercely and fearfully. After several minutes he broke off abruptly. 'Does Ranulf know this?'

'No. The bloodied clothes were in my saddle pack by then. I've buried them on the moor. I confess that I may have perverted the course of justice by doing that.'

'So what's she wearing now?'

'My best shirt,' was the dry answer. 'It goes down to her knees even when belted.'

'Were her own clothes - torn? Or damaged in any way?'

'Nothing out of the ordinary. A couple of bramble snatches maybe, no more. No I don't think she was stabbed.'

Again the Prior prayed. It was as if he were giving himself time to think. His next question was one Will had not thought of. 'Was there blood on the pony? No? You would have seen it if it had been there, wouldn't you? On its white coat?'

'Yes,' Will admitted, then against his wishes his next thought came out, 'unless it had been washed. I - remember now that she mentioned that *she* had fallen into the river. I thought she meant the Black Burn here, or another burn along the way.'

'And now what do you think? Come, my son, this is *your* confession.'

'Och, the Divvel be cursed! Now I'm wondering... Did she take Nicol from the mill yard and put him in the river? Into the Lossie? Somebody did. The burn water is low just now and could never have swept a body so far so fast. It's what - a mile? She could never have carried Nicol all that way on her back either. Besides the blood was on her front. So she must have used the pony. It's a wonder she wasn't seen by half the countryside!'

After a pause the Prior began to muse. 'The pony went missing during the noon dinner, according to Brother Stephen's evidence. Our working folk also go home to eat then and are gone for around an hour. She would have known that, and she certainly knows the quiet paths, among trees, behind hedges. She did not, in fact, need to leave Priory land. In spite of de Chisholm's implication over supper tonight, he does not govern all the land on the west bank of the Lossie. Upstream of the Black Burn the land is ours.'

'What I don't understand is why she bothered. If she was wanting to, well, to cleanse Nicol, why not in the burn right beside the mill. Why take him all that way?'

Thomas swallowed and the Adam's apple in his long, thin neck bobbed in pain. 'She took Nicol to where his mother died. Poor child! The mother was hers, too, of course.'

'Ohh...' Will shuddered. 'She said... Oh, how easy it is to let things slip by! She told me Nicol had gone back to his mother. Now I know what she meant.'

'You couldn't have known.'

'Poor, poor bairn!' After a few moments Will asked, 'When did the mother die?'

'I wasn't here, but I'm told it was about a week after I left for my confirmation in Burgundy. Father Gregory was in charge. On that occasion the body was washed on to de Chisholm land and Robert's father handed the case over to the Bishop for trial.'

'And the verdict was suicide. Ranulf told me.' He did not mention the rest. 'Thank you, Father. May I have a penance?' When this was given, Will stood up. There was another possible scenario for Nicol's death but neither man dared to voice his fears. Nevertheless, it hovered in the air between them until Will veered away from the black thought with more blunt words.

'Thomas, you're still tired. But thank you for listening.'

'Thank you for coming to me, my friend. In spite of my weariness, and in spite of the horrors visited upon us, I feel a rare uplifting of my heart tonight.' Will could not think of a reply, until Thomas gave a gurgle of laughter. 'How pompous I sound.'

'Maybe you need a friend to knock the stuffiness out of you. - Or shove the stuffing back in, maybe?'

'How right you are. But there is still more information you ought to have.'

'The reason why Francie's special? Apart from her tremendous spunk, I mean. She's no ordinary peasant bairn, is she?'

'No. She isn't. Her grandmother was a de Chisholm.' Thomas watched that news blow Will's wits sideways. 'Isabella, her grandmother, married far beneath her when she married Hector. Across cultures too. Hector is a Mac Fearchar, a Gaelic-speaking highlander. Their daughter Amelia was born a couple of months too soon, I fear, and Isabella died a few weeks later. The miller had to raise

Amelia on his own because the de Chisholms had disowned his wife. She went to him without a dowry and at that time he was just a soldier of fortune, selling his skills to whoever would buy them. Of course, with a child to care for he had to give up that way of life and find a new profession, which he did thanks to the de May family. Hugo's father, I mean. He was a burgess in Inverness, but he had been Hector's army captain at some stage, I believe.'

It was Will's turn to stand up, taking a turn round the Auditorium and back while he digested the new information. The room was growing darker but filling with the warm glow of a pink and dove grey sunset outside. 'They were beautiful, these women? Aye, of course they were. Just look at the bairns. I fancy the miller was a fine looking man many years ago, before misfortune ground him down.'

'I know Amelia was considered the loveliest lady for miles around.' Thomas had to be prodded before adding the rest. 'No, I don't know who Francie's father was. He never declared himself. He certainly never produced a ring.'

'Hm. - But didn't he produce the pony?'

'Did he? Hugo de May delivered it. There's is no doubt about that. But there's no reason to suppose any more than that. Besides, although the de Chisholms disowned Isabella publicly, there were still gifts of some significance which came Amelia's way, especially after Isabella's father died - as a very old man still stubborn in his unforgiving, I understand. So why not gifts to Amelia's children?'

'From the de Chisholms, you mean?'

'I do. Robert's father was Isabella's brother, which made Robert and Amelia full cousins. But there's more. - I cannot govern your silence as you governed mine, Will, but I beg of you, treat this as equally sacrosanct.'

'You have my word.'

‘Then - no. First let me tell you that it is no secret that Hugo was the middle of three de May brothers. I have to hope he still lives. The father died not long after the youngest was born and the family's fortunes sagged badly, although the mother did well to give all three an education of a kind, thanks to the church. The eldest is Ranulf. Little wonder that he was so upset at the thought of his brother drowning in a bog. And the youngest is Brother Michael. Yes, our kiln master here at Pluscardyn. All three brothers knew the miller's family well, including Amelia. As I said, their father had been Hector's officer and it was he who found a place for him at one of the Elgin mills so that he could raise his child.'

'So this familiarity predates the de May brothers entering the church?'

'Father Gregory tells me so. He has been here for nearly twenty years and I have no hesitation in believing him.' Thomas dried up, embarrassed.

'Ah, you mean they are candidates for the post of Francie's father. Or one of them.'

'I believe so. There seem to be no others - unless you include Robert, which I doubt because of the consanguinity. I feel wretched about maligning the de Mays behind their backs like this...'

'But others are saying it so it's better I know.'

'I am expected to be more forgiving.'

'It's truth we're after here, not charitable blindness. No other candidates?'

'I don't think so, but Francie was born before I came here. So was Nicol, just.'

'Same father, d'you think?'

'No.'

'Ah.' Will waited. 'You sound very sure. So you know *his* father, then?' Thomas said nothing at all. 'And the confessional keeps you quiet. Very well, which of the de May brothers do you think could be Francie's father?'

'I can only speculate.'

'Then speculate. Because I can think of one reason why Nicol was killed by Francie's father.'

'Can you?'

'And you've thought of it too, only you're too Christian to put it into words. Nicol was a millstone round everybody's neck. The miller was coming to the end of his tether, with Nicol getting bigger and harder to cope with. No matter how much Francie tried, she couldn't really look after Nicol well enough to protect him from her grandfather's rage. She did love Nicol, didn't she?' And there was that horrid question flitting between them once more. This time Thomas did not duck it.

'Totally and without judgement. Please, don't ask me if she could have killed her brother for his own sake.' The Prior was pleading. 'Or for her own.'

'Why not?'

'I will not answer.'

'It should be asked nevertheless,' Will insisted quietly, though far from happy about it. 'Others will. But if she didn't, who might have killed Nicol for *her* sake, maybe fearing that she'd put herself between Nicol and the miller once too often?' He held Thomas's eye. 'It couldn't have been Ranulf for he was a full day's ride away and he hadn't left Mortlach for weeks. I took the trouble to check - only then I was wondering about a link with Hugo's death, not Nicol's.'

'You think Hugo is dead, then?' Thomas was deliberate in changing direction.

'I - fear so. Now, what about him? He returned to Pluscardyn after his abortive chase to Finderyn. That would have put him back here at some time around the noon break. And then there's Michael, there on the doorstep all the time.

And mind, whichever one is Francie's father, the other two are her uncles and they probably cared for her a lot. So who is your candidate as Nicol's killer?'

'My candidate is the grandfather.'

'Still?'

'It always was. Will, I am not breaking the silence of confession when I say I know he has come near to it many times. He has openly admitted to the tyranny of his temper. And to his fear and despair.'

'Would it help to know who Nicol's father is?' Thomas was silent again. 'Sorry. I won't ask again. But - why are we not searching for the grandfather?'

'We are. That was one reason why I called on the Bishop today. I feared that Francie might be with the miller. Or dead somewhere. Everybody did. Strictly, the miller is still the Bishop's man, as Robert de Chisholm said. And between ourselves, Hector and the children were brought here to Pluscardyn after Amelia's death so that Michael could keep an eye on things. It was convenient that the mill and the kiln stood side by side. As you say, he was on watch all the time. But now, the Bishop has sent out men to scour the roads and towns. They will check all the harbours and the woods and fields. And the river banks in case the miller follows where his daughter led, or in case Francie is also a victim. I - haven't yet sent to the bishop that she is safe.'

'Have you any idea where the miller might be?'

'Those *were* my ideas. The Bishop didn't seem too interested - except in capturing you. Beware, my friend. You are in danger of being made the scapegoat, perhaps for reasons beyond this tragedy. I strongly advise you to remain under our protection until you have secured all the evidence you need to prove your innocence and your right to ride away freely.'

'Och Thomas, you're a nuisance! I'm supposed to be in Aberdeen in five days' time and I can't see my family being pleased if I reach Druminnor just in time to leave again.' His heart ached over somebody else who would be cross. He was desperately anxious not to give Bethoc Gordon the impression that his love for her was light. Her father was hardly likely to look well on his offer of marriage either, if he could not stand still for long enough to declare his intentions. 'And what'll I *do* here while I wait?'

Thomas laughed outright. 'Alexander and Stephen both complained of your prowling this afternoon. But I think I know of a job to keep your restless mind busy. Very busy indeed!'

Once that was explained, and accepted with relish, they parted. Neither commented on how late and dark the hour was, but Will was glad he would be able to sleep until he was rested. Thomas had to be up in three hours' time. Who would be a priest? As they parted Thomas added one more request.

'Please attend at the Chapter House at ten tomorrow morning.'

Everyone was up before Will that Saturday morning, including the Bishop's Investigator of Crimes. He, like Ranulf, was another Sub-Prior of the Diocese of Elgin, Father Symon, a bumptious little man as round and well-feathered as a Christmas goose. His charge was the parish of St Michael's in Dallas, of all places. He came prancing on a pretty, speckled pony in comfortable time for Prime, leading a well caparisoned retinue of six men at arms, a scribe and a clerical assistant. When the Sheriff of Elgin's procurator fiscal turned up ten minutes later with another boisterous troop of arresting officers and a clerk of his own, the Investigator was outraged but had no option but to accept their presence. Sandy Watson, a long skinny man with a beak of a nose and a way of walking highly reminiscent of a heron wading in freezing waters, was clerk of the Guild of Hammerers and an ironmonger by trade.

Both teams were clad to impress, the townsfolk in bright robes, the Bishop's men more sober in hue if not in richness, and both sporting a fair number of fine jewels. Their separate plumages were far less distinct from each other than either was from Father Thomas's restrained simplicity. Were it not for his contained authority, he would have been likened to a drab pigeon caught among a quarrel of gaudy partridges. Clad in his white woollen tunic and cowl, he stood alone before the great altar to receive them.

The service ran its due course in spite of the Investigator's coughing restlessness, employed deliberately to indicate that he wanted to get on with his own much more important business. Given half a chance he would have impounded the unexpected Will and departed forthwith.

When it came to examining Nicol's body Prior Thomas led the way to the last chapel, having stated that no more than four people would be allowed in. He invited the Investigator and the Sheriff to accompany him, and Will as the accused perpetrator. Again it was not what the Investigator had intended but again the Prior's will prevailed, in part because they were inside the church with a hostile gathering of monks watching Symon's behaviour. Only after a bad-tempered skirmish did the bully accept that neither his clerk nor his assistant could enter with him. Even he had to concede the limitation of space. He would have to make his own notes. Thomas's silent dignity shamed them with the deep respect he was exhibiting for the murdered child.

Thomas also asked the rest of the congregation to leave the church before the viewing. Only when the great chamber was empty, with Father Gregory standing in the doorway, solid and forbidding, did the Prior pull back the curtain. Nicol's body seemed to Will to have floated still farther away from the vibrancy of life. Even the wounds, when revealed, had begun to shrink into unreality, almost disbelief.

The Investigator bent to examine these closely, then pulled back as the smells of putrefaction hit his nose, despite the herbal oils they had used on the body. Sandy Watson smirked, choosing to move the sole candle to a position as close to the body as possible. Above the two bent heads Thomas caught Will's eye. They stood in the archway making no effort to interfere as the officers ran through almost all the points Will and the choir monks had covered the day before.

They did not, however, ask for the body to be turned over. When it looked as if they were preparing to leave, Thomas raised a hand. Stepping out into the aisle of the main church he beckoned and Brother Alexander came forward with two weapons.

'Yes,' Will confirmed when asked. 'They're mine.'

'Then ye must have used something else for these wounds,' the Sheriff announced cheerily, well aware that he had been summoned to spike the Bishop's plans.

'I was miles away and can prove it,' Will countered, and repeated his defence.

'I shall check that with Hugo de May when he returns,' the Investigator threatened. That gave Will a shock. Given the circumstances, Hugo's death might be employed against him, or even laid at his door.

'There are at least ten more witnesses, either at the Dallas Inn or Dallas Castle. One of them is George de Leslie. Isn't he some sort of Deputy Sheriff of Murray?'

'What were you doing at Dallas anyway?' the Investigator demanded, annoyed that he was losing command. He was beginning to fear that he might have to return without his prey. The Bishop would not be pleased.

'I was on my way to Balvenie,' Will repeated with heavy patience. 'My father will be waiting for a report on his castle garrison there.' They saw a jolt as the Investigator realised at last who Will was. Impounding the son of the realm's Shield-bearer was not what he had anticipated. If he tried, and it turned out to be a mistake, all kinds of complications could ensue. 'And I had a book to deliver to Father Ranulf from the Bishop himself. Didn't he tell you that?'

Obviously not. Symon the Investigator was becoming angrier by the minute, to the growing glee of the Sheriff. Conscious of this, Symon turned again to leave, but this time it was Will who stopped him, while avoiding Thomas's eyes.

'Before you go, gentlemen, there's something more you should see. I'll not have you accuse me of hiding evidence.' He knelt and gently turned the body over so that both visitors could see the ninth - or first - damning wound. It too had stiffened, but was still plainly different from the rest.

'Now that's a significant injury,' the Bishop's man declared, surprise and hope recharging his voice.

'Aye, but nae made by either o' these beasties.' For the first time the Sheriff took an active part. He picked up Will's sword and held it close to the wound. It was visibly too broad to have caused the damage. Then he picked up the dirk, turned it over to look with a specialist's eye at the handsome Cordoba blade, before holding it, too, above the wound. The size approximated much more closely.

'Na, still nae right.' He shook his head, making to rise. The Investigator snorted.

'It's exactly right!' he challenged, seeing a faint hope of success after all.

'Ye think so? I'm thinking I've seen a good many more pricked corpses that you have, Father Symon. You being a man o' the cloth, like, and ordinary folk more inclined to murder than kirk folk. - Father Thomas, d'ye hae a cheese?'

'A cheese?' the Prior stammered.

'Aye, a nice, ripe, moist, firm cheese. Just bring it here.'

That took Brother Alexander ten minutes to fetch, during which time the two examiners bickered about their conclusions and the Sheriff continued to fiddle with Will's dirk, his eyes gleaming with admiration tinged with envy. Will meanwhile laid Nicol on his back. A couple of times his eye met Thomas's, each wondering what would happen next.

When the cheese arrived, the Sheriff gestured to Will to turn Nicol over again while he put the cheese on the floor so that its surface was more or less parallel to the point where the slim knife had entered. It made a weird miniature copy of the body - and Will began to guess what the Sheriff was up to. Eyeing the wound the man lifted Will's dirk. 'How deep did it go? It has atrophied now, so I canna tell.'

'Brother Infirmarian says it reached the heart.' This again was Will. Thomas was rooted to the floor and his face was acquiring a tinge of green. Eyes down, neither visitor noticed. The Sheriff slid his fingers along the blade till the tips were at the point he estimated would be level with the child's skin, leaving the exposed inches at the point which would have been thrust as far as the heart. He held it like a dart with the handle lying along his wrist.

'Now...' With a soft thwack he plunged the dirk into the cheese until his fingertips touched the rind. The thrust was so sudden that the other three jumped in spite of their anticipation. Will felt his gorge rise and he had to struggle to establish control over his stomach. The killing blow on Nicol must have been horrifyingly similar.

'Now then.' Sandy Watson had not finished. 'Father Symon, lay your fingers either side o' the knife, will ye, and push down. Haud still, now. I want to pull the knife out as straight as I can.' The blade came away from the cheese with a soft, sucking gurgle. It was that which did for Thomas, and very nearly for Will too. The Prior withdrew rapidly and they heard him vomit outside in the main aisle, but Will was tethered by the weight of Nicol's body on his knee.

Inside the tiny chapel the investigators were comparing the two knife wounds, on the body and on the cheese. Even while he was gulping what air, foul as it was, that he could into his heaving chest, Will was relieved to see that the cut in the cheese was broader than Nicol's wound. The difference was not great but was undeniable, and the realisation helped enormously with his breathing.

'Very well.' Symon of Dallas blew his chagrin out through his fleshy nose. 'Put the body down again, man. I accept that neither of these weapons was used in the crime. - But that doesn't mean the accused is innocent.'

'Ach, g'away man...' The Sheriff's patience was running out.

'There is a witness who saw him in the yard at the estimated time of...'

'Saw somebody, but that was from twa hunner yards away and...'

'Please, gentlemen, do your arguing outside God's house, if you will.' Barely recovered, Thomas's white face was furious. 'No. Leave the cheese where it is. And the knife, Captain. I shall arrange for other witnesses to view them for further and independent confirmation before the child is committed to God. This afternoon.' Neither of the visitors argued.

The Bishop's party rode off in defeat, but the Sheriff remained with his men. It was more to satisfy his own curiosity than out of any doubt he had about either Will or the monks, including Michael. Sandy Watson wanted to conduct another experiment. Still shaking with the after effects of the previous one, Thomas left him to it. Brother Mark was summoned, to his disgust, to clean up the mess on the church floor and Michael was delegated to help the Sheriff, since Sandy Watson's plan was to reconstruct the purported sighting of Will at the mill as viewed through the North Gate from the refectory. Before Chapter began, Will himself nipped out to the South Gate to ask Camus if any news had come from Ranulf. Nothing.

It was almost unheard of for outsiders to attend Chapter meetings in any religious house, especially a closed one. Chapter was for internal discussion and self-examination. Inevitably Will's presence raised fierce objections. In the midst of the uproar - for Chapter could not, of course, be conducted in silence - Will was all for leaving but Thomas laid a hand on his arm, gripping until the thin fingers hurt him.

'Please, Will,' he muttered. 'Please resist their outrage for just ten minutes.' Then turning towards his flock he raised both hands. 'Please, my sons. Please listen to the news which Captain Forbys has brought.'

Will gulped. He had not intended to make a public announcement about anything. Then he realised that Thomas was handing to him the task of giving good news, in order to allay the monks' sense of affront. Discomfort made his handling inept.

'Uh, brothers, I want to tell you that Francie, the miller's granddaughter is safe. I have no idea what has happened to the miller himself. I don't think she knows either. But she took the pony from the Priory and finally caught up with me near Knockando.' Was that saying too much? The atmosphere became charged with relief, but it was not quite total.

'Where is she now?' Brother Mark demanded. 'Why didn't you bring her back?'

Annoyed by the hectoring tone Will lost his awkwardness. 'Because she was terrified! She refused to tell me anything, but I think she knows who killed her brother. If she does, she herself could be in danger.'

'You mean Nicol's killer wouldn't want her bearing witness against him?' This was Mark again, only a little less aggressively.

'Then why are you telling us now?' The Cellarer asked. His initial reaction had been relief, but now it switched to alarm. 'If monks can't be trusted, I don't know who can.'

'We're human like everybody else,' Father Gregory slipped in, trying to calm everyone. 'But I at least am glad to know she is alive and unharmed. I am sure I speak for all of us and thank you for the reassurance.'

'But where is she?' the Sacristan repeated, then scowled when he realised he was receiving critical glances. 'You said you trusted us.'

'She is in the safest place I could devise at short notice. Forgive me if I say no more for now, but any one of you might be asked if you know. If you don't, then you need not lie. Nor can you be trapped into saying more than you wish. The only reason I said anything was that I realised how worried you all were about her.'

When he stepped back, the Prior added, 'For Francie's sake, please do not pass this information on. Let us not even talk of it among ourselves for even walls appear to have ears. - Certainly Francie seemed to be privy to far more than she should have been.'

He stopped short. Only after much clearing of his throat did he proceed. 'Now, I have another matter concerning Captain Forbys which I wish to raise. - Yes, Brother Mark?'

'Why is he here? What has happened to the message to the Pope? If that falls into the wrong hands we shall undoubtedly suffer, as a house and as individuals.'

'Ay, yes.' The Prior moistened his lips. 'Captain Forbys, is there any chance of overtaking the messengers?'

Will blinked. 'None whatever. Why?'

'The Bishop gave me uncomfortable news yesterday. He has just heard that the Pope has removed his court from Avignon to Rome.'

Chapter 10 - A Regime Change

While the monks exclaimed in a spin of dismay Will thought hard. He did not sound too perturbed when he could finally make himself heard. 'Your letter is well on its way by now, I promise you. Far beyond any danger of being discovered. Given this kind of weather it could be on Gascon soil within a fortnight. It's the land travel across France that takes the time, especially if there is unrest.'

'But if the Pope isn't there...' Mark fretted.

'Somebody in Avignon will tell the courier when he asks and the letter will be sent on. I'm sure it will reach the Pope, Father Thomas. But I doubt if your reply will arrive back here by the date you specified. I'm sorry. There's nothing that I or anybody can do about that.'

Thomas shrugged and grasped the opening. 'Then we must make an even greater effort to ensure our independence for ourselves. My sons, you are all aware of how Father Gregory has been struggling to discover the truth of our own foundation. He is by far our best scholar but...' When the Prior broke off in discomfort Father Gregory completed the sentence with candour.

'My sight is giving up. After ten minutes of reading, the letters begin to scramble around like scurrying ants. By the time my eyes have recovered,' the old man shrugged in an odd mixture of amusement and despair, 'my brain has forgotten what I read in the first place. Forgive me, brothers, but the task is becoming hopeless.'

'What about Brother Daniel?' Will suggested.

Thomas shook his head. 'Daniel doesn't read.' Seeing Will's astonishment he smiled faintly. 'It's true. He is an excellent and accurate copyist and a superb illustrator but he would not be able to read back what he has written.'

Daniel's expression was one of shame. When a heavy sniff came from Brother Mark, the abject look intensified the man's heavy, dark ugliness.

'I have yet to detect an error,' the Cantor interposed smoothly in Daniel's defence. 'His work for me has never once been less than perfect.'

'What a wonderful gift,' Will murmured, without thinking, then felt glad when the silent man flushed with pleasure at the praise he was receiving, perhaps for the first time in his life. Possibly for the last as well, Will feared. The sin of Pride was guarded against most severely in this house. But it came to him that someone other than Daniel must have chosen the Beatitude text for him to illustrate.

'He uses it well for the glory of God.' The Prior cleared his throat. 'The point I wish to make is this. We have in our midst a man who is both scholar and negotiator, with a knowledge of Latin which is both broad and deep. He has considerable familiarity with the management of business matters, including some of church significance, and he is also well used to handling legal documents in all their complexity. In other words Our Lord has sent us someone who is familiar, in practical ways that none of us are, with the caveats and codicils inserted by one party in the hope of gaining advantage over another. Why don't we make use of his skills?'

'And tell him all our secrets!' Mark seemed appalled, but the other monks looked thoughtful. 'I'm a Latin scholar,' Mark claimed. 'Let me do it. Our charters shouldn't be made privy to outsiders we have no reason to trust!'

For a moment Father Thomas's eyes fluttered shut. Weary, and unable to think of a gentle rebuttal, he was forced into being unkind. 'I am sorry, Brother Mark, but your Latin is at best mediocre, and your vocabulary limited to church matters.'

'Father Gregory could guide...'

'Besides,' Thomas cut into Mark's importunity, 'a charter is a public document. As such it should be open to scrutiny by everybody. That way lies the assurance of justice.'

'But why should we trust this man? Where on earth would he get to know about church management?'

Thomas had been hoping for this question. The tension in him eased as he let Will explain.

'I have been lucky enough to study under two wise scholars. One is a Knight of the Order of St John of Jerusalem, - that's the Teutonic Order. He traded with my grandfather in Danzig on behalf of his Order. The other is Father Jehan of Stettin.'

Gregory and Stephen both gasped at the second name. It was left to Mark, once again, to demand who Jehan of Stettin was.

'He is the scholar priest who has been designated to deal with the secretarial side of the current negotiations going on in Stralsund.'

'Stralsund in Sweden?' Mark's fine brow creased. 'You don't mean the treaty they're trying to hammer out to end the war between Denmark and the German League? He's - actually in charge?' It was an awesome responsibility, all the more demanding since the hostilities had been going on for almost a decade.

'Yes.' Will scratched his head with a touch of anxiety. 'I myself am supposed to be there by the second week in June to lend a hand.' In other words, Will's credentials were solid.

'How did you come to study under him?' Mark made the demand downright rude.

'He is currently the chaplain in residence at the Hanseatic Kontor in Bergen. That's where I did much of my merchant training. - It's a complicated story.' He was glad when Thomas intervened to divert Mark's drift, for the Sacristan was surely looking for a means of discrediting the young merchant. Furious at being baulked, Mark had one last try.

'What about yourself, Father Thomas? You are a scholar.'

'But I have no knowledge of law. We each have our own skills and our own limitations and these we should acknowledge.'

Yet again Father Gregory's calm voice soothed the company. 'Is Captain Forbys willing to undertake this scrutiny?' Thomas raised a tired hand in Will's direction.

'Only if you all agree to it,' Will prevaricated, expecting the rumpus he got. Eventually they all did agree, even Brother Mark when he realised he was seriously outweighed.

'Good. I shall ask him to begin straight away.' Father Thomas closed the matter. Will had been sensing the tension in the Prior rise throughout the discussions but he would never have anticipated what happened then. 'Let us move on to the next matter. It is equally urgent.'

There was a small lectern in the middle of the Chapter House. So far that morning it had not been used but now Thomas stepped up to it. Pulling the ruby ring from his finger he laid it on the surface and stepped back until he had become part of the circle of astonished monks around the room.

'Brothers, forgive me.' Not sons. At least two men drew a sharp breath as the significance of Thomas's actions sank in. 'I have failed you all. I have been failing you for many months now and have known it in my heart. I ignored that knowledge, concealing it beneath spurious justifications. Out of the sin of Pride I have been unwilling to fail where I myself had led. As a result an innocent boy came near to dying. Through pride and carelessness I allowed a young, healthy, gifted youth to be starved to within days, if not hours, of death. That has convinced me that I am not fit to lead this community and I ask...'

'I'm not staying to listen to this rubbish!' Will headed for the door.

Instantly, the Cellarer turned on him. 'This is your doing, you - you loud-mouth *boy*!' It was the worst insult Alexander could think of.

Will gulped, then gulped again and turned back to the bewildered faces. Alexander was right, of course. 'Then I'd better try and undo it,' he mumbled. His dry throat made the words croak.

Yet again it was Father Gregory's voice which controlled the storm. 'We shall allow you ten minutes, Captain.' Everybody accepted that decision and waited for the next step. Even as he began to sort and select the words he would use, Will again wondered about the old man's position in the community. Should Gregory, perhaps, have been Prior, with Thomas as his deputy learning the ropes, learning especially how to be at peace with himself? He felt sure that Thomas, when fit and well rested, was the best Prior for the future of the house, from what he could see of the others, although Gregory would undoubtedly have been very able despite his age - except for his inability to read the documents he needed to.

Now, however, it was up to Will to persuade them all, Thomas included, to ditch the daft rule of under-eating with which they had saddled themselves. He already knew that it was Thomas, presumably in the white heat of zeal in his new incumbency, who had brought the idea back from Burgundy. He had discovered the original document detailing the regulations on which the very first Valiscaulian Priory had been founded and had somehow persuaded his flock at Pluscardyn to try out the system as a particular devotion to God. This old Rule had, after all, been given the sanction of the Pope of the time.

Will looked around him, seeing a range of emotions in the men's eyes. 'Brothers of Pluscardyn, I must first thank you for your hospitality to me. During my visit here I have been treated with generosity and respect. In particular I have been very well fed. The fare has been simple but the best ingredients were used and the cooking excellent. I - would not dare to criticise the way you choose to run your lives unless I had a real fear for your well-being.'

How to do it? He chewed the inside of his bottom lip till it hurt. Absolutely the last thing he wanted to do was to offend the men staring at him now.

'Brothers, it was when I noticed that there was, oh, four times the quantity on my plate than there was on any of yours that I began to wonder. At first I was deeply embarrassed, thinking that I had been given what should have been yours; that there was not enough to go round. Then, when I realised that was nonsense because this is a very rich establishment, I began to worry. I looked around and noticed how thin you all were, that your eyes are sunken and your faces grey and lack-lustre in spite of your frequent outdoor work. Many of you have lesions on your skin which is a sign of general ill health. – I recognise that because my background training as a boy was under an apothecary. If this were a ship and you were my crew I would be doing something about your rations for fear of sickness breaking out among you. Certainly you would not be able to do the work I expected of you. You would not have the strength.'

'This is not a ship,' snapped the Sacristan.

'Isn't it? Is a church community not a ship of God?' They were all familiar with the allusion. 'And would God not expect you to maintain the best health you could, in order that you could do your work for Him to the highest standard possible?'

'That's what we are trying to do,' murmured Gregory. 'We did not go into this lightly, Captain. The Rule we are trying to adhere to was prescribed by no less a mentor than Pope Innocent the Second. - The same Pope who gave the Blessed Saint Francis his Rule, which is not so very different.'

Will had another chew at his lip. His answer was oblique. 'Think of last night in the refectory. No, think of all of us gathering in here just before we paraded in for the evening meal. Try to remember what your impression of Robert de Chisholm was. Did he not strike you as a big healthy fellow? Tall, handsome, glowing with well-being. A big, fat man even, compared with any of you? - You must think of me as a great lump of lard.' There was a stir of discomfort. 'Well, the folk outside your gates consider Robert a slim fellow. I assure you, they do.

'Now think of the poor folk who come to your gate to be fed. Think of any one of yourselves working among them, handing out soup and bread. How do you compare with them? Not much difference, I'd say. In fact they are probably better fed than you are.'

'Gluttony is a sin.' This mutter came from the Cellarer. It was, after all, his job to provide what they all ate, and yet Will had gained the impression that he was one of those most worried by the tightness of the provisioning.

'Then it's a sin none of you could possibly be charged with!' Will snapped back, more out of nervousness than annoyance. He feared that he was making no impression on their stubbornness. If so, they would call it their conviction. 'I'm sorry, Brother Alexander.' His hand went to his beard, which was no longer than the last time he had reached for its comfort. 'Look, you are one of only three men here who may leave the precincts and go into the world outside. The rest of you have no opportunity to see for yourselves any comparison with normal folk. Except the starving poor who come to your gate, I suppose. And because you live in close contact with each other, seeing each other every day, you may not have seen how you have all lost weight to an alarming degree. How much more do you think you can lose? For lose you must on the amount you eat. Surely there is a limit? Every one of you is skin and bone already.'

'You arrogant puppy!' Mark exclaimed. 'Who are you to...'

'Brother Sacristan, let him finish without interruption.' Father Gregory was again obeyed and Will continued.

'Father Thomas explained to me that the Valiscaulians were founded by a Carthusian priest who adopted the original Carthusian Rule with very little alteration. In its original form, it is very severe in its restrictions, the most demanding of any Rule devised.'

'Not all of us follow the most extreme form,' Thomas interrupted. 'Only the choir monks. The labourers could not do their work on the restricted diet we...'

'Can you do yours? This diet was devised for men living in Southern Italy where the climate is benign, far better than here and with a much longer growing season. In fact, I have a feeling that even there it proved too onerous. I believe that a later Pope ordered that the original Carthusian Rule itself had to be relaxed because it was indeed leading to too much illness. The monks were succumbing to every epidemic which came anywhere near them. - Brother Stephen, when was the last time you had a singing service without having it blanketed out by coughing and sneezing?'

There was a long, uncomfortable silence. 'What happens if there is an epidemic of disease in this neighbourhood? Plague, perhaps, or one of the rosy sicknesses? If all of you become ill, what will happen to the destitute people who depend on you for sustenance? What would happen to the Priory itself?'

And there, he realised, was the lever he needed. 'It would be just the excuse the Bishop wants. Do you know what the men in Elgin call Pluscardyn? The House of Scarecrows. The Cathedral Dean even asked me to stay for a good square meal. Oh, I told him how well you fed me, but I am certain the Bishop is hoping you will run into trouble so that he can take over your management. Are you prepared to risk that? Is that what you want?'

After another pause he added, 'I think I've said enough,' and left, fighting a forlorn desperation. It was for the members of the convent themselves to decide how they should live their lives, not him. He should never have allowed himself to be goaded into speaking and he hoped he had not made things even worse than before for Thomas.

Nicol's funeral was held in the main church of the Priory immediately after the noon meal. Unexpectedly it was packed with mourners for news had travelled far and fast. It was strange to see the simple, elegant building so crammed full. All the monks sang for him, mysteriously without a single sneeze or cough, and a special solo was given to Brother James as the youngest of the community. Now recovering slowly, he had begged to be permitted to do so, for he, too, had become close to the children at the mill. Like Justin, whose open face was awash with tears, James had learned to love the witless boy and his lively sister. It turned out that James had a baritone voice of deep, compelling beauty. That day he used it with such resonant intensity that many in the congregation were also reduced to weeping.

Among these mourners were Priory workers who had come from considerable distances, and a surprising number of townsfolk had walked the miles from the borough of

Elgin, where the family had once lived. A greater surprise for Will was a group of five members of the de Chisholm family. Robert and his wife had ridden over with two younger sisters, both in religious garb, and a very old lady too familiar with bereavement to find it overwhelming any more.

The wife was a dark girl with the blue-black hair, sky-coloured eyes and white skin found among certain Celts. She would have been attractive if she had at least hidden her pout which left no doubt that she could have found better things to do than spend the afternoon in the company of monks whom she did not regard as men at all. When she saw Will, however, her demeanour changed. Not immediately. The blue eyes brushed over him and moved away. An instant later, when he had already turned his attention to the old lady, he sensed the eyes had returned to examine him with a sharp interest. Deliberately Will ignored her, concentrating on the elderly relative who insisted on tottering right up to the little coffin where she remained standing, with the aid of a stout stick, throughout the service. Will was amused that Thomas backed away immediately from any confrontation.

'My grand-aunt Amelia,' Robert murmured in Will's ear as she faced the Prior in defiance. 'Would you believe it? She remembers Bannockburn. She even remembers Stirling Bridge, or so she claims.' Since that battle was fought in 1297, Will's eyebrows crawled up towards his hair.

'Impressive! She's making a point, I suppose.'

'Nicol's mother was named after her. Of course she's making a point. I remember the curses she poured on Isabella's father for being so harsh, especially when Isabella died. Said she was black affronted to call him brother - and that's a mendaciously mild paraphrase. The real thing would curl the pages of the Prior's Bible.' He managed to turn a laugh into a more seemly cough. 'All but danced on my grandfather's grave, she did, when the time came at long last. She's quite convinced they'll not be meeting again.'

Good for her, thought Will. Was this where Francie inherited her spunk from? But then, Isabella must have had considerable courage, too, to make a tocherless marriage with Hector in the face of such opposition.

'Introduce me afterwards, will ye?'

Robert duly did so. He did not introduce his wife, but whether that was deliberate or not Will could not tell. Again he concentrated on the older lady. The wife, however, had her own way of attracting his attention. When Robert became engrossed in a conversation with Thomas and Gregory, the girl turned away from his side - and his line of sight - and sent across the grassed courtyard such a searing look of sensual invitation to Will that his innards were scorched. His face grew hot with shock and his loins shrivelled then swelled embarrassingly. Thomas must have seen his shifting expressions over Robert's shoulder and guessed at least vaguely at the cause, for his eyes opened a little more widely despite his tiredness.

'And him a priest,' murmured an acid old voice down around Will's midriff. 'I wonder where the honourable Prior came from, eh? And I wonder every day if Robert realises what he took on when he married that hot witch, Maura.' Lady Amelia's faded blue eyes snapped with distaste as much as curiosity.

Only partially recovered, for he was as susceptible as any other young healthy male, Will was allowed to lead Lady Amelia on his arm as the small burial party walked to the graveyard for the internment. The stick came near to being used as a weapon if anybody got in her way. Carved in black bog-oak it had a knob tooled heavily with gold and the ancient, freckled fingers were bedecked with fine rings.

'Francie,' he murmured to her, dropping his head to keep his words between just the two of them, 'is safe.' The shrewd old eyes immediately flashed up at him. 'Say nothing to anybody else for now, if you please.'

'You mean she's...' She dropped her voice even lower than his in a parody of conspiracy. '…not with Hector? You're sure of that, aren't you? So there is a God after all!'

Seeing Will cringe at the sacrilege voiced in public she cackled, not caring who heard or what they thought. Embarrassed yet again, Will sought support from the only two monks now in the group apart from the Prior. Brother Michael had an unaccustomed glint in his eye, a touch of wary fondness maybe. Now reassured about Francie, he was beginning to think he might have been mistaken about seeing Will at the mill, especially after the Sheriff's re-enactment. Father Gregory was actually smiling. He came towards them.

'Stop tormenting the boy. You are a wicked old woman, Lady Amelia.'

'I'll still get into Heaven before you will,' she returned. Purloining a discomfited Michael's arm she flounced off in a manner only an old lady could get away with. And Francie.

The Sub-Prior grinned after her. 'Did you warn her to keep the news to herself?'

Alarmed, Will demanded, 'Will she?'

'Oh, to the death! Now, can you guide me over the rough ground.' It was only then that Will realised just how poor Gregory's sight was.

'Of course, Father.'

'No, Captain,' the old man corrected. 'I am *Brother* Gregory. There is no room for two father figures in one house?'

Will had to agree. Since Thomas had just led the service with the Prior’s ring in its proper position and with the solid support of his community, it was plain that he had been reinstalled in his proper position.

After everybody had gone home, Will settled down in the Scriptorium to study the old documents concerning the Priory's foundation. By Vespers he had worked his way through all nine of the charters in the Priory's possession and covered one hundred and thirty seven years of legal fencing. There were a few jinks and anomalies in the history, some amusing, others revealing the venal personalities of participants in more than one era, - and a problem which could spell trouble.

Perhaps more information held in the mother house in Burgundy could clarify the situation but it would take time for somebody to go there and find out. If the Bishop were indeed determined to force visitation rights on the Priory in the near future, these might have to be conceded before such papers could be fetched. Once a visitation had taken place it would be much more difficult to deny the Bishop the right to do so again, and virtually impossible to prevent him from claiming a considerable portion of the Pluscardyn rents, by right of the implied overlordship these visitations contained, however contentious.

Will attended the evening meal, once more held in silence apart from a reading, and with slightly more food on the monks' platters. The atmosphere was more relaxed than he had yet experienced. He also joined them at Compline, after which they all headed for bed while he begged the key to the Library which adjoined the church.

It was some time after seven, when the rest of the house was asleep, or should have been, that the first of the bridges Will had broken was tentatively mended. A tap on the Library door heralded the Cellarer. He poked his head in to check Will was there and alone, then he disappeared only to return a moment later with a jug in one hand and a wooden plate in the other bearing a fresh oaten loaf wrapped in a white napkin. Alexander had even found a small pot of damson preserve left over from the winter stores. The monk looked as uncomfortable as Will felt.

'I hope the night won't be that long,' the younger man ventured. 'But I'm most grateful.' He laid down the quill Daniel had supplied him with, but Alexander did not take the hint, backing instead towards the door with a goodnight nod. They were, after all, into the sacred Great Silence of night.

Will enjoyed the hours that followed. Evening light poured in through the open windows, along with the drowsy twittering of birds as they settled their restless first broods under the eaves. The Priory slumbered, once more at peace with itself he hoped, as he worked his way through several volumes chained to their stands, scanning and searching, now and then slowing to read more deeply as a particular topic, usually extraneous to his search, caught his interest. It was growing almost too dark to see the lettering when another knock came. Again it was Alexander, looking rumpled and sleepy in his night cowl and wearing sandals but no socks. This time he brought a tallow candle and flints.

'We're not supposed to use a naked flame in here but...' When he lit it, Will noticed how swollen and misshapen his scabbed feet were, and covered with a weeping rash which looked itchy and sore.

'I have to admit that my mind has been sharpened rather than wearied by the reading. It is whirling too much to let me rest. But you should not have disturbed your own rest for me.'

'I - wakened and couldn't sleep again. What are you looking for here?'

'The Pope who brought the Carthusians to their senses. - Uh, I'm sorry. That was uncalled for.' The Cellarer had gone stiff. 'But, Brother Alexander, I'm glad that you have given me a chance to say something that needs saying. Please don't think that I was blaming you for the mess James was in. I'm sure nobody else does either. You obeyed an order, as you are required to by the Rules of the house.'

Alexander's lips turned downwards. 'But I should have checked. My own senses told me it was too much, too severe, and I did nothing about it.' An awkward pause acknowledged that nobody else was free from that reproof either, but it would not be voiced. Accusations against others were not permitted here unless the individuals themselves indulged in public self-criticism. Will thought they probably would, if not in Chapter then in confession, and by the end of it Thomas was going to find the repetitiveness wearing and painful.

'Nobody's blaming you either,' Alexander burst out, bringing Will's eyes to his. The words had been difficult for him to utter. 'We - mean to learn from it.'

'The last think I wanted to do was disrupt the peace of the Priory,' Will mumbled. 'I admire your wish to set yourselves high standards and stick to them. Few folk do either. It was just... Well, let's leave it now. It's over.' After a moment, he added, 'I thank you for coming to make peace with me. It's more than I deserve.'

Alexander shrugged. 'As you say, it is over. But I have another reason for coming to you.'

Will's head shot up, almost expecting what came. 'To tell me who your traitor is?'

'It has to be one of two people,' the monk agreed dryly, no longer surprised by Will's grasp of matters. 'And I'm one of them.'

'If you were responsible, then I am assured that it was inadvertent. As you say, only two people left the Chapter House last Wednesday morning within the space of time after the document was signed but before I left with it. You went to the kitchens to order travel food. Even if you did not say who it was for, the men in the kitchens would have realised it had to be for me as I was the only visitor. They would also have realised I would be leaving shortly and could easily have informed an outsider if they were so inclined. I do know that somebody learned that I had left here and followed me. The other man who left the Chapter House alone was the Sacristan. He went ahead just two minutes earlier than the rest of us to prepare the church for Prime, to which we processed together. I cannot think that is long enough for him to pass on any message to an outsider.'

Alexander's cracked lips thinned. 'He's not the brightest, but since you turned up last Sunday he's had three days to think up a way of giving a signal of some sort.'

'He wouldn't have known the Prior planned to send a message away with me. He didn't even ask me till Monday evening.'

'The Prior was going to take the first chance he got, I can tell you that. He was convinced that God would send him somebody to carry the message to the Pope for him. He was right. You turned up. I doubt if the Prior will tell you this, but I think you should know that Brother Mark is the Bishop's man.'

Will took a moment to digest that. 'What do you mean?'

'When the elections for the Priorship became necessary, the Bishop nominated Mark for the position.'

'But it was an internal election, wasn't it?'

'It was. But Bishop Barr tried to intervene. You see, Mark came here about six years ago with the express intention of working his way into the post. Our last Prior had also been, well, a bit over-awed by the Cathedral's influence, especially during the reign of the Bishop before this one. Understandable, I suppose, with the country at war with England every other year and our mother house in Burgundy very far away. Then, of course, the Pest struck.' They were both silent for a little. The plague had not only wiped out nearly half of the population in both Scotland and France, but the entire social structure had been undermined, especially people's trust in the church. 'Maybe that's why they did it,' mused Alexander. 'That particular Prior and Bishop were both involved in drawing up a charter about a generation ago which we now want to overturn.'

'That was the letter to the Pope, I suppose. - No, don't answer that.' Alexander had raised a hairy eyebrow.

'Now, Thomas had already been here about eighteen months when Mark arrived. He was spending his time beavering away with his books and was showing no ambition for office. Gregory was seen as the obvious successor by us anyway. Only, when the time came Gregory refused to take it on permanently because of his bad eyesight and his age. He was even older than the Prior who had just died. We realised then that we had to find somebody to challenge Mark and once we started looking at each other as candidates, Thomas stood out head and shoulders above us.'

'But the Bishop said he was too young? Too inexperienced?'

'You've guessed it. Anyway none of us thought much of being under Mark's thumb so he was on a loser from the start. Besides it was taking the Priory in the wrong direction.'

'Away from its independence from the Bishopric? Out of the king's protection?'

'Well, not exactly. You see, we didn't want to become involved in politics of any kind. That's not why we entered a Priory.'

'Politics? You mean the struggle between church and state? But aren't you always likely to be drawn into that to some extent?'

'No, not that either. Though what you say is true. So far, we in Pluscardyn have managed to keep our heads pretty low in that scrap. No, it's Mark's background we don't like. You see, he's a Douglas.'

Will frowned. 'But I thought the Douglases were a spent force in the North. I know they're still powerful down south.'

'And there you have it. They're looking for a toehold to get them started again here in the north. I don't know if even the Bishop realises it, but that's what Mark is after.'

'Hm. Power.' Unlike an Abbot, a Prior is not regarded as a prince of the kingdom, but he could claim a seat in Parliament, and the Scots Parliament had a growing influence in the land which even the king could not ignore.

'Yes, power. And not just for himself. He's a first son too, an only son. As a monk he cannot have personal possessions, of course, but he can deploy anything he inherits, be it wealth or influence, in any way he pleases. You can be sure it will go back to the family, the Douglases being what they are. I'm pretty sure the Bishop didn't realise that either. But I am also sure the Stewarts do.'

'You think His Grace expects Mark to hand over any inheritance to the church? In thanks for supporting his bid for the Priorship?'

'Maybe not anymore, but I'm sure that's the way it began. He'd have been disappointed though, even if Mark had become Prior.'

'So what happened over the election?'

'Nominations were accepted only from inside the house and the only nominee was Thomas. So it was a foregone conclusion.'

'In spite of his inexperience,' murmured Will. The change of tack was sudden.

'We've done our best to support him,' the Cellarer growled. After a few moments he added, 'Well?'

'It can't have been easy for him to become father to a community of men who were almost all older than himself.' Will trod delicately but the words still brought a flush to Alexander's face. He was revealing that he was very far from being a fool. His analysis of the problems had been shrewd, and although he made no claim towards scholarship he did have a fair background knowledge of political affairs in spite of his disaffection for them. It was only after careful thought that he continued, 'He would have had nobody to turn to, would he?'

'Well?' Alexander became more belligerent. 'You might as well spit out whatever criticism you've come up with now.' Their eyes locked.

'I - have a notion that he is deeply lonely in his position of authority. I'm sure that's the only reason he and I hit it off so well last Sunday afternoon. Since I was an outsider, and since by chance I had interests in common with his, there was no barrier. We talked man to man about books we had both read, nothing more. Maybe if you could... Oh, I don't know. I'm sure you could find a way to... Look, Brother Alexander, it's obvious to me that you are all pretty fond of Prior Thomas as a man. Maybe if you could break through the carapace of the position and make better contact with the person inside, it would - help him. Help you all.'

Alexander rose abruptly, pushing back the stool so that it clattered in the night's quietness. They both froze for a moment before the monk turned to hide his quivering lips by walking towards the window and looking out at the dusk. When he had recovered he returned to stand beside Will. Equally upset Will looked up, knowing his eyes had turned into black holes, knowing he had said far more than he could ever claim the right to have done. He knew, however, it was the best he could do, and thinking that it might well have been said to the best person, for all his crabbit aspect. Alexander was in any case the only monk who had given him the opportunity to say anything at all on the subject. Had he come deliberately for this? Even if subconsciously?

'You'll be needing another horse,' was all Will could think of saying to lighten the atmosphere.

'*I* have never had a horse.'

'The use of, then. I could leave you mine.'

A look of fright came over Alexander's face. 'I could never manage a big beast like that!'

'Well, do you know of a pony for sale which might suit your purpose? Those feet are never going to heal if you take them travelling on the provisioning journeys you need to make in the next few weeks.' He knew he was taking a risk.

'You're a blunt brat!' Suddenly, out of the Cellarer's rage and hurt came a smile. 'But yes, I do know of two possible ponies. They're from the same mare that foaled Francie's. The person to ask is the blacksmith on the other side of the bridge from the kiln.' He watched, frankly fascinated, as

Will's eyes returned to normal, then he also chanced a forbidden topic. 'So the rumours are all wrong, are they? You can spend some of those riches you've inherited?'

Will laughed outright, but softly. 'I think my grandfather must have had some great sins to atone for. Oh, it's perfectly true that I cannot spend the House of Bromse money on anything except Hanseatic business but I do have a small allowance for clothes and keep. If the trustees found I have gone over budget or spent a penny on something they consider inappropriate, then I'd lose the lot. In that respect I have to remain a child until I am thirty. Thirty!'

'Oh well. Maybe by then you'll have matured enough not to waste it,' Alexander taunted, the smile still lingering at the edges of his mouth.

'The exception, as you've guessed, is donations to Holy Mother Church. I can give what I like to that, within reason. So I shall give a horse to Pluscardyn Priory. - By the way, how did you get rid of the coughs for the funeral?'

Alexander's mouth opened then closed with a snap. 'That's my secret.' When he began to look uncomfortable, it was Will's turn to smile.

'Let me guess. Honey? I'm sure the Infirmarian would have allowed that. And some galangal, maybe? And - I do believe you've found a local warlock who makes *uisque bha*. Oh, come on. It's time we went to bed!'

And so next morning, straight after Prime and forgetting it was Sunday, Will took himself down to the smiddy. Used to rising early, the blacksmith himself had long been up and about. A stocky, middle-aged man, he was now feeding several horses lodging in his small field at the back of the forge. Two were greys, small but sturdy.

'It's nae for me to say. Nane o' them are mine, but he could hae whichever o' the greys he wants,' he agreed cheerily. 'I'm sure Lady Amelia will sell. She comes ower here herself every other day to exercise them so ye can be sure they're well-mannered. Naebody's going to tangle with her, horse or man, I can tell ye!' The words told Will far more than the blacksmith realised and also gave him an excellent excuse for calling on the lady. Further questioning produced another reason for doing so which was much more private.

Will wandered over to look at another horse in the field, a fine, light hunter which looked as if it would have a good turn of speed over rough ground. That the stallion had been used for doing so recently was borne out by a number of bramble scratches along the roan withers which had barely begun to heal.

The animal had been given a casual grooming but closer inspection revealed that small patches of blue clay still clung to its belly and to the feathers above one hoof.

'Aye, they had him out hunting on Friday. Half ridden into the ground he was when he came in, poor beast. And through the river. They left him here to be reshod.'

Will picked a small ball of the clay out of the stallion's coat and rubbed it thoughtfully between finger and thumb. 'A big hunting party, was it?'

The smith gave an elaborate shrug. 'I saw nae others, but the castle is the other side of the hill so I wouldna.'

'But nobody has brought another horse to you needing shoeing?' He shook his head. 'Is that usual?' The man thought, then pursed his lips and shook his head again. 'So they hunt hard here?'

'Ye can say that again. Mind, it's even worse when the king comes to hunt in the Pluscardyn woods. Thay courtiers thrash their beasts to death, given half a chance. As well they dinna come more than once in a twa-three year. No, near five year since the last time, come to think.' He clapped the stallion on the shoulder then ran his hand along its back, obviously preferring to see animals treated well even if it did mean a drop in trade. 'But this cratur was in an awfa state when he came in.'

'So whose horse is it? Surely not Lady Amelia's?'

'Guid sakes! She'd thrash me if I did that tae a horse! I wonder she disna thrash Robert. Aye, it's his beast. His best and all, so why he treats it like this I canna work oot.'

Will kept his thoughts to himself. 'I'll ask Brother Alexander to come this afternoon and choose which of the greys he wants. Then I'll head over and deal directly with Lady Amelia myself.'

Will's next stop was at the quarry cut into Heldon Hill, where the fine cream stone was being excavated to build many of the fine new buildings going up in and around Elgin. The quarry master, who was a Priory man highly regarded for his local knowledge, kept Will chatting over his cottage fence on all manner of topics until a sharp, damp wind and hunger sent him indoors for the noon meal. Hidden among enormous quantity of blether were several nuggets of information which sent Will's speculations chasing along very dark lanes indeed.

Again the Priory meal, rather larger than before, was eaten in silence, and this time there was not even a reading. It was very comfortable, leaving each man with his own thoughts while still enjoying the company of others. A more elaborate church service than usual was followed by the weekly relaxation in the Auditorium, where the Cellarer had lit a fire to combat the sudden plunge into unseasonably chilly weather. A couple of the older men reverted to their rabbit-fur line cloaks. Will approached Alexander immediately.

'Brother Alexander, I must thank you for the information you gave me during our conversation last... evening.' A suspicious itch made him throw a hasty glance over his shoulder to see the Sacristan watching them coldly. 'Much of what you told me complemented what I had been searching for in my reading. I am grateful to you for bringing it to my attention. - And if you wish to choose the pony of your choice I shall arrange things with Lady Amelia before I leave.'

'I half expected you to leave this morning,' the Cellarer told him quietly. 'Now that the threat to your neck seems to be lifted.'

'I am waiting for information.' Alexander looked up and held his eye but said no more. 'If the rain stops, could you visit the ponies this afternoon perhaps? We could go together.'

'Then let us go now.'

He struggled to his feet, which gave Will a chance to exclaim loudly enough for the Infirmarian to hear, 'How are your feet today? Any better?'

'Feet? What's wrong with his feet?' The old man may have been almost as blind as Gregory but he was neither deaf nor stupid. He insisted on the immediate removal of Alexander's shoes and socks then stooped over the feet in question, squinting from less than two feet away. 'Oh my! Oh my-oh-my. This won't do. You should have come to me long ago, you idiot...' He trailed off, remembering he was not supposed to criticise, far less insult, according to the Rule in use. The freer, easier days of the past were gone. 'Come with me, Brother. At once,' was his compromise.

'Tell you what, Brother Alexander,' Will offered, seeing the Cellarer unable to honour both commitments, and realising that Thomas was watching the interplay with interest, 'I'll fetch the ponies up to the door.'

'No need, Captain,' Alexander confessed. 'I think the smaller one is the better option, the one with black on his nostrils. The mare is better left for breeding.' Shame-faced he hobbled after Brother Infirmarian, and Will was left to field any questions Thomas might have on the matter. The Prior made do with a smile quirked at the fire.

Alexander and the Infirmarian had just left when Justin came running in from his porter duty at the South Gate to say a messenger had arrived from Mortlach.

'Bring him in here,' the Prior told him, then realised this might not be wise.

Justin hopped from one foot to the other. 'I - think his message may be private. It's for Captain Forbys.'

'There should be no secrets within the community,' came a mutter. It was Brother Mark, of course, and Will caught spasms of annoyance flitting across at least three faces. Whether it was impatience with Mark himself or a growing irritation with the strictures of the Rule they were following Will could not guess. Whatever it was, the earlier comfortable camaraderie had been wiped away by sudden anxiety. Thomas knew, and all the others must have guessed by now, that Francie had arrived at Mortlach with Will, and every one of them jumped to the conclusion that this message could involve her.

Will turned to Thomas. 'Perhaps we ought to bring the messenger in here,' he murmured. Thomas looked at him for a long time, both of them acutely aware of the presence of Brother Michael. Then he nodded, and Justin disappeared to bring in the visitor.

'We ought to explain what has happened to the Bishop's messenger,' Thomas said, glancing directly at Michael, who began to rise as he sensed the dark expectancy in the two of them.

We don't know for sure,' Will objected, then sighed. 'Brothers, I think you all know Hugo de May. Forgive me for not telling you this before now, especially you, Brother

Michael, for I have learned that you are Hugo's blood brother. After I reached Balvenie last Wednesday night Hugo caught up with me and we spoke for a short while before he set out again for Mortlach. Among other things, he told me about my name being linked with the death of Nicol. At the time Francie was curled up beside me sound asleep inside a blanket and he did not see her. Perhaps if he had, he would have stayed. As it happened, he left but never reached Mortlach. When we arrived there next morning Father Ranulf had seen nothing of him. The night had been filthy and it...' Michael let out a great howl of pain and Thomas wrapped an arm around his shoulders. 'I'm sorry. It looks as if he went off the road into a bog and was unable to get himself out again.' As far as it went it was true. Surely it was enough to prepare them for what was coming.

'Didn't you try to find him?' demanded Mark.

'Yes, of course we did. I searched all over the moor until late on Thursday. First thing on Friday morning I went back to Balvenie Castle and arranged for the soldiers there to set up a search with grapples at the most likely place where he could have gone in. I've been waiting for news ever since I got back. - I have to say that since it has taken so long in coming I was beginning to hope that he had survived after all.'

Footsteps slapped on the stone slabs of the corridor and Justin ushered in someone Will knew. 'Ah, my barber. Brothers, this is David, one of the novices under Father Ranulf. Come over to the fire, lad. You're shivering.'

David looked around rather wildly, brushing his black gown free from bits of gorse and leaves as best he could. His face was flushed but very unhappy and his eyes overbright. 'I told Maister Camus - didn't the lad tell you? I - was to speak with you in private, Captain.'

'Aye, I got the message, but on reflection we decided that a public telling would be best.'

'But... I really think I should speak to you alone, at least at first.'

'The brothers know why you're here, lad. We've been waiting for the news.'

'Not this news.' David's eyes rolled upwards. 'Never this.'

'You mean they haven't found Hugo?' demanded Michael.

'Oh - I don't know. They'd only just started when I left.'

'What do you mean, only just started!' Will growled. 'They were to begin on Friday.'

'They didn't have grapples so they had to send to somewhere else for them.'

'Send somewhere else? - They've been stringing you along!' Will was furious. 'I'll string them along when I get back there, every last one of them, the lazy...'

'Captain,' Gregory broke in anxiously, 'if it isn't Hugo who has brought David here, perhaps we ought to hear what has.'

Will swallowed his rage, struggling not to choke on it. 'Of course. Well lad?'

David was shivering more than ever and a touch to his hand confirmed that cold was not the cause. His skin was burning. When his eyes filled with tears everybody became stiff with foreboding. 'It isn't the messenger who's dead, it's... It's Father Ranulf.'

The silence which followed was filled with horror. Even Gregory was stunned into stupefaction and it was left to the Prior to take charge. Still with one arm around Michael he found from somewhere the self-possession to speak quietly to the gathering. 'May the Lord our God receive his soul. My sons, we must hear what David has to say and then consider what action is now necessary. David, is there anybody senior at Mortlach who can take command?'

'Only Captain Forbys from Balvenie. Captain James Forbys, I mean.'

Thomas looked at Will who shook his head. 'James hasn't even been able to organise a grapple party.'

'That's what we thought,' David nodded.

'We?' The Prior took charge again.

'The four of us novices there. We thought... Because of how things are we thought we shouldn't tell too many people straight off. So Cormac has gone to the Bishop and I've come here. Kenneth is the oldest so we left him in charge at the church with Father Ranulf inside.'

Father Thomas nodded, looking so intently at the boy that he in turn calmed down a little. Thomas's actions seemed instinctive, perhaps emulating Gregory's habitual tranquillity. The effect impressed Will.

'And Walter?' he prodded.

'Oh, he's out looking for the bairn, Francie.' That created another dense silence.

'Why?' This anguished query came from Michael.

'We think she's run off. She was gone before we found the Father.'

'When was that?' asked Thomas.

David gulped as they came nearer to the actual details of the priest's death. 'About three in the afternoon.'

'You mean yesterday?' Will demanded.

'No, Friday. The day you left.'

'Where did you find him?'

'At the back of some old hurdle fences. After you left we began sorting and stacking them ready for repair but it came on rain and he sent us off to study for an hour till it eased off. But when we got back he wasn't there, or so we thought. One pile had slipped over but instead of starting stacking again we went back to study for it was raining quite heavily by then. We thought the Father had gone to visit some of the sick folk in the village out by. He was meant to but - he never got there.'

'When did you find out?'

'We didn't realise till afternoon. He didn't come back for dinner at noon. That does sometimes happen if he has some distance to travel, but he's usually there for the service. When he didn't turn up for that we just sat and prayed instead, then went back out to set up the stack of hurdles again and...' He tailed off, his wide hazel eyes seeing nothing of the Auditorium of shocked men around him.

'...found him lying behind it. Or under it, really. He was dead.'

'Have you any idea how he died, my son?' Thomas said gently, again trying to ease the telling for the boy. Blood had already been pounding in Will's ears for ages.

'Oh yes. It was obvious. Somebody had stuck a knife in him.' This time the silence seemed to scream.

Chapter 12 – Why Ranulf

'Why Ranulf?' It was a despairing Michael who whispered the question they all wanted to ask. 'He was such a good man.' Inevitably, it was Mark who answered with an oblique snipe.

'Well, now we know where to look for Hector.' When this was greeted with disapproving looks the Sacristan gave a shrug. 'Isn't it obvious? The miller has taken his revenge for the deflowering of his daughter and all that followed in its wake, the Gowk Bairn included.'

'Nicol was certainly not Ranulf's child!' Brother Gregory was stung to a sharp answer for once. 'Ranulf had been in Rome a full year when Nicol was born.'

'He was around when Francie was begun, though, wasn't he? And both his brothers for that matter.' A peculiar hiss came from the far corner of the room, accurately expressing the disgust of all of them at Mark's insensitivity towards Michael. It came, surprisingly, from Brother Daniel who never spoke and who normally kept himself out of the limelight and alone. He did not even sing in church, just hummed along with the psalms and canticles. Now he sat with his dark eyes blazing.

The Prior stood up, giving Michael a last supportive tap on the shoulder, and faced the gathering. 'This is becoming disorganised, my sons. Allow me to request Captain Forbys to make the enquiries of Brother David, since he is the only one among us with experience of the law.'

'Not this kind of law!'

'Are you not willing to undertake it?' And before Mark could complain yet again Thomas inserted swiftly, holding the Sacristan's eye, 'You will be given complete freedom from interruption.'

Will took a deep breath as he considered. 'Only if that is the general wish.' It was, and once again Mark kept his minority dislike of it unvoiced. 'Then first of all, I think we should let this laddie have something to eat. He has come a long way and must be tired and hungry.'

'I couldn't swallow anything,' David muttered. A closer look suggested that there was a touch of shock in him not unlike Francie's.

'A drink at least,' the Prior insisted. 'Brother Justin? Please fetch something from the kitchens. Milk perhaps. With honey in it. Captain, we might as well continue.'

'Then let's start at the beginning.' He signed to David to sit within the circle of men on the stool which the Cellarer had vacated. 'Now, on Friday morning I myself was up and off from Mortlach just after dawn. I'd reached Balvenie by six of the morning and had crossed the Spey before nine.'

'I know,' the lad agreed. 'The ferryman told us.'

'I didn't see anybody before I left except for Father Ranulf and Walter.'

David flushed. 'They're good in the mornings.' Obviously David and the other two lads were not.

'How was Father Ranulf that day?'

The question was unexpected enough to yank David out of the inward-looking malaise which was threatening to engulf him. He started, then pulled his wits together in order to think. 'Worried about the messenger. He kept looking for the soldiers to come and when they hadn't appeared by Prime he became irritated. And that's not like him. He's always good-tempered. Usually.'

'Would you see the soldiers from where you were stacking the hurdles? The place where the messenger went off the road is half a mile to the west of the toun.'

'Oh yes. We were up on a hillock. I think we were working there just because it overlooked the valley and the peat bog.'

'Between the kirk and the bog?' Will thought he remembered the spot.

From that point Will took him through the timing of the boys' Friday morning. In the middle of it Justin returned with a mug of milk and bread spread with honey - which David was able to swallow with greater gusto than his earlier expectations had promised, much to Will's relief. He took another breath, wondering if his next suggestion would test Mark's patience too far.

'Father Thomas, may we include my three men outside the gates in this enquiry? They know the area and the people around Mortlach and might be able to answer - or ask - questions which I don't know are relevant.' Thomas again stared Mark down, although he was not the only monk to look doubtful. Camus might have been acceptable, but the Highlanders created mistrust.

'Mm. I suppose it does make some sense,' Thomas pondered. 'Very well.' He raised an eyebrow at Justin who again disappeared.

Will began again. 'Now, David, exactly when was Father Ranulf found?'

'In the early afternoon.'

'And he was lying on the ground?'

'Yes. But several of the hurdles had slipped over him so we didn't see him there to begin with. We still thought he was out visiting. It was only when Cormac went round the back to begin the lifting that he realised... He saw a foot, and a bit of a cloak...'

'Have you any idea how long he had been lying there?' David shook his head. 'But the last time you saw him was when he sent you all indoors out of the rain?' The boy nodded. 'Did he come indoors with you? Maybe to settle you down to the work you were to do?' The head shook again. 'All four of you boys went in together?' Another nod, then an adjustment.

'Two of us visited the bushes first.'

'Which two?'

'Walter and me.'

'Which one of you was last inside?'

'Uh, we were together, but I - think it must have been me last for I shut the door.'

'And in that last moment before you shut it, do remember seeing the Father?'

David thought for a moment, then shook his head slowly. 'No. He wasn't in sight.'

'So what was the very last sight of him that you did have?'

'When we left the stack of hurdles. He was bending over having a look at a couple to see if they were worth mending or just good for burning.'

'Bent over them, was he?' He nodded. 'How heavy was the rain then?'

'Oh, just spitting, but the clouds were black and the wind had begun whipping up cold. - There was all summer to do the hurdles, so they didn't have to be done in a hurry that very day!'

Will nodded his understanding, then turned to watch as Camus and the two Highlanders entered, escorted by a chary Justin. With not enough seats to go round Camus leaned his long, louche frame against a wall, tipped his right toe casually across his left boot and crossed his arms. Seeing him relax in the gathering, the Highlanders followed suit. Possibly brothers by their similar looks, they found spaces for themselves to lean against, but stood more rigidly to attention. Handsome they were with their heavily lashed blue eyes and chestnut gold hair and neat whiskers framing high cheekbones and long, firm jaws.

All three soldiers wore travelling plaids, of differing setts using blue, green and black threads. In the warm atmosphere it took no more than three minutes for them to shuck these heavy woollen blankets off their shoulders and on to the floor in front of them where they slowly began to release a strong musty smell, part the waterproofing sheep's lanolin, part unwashed man. With slight guilt Will remembered they had been quartered out of doors since leaving Balvenie on Friday.

Thomas, after checking that the MacIntoshes could understand some Scots, gave a succinct description of what had been uncovered up till that point before handing over once again to Will.

'Okay, David. You said it was immediately visible that the priest had had a knife stuck in him. Was the knife still there?' He sensed a stiffening of the newcomers.

'No.'

'Did you find it nearby?'

'No.'

'Did you look?'

'Did we ever! We hunted high and low but there was nothing that would have done the job. Or nothing we could find. We knew somebody was going to ask.'

'So how did you know he had been knifed.'

'The hole in him and... the blood. It didn't seem too much at first, but when we moved him there was plenty more underneath that had soaked into the ground.' After an uncertain minute David got himself in hand, stomach and all.

'So what did you do? - You were all together, were you? The four of you?'

'Yes. We'd been together all day.' The boy flushed. 'When we finally went out to do the hurdles it was afternoon. We'd been larking around,' he admitted, 'and at first we didn't believe Cormac and jeered at him for his black joke...'

'I'm sure Father Thomas will absolve you,' Will grimaced. 'Now. Can you remember this? How wet were the Father's clothes?'

'Wet?'

'Yes, wet. It had been raining, hadn't it?'

'Oh. Yes. Not as much as all that. The storm didn't really set in, just sort of went over westwards. We - just preferred to study rather than go out and hump hurdles.'

'Was the grass wet?'

'Yes, fairly. And yes, his cloak was wet, but in patches.'

'Patches?'

'Where the rain had got through between the hurdle slats.'

'Another question. I want you to think carefully about this one. When you picked Father Ranulf up, was the grass beneath him wet.' Seeing the boy's face blench he hurried on. 'I mean wet with rain? And the part of his cloak which was against the grass and not touched with blood? Was that wet or dry?'

David looked surprised. 'I - think it was dry. So was the grass. Except for the blood.' His teeth gritted but he stuck his chin in the air, determined to continue.

'Do you remember, or do you know, when the rain began?'

'We discussed that. We think it must have been about half an hour before we went out again. I mean when we went out the first time.'

'Which was when?'

'Nearly midday. Cormac went to check whether one of us should put the broth pot on for dinner.' Will nodded, already aware that Father Ranulf kept a large pot in constant use, topping it up with whatever came to hand and cooking it up regularly twice a day.

'And he wasn't in sight? Was it raining then?'

'Yes. That was probably when it was hardest. Which wasn't that hard.'

'So, Father Ranulf must have collapsed on the ground before the rain had properly begun. Say within half to three quarters of an hour of your going inside. How warm was his body when you found him?'

David swallowed hard. Twice. 'Not very.' Hardly precise. 'We - didn't check straight away, you see. Anyway that was not when we found him. We thought he had gone visiting because we couldn't see him anywhere and he had said he was going. Like I said we put the broth on anyway, then ate it. It was maybe two hours before we found him. Then we spent maybe ten minutes, no, probably more, deciding first that he really was dead and then what to do about it. There was - something about his colour that made us feel sure.'

'Was it possible that the ground he was lying on could have been sheltered from the rain? I mean before he fell on it? That could have made a difference to the timing.'

'No. It was right where we had all been stepping around the pile of hurdles.'

Will grimaced. 'So a mess of footmarks. Did you think of examining these before stepping among them again?'

'Yes, we did.' David looked anxious, as if expecting disapproval for wasting time. He had, of course, seen Will and Ranulf examining the footmarks where Hugo went off the drove road and into the bog. 'We left him lying for quite a while as we did it. He was so obviously dead, you see. There - was no longer any hurry to move him back to the village. And we thought we should look for any clues before we messed them up with our own feet again.'

'Well done,' praised the Prior, and the boy looked both abashed and pleased.

'You didn't think to write things down, did you?' Will asked.

'Of course! Cormac made us all write down what we saw first. Before we even spoke about it, in case we changed each other's minds.'

'Better still! Where are these testaments?'

'Gone to the Bishop. Cormac took them with him.'

David was no fool. He must have wondered at the change in the air and in the quality of the silence. After a moment he began fishing for something up his sleeve.

'We also made transumpts. Father Ranulf insists we always make copies of important things.' Suddenly he realised that the present tense was no longer correct and his eyes filled with tears.

While he was fighting to control these, Thomas reached to receive the single sheet, catching Will's eye as he did so. 'That sounds a sensible principle,' he murmured. 'Shall we do the same? We shall need a scribe.'

'I'll do it,' offered Mark.

After a stiff moment Thomas agreed, adding, 'And I shall do it also. Two copies should ensure we get things right, just as the boys decided. Brother Daniel, may we have the materials, please?'

Daniel heaved his heavy frame up on to his feet. Instead of heading directly for the door he came to Will's side and plucked at his sleeve, jerking his head towards the door to ask him to go too. Puzzled Will followed, receiving a nod from a surprised Thomas.

'We shall look at this multiple transumpt while you are gone.'

As they hurried through the church to the steps leading to the Brothers' Quarter, the gilded vessel swung lazily above them on its chain, its white kerchief stark and pure in the gloom. The bustle of spring birdsong echoed to the roof from the doorway, and among the twittering from sparrows and chaffinches came the captivating musical variations of a thrush and the subtle threnody once more of the gowk, the cuckoo on the hill. Why was he mocking now? What idiocy was Will committing this time? For an instant he wished with all his heart that he had said no to the task of delivering the Pope's letter and just headed over the hills for home. This very minute he could be courting Bethoc; maybe by now he could even have won her. Oh, joy! Instead he was knee deep in a mire entirely not of his own making.

An impatient grunt from Daniel hurried him up the narrow stairs and into the Scriptorium. The monk made straight to a large table at the far western end where three books were laid out, each open. Beside them were two tools and it was to these that Daniel drew William's attention. One was a garden trowel, the other a straighter, pointed version used by a builder.

Seeing Will take note of them and frown, Daniel then pointed at an illustration in the nearest of the books. It showed a gardener going about his work, using a trowel to plant what looked like onions. The second book came up with a craftsman using the second version for mortar in the raising of a wall beneath a church tower. Will looked at both pictures closely, admiring the meticulous detail.

'Did you do these? They are exquisite! I don't believe I have seen work to equal it.'

Daniel brushed aside the praise with a quick sweep of his hands, then pointed to a third picture. This scene was in a pottery, just as the pots were being put into the kiln ready for firing or being removed. Again there was a tool being used, a trowel of a sort which was being slipped under the hot bowl. Daniel picked up a sharpened quill, dipped it into a pot of dark tincture and drew another tool, discarded on one side of the bench by another potter, meticulously drawn. Still a trowel but...

'The shape is odd!' It was straight on the left and sharply angled on the right with a high shield to protect the potter's hand from the heat of the kiln. 'It matches - the wounds in Nicol's chest,' Will finished hoarsely. Daniel gave a solemn nod. 'You prepared these for me to see, didn't you?' Again the artist nodded. 'You do know, don't you, that those wounds were not what killed him? That he was probably dead already when they were struck?'

Daniel waited, expecting him to follow the argument through. 'So you believe that a potter's trowel was used to attack him after he was dead? That - two people were involved, perhaps?'

Daniel stuck out his bottom lip before lifting two fingers, then after a moment three. Will's heart plummeted.

'So, first the person who made the first strike from behind, the killing blow. Yes? Then - whoever hacked at him from the front. And then Francie?'

Daniel looked shocked. Shook his head. Then hesitated frowning.

'Don't you think she was the one to take Nicol's body to the river?'

Daniel's frown cleared immediately, then he gave a slow nod, tucked praying hands under his chin and nodded again. He was not intending to charge France with wrong doing. She was not the third person he intended.

'Then why three people?' Daniel tapped the picture of the pottery then, impatient with Will's obtuseness, turned to a shelf where three more books sat on the south wall where the sun could never shine on them. He took one down and opened it, searching swiftly through the pages as if certain of what he sought. It turned out to be a map. To Will's surprise it was of an area he knew well, the eastern Baltic Sea with Danzig just left of centre.

'Yes, I know this area.' Daniel's finger brushed to the right, then he brought his left hand to join it, as if picking up pieces from the various cities to the west and placing them down on to the Danzig area before looking up, again challenging Will to follow the signs. 'Is the Rule really as severe as all this?' Will complained, irked as much by his inability to understand than frustration at having to do without words of explanation. 'Why don't you just tell me?'

The answer shocked him. Daniel pulled himself upright, his ugly face setting like stone. Then he opened his mouth. His tongue had been ripped out at the roots.

Will swayed, then hurried to apologise, only to be stopped yet again with an angry sweep of Daniel's hands. Nevertheless Will spoke furiously, 'Whoever did that to you is evil!'

Daniel ignored him and tapped the map again, urging him to think harder. Swallowing his nausea Will bent his head and deliberately muttered his thinking out loud. 'So, something comes from the West to East, and... Ah. The German traders and settlers? They settled the Eastern areas and...' Daniel's right hand was again drifting eastwards, tiptoeing, slinking? Cowering almost as the left hand approached. It was alarmingly expressive. 'Is it the Slavs you mean? Good. The Germans came and drove out the Slavs, or Christianised them.' This time, accompanied by a nod, the fingers of the right hand were turned upwards only to be enclosed by the left fist. 'All right, then. They were enslaved. Or taken into servitude. There are still plenty of them left in Danzig, you know.'

Daniel touched his lips. After a moment's thought Will guessed, 'The only way they have of objecting is by refusing to learn our Low German. If the settlers want to communicate with them they have to learn at least a few words of their Slav tongue.'

Daniel poked Will's chest. 'Yes, as a matter of fact I can speak a bit of it. Why?'

Here the monk looked very pleased. First he pointed at the picture of pottery in the book, then he led Will to the high window and pointed down to the North-East where the mill and the kiln nestled far below by the bridge. Comprehension hit Will like a blow.

'Are you saying those two workmen in the glass-kiln are Slavs? I wondered why they didn't come out when Francie shouted for help. So they are still playing their old game of refusing to understand a foreign tongue, are they? And you want me to go and talk to them. See if they saw anything on Wednesday morning. - You don't think they were responsible for anything, do you!'

Daniel stood very still for a few moments before shaking his head, very slowly.

'But you're not quite sure. So - are they Christians?' A shrug, grimace and wobble of hands suggested they might not be, or might pretend to be but be keeping up their pagan beliefs underneath. 'I wonder if... Well, I know that some of the local folk are superstitious enough to regard Nicol as a Devil's Child. The Slavs are highly likely to think the same way.' Daniel nodded, but with another shrug to indicate that his opinion was conjecture only. He was trying to be fair.

Will was forming a high respect for this saturnine monk, even a real liking. After a long pause holding the dark eyes, he made a decision. 'Right, as soon as we've dug all the information we can out of David, I shall wander down to the kiln and have a word with them. Oh, don't worry. I'll play the innocent, just in case they are involved, - but somehow I doubt if they were.'

Outside the door of the Auditorium once more he paused to murmur, 'Thank you, my friend. This might be a very important break-through. Especially if the Slavs can tell me of any other visitors to the mill on Wednesday morning. I think Nicol's death might be connected with others. And yes,' he admitted soberly, 'I think Hugo probably is dead. What I want to know now is whether he has been skewered as well.'

Chapter 13 – New Witnesses

On entering the Auditorium, the pungent smell of the soldiers' plaids struck Will's nose.

'Brother Justin,' he chanced, gesturing to them heaped on the floor, 'is there anywhere else where these could dry off? I'm sure the soldiers would be grateful.' Justin's eyebrows only just remained in place as he bent to pick them up and Will did not dare meet Thomas's eye. Or Camus's, come to that.

As it happened, David had little more firm information that was noteworthy, apart from the testimony already written into the transumpt. That was interesting, however. All four boys had seen the imprint of a single unknown footprint, all describing it as large with a rounded toe and a distinctive heel which was broad and square, like a leather riding boot. Will thought of his own boots and looked at Camus's and those of the Highlanders. Any one of them might have made the depression. He knew he himself had not been near that particular spot.

Almost laughably, David described how Walter had taken some melted mutton fat all the way out from their kitchen and poured it into the print so that there would be a model of it when it cooled. But who could tell? It might just serve a turn.

Three of the boys wrote that they considered the pile of hurdles had merely fallen across Father Ranulf when he either collapsed or was pushed against it; one, Walter again, wondered if the hurdles had deliberately been shoved in a hurry over the body to conceal it, perhaps hoping to delay discovery and allow the killer more time to escape, but even he admitted that the pile was unstable to begin with.

None of them gave any indication that Ranulf might have chased the boys indoors because he had seen something or someone on the road. On the other hand, when this was put to David by the Prior, he took a very long time to think before agreeing that yes, this could have been possible. Ranulf was not in the habit of molly-codling his pupils. Normally he would ignore rain and expect them to finish the job they had started. On reflection, David did think their dispatch indoors had been both sudden and out of character.

Then there was a discussion about the position of the priest's body. Again the boys' descriptions more or less matched, although none was entirely explicit. The Prior suggested that David should demonstrate, and there he was lying face down on the floor with one arm trapped crookedly beneath him, the hand turned inward against his breast as if in pain, and the other flung out level with his head when Brother Alexander and the Infirmarian returned. The latter, too short-sighted to see the boy's alert expression, immediately jumped to the wrong conclusion.

'Oh my! The poor child. Let me...'

'No, no, Brother Infirmarian, he is only acting.' Thomas once again demonstrated his mastery of language by bringing the two absentees up to date in an impressive minimum of words. By this time both he and Mark were scribbling away on either side of a small table brought in to support their materials. Mark's transcription was very much more laborious.

There was one essential question which Will longed to bury, knowing it would bring David distress. He made it as impersonal as possible. 'What about the wound? Just one wound, was it? Did you look at that carefully?

'We - washed him and laid him out before the altar.' David swallowed. His throat had the large, awkward Adam's apple of a youth and it seemed painfully distended to the men watching it bob up and down. Of course the boys had seen the wound, and no doubt had struggled to examine it and not look at it at the same time.

'I'm sorry, David,' Will said softly, 'but could you describe it?'

'It's - in the transumpt.'

'Yes, but I want to hear if your memory now is exactly as you wrote down. When did you do that, by the way? Yesterday?'

'In the morning before we set out. The transumpt that is. We did the first notes on Friday. '

'I am assuming that you have walked here.' The boy nodded. 'So you have had two days journey during which to forget.' David frowned, bristling very slightly. 'If, for instance, you saw another puncture like it, how sure would you be that it was the same size? The same shape?'

'I'll never forget it!' the boy declared, his eyes growing wild. 'Never!'

Will's eyes met Brother Alexander's. 'It's in the pantry.' The Cellarer knew what was coming and forestalled him acidly. 'And no, it has not been chopped up for supper.'

'Brother Justin?' The young man rose, grimacing wryly at the bewildered young Franciscan. Will's soldiers were just as puzzled. 'May I ask you to fetch that cheese?'

When it arrived, still cold from the slate slab, David stared at it in near horror. The puncture in it still had an uncomfortable similarity to a real wound. 'I - think it was just like that,' he whispered. Will's innards twisted but he remained rock still and expressionless. Nobody else moved either, every face blank. After a moment David recovered and looked again. He even reached out to take the cheese between his trembling hands and carry it over to the light from a window to look more closely. 'I - don't know,' he muttered to himself. 'Maybe this hole is too large. A little too fat.'

Behind Will, Camus cleared his throat. 'Could it have been made by a sporting weapon? Not a fighting sword at all?'

'Ah, yes! I used to have one of those.' This first comment from Brother Gregory surprised Will, although perhaps it should not have done. The three faint scars across his tonsure already testified that he had been a fighting man. The admission told him something else. Once upon a time Gregory, in addition to acquiring an excellent education, had also been able to afford a sports sword, very much lighter than the fighting weapons used in the schooling yards, but also expensive; it was the first inkling Will had that the old man had come from the upper classes, at the very least from gentry. Belatedly it struck him just how egalitarian this little community at the Priory really was and he wondered if this was one of the prime objectives of its founding fathers.

'Do you mind if we try an experiment?' It was the Cantor who spoke, the first of the brethren to take any initiative in the investigation. 'The nearest tool I have seen to fit that hole is my hive knife. May I fetch it?'

They all sat in silence while Brother Stephen was out of the chamber. When he returned he handed it to Will, whose investigative role seemed to be fully acknowledged by them all by then. Even Brother Mark sat motionless and silent. What the three soldiers behind him were thinking Will had no idea. He was uncertain just how much the Highlanders were understanding.

First he pointed the knife towards the puncture in the cheese. Then, slowly and carefully, not wanting to reproduce the macabre squelching noise the Sheriff had gloried in, he pushed it through the rind a couple of inches away from the hole already there and into the firm curd up to the hilt. Equally slowly he pulled it out then laid the cheese down on the table. There was only just room for it between the two sets of papers.

Everybody stared at it. Brother Gregory stood up and bent closely to examine the two punctures and nodded. He was followed by the Infirmarian. After catching Will's attention with a cough, Camus heaved his back from the wall and he too stepped forward to have a closer look before returning to his previous position, arms folded and chin on chest. His stance was deceptively disinterested but Will realised his sharp eyes were taking in every movement.

It was the Infirmarian who broke the silence. 'This knife is too short to kill a man.' The implication was that the punctures looked very similar. Indeed, they did. 'It might have been long enough to kill Nicol, though.'

David gasped, then swooned as the implication of this hit him. After a moment Will asked, 'Where is it normally kept?'

'In the tool shed.' He remembered seeing that built against the wall of the kitchen garden.

'Is it kept locked?'

'Not usually. We are always in and out fetching things.' The older man sounded apologetic.

'So anybody could have gone in and taken it last Wednesday?' Out of the corner of his eye he saw Mark's head jerk up sharply, his mouth open. Thomas raised his hand a couple of inches to hush him. Will went on. 'On Friday I know it was in use here in the Priory garden for I saw you and Brother Mark working with it on the beehives. It could not possibly have been up in Mortlach at the same time. I presume that nobody touched the bees during the week before Friday so this must have been in the shed.' If Mark was keeping his mouth shut, the least he could do was meet him half way. 'Does anybody remember using it for anything else between Wednesday morning and Friday?'

Nobody did. But Will's stomach was on the way down into his boots again. He was sure he was not the only one there who knew that someone else had been in the garden. After another long pause, a particularly painful one this time, it was Prior Thomas who spoke the words none of them wanted to hear. They ached with sadness.

'Francie would have known where the knife was kept.'

It was only later that Will realised that neither Thomas nor Mark wrote that down before they broke up for Vespers.

He excused himself and set out for the mill. Camus followed, detailing his men to watch a gate each before lengthening his stride to come abreast of Will.

'This is getting uglier by the minute.'

'Mm.' Will agreed, glad of the young man's company. He felt able to relax with him for they had a good deal in common. They walked in silence, each teasing at the evidence so far uncovered, till, 'Tell me, what the divvel is James Forbys playing at? Surely any self-respecting castle should have grapples in the cupboard.'

'Maybe not. Remember Balvenie used to be a Comyn holding. It's been leased to your father but only because the Comyns have been disenfranchised.'

'Serves them right for swinging behind the Balliols,' grunted Will, his mind elsewhere.

'Your father might be fearing the day the pendulum swings back. The Comyns might yet worm themselves into favour again and ask for the return of their property.' That brought Will's full attention back.

'Has that anything to do with the fact that it's full of MacIntoshes?'

Camus gave a rolling shrug. 'They'll be Comyn folk on Comyn land. Where else would they go, if they're not to starve?' After a long look Will turned away, setting the matter aside for the time being.

He had half expected the mill to feel sinister or threatening but, on that dank Sunday, the late afternoon lent it an air of dereliction which seemed the product of far longer than the four days since Nicol's murder. Had the place imbibed the terrible despair in the miller after his daughter's suicide many months ago? Now it was a place of tragedy, not evil. It even felt sacrilegious to enter the yard alone, uninvited, without another living soul to accompany him, for Camus stopped short in the roadway. There was no longer a trace of what must have been a copious amount of blood. No tools were left out. The bags of corn which had awaited their late grinding had gone. He wondered if the miller's possessions had also been removed, and the traces of the children who had lived here.

The pottery yard next door was also empty, except for several empty crates but the door stood open. Hot air wafted out, for a kiln is a fickle contraption to light again once put out and this one, he had already been told, was kept burning constantly. Besides, both pots and glass needed long cooking and there was no reason why that should not be done over a Sunday. It did puzzle him how they managed to get one kiln to do both jobs, for the temperatures required were starkly different.

There was nobody inside the workshop which was no more than three walls and a roof leaving the fourth wall wide to the weather. When Will tried the low turf cottage behind, that was also empty. He ducked to look through the doorway, remaining bent for a few moments while his eyes swept round the interior. It must have made a miserable shelter during the bitter winter months.

At the back on the earth floor lay a rumpled mattress stuffed thickly, he guessed, with prickly heather not chaff, and against the side wall hung a couple of garments, one very long which swept barely an inch off the ground. Apart from that there was nothing. Absolutely nothing. Not even a crucifix. Did the two men cook on the kiln somehow? He looked more closely at the workshop interior as he returned to Camus, seeing enough to prompt questions rather than answers.

'Let's go for a walk,' he sighed to Camus. 'I've been shut up too long.'

'Reading. I know.'

'How?'

'I saw you through the windows. From Heldon Hill.' Camus grinned. 'You looked just like a schoolboy chained to your lessons!' They crossed the bridge on to the road which took the bulk of the traffic passing by between Forres and Kinloss in the West and Elgin and Spynie in the East. Their long legs were soon striding off it and upwards through the rising lushness of spring bracken fronds.

'There, see?' Camus pointed down at the Library windows, then swept his fingers to the Scriptorium on the top floor, its high window opening to the clear North light. 'I could see you up there only when you were on your feet.'

'What were you doing up here?'

'Being conscientious, guarding against your spies. Well, taking a walk to relieve the boredom really.'

'Find anything?' Will looked back. They were already high enough to see over the Priory wall into the garden and, right enough, it was possible to see the windows of both the Library and the Scriptorium above it. Anybody passing inside the windows would have been obvious, and he had done a great deal of pacing up and down as his mind teased out the details of the charters he had been studying. His eye returned to the road, now running below them.

Could the people passing by on it also see into the Library? He thought not. But they certainly could see the Scriptorium on the high upper storey. Could this be how a message had been sent out of the Priory? A signal sent? But by whom? Brother Mark could not have had time to climb to the Scriptorium on the first Wednesday morning and be back to join the congregation for Prime. The Cellarer could have, but he had gone in the opposite direction, as proven by his coming back with Will's travel provisions. Besides, everybody would have seen if he had taken an elaborate detour past the Chapter House door towards the church.

Before turning back to follow Camus he looked at the beautiful, simple lines of the great building, with the church at the heart of the community. The lack of ornamentation contrasted severely with the ornate embellishments on either the cathedral in Elgin or Kinloss Abbey. He knew which he preferred. Just above the sill of the end window he caught a glimpse of the gilded chalice hanging on its chain inside the chapel, freed for the moment from its white coverlet, for the monks would be in there right now, praying with extra fervour in the face of the tragedies which had struck so close to home.

Suddenly, very near, the cuckoo's clarion rang out, a loud complaint against their careless invasion, a gowk's jeering yet again. 'Oh, come on. Up to the top of the hill, then I'll try the kiln again.'

The sun was already setting, but only in the Vale of St. Andrew tucked behind the Heldon Hill. From the ridge above, the two young men gazed towards the northwest in startled awe over the spectacular Laich of Murray spread below them, its rich fields tumbling towards the shore. From the two ports of Finderyn in the West to Spynie preening itself in the east on the shore of its great sea loch, and across the piercing blue Firth to the Earldom of Ross tapering towards Orkney far in the north, the citizens and serfs, lords and lairds alike would be bathed in sunshine for many hours yet while the monks of Pluscardyn slept.

'Lec,' said the taller man. He was very tall, at least two inches taller even than Will, but narrow as a yard brush. Will's approaching steps had cut off soft laughter inside the hut, and by the time he had reached the door Lec was already there to bar entry. Both faces had been wary, defensive yet with defiance lurking beneath the surface. The tall man had been surprised to receive a greeting in Low German, the tongue of the Hansa, but had deliberately refused to answer. It was as Will expected. Lec had been shocked, however, when asked his name in a rough but comprehensible Slav dialect. 'Hus.' A scarred thumb was jerked at the other man, small and broad in build, but almost as thinly fleshed as Lec. Both had the round flat faces typical of Baltic Slavs, but it quickly became apparent that their language was some way removed from the version Will spoke.

'I,' Will pointed to his own chest, 'am Villi Vorbus. From Danzig.' He refused to be intimidated by the cool distaste on Lec's face, again unsurprised at the reaction.

'You lose samples? You want more?'

'Not at all. They have gone to Bruges with my fleet captain. And yes, I think I can use some more. If you have some. Your work is good, very good.'

Lec pouted, which did surprise Will a little. He had expected the man to be proud of his work, but the moment was quickly over. With a quick, 'I get them,' Lec stepped straight towards Will, obliging him to step backwards out of the doorway to let him through. Hus still crouched by the bed, his moon face stiff and his eyes gleaming with apprehension in the gloom. Perhaps he had not understood the conversation. Lec gave a jerk when he saw Camus slouching against the old oak by the bridge. He flung Will a quick squint then strode on towards the kiln, his movements heavy with disdain.

When they entered the building the glassmaker began rummaging among a pile of oddments while Will eyed an open ledger on the slate shelving, alongside baked clay bowls and jugs cooling on straw from the last load from the kiln. Will's cargo had already been entered as despatched for Lille.

Searching for the right vocabulary he said, 'May I ask you something?' When Lec looked over his shoulder at him he took that as agreement, although it might not have been. 'Did you see or hear anything unusual last Wednesday morning?'

Lec's frown was meant to indicate lack of understanding. Will knew from the recalcitrant behaviour of Slavs in Danzig that this might or might not be the case. 'Wednesday? The day of Woden?' Lec's eyes narrowed at that but he made no effort to deny that he was a pagan, even here within the Christian community which employed him. He certainly knew when Woden's Day was and shook his head. Well, it was something, Will supposed. There was many a Slav labourer or serf in Danzig who would not ever converse with the Germans who had ousted or enslaved them, not even in Slav.

Lec finished his search and reached for a strip of leather with which to wrap the little coloured droplets. One tumbled out and fell at Will's feet. He bent to pick it up and held it between finger and thumb against the light. It was a bead of crimson blood.

'Pretty,' he murmured. 'Just the same four colours? Do you make any others?' Again came that odd pout, this time with a wide splay of hands. 'Ah well, I am sure these will create interest. I was hoping...' He repeated his earlier question, this time touching an eye then an ear, half expecting the man would grab at the chance to take offence. But no. Lec looked deeply puzzled.

'You,' he frowned. His face, though round, was very thin and the skin deeply lined, almost as if it had been patched on to the framework of bones, or at least slid on over the skull and left to hang loosely on the hump of a nose and high cheek bones. A quiver set the lines in motion and, just for an instant, Will thought he saw himself in the strange expression they formed. 'You came here. You went to there.' He pointed at the wall separating the mill from the yard where they stood. 'To children shouting.'

Will took a deep breath as he nodded. 'What happened after I left?' The breath remained within him and the blood began to pound in his ears.

Lec stared at him then, oh so slowly, shook his head and pursed his lips.

'Did Brother Michael stay with the miller?' This time came a nod. 'How long?'

Lec reached out and tipped the hourglass by the ledger just once.

'An hour? Then he came back?'

Lec pointed towards the Prior buildings.

'Yes, he went for dinner. Did you go to eat then as well?'

'We eat here. We watch glass.' This time Lec pointed to behind the kiln, which by no means filled the stone building protecting it from the weather. Whoever had built the kiln had been determined that it should not cause any other buildings to catch fire, even if it blew up itself, but now Will saw a little stove arrangement off to the side; it seemed to utilise the heat coming from the flue and there was a small pile of eating utensils beside it.

'Did you see the miller? Or either of the children?' The head shook. 'Did you hear anything? Did you hear Nicol calling, or crying? Or Francie?'

Looking more puzzled than ever, Lec shook his head to every question and Will began to believe his reaction was genuine after all. A nasty suspicion crept into his head.

'Uh, you do know what happened on Woden's Day, don't you?'

'You come.'

'Nicol was killed.' It was brutal to put it so suddenly, but his shaky command of Slav left no alternative. Lec's eyes bulged, then he sprang back, fully expecting that he and Hus were about to be accused. Slavs had learned to expect being made the scapegoats.

'No, no! All I want to know is did you hear or see anything. Are you sure you didn't?'

The strange face froze, staring on, the bulging eyes never leaving Will's face. 'You?' Lec finally whispered as if faced by a spirit from hell.

'No,' Will snapped, 'not me! I was miles away. But somebody did it. I don't think it was you, and I don't think it was Brother Michael either. I'm not even sure it was Hector.'

Again the lines on Lec's face quivered and this time the flash of instinctive mimicry was of Hector, an angry Hector but a despairing one who looked as if consumed by guilt. The impression was over almost before it was begun, but Will's throat went dry. Did Lec know more than he was saying after all? A moment later the reflection was of the empty angelic face of a church putti. The sudden likeness was eerie.

'Nicol? Devil child? Should have been dead long ago.'

'Not a devil child,' repelled by the idea, Will felt obliged to argue. 'A child of God like every other child.'

'Dead now? How?'

It was unusual for Will to have to look up to anybody, but he held Lec's eyes for several long moments before turning to search among the tools on the shelf. There were several of the strange triangular trowels in different sizes, all straight edged on the left and sloping sharply on the right, but he could find nothing with which to demonstrate the first fatal blow. At a loss, he settled on doing a mime. First he held up one finger and proceeded to draw his phantom sword and wipe its blade between finger and thumb, holding these up to indicate that the blade was very fine then turning them at right angles to show it was narrow as well. Then he turned Lec round and indicated how the blade had been slipped up under the ribcage and straight into Nicol's heart. Lec watched frog-eyed over his shoulder.

A moment later the Slav demonstrated that he was a far finer mimic than Will could ever be. With back pulled straight, head high and arms slammed straight by his side he quite literally turned himself into a soldier. Not any ordinary soldier either, but an officer whose merciless glance flicked right then left seeking the slightest deviation from discipline. Will's mouth fell open. Hector.

'Yes, you may be right.' Lec resumed his own persona. First he mimed a blow with one hand then raised one finger of the other hand, his eyebrows raised. When Will nodded, he gave a sharp upward shove with a finger in the direction of Will's rib cage. 'Uh, yes again. Someone who knew how to kill with one stroke. And someone strong enough to do it.' He had no need to add that Hector might fit that picture very well indeed - except for the officer element. Or had he been an officer? But even if he had, he would surely never have owned a sword with such a slender blade? Lec watched him thinking, his own frown deepening.

'But after Nicol was dead,' Will found himself saying, far from certain that he was doing the right thing to reveal more, 'someone took one of these and...' He selected the trowel he estimated nearest the correct size then struck towards his own breast in roughly the same positions as the blows made on Nicol's body, carefully counting out the blows with the other hand. Lec's expression became one of disgust.

'One person? Or two?'

'I don't know. Perhaps three. When Michael went to the Priory for dinner Nicol's body was taken from the mill yard and put it into the river Lossie. There was nothing but a pool of blood left.'

'Michael?' Lec whispered aghast. Then he shook his head at his own idea. 'No. Michael came back from mill and we heard children, Francie talking. Michael not go back to the mill.'

'Were you here in the kiln all the time? I know you were preparing a new batch of glass when I was there earlier. It needed all your attention. Both you and... Hus, is it?'

'We not stop till late afternoon except to take many drinks. We need when work so hot.'

Will nodded. The strangest thing to others would be that Lec and Hus had not known what had happened so nearby. But it did not surprise him. Not now he thought about it. The pair were doing exactly as he had observed other Slavs do again and again in the Eastern Baltic lands. Having been driven from their homes by usurping German traders, they had been disinherited from everything that was theirs by right, or so they thought, and forced into servitude, even slavery. The only freedom left to them was their language. By refusing to speak anything but Slav they forced their conquerors to bow in this one thing, obliging them to learn at least enough Slav to enable orders to be given, arrangements to be made, information to be passed on. The two of them were doing exactly the same here, keeping themselves strictly in isolation, refusing to speak Scots, or

Latin or French if they had any at all. As a result nobody even tried to talk to them. Will thought he knew why they wanted it that way.

'How did you come here?' he asked.

Lec's face stiffened. 'Ship.'

'Why?'

'Captured by Knights. Sold to pirate captain to fight against Danes.' His lip curled up. 'For you.'

'No, not for me. I do not like many things done to your people. Do the monks pay you well?'

The lip curled again. 'No pay. Just food, clothes.'

'So you are bonded to them. For how long? Ah, you have not been told?' In other words they had been too stiff-necked to ask. 'Where were you captured by the Knights then?' They were talking about the Teutonic Knights who regarded the Christianising of the East as their Crusade, right down to treating the recalcitrant ones who refused their Great Gift as animals, as had obviously happened here.

Lec's mouth tightened.

'You must have learned your skills somewhere.'

'Vilnius. Home of Hus. I from Kirkegaard.' That was all Will would get. Lec turned away, set on removing himself from the inquisition and caring not a pin for any offence he might give.

'But the third person involved in Nicol's death? Have you any idea who that might have been?'

The man shook his head fiercely. But again, just for an instant, another likeness hover on the man's face and Will saw his eyes fill with tears.

Chapter 14 - Paying Visits

Sick at heart, Will returned to join Camus.

'That dumb show was pretty plain.' Camus unpeeled his shoulders from the oak tree. 'Nothing?'

'Nothing admitted,' Will grumbled. 'But maybe they did see nothing at all. That pair have isolated themselves from the rest of the sane world. Oh, come on, let's see if Brother Alexander has left anything out for us to eat.'

A substantial cold meal was waiting for them in the Guest House and the Cellarer had also had five beds prepared. In one of them David was sound asleep, white-faced and exhausted by shock and travel weariness. Camus agreed to use another. His two MacIntoshes elected to remain independent, despite the discomfort of sleeping out of doors on a damp, cool night. After rejecting an initial inclination to go visiting further afield before turning in, Will contented himself with a walk round the garden where the female cuckoo was back at her game of snatching the last of the late bees returning from the fruit blossoms. Again her mate called from the hill and again Will was convinced he was mocking the poor success which the human gowks in the drowsy valley were making of teasing out the pieces of the puzzles before them.

He was up by five next morning, which felt early although a whole three hours after the monks. He intended to call on Lady Amelia, buy the horse then leave but, despite an urge to quit the investigation and head for his parents' home, Will found himself promising Thomas that he would be back in time for Chapter at ten.

Quarrelwood, the sturdy seat of the de Chisholm family was one of the most attractive of the liens from the Earldom of Murray. It sat on an elegantly wooded ridge looking north and westwards over the richest farmland of the Laich of Murray which was cut by a sweep of sweet water. This ribbon of small lochs had once been the River Eryn but many decades ago it had broken a new mouth for itself farther west by cutting due north into the Firth. The ensuing catastrophe for the fisher folk and traders had drowned and destroyed an ancient, earlier shore village which had sat on a spit of land between the sea and the river. Until then the river had flowed sluggishly eastwards, parallel to the shore and skirting the Abbey lands of Kinloss before meandering on for a couple of miles to enter the most westerly curve of the Bay of Spynie. So legend said.

Farther east the river Lossie also entered the same bay by the Bishop's palace of Spynie, but the flow of the two rivers into one estuary had been both benign and threatening. While both poured their waters into the bay there was enough water to keep the mouth open, creating for Spynie a superb, sheltered haven for shipping, but the rivers also brought down huge amounts of fine sand which needed constant dredging. Out at sea, this silt was also swept into gigantic banks by the powerful tidal flow into the Firth from the German Sea, westward-growing banks becoming ever less stable as they were piled adjacent to the shore, a constant perennial process. Sooner or later these banks would become offshore islets, or dunes; sooner or later these would be breached in turn by storms, causing major changes to the shoreline and the land behind. Will had seen this process happening along the entire southern shore of the Baltic Sea where islands came and went within generations.

The ancient eastern exit of the Eryn into Spynie Bay had long been silted up by now leaving shallow, diminishing lochs with four clear islets rising above lovely marsh meadows; one was the home of badgers for some reason, another held the few crumbling remnants of a monastic cell from the old Culdee church. Now all that was left of the river was the delicate receding waters still lapping the moat of Duffus Castle two miles north. There he could just see signs of desultory repair under way, for the old pile had been left in a sorry state by English battering.

Until the last minute Will was hidden from the old fortalice of Quarrelwood by a spread of birches and alders interspersed with ancient, stately oaks.

'Aye, Willie. Come to call on my wife, have ye?' Robert de Chisholm strode round the corner to see who was clattering to his door. 'Ye'll nae find her about at this hour, laddie.'

'I've come to buy a horse from Lady Amelia,' snapped Will. 'If she'll sell.'

'She will if ye offer her enough.' Robert grinned, seeing he had hit a sore spot. Plainly he did know what his wife got up to behind his back, but it did not seem to bother him today. In spite of the early hour, still not long after six, he was got up in leather and steel and his brow was glistening with sweat. 'Fancy a turn in the yard?' To one side a couple of tough-looking henchmen were setting up a target while a third began to peel off the padded leather tunic he had worn during the practice fencing bout which had just finished.

'I dinna carry my armour with me.'

'Ye've got your sword though.' Robert eyed the weapon, which was a good deal smaller and lighter than the hefty broadsword Robert was now leaning on. 'If ye havena brought it for a joust, I'll be wondering if ye thought yourself less than safe in coming here.' That, he implied, would be considered an affront. He headed towards the yard again, leaving Will to trudge after him, his horse's reins over his arm.

'Right now is not the time to leave any weapon lying around. Haven't ye heard that Father Ranulf up at Mortlach has been killed? Skewered, like Nicol.'

Robert stopped in mid-stride. It took him several still seconds to turn and ask, 'When?'

'Friday. A few hours after I left.'

'So how did ye find out?'

'One of the Mortlach laddies came in yesterday afternoon wi' the news. Another o' them has gone to the Bishop.'

'Hah! And the Bishop'll want to muscle in, I'm thinking. This time he'll maybe manage it, whatever Prior Thomas says - Ranulf being one of his own Cathedral chaplains, like. He'll try and include Nicol's case and all.'

'I canna see a link.'

'No? Ye said it yersel. Skewered like Nicol. A blade, laddie, a blade. I had a notion ye fancied yourself as an investigator.'

'Just an enquirer.'

'Well, well. But can ye nae see?'

'How do we know if there was any similarity at all between the blades?' Will phrased it as a question, not wishing to stray into lying. 'All we can say is that they were both stabbed to death.' He waited a moment before adding, 'I suppose we'll find out soon enough.'

'Why?' Was it Will's imagination, or did that question sound sharp?

'Won't they bring Ranulf's body back to Elgin? Then anybody who saw Nicol's wound will be able to testify whether they look at all alike.' He was not sure whether he was glad or sorry that Thomas had insisted on so many people seeing Nicol's body before burial.

'You included?' That definitely did sound grumpy.

'I was thinking of Father Symon, the Bishop's Investigator. He's keen, even if he's not that sharp. Not as sharp as Sandy Watson from Elgin Toun I'll warrant. He viewed the body and all.'

Wasn't it Robert who had twitted Will about the popularity of his neck? Now he jerked his head to the left and led Will through the gate in the outer defences. In the bailey a couple of young squires were exercising with wooden swords and several lower retainers with practice pikes and a swinging punch-bag. The men at arms followed the men in, leaving the target ready for use. A more mature and muscular trainer than the rest stood waiting for Robert's return. Before they reached his hearing Robert murmured, 'I've been wondering, could more than one person have been involved wi' young Nicol's death.'

Now that was interesting. Robert, like most folk, had not been told about the trowel slashing and his viewing of Nicol's shrouded body had been cursory. 'Why?'

'One tae stab the wee gowk while he was still at the mill. Didn't ye say there was a pool of blood there? And then anither to dump him in the river. The killer would have got out pretty quick after the deed, wouldn't ye think? And if he left blood in the yard he's bound to know that folk would realise the bairn was killed there anyway. Why run the risk and tak him tae the Lossie?'

Will had thought about that a great deal. 'A message of some kind?'

'Saying the bairn had driven his mither to drown hersel? That would surely make it Hector, then. Like I said on Friday.'

'Why would he kill Ranulf? If there is a link.' He left Hugo out of the picture.

Robert threw him a leer. 'The local punters lay odds on Ranulf being the saint who defiled the miller's darling daughter. At the tender age o' fifteen, an' all, and him already a priest and near ten years older.'

Will caught his breath, holding the knight's eye. That would explain a great deal; the pain, and the near-blasphemous resentment over Amelia's suicide and subsequent atrocious burial; the instinctive, angry protectiveness of Francie when he thought Will was abducting her. But it hardly explained Hugo's death.

He had also begun to wonder if Brother Michael was in danger. So had Thomas, for he had agreed instantly to keep Michael within the Priory precincts in the meantime and Michael, still distraught after David's ghastly news, had not been difficult to persuade. He seemed to have forgotten for the moment that he had seen, or thought he had seen Will in the mill yard. At the back of Will's mind was lodged the fact that when Ranulf's body was found, he himself had not been gone from Mortlach for long. That might enter Michael's mind too, although Will could call on Camus for an alibi, and half the Balvenie garrison for that matter.

'Right. Up wi' yer sword, laddie.' Seeing his visitor was off deep in thought, Robert turned suddenly to face him, his eyes alight with challenge.

'But I've already told ye I've nae...'

'Ach, ye dinna need armour.'

'Well, you tak yours off and mak it fair.'

'Nae time, laddie, the battle's on!' And he gave Will barely enough to draw his breath far less his weapon before he charged. Instantly Will was alert. Every nerve jangled. Every muscle responded to the thrill of danger. The very first thrust of the murderous two-hander nearly ruined his last clean shirt.

Afterwards, Will could never decide on what Robert intended when he forced the fight on him. Woefully under armed and unprotected, Will made a poor opponent. He was trained in swordsmanship, of course, merchants had to be, but out of practice and he had never fought in earnest. Under the circumstances it was never going to be to Robert's credit that he was dominant within seconds. His fighting was also dirty, thoroughly at variance with the code of chivalry. The very fact that a knight had taken the challenge to a merchant, however ambiguous that claim, was distasteful.

Later Will wondered. Did the man have some inkling, some resentful premonition of what was to follow that day? Or was he trying to soften up the visitor in preparation for a later conquest elsewhere? It seemed incredulous. Or could it have been that Will's embarrassment when twitted about Maura had set a chain of speculation going, arousing jealousy, a jealousy not yet justified?

Or was it something completely different? Was Robert afraid that Will suspected him of having a role in the chain of murders taking place? More pertinently, might Will be following up the case with more curiosity than a knight with undisclosed secrets could tolerate? At the very first swing of the hefty broadsword that was the dread which drenched Will, that Robert wanted to shut him up or at the very least warn him not to go poking his nose in.

Whatever it was, for ten minutes Will truly believed that he was going to die. Throughout the contest none of the onlookers moved a muscle. All were de Chisholm men, whatever they thought of their lord and his breach of good behaviour. If it came to an enquiry over the death of a visitor during a practice at arms, Will had no doubt what their answers would be. Whatever Robert told them to say. Accident. Pure accident. Even if the Bishop asked with the obsessive weight of the Church's sorcery behind him as well as the Law of the people, they would still stick to their lord's command. Robert fed them and their families.

Deliverance came none too soon. Will had his back to the bailey fence with the hideous weapon pressing flat across his shoulders just under his chin. Robert's clear grey eyes glinted, steady and mocking, as he gazed with frank fascination at the devilish black holes which Will knew his eyes had become the instant the first strike was made. How long the lady Maura had been watching he had no idea, but that was the moment when she slid a slender blade between them. It hovered beneath their noses, scintillating in a reflected ray of sunshine. Both men froze, still eye to eye, each waiting to see what the other would do. In theory, Will might still have heaved the great sword away from him and continued the fight. In practice, both knew his strength was gone. In any case Will was much too shocked at finding a possible murder weapon presented so openly. From his very stillness, perhaps Robert was too, but his eyes never flickered.

After several seconds Robert stepped back, lifting the broadsword away and letting the point clatter to the cobbles, careless of any damage the smith would have to repair later. Although sweating, he was not even out of breath. Recovering fast, Will slithered sideways away from the wall behind him, away from the girl in the blue dress which matched her eyes. A glance showed him that she held the sporting blade in one leather-gloved hand. A second was still in the double sheath slung by her side. His own sword had just been twirled out of his hand by Robert and tossed to where it now lay yards away. The trainer was bending to pick it up, his eyes admiring the Spanish tooling.

'Ye've fought a left-hander afore, I see,' was Robert's dismissive comment as he turned away.

Will caught the tip of his tongue between his teeth and held on tightly. If he used it at this particular moment, his words would have shattered the peace of all Christendom.

Taking another step backwards he brushed his hands, trembling at last, down over the front of his shirt.

He knew now how strong and skilful Robert must be. A broadsword is a hefty two-hander with spectacular killing power and this one was made to be wielded in deadly blood battles. It was at least half as long again as Will's own light weapon and probably more than twice the weight. The edge, he was certain, had been repeatedly hammered and heated to introduce some carbon along the cutting edge; the resulting annealed steel would have been sharpened fit to slice thistledown. Accidentally or otherwise, Robert could have killed Will with a careless swipe any time he liked. As it was, there were no more than a few scuff marks on his shirt. Not a single nick spoiled its smoothness.

His pride was another matter. That had been punctured in a thousand places and out of each and every lesion was beginning to pour a vitriolic rage. He bit his tongue even harder, only just mature enough to realise that uttering even a single word would be self-defeating. Robert was waiting for his outburst as he walked away, hugging his victory inside himself and counting. Nothing on earth would make Will oblige him.

'My lady.' He managed a bow or sorts but a pleasant expression was beyond him. 'Direct me to the apartments of Lady Amelia, if you please?'

Her blue, blue eyes searched his face and the slow smile she gave him was enigmatic. Then she pointed north-eastwards with the slim blade. Its tip was permanently blunted by being hammered into a small thick spoon shape for sport. 'Rassie Castle. Half a mile away. You're not staying for a stoup?'

'My time is short.'

'Like your manners,' she murmured very softly, maintaining the mockery. He drew in a deep breath, his lips slightly parted, for he was still out of breath although he did all he could to cover the fact. She too was transfixed by his black eyes.

'With some justification, my lady. If you witnessed it all you will know the reason.' He too lowered his voice, not sure why but aware that Maura's magnetism was again beginning to confound him in ways he could not handle well, especially given the trouncing her husband had just inflicted on him. 'If you will excuse me...'

He retrieved his sword from Robert's trainer and headed for his horse. When Robert made his charge Will had dropped the reins rapidly and nobody had bothered to tend to the animal. It had skittered away then wandered back on to the hillside where he was now grazing patiently. As Will rode off, boiling, he felt Maura's hot eyes follow him, but he did not turn round. Why did he have the feeling that the whole unsavoury incident had been staged? By whom, he did not dare guess. He wondered, too, whether that second sporting blade inside its pocket had also had its tip mutilated, or not.

Rassie was a pretty little castle set on the low ridge which ran between Pluscardyn and the sea. Most of the oak forests crowning it had been felled to provide sheep land which overlooked the rich dark loam of the Laich farms. Lady Amelia was plainly in favour of getting as much profit out of her share as possible for around the castle walls the adjoining hamlet was humming with Monday morning activity. More steadings were scattered nearby, separated from each other by their surrounding fields from which grazing animals were firmly fenced out by hedges and well-built rubble walls. Here and there the tenants were making it evident that they were attending to their business and it was still well before eight.

‘Breakfast? Ah, good. My farm folk will be in shortly to eat so if we want peace we’d better take our food into the solar.’

Lady Amelia did not stand on ceremony. Handing Will a large platter she took another, both laden with fresh oaten bread and sheep’s sweet-milk cheese. A servant followed with a jug of surprisingly strong ale with a nip in the taste of it, and another of water, and led the way out of the great hall where trestles were being raised to feed the tenantry. It was much earlier than most folk ate but this lady was obviously a law unto herself. She also insisted on no business over the meal, instead preferring small talk which she conducted in flowing court French. Will grew alarmed at how easily she winkled out of him a mass of details about his own background, and at how much more she already knew. When he dared to say so she laughed, an infectious trill, before explaining that she knew his father well and had also met his mother on a couple of occasions.

'A very clever woman. Such a pity that she does not come to court. It needs all the livening up it can get at times.'

'I think you must know why, my lady,' Will chided gently. Dolinda Bromse was German for a start. Born into trade to boot, she was despised by the noble lords clustering around the King, even more so by the ladies - although most were eager enough to take advantage of the profits they could make by employing such figures. Worse still, Dolinda, it was rumoured, was in trade in her own right, and her a woman. A Lady!

The trill of laughter returned. 'And I repeat. The court is the poorer for it, but I don't suppose for a moment that she is. Shall I tell you a secret? Only she and I know, but she is my trading agent! She buys silks and velvets for me from Bruges, even from Florence. How about that?'

He smiled into his second tankard of ale. It was not for him to confess about others he knew who hugged their secretive trading through Dolinda with equal relish. His mother did not take on many customers, fearing she might arouse the suspicions of the scrutineers of her son's legacy. She did just enough trading to keep the wolf from her Scottish husband's door. For all his ancient blue blood Will's father's silver was scarce indeed and those five younger Forbys sisters had to be fed and educated and would soon need to be kitted out with dowries and marriage chests.

He himself was not allowed to give them help out of his Bromse fortune, not a single penny. It cut him hard to see them all go without. Even worse was sensing the disapproval of other folk, who considered him mean. They were not aware of the rapacious suspicion of his grandfather's trust members, one of whom could become the recipient of the entire fortune if he overstepped the prescribed mark. He wondered if Dolinda had explained this to Lady Amelia. On the whole he thought not. His mother was a proud woman and wise enough to know that her cash-strapped husband was an even more proud man.

'Now, dear boy, tell me why you are here.' Will explained, offering what he hoped was a good price for the pony with the black nose. Lady Amelia refilled his tankard to the brim before declaring, 'I shall take nothing. I intended to give him to the Priory in any case. God only knows why He gave Brother Alexander the feet He did if He expects him to traipse round the countryside on them!'

Will winced at her disrespect for the Deity, then grinned, realising he agreed.

'If you wish to make a donation in lieu to the monks, that is entirely between you and them,' she continued. 'Now, how about telling me why you arrived in such a hurry. Oh, I was watching from this window as you came riding at full tilt.

Did you have a witch on your tail?' She went to the window now, stepping up on a little stage put in to raise her tiny stature high enough to let her peep over the sill. A moment later she looked back over her shoulder then laughed again. Her actions had been a device to bring Will's eyes to the light and now, of course, they betrayed him. 'Well, well! So it was Maura! I suppose you went there to find me.'

'I - crossed swords with Robert,' he muttered.

'Did you now. That's easily - what?' Her voice sharpened. 'Literally? From what people say of his swordsmanship, that was not very wise.

'I got no choice.

'I wonder why?' She was intrigued.

'He neglected to explain.' His rage had come surging back, probably fed by the ale, but he was not so far gone as to utter indiscretions. Not yet. 'He - probably wanted a change of sporting partner, that's all.'

'Oh, probably.' The words dripped disbelief. She tried a couple more gambits but when she realised she had learned all she would about the incident she changed course. 'So who do you think killed poor Nicol?'

She asked the question lightly enough, although a thread of compassion coloured her voice. Will dropped his eyes to his boots and kept them there for more than two minutes, waiting for the slight reeling of his brain to settle. When at last he looked up she had begun to frown. 'Surely - you don't think it could have been Francie!'

He drew in a slow breath. 'The most immediate candidate is Hector. But there are others. Several others. And - it is just possible that Francie is one of them.'

Chapter 15 - Confrontations

'No! That I shall never accept!' The lady shuddered with outrage. Her faded blue eyes flamed suddenly as if a blaze had been ignited within her. 'Oh, I have no doubt she was the one who took him to the river. It is an old tradition, you know, a sacrifice to flowing water. That way the passage of the soul is eased on its way to Heaven. It is especially effective when the lands of three lairds meet.' A tingle ran down Will's back. This was the case at the very spot where Nicol had been found; and where Amelia had, or may have, drowned herself. That was confirmed by Robert's spat with Gregory over supper on Friday night.

Amelia added, 'Francie may be a de Chisholm, Captain Forbys, but she is also a Mac Fearchar like her grandfather who had much of the rearing of her - and all the rearing of her mother. He comes of Celtic folk and has some very queer Celtic fancies. And don't forget that Francie's mother died by water less than two years ago. It had a terrible effect on the child.'

'But... I don't know if you have been told this, my lady, but before I left on Wednesday morning I came on Hector beating the children. The laddie had fouled himself and for some reason this time was the last straw for his grandfather. Heaven knows how often they had cleaned the bairn already that day. I didn't fully understand what was going on at the time, but now - well, I believe that Hector had reached the end of the road. The way he was wielding that flail - he was within a breath of killing one of those bairns. Or both. The only thing that stopped him was the point of my sword, you know.'

She could no longer keep back the tears but the flare inside her was in no way doused by them. 'You're saying Francie understood that? That she might have...' Putting the thought into words was beyond her.

'Nicol was getting beyond them all,' Will said bluntly, 'and he was never going to change. She might have seen it as the only solution.' He could not bear to be explicit either. 'For everybody.'

'No,' she repeated, beating her fist into her palm. 'No, no, no. - Why are you looking at me like that?'

'If you had been Francie, if *you* were that brave, spunky child and were terrified that your grandfather would kill your brother and you knew it would bring the full rigour of the law on his head - what would you have done? If there appeared to be no other way out?' The cruel challenge made a ghost of her. She looked as crushed as Francie had on the journey to Balvenie. It took her long minutes to batter the challenge back at him.

'It's not enough,' she muttered. Slowly a cool calmness returned and her eyes narrowed. 'You must have more information. You have? Yes, I see it in your face. Please tell me. I know how to be discreet, if that is your...'

'Brother Gregory assured me of that.' Will saw no way out. 'Very well. There is more. A great deal more. First, I must tell you that Francie has disappeared again. I think… I hope she has not come to harm. With all my heart I hope that. Since her pony is missing again as well, she may be safe enough. I - was wondering if you could suggest anywhere she might have fled to? Or what manner of place?'

After a few seconds Lady Amelia suggested his own home.

'That was our plan,' he admitted. 'I even prepared a letter for my mother to go with Ranulf when he took Francie there.

It's no more than a good day's journey from Mortlach to Druminnor.'

'And has the letter gone missing too?'

'All I can tell you is that the laddies at Mortlach have no memory of seeing it. Or David hasn't.' That made her frown and prepare for more bad news. 'You see, uh, I'm sorry, my lady, but I have to tell you that Father Ranulf is dead. He - was found collapsed by a woodpile on Friday afternoon.' Still as stone she waited, wide eyes watching him swallow hard. 'Two of the novices set out on foot on Saturday morning. They stayed overnight at Knockando then parted company at the Palmers' Cross, one heading on to Elgin to tell the Bishop and the other to Pluscardyn. Of the two left at Mortlach, one is still there with, um, the body and the other is scouring the countryside for Francie.'

'You might as well tell me the rest.' The old lady returned to her chair, her bird-like body collapsing in bleak misery against the support of tapestry cushions.

'Ranulf was stabbed.'

'Like Nicol?'

'It sounds like it. I can only judge by the description young David gave us. A single blow from a long slim blade, struck upwards into the heart from behind. Death would have been swift and inevitable, according to the Infirmarian.'

'For both of them?' An odd relief coloured her voice. It grew as Will nodded. 'A single blow?' He nodded again, discarding the slashes from the kiln trowel as irrelevant to Nicol's actual killing.

'So by somebody who knew what he was doing, then. Hardly fits Francie, does it? Would it have taken much strength, to kill a man that way? How much was needed?'

The morning's swordplay with Robert entered Will's mind. He did not really know, never having killed, nor even wounded. A straw punch bag took some stabbing, however. 'Quite a bit, I would think.'

'More than a child could manage? And more than the strength to kill a child? A trusting child?'

'I doubt if Ranulf was trusting,' Will grunted, then immediately regretted it.

Her nostrils flared. 'Go on!' She was becoming angry at his prevarication. 'Captain, I want it all, do you hear? I'm not a lily-liver.'

'Ranulf had been a doing a routine job with his novices. Just minutes before finishing it he broke off and for no reason they understand he sent his novices indoors to study. It was uncharacteristic, according to David. I conjecture that he saw somebody on the road whose company he did not want to share with the boys.'

'Who? Any guesses?'

He shrugged. 'Somebody he recognised, or why else would he take protective action. I do know he would have been watching the road for the soldiers...' He realised he had missed out a bit of the story and glowered at the tankard before him. It was half empty once more and the lost contents were no doubt responsible for his lack of logical telling. 'Let me go back a bit.' He outlined how first Francie then Hugo de May had overtaken him on the road to Balvenie, explaining all that followed. During the telling, especially when he came to the need to grapple the bog, she shrivelled before his eyes, shrinking into her chair like a winkle retreating into its shell. 'I'm sorry, Lady Amelia,' he finished, almost shaking with regret, 'I wish I could have spared you this.'

'I hope somebody is looking after Michael.' The murmur was almost an aside but it sent a jolt through Will.

'Why?' The sharp question was out before he could catch it but it was enough to make her head snap up in turn.

'Haven't you warned Prior Thomas to keep an eye on him?'

'Yes, I have. But I still want an answer. Do you know of a reason?'

'Michael would be as much of an impediment as Hugo or Ranulf.'

'Impediment to what?' Will demanded. Had he uncovered more than he expected? Amelia's mouth opened, then her teeth clicked as she closed it, indicating that this was not Will's business. A moment later she grimaced. He had been frank with her, she was realising, and deserved the same in return.

'Francie is my heir, Captain. And I have been foolish enough to make that known.'

Will closed his eyes. Then he shook his head to clear the ale fumes from his brain. 'To whom did you make it known?' he asked delicately, his heart plummeting.

'To the family, of course, to secure Francie, the family and the legacy. Others may not see it that way.'

'Please, explain.' A request sounded better than admitting he did not follow her reasoning. Again he wondered if he would have been more acute if he had drunk less, or drunk more water to quench his post-exercise thirst instead of what he suspected was ale which had been doctored.

Lady Amelia sighed then pulled herself erect in her chair. 'I had hoped that Robert and his wife might take Francie in, adopt her if you like.'

'And Nicol? She would never have left Nicol.'

'Yes, Nicol too. - Yes, maybe I was hoping for miracles. I could see Hector was near to breaking point. It was only a matter of time before something like this, this tragedy happened. I wanted to prevent it but I've left it too late. I would have moved sooner only there was always the hope that...'

Will licked dry lips, sensing a link with his skirmish with Robert but he could hardly force the lady to tell more than she thought appropriate. This was private family business. From outside, chatter and laughter drifted in through the narrow window as the tenants below clinked and pattered their way back to work.

'Oh, I might as well tell you everything,' she sighed at last. 'You see, it looks as if the de Chisholm line is dying out. We make weak breeding stock. I had no children in spite of three husbands - and the wealth they left me, of course. - You know, widowhood is undoubtedly the only way a woman can be truly free and independent. I shall tell Francie to choose an old man as a husband. - Anyway, there is Robert eight years married to a young, healthy wife and not a single quickening. His sisters have entered the church,' she added with some disgust, 'so there'll be nothing there. Their father had no siblings except for Isabella and their grandfather had only me as a sister.'

'Robert might marry again.'

'A fat lot of good that'll do him,' she snapped. 'Besides he adores Maura. Oh, I admit that has not stopped him entertaining a long line of other ladies away from home, even to my limited knowledge, but if you want proof that the fault is in him not one of those women has produced as much as a rotten egg for him.' It so happened that Will himself knew examples of Robert's unproductive liaisons, but that was one indiscretion he did manage to keep behind his teeth.

Lady Amelia was watching his reactions and the blaze returned to her eyes. 'There may be hope in another direction,' she speculated. 'I have a suspicion that Maura has begun to entertain elsewhere if she can get away with it. At least she has the sense to choose appropriate men with the best of qualities - especially discretion.' Then the blaze died.

‘But still there's no sign of a pip. So no, Captain, I doubt if there will be another de Chisholm generation.'

'Except for Francie.'

'Except for Francie,' she agreed heavily. 'And Nicol, of course, till last Wednesday. He was a de Chisholm too, although of course he would never have... Well, all he would ever provide was a burden.'

A burden which somebody had removed. They sat in shared silence aching with sadness while Will tried to sort out his befuddled wits. There was no need to point out that the de Chisholms would not have wanted to take on that millstone, however much they might wish for the rest of the package. Perhaps it should be put into words. 'You are suggesting that somebody might have killed Nicol so that Francie would be freed for adoption, fortune and all? That might motivate several people.'

She held up her fingers and ticked them off. 'Hector, for Francie's sake - on top of his other justifications. Robert, with an eye on the fortune if he were Francie's guardian. Maura, likewise, with the added wish to avoid being burdened with a healthy but idiot child to look after, a child who might survive for years more if looked after in the way Francie would insist on.' She hesitated, perhaps regretting putting that into words.

'And the three de May brothers? I've been told that one of them is Francie's father. Surely he would have first claim before any outsider could adopt her? And the other two would be her uncles. Paternal uncles. I imagine they'd have a better claim to be her guardian than a cousin. Come to that, surely Hector has first claim? He is her grandfather and has brought her up since...' He stopped to think. 'Hasn't he? Been her replacement father during her childhood, I mean? I've been assuming that Amelia remained with her father.'

'Much of the time.' Her hesitation was oddly uneasy. After a moment she went on. 'Ranulf is Francie's father. I gather she thought it was Hugo, but she might have been encouraged to think that because Hugo is the only brother not in Holy Orders. Oh yes. It sounds unlikely but Michael has taken his full vows, even although he has nothing like the education or intelligence of his brothers. He was a come-lately child, born just after his father was killed in battle. What money there was ran out long before he reached the studying stage and he had to rely on charity. He is not, I think, a practicing priest.' She rose and walked to the window again, then turned and walked back as if she had forgotten why she went there in the first place.

'I've no doubt that Ranulf and Amelia wanted to make a life together. They were well matched, too, in spite of the age gap and Amelia's young years. Ranulf had already applied for a Papal dispensation when Francie was conceived, you know. He wanted to leave the priesthood and explained quite openly that he wanted to marry.'

'But the Pope said no?' Will's words came out dry as dust.

'I think they were unlucky in their timing. Too many priests had been leaving for just that reason and the Holy Father ordered the Scottish Convention of Bishops to crack down on it just at the time when Ranulf's plea went in. Somebody had to become example. There might also have been some internal ill feeling inside the Convention, with the other bishops keen to rap the fingers of the Bishop of Murray just at the time when Ranulf was a servitor there.' She sighed. 'I doubt if we shall ever know.'

'Could he not have just gone? Disappeared with Amelia to another country perhaps? They could have married somewhere else and be done with it. Nobody would have annulled a marriage with a child, surely? There wasn't any other reason for debarring their marriage, was there? No consanguinity for instance?'

'None at all. But if Ranulf left the priesthood without a Papal sanction he would be labelled an apostate. He might even have been excommunicated, and certainly the same fate would have befallen any cleric who married them in the face of the Pope's injunction against it. Knowing that, Ranulf would never have asked a fellow priest to perform such a service. You have to remember that he had been received into the church as a small child and had taken the full vows. You don't reject those easily.' She swivelled her eyes to his, well aware by now of his heretical leanings. 'Nor the griping superstitions that go along with them.'

'Even if it left Amelia branded as a whore and their child a bastard?'

'Nobody branded her a whore!' Lady Amelia countered sharply. 'And there are worse states than bastardy, judging from the number of bastards I know. Just look at those hanging around the royal court for a start.'

'Most of them Stewarts,' Will mumbled unwisely. The silence grew thick.

'Wasn't your father's first wife a royal bastard? Your brother Jock's mother?' Lady Amelia meant him to squirm, which he did, but she left off her baiting almost immediately. In other circumstances she would have hounded him till he yelped, he was sure.

'Oh, never mind. What matters is that Hector was devastated. Up till then she could do no wrong in his eyes. She was so like her mother, you see, lovely to look at and with the same sweet nature. It really was little surprise that she had Ranulf at her feet, and many others I'm sure. But to Hector she remained an innocent little girl till it was too late, in spite of the wooing going on under his very nose. He was so angry when he discovered her state that... Well, I am glad to say that when she ran away she came to me.'

That made the best of sense to Will. He drained his tankard and barely noticed the lady filling it up again from the refreshed jug. Perhaps nor did she.

'I ought to tell you that in spite of what you might think, in spite of everything that has happened, Hector is not a bad man. Far from it. He was a good and kindly neighbour to many folk and often bothered when others didn't. However much he adored Amelia, he didn't spoil her. Brought her up to be a polite, useful citizen and never a Sunday service was missed. Made her toe the line when she was wilful, which was rare. Taught her letters and numbers as far as he could himself, then asked me to take her beyond what little he could give her. When Francie's turn came, he did the same with her.'

'So Amelia did return to him?'

'After a few weeks. Once he had calmed down. He was deeply glad to have her back, but deep down he never really accepted the shame she had brought on him. Or on herself as he saw it. He began to drink more than was good for him just to stop himself thinking about it.'

'And Nicol?' That earned him a long, cool stare.

'Let's leave Nicol out of it, shall we?' That was an order.

'Well, what about this question? How did Hector react when Nicol was born? - Or did the bairn's lack of wits not appear until later?'

'Later. Much later, although he was much too easy as a baby. Perhaps we should have been warned. But to go back, Amelia and Francie stayed with me throughout her second pregnancy and for a year after Nicol was born. Then Hector injured his arm one day, catching it between the millstones. Amelia went back to nurse him intending to return here when he had recovered. She ended up remaining with him until - until she died.'

'I heard she drowned.' Then out popped another unforgivable question. 'Do you know if she died by accident or design?' When she closed her eyes in pain he felt utter shame. 'Please,' he croaked, 'don't answer that.'

'I can't. I've no idea what the truth is. But if you are asking me if suicide was a possibility I - must admit it was. Her life was - beset with intractable problems.' She sighed before adding something Will could not fathom. 'Death might have become her only way out, but she didn't tell me.'

'You - don't mean that was murder too, do you?'

Her sigh was wry, seeming to dismiss this suggestion as ridiculous by rising to check the height of the sun in the sky. 'Captain, did you say something about being required for a Chapter meeting? I have had enough for just now. Tell Brother Alexander I'll be over in the afternoon, will you? He shall take over the care of the pony from today.'

He stumbled several times on the way down the steps from the solar. It alerted him to the need to concentrate harder on where he was putting his feet. The Hall seemed longer than when he arrived and the fresh air, when he reached it, was like a draft of new wine which left his head reeling so that he was glad of the stableman's cupped hands beneath his foot to help him into the saddle. Take your time, he warned himself, gripping the reins a touch too firmly. Lady Amelia's brewer must have had a wicked sense of humour. As he rode off, he fancied there had been a glint in her eye in spite of her anguish. She was right. If he didn't allow himself time to sober up he would make a dismal presentation before the monks; it was his report on the charters which they wished to hear, naturally and preferably before the Bishop came to call.

Choosing a track along the top of the ridge, he meandered among the few good oaks still left standing. He had gone barely a mile when he realised that he had company. The light grassing of the pathway indicated it was almost unused but once, then twice, he caught the chink of hoof on stone. A third click sounded closer, and the fourth closer still. Alarmed he drew his horse off to one side so that he had protection for his back from the broadest tree trunk he could find. Loosening his sword in its sheath he checked that his dirk was ready for instant action before glancing backwards but he was in a vastly poorer condition for fighting than he had been even at Quarrelwood.

'You found her at home then?' It was the lady Maura, this time with no more protection than a small dagger at her belt - and her smouldering, challenging eyes. They echoed the smoky blue of her robe and her eyelashes matched the loose blackbird hair she tossed back. Her delicate Celtic skin glowed like alabaster, in contrast with lips red enough to make him wonder if she had bitten them to encourage the inviting ruddiness as she approached him. A twitch at their corners confirmed that she had seen his preparations for defence and when he was foolish enough to let his mount yank the reins out of his hand the smile broadened.

'And I do believe you've been plied with her magic brew!' He realised then that he had been deliberately waylaid. Leaning over she grasped his bridle, bringing the horse back under control while nudging it farther into the wood. Sliding her fingers along the leather, she took possession of the reins and turned to guide both animals. She kept Will's on a long lead, nudging it southwards and down the gentle slope along a narrow, overgrown sheep lane he had not noticed. Her destination was a tiny stream in a hidden, sun-drenched hollow. Her skirts brushed a tangle of butter-yellow early honeysuckle, tossing its overwhelming perfume into the air around him until all his senses sang; several crab apple petals drifted from the very last blossoms to twirl and rock through the air then settle like snowflakes on the glossy black head ahead of him. The bank side was firm underfoot but overlaid with a cool, resilient blanket of mosses and herbs, intricately intertwined, and the waters burbled over smooth stones in an idyllic dappled shade; a veritable bed of temptation, his woolly mind warned.

'Dunk your head into that, Captain Forbys. You don't want the scarecrows to see how confused you are, do you?'

The taunt about the monks irritated him more than her accusation about his condition, but he saw the sense in her advice. The chill of the water was piercing, but when he cupped his hands and drank, it tasted like ambrosia. When Maura knelt laughing beside him he offered her a mouthful. It brought her very close and he caught the exotic smell of her, a bouquet of all the sweetest and most seductive flowers of spring with, rising from beneath, the treacherous, intoxicating musk of warm female flesh.

Catching his breath, he plunged his swooning head into the water again but this time the iciness served only to excite him further. He emerged to find she had whipped off her wimple, which had already been relegated to the status of shoulder scarf when she arrived, and used it to rub his hair dry. So that was what it was for. The result was inevitable. Their relative positions brought her full breasts level with his face and - fool that he was, the utter, utter fool - he leaned forward and kissed the hollow between them. Such soft, warm velvety skin it was. Her perfume engulfed him and made his head spin and swoon. When his lips kissed again, resting even longer against her breast where it began to swell out of the bodice, he felt a ripple of excitement run through her, a silent erotic laughter making her tremble in response to his homage. She dropped her head so that her hair fell across his face, caressing and aromatic, and in an instant he was wildly inflamed, struggling for control.

'Lie with me,' she murmured, sliding her fingers round the back of his head. They held his lips against the precise spot where her blood was throbbing with increasing pace, waves of excitement sending swift flushes of warmth over the breasts beneath his skin and stifling him with desire. His own hands, quite without his intending them to, had already encircled her waist and the world was beginning to flare into flames all around him, above him, inside him, bursting for release.

From far above a buzzard mewed, the cry of a cat, or a lost infant bleating at its betrayal. The last vestige of his sanity heard its call and responded. 'No,' he muttered, drunk with far more than liquor. He dragged himself away. 'No. You have a husband. He'll really kill me this time!'

'You think so?' Wide-eyed with shock she too stepped away, leaving his desire flaming more wildly than ever. It amazed him to see her eyes fill with angry tears. 'Don't you know the situation between us? The rest of the world seems aware of it. I want a child. I need a child!' Despair and shame were dragging the words from her.

'Not like this, surely!'

'There is no other way,' she whispered. 'Not for us, for me. Please... Are you not man enough for it?' She brushed the tears aside, forcing herself suddenly to smile through them. The stubborn effort at a jaunty scorn drove a shaft of pity through him. What is a woman worth, after all, if she cannot provide her husband with an heir to maintain the inheritance of his blood and, even more crucially here, his land. 'I am exceedingly careful about my selection of partners, Captain. Always good, clean, upstanding men of quality. Intelligence too, if I can find it. And discretion, of course.'

She glided close again, so close that he could feel the trembling of her clothing, without the actual weight of the body beneath making solid contact with his. It was profoundly arousing. Reaching to stroke gently at his shorn beard, she dropped her head on one shoulder in coquettish supplication exposing her long white throat and the swift throb of the pulse at its base. 'Believe me, I have found very few to suit me. Very few indeed. None of those qualities is easy to find. If I find them all in such abundance in one man - the only time, I should tell you - I am hardly likely to pass it by, now am I?'

'And if you produce a bairn the image of me? You're hardly likely to find anything more obvious either, are you? In heaven's name, woman, just look at me!'

She laughed, sensing now just how gossamer thin his resistance really was and leaned fully against him so that he could feel the thundering vibrations of desire run from her body to his. He was losing the argument. 'It would be a good fifteen years before any scarlet beard appears. Long enough for everybody to have forgotten you. Robert will be too used to having a son of his own to give it another thought. Or if he does, by then he would never wish to challenge it.'

'And if a child inherits my devilish eyes? That would tell everybody pretty quickly, I'm thinking.'

Taking his face between her strong fingers she turned the eyes to hers. Slowly, slowly she drew his head down for her kiss.It was the ale which undid him. He had taken far, far too much for discretion but not nearly enough to render him incapable. Nothing like it.

He was, of course, late for the Chapter House appointment.

Chapter 16 – Evaluations

Camus tried to waylay him as he lolloped up to the North Gate.

'Later, lad. See to my horse, will ye?' Dodging through the beggars who were already gathering for the distribution of food at noon, - although it could not have been long after half past ten - he hurried to the Guest House. His brain was churning his wits into sour curds after all that had already happened to him that morning. First he dunked his thumping head into a bucket of cold water provided for ablutions, then scraped his trimmed hair as flat as it would go, grabbed the notes he had made on Saturday evening and set off at a run across the courtyard towards the main Priory buildings. Through the open Chapter House door a solid silence surged along the corridor stopping him like a wall. After two deliberate breaths to recompose his wits, he drew a painful third gulp and stepped forward to face the disapproval of a dozen patient faces.

'I'm sorry. I - was unavoidably delayed.' It sounded lame beyond belief and, to his own ears at least, perilously dishonest and revealing. Could they smell the ale on him, or even the woman? To his chagrin not a word was uttered. Thomas, flat faced, raised a quiet hand towards the lectern and he pulled himself together.

'Gentlemen,' he began, and was immediately alarmed that his tongue had acquired a lisping life of its own, 'you have nine documents here in the Priory. There may be more elsewhere, in Elgin perhaps, or in the King's hands or in Burgundy where your mother house lies. The early charters held here deal with the foundation of Pluscardyn Priory and the limitations and obligations laid on the monks within the convent. Most of the rest cover later gifts and exchanges of related properties, or the settlement of arguments over who owns what, or more often who owes tithes to whom. I found a reference to at least one more document which I cannot find in the Scriptorium or the Library. Is there anywhere else in the Priory where it might have been kept?' Several doubtful heads shook. 'Then either it is elsewhere or it has been lost or destroyed. I suspect it is minor and will presume to ignore it.

'Before I begin my report, may I tell you that I have also received a cache of documents, mostly copies, from Elgin Cathedral. They were being held against the danger of fire here. I enquired about them from Father Symon on Saturday morning and they were delivered here yesterday afternoon.'

'Can't we find somewhere better to leave them than in the Bishop's pocket?' Brother Alexander blurted out, scarcely hiding a swift frown towards the Sacristan. When the Prior's eyebrows rose in slow rebuke Alexander's annoyance withered. 'I mean - if they have access to the details... How are we to know they haven't been tampered with?'

'They arrived as they had been delivered, my son, in a sealed coffer. The Priory seal on each has been untouched for twenty five years. I was told that the coffer has been in the Cathedral's care since the last visitor from Burgundy, a representative of our own Prior-General. Please continue, Captain Forbys.'

'Inside that box,' Will continued, glad that Thomas was relieving him of giving answers which might need some sharpness of wit, 'I found copies of just seven of your own documents and charters but also of two from your mother house in Burgundy. The earlier one is the Bull of Pope Innocent the Third confirming the foundation of the Order of Valliscaulians in 1206. A copy of their original Rule, based on the Rule of St Bruno of Chartreuse, is attached to it. It's the same Rule which Father Thomas brought back from France eighteen months ago, in turn based on the Rule of St Basil, I understand.

‘But seventeen years later,' Will held up the only original vellum he had found, ‘is a change to that Rule. The monks at Vallis Caulium in Burgundy had kept the original tenets up for ten years before being forced to amend it themselves because, like you, they found it, er, undermined their strength.'

He glanced around the room. Most of the faces bore some relief at this news. Young David from Mortlach stood out like a black crow in the white flock. Since these matters did not affect him directly, he was the only one with his eyes cast down. He might have been half asleep. Will handed the scroll to Thomas.

'You'll see that this order applied to the Carthusians and their sects, not just your own Order. As for the rest of the documents, I'll give you only the important details from the Pluscardyn charters. There is some variation of spelling but the places referred to seem clear enough.' A careless brush of his hand sent his notes fluttering to the ground. Agonised by shame at his clumsiness he bent to gather them up, squirming all the time under the company's cool observation.

He began again, wiping the back of his hand across his sticky brow. 'The first document, dated 1230, confirms that King Alexander the Second of Scotland has begun the process which led to the establishment of a monastery in the royal forest of Pluscardyn. Right here, in other words. The document makes it plain that the convent shall be self-contained. He explains clearly that the monks will elect their own Prior from among their number and they will be answerable to the Crown, not to the Church, although the Prior-General of the Burgundian mother house will be their religious superior. In other words, the Priory is to be under the king's particular protection in Scotland, not the Bishop's.'

He reached to pull at his beard, forgetting it was so short. 'I shall quote the King's words from the first charter.

And we have taken the aforesaid brethren and their house and all their men, and all the possessions and goods of them and their men, into our firm peace and protection; and we firmly forbid that any one inflict any injury, trouble or grievance upon them upon pain of our full forfeiture...

And it goes on at length to say what would happen. It's all plain enough. There is no doubt about what he is saying.

'Then comes the Papal bull of 1232 confirming your religious foundation. It probably arrived here along with the King's own confirmation of the temporal lands and obligations.

'Now, at the end of that year in February 1232, just before New Year, another confirmation was written by Bishop Andrew of Murray and signed by local bigwigs in Elgin, including the King's Sheriff, then one Sir Andrew de Moravia. I presume that was drawn up at the King's behest to confirm that they understood what the King had done and agreed with it. However, some of the land that the King had given to Pluscardyn had formerly belonged to the See of Murray and that Bishop tried very hard to use that to lay a claim for himself over the monks. Whatever the reason, he declares in his charter that he has…

…taken the monks into his own care and protection.

As far as I can see, he also does some adjustment of the possessions. A number of lay landowners were equally deprived and I don't suppose they were any happier than the Bishop was.

'It's after this event that I think there is a missing letter. Possibly two, one from the King and then a reply from the Bishop, in which they argue about the final status of Pluscardyn and the Bishop's position with regard to it. What matters is that the King issued another charter in 1236, probably the most important document of all for you. In it he is very specific indeed about what possessions he wants to be given to the Priory. He appears to be rapping the Bishop's knuckles. I did wonder if the King wants the monks here to be his spies throughout the entire region of Murray because they are given many small benefices scattered all over the place. What's more, he wants them to remain independent of the other Church settlements nearby as well as of all the lay landlords. It's very cleverly done. Very strategic.'

He looked up and spoke directly to his audience. 'Another thing I noticed when I was reading this document, the King makes particular mention of his forest rights. This Priory is built in the middle of a royal forest. It was already called the Vale of St Andrew which means that somewhere around here there was a church already, but probably of the old Belgic faith which the King wanted to have replaced with a Catholic institution. You use an old well called Saint Margaret's Well, don't you, although you are dedicated to The Virgin Mary and Saint John the Baptist? And am I not right in thinking that the Kings of Scotland still maintain the right to hunt here, a hundred and forty years on? Does King David ever come?'

'He was here less than a year ago,' Thomas confirmed. 'And Robert the Steward has been here many times.'

'Then that must be significant,' Will declared. He felt a stiffening in Brother Mark but kept his eyes on his notes. 'I imagine the King won't want the Bishop making free with his hunting grounds.' He thought for a few moments before adding, 'Nor yet the Earl of Murray, I suppose.'

The Prior frowned. 'We are allowed the normal forest rights of a tenant, feeding pigs on acorns, trapping small animals for meat and fur, copsing, that sort of thing. But we are also obligated to maintain the forest as a royal hunting ground. We ourselves must not take any of the large wild animals - that's deer or boar. Nor may we allow others to hunt them.

'Not even a bishop,' Thomas added slowly, and pursed his lips as he thought of more possible scraps of evidence. 'We are allowed to snare wolves, which would surely acknowledge us as stewards of the King's land and venery. And we also hold the mineral rights of the forest, in particular the right to quarry freestone for building and to mine for lead. And we pay no tithes to the Bishop - although,' his eyes flared with hope, 'it might be significant that at present he is paying us multures. They're from a mill of ours which he is using in the town of Elgin. He's also due us tithes on wheat being grown by his tenants on our land. Perhaps the most important factor is our right to hold our own legal court - and to be fair no Bishop has tried to stop that. Not so far. All of that indicates independence, doesn't it?'

Will nodded, then gave a sickly grin. 'On the other hand there's another sentence stating that the monks must...

never use their possessions and privileges for civil purposes of peace or war contrary to the King and his throne.

Sounds almost like a threat if you don't toe the King's line.'

The atmosphere had lightened tremendously. Only Brother Mark was peevish. 'Why was all of this not known before?'

'It was.' Thomas and Gregory spoke together. It was Gregory who continued. 'Most of it. But one of those charters, the King's declaration of 1236, was not here. We had no idea it existed. We believed that the Cathedral chest contained only copies of what we had here already.'

Mark grunted. Then he frowned. 'Who asked for the chest to be sent?'

'I did, last Friday,' the Prior said. They all knew he had visited the Bishop, a commitment made before Nicol's death, but which had taken on an even greater significance as a result of it. 'I must say that I was surprised when it arrived so quickly. Perhaps Captain Forbys's request to Father Symon pushed the matter along.'

Brother Stephen was the next to ask a question. 'Which charters do we have which were not copied for the Cathedral chest? You said we have nine but the chest had only seven.'

'One is just a readjustment of fishing pools, an exchange made with the burgh of Forres. Another three are of similar insignificance. What is more serious, though, is a document they had but you did not. It is the very first foundation charter drawn up by the King.'

'The original?' Gregory took up the questioning, his voice sharpening.

'Yes.'

'Why should that original have been held by the Cathedral without a copy lying here, I wonder?' Gregory sounded as if he might know an answer.

'Or why that way round?' Alexander demanded. 'We ought to make sure the original stays here when the box goes back. I'm sure Daniel can do a good copy for them if they want it.'

David from Mortlach was sitting up now and taking notice. This mystery was nothing like as boring as he had expected. Not being a member of a silent order he had no qualms about asking a question of his own. A perspicacious question it was too. 'Could the copy have gone to France instead of here?'

'Why?' Alexander looked dumbfounded, perhaps at the impertinence of a boy daring to poke his oar in.

'Well, didn't Prior Thomas say the copies had been in a box in Elgin for twenty five years? And that it was left there when your Prior-General came from France?'

'His representative,' Father Thomas corrected. 'Are you asking if he took it?'

'Maybe. Maybe he did a deal with the Bishop or something and wanted to show it to his Prior-General in France. - What have I said?' Sensing alarm the lad looked around in some bewilderment.

Thomas caught Will's glance. It was their first honest eye contact since he had entered the Chapter House. 'I think we are being waylaid into dealing with things out of sequence, Captain. But thank you, David. We shall deal with that question shortly.' He nodded to Will to continue.

'Right. After the King's reprimand of the Bishop in 1236, if that was what it was, the Bishop then writes another confirmation in 1237 in which he finally releases the lands which the King declares must go to the Priory. Those two documents I believe will be your strongest pieces of evidence if this ever comes to a public examination.

'The next significant letter is from Pope Urban the Fourth in 1263. In this he states clearly that he takes the Priory of Pluscardyn with possessions under *his* protection. Now while that means you will have to pay tithes to the Pope himself, it is also plain that you owe allegiance to the Pope directly and not through any Bishop. Um, I'm not sure where that leaves the King. The King by now is the next Alexander, the III, and he has just given Haakon of Denmark a trouncing when he tried attacking Scotland. Maybe some political deal has just been made with the Pope, but that is not our problem at the moment, especially as at the same time Henry III, the king of England, is trying to persuade Alexander to do homage to the English throne.

'Apart from one other document, all the rest deal with disputes on individual holdings between the Priory and various other landowners, mainly with neighbours or burgesses of Elgin. There were probably many more such papers and I regard them as having little significance in your claim to independence.

'The last document, however, is the one which is worrying. It is dated the twentieth October 1345. In it the then Bishop of Murray claims the right of visitation at Pluscardyn. Am I correct in thinking that this means he wants to come and examine your way of life and your finances? If so, the Bishop would act as a superior. And in return for his protection you would have to pay tithes and taxes to him.'

'Quite right,' Thomas agreed. 'The last is exactly what he is after, plus the power.' Again his eyes met Will's, both of them sensing again that Mark disliked this entire enquiry. He would be finding the aspersions being cast on the Bishopric especially unpalatable. It was puzzling, however, that he was not interrupting more, not even to give the other point of view. Since Mark was not doing so, Thomas himself felt obliged to add, in pursuit of a balanced argument, 'We have to remember that around that time Scotland was in great danger. After King Robert died he left an infant son as king. There followed virtual civil war with Edward Balliol as the puppet-king ruling on behalf of Edward the Third of England, the one still on the throne there.'

'He found the throne slithery,' Brother Gregory murmured. ‘Baliol, I mean, ‘like his father, Bleary John, both of them more often off it than on it. In any case, by the time that this 1345 paper was written, Scotland had had King David back from France for, what, four, five years.'

'But still young and green,' Brother Stephen entered the discussion again. 'And the English were making too much headway in their battles against the French, which made it neither easy nor safe for Pluscarden to keep contact with its mother church.' He looked at the Prior.

'Mm. Perhaps the monks felt they needed the protection of somebody nearer home,' Thomas mused. 'Maybe they said so to the Prior-General's delegate from France.'

Gregory waded in again. 'And we all know what happened soon after. At the request of the French King, David attacked England hoping to draw some of their troops back from France. I know. I was there at Neville's Cross. I even saw the King blasted in the face and captured.'

Gloom settled like a blanket over them all - and still Mark said nothing. He just sat there with his eyes slightly glazed, concentrating on everything being said.

With half an eye on Gregory's scarred head Will went on carefully. 'It appears that the Bishop, at least, considered they needed protection, and the Prior-General's representative agreed. Perhaps David here is right. They did do a deal. The 1345 document suggests that. But the way I see it they did not do it correctly. Or they didn’t complete it. First of all, although the Prior allows the agreement to be drawn up he signs nothing. He can’t have been happy about it because he insists that the final ratification on behalf of Pluscardyn can be done only by the Prior-General himself, not by his representative without consultation with Burgundy. Secondly, the King is not involved.'

'Because he was in England!' At last Mark objected.

'So he was, eventually. But this document is dated the year before his capture. He would have had time to sign if he wished. In any case, in England he was not held in isolation, not even in prison. He lived in a palace and received regular couriers from Scotland. He did business all the time from there. If you look at other state and church transactions during the next eleven years you will find David is still signing papers where it matters to the state. But we don't have his signature on any document stating that he gives up his claim on Pluscardyn. Nor does Robert Stewart sign anything on his behalf and he was the Guardian of Scotland, and heir presumptive. As far as I can see, neither does the Prior-General sign anything on behalf of the Order of the Valiscaulians. In other words, this 1345 document is nothing more than a draft.'

'Which was never ratified.' Thomas was looking much happier.

'Exactly.'

'There is one more thing I can offer which might help,' Thomas said. 'It is very minor, but when the king came to hunt last autumn we entertained him here. He acted as if he still regarded this as his own foundation. Towards the end of the year, on the twenty fifth of January, I exchanged an indenture with Sir Robert de Chisholm over the multures of Quarrelwood. I had mentioned the problem of suzerainty to the King when he was here and he asked if I would let him know how the matter was finally settled. Surely he would not have asked if he had considered the Priory under the protection of the Bishop?'

Robert de Chisholm again. Will's lips tightened. Inevitably he thought of Maura. - No, he mustn't! Then Lady Amelia and her inheritance tugged at his attention, and poor little dead Nicol, and the other men already dead and perhaps more still to die. How did they all tie together? Was there a link here? It seemed highly improbable, and yet, and yet... Robert de Chisholm's name had jumped out at him from the letter to the Pope.

With his mouth already opening he looked at Thomas. The Prior looked back and, still holding Will's gaze, he turned his head very slightly to one side only. Towards Mark.

'I - think that's all I can tell you,' Will finished lamely.

'Then let us proceed to our prayers.' Thomas closed the proceedings. 'May Our Lord guide us through the maze of facts you have brought before us, Captain, and help us to understand how best to use them. I thank you for your work on our behalf.'

Will was the last but one to leave the Chapter House. The last was Brother Alexander who laid a hard grip on his arm.

'Not a bad job, Captain. I wonder how much better you would have done if you'd been sober?' His whispering was rich with anger. 'I wonder you dared to come before us in this condition!'

There was nothing Will could say to that. Alexander had stepped close so that he could smell the fumes. Out of the blue he made a decision. 'You are a priest, aren't you, Brother Alexander?'

'I am.' The Cellarer looked surprised, disbelieving.

'Will you hear my confession? Please?'

'Good Heavens... Why me? Why not your...' Alexander clawed himself back from his rage, forcing calm upon himself with a wipe of his hand over his face. 'Forgive me. I'm being unjust. But why me when you are so close to the Prior? Ah, you are ashamed of something and you don't want to tell it to him. If that's the case, perhaps you should be telling him as your self-punishment.'

Will grimaced. 'It isn't that. It's... It involves somebody else, you see, and it's just possible that she will... Damn.'

Alexander stared. His imagination was plainly whirling through all manner of scenarios and his anger returned with a clattering of his teeth. 'Then come to me at the end of the service, if you haven't thought better of it.'

That obliged Will to attend the service instead of heading off to mend his head, which was thumping worse than ever. The smell of cooking drifting in from the kitchens did not help at all and he had an uncomfortable feeling that Alexander was quite worldly enough to know this and intended to make him suffer a touch of Purgatory on earth. When the rest of the house headed for the refectory he waited in the small chapel nearest to the door which Alexander indicated before disappearing to set in motion the serving of the noonday meal.

'Right, what's this all about?'

'Father, I have sinned.' And there he stuck.

'We all sin, my son.' A pause followed the dry rejoinder, and lengthened. 'Is that all I'm getting? I can't absolve you on that.'

Will dropped his face into his hands for a few seconds. Maybe he should not be admitting this at all. Maybe he should be suffering in silence, making that his personal flagellation. If it got out, and if there were a child... Surely not!

'Captain, are you sure you want to do this? And are you sure it's my absolution you want, not Father Thomas's?'

He looked up. Not Thomas's. 'I'm not sure of anything, but I think you would be the best person to - talk to because... I think you might understand better.'

'A trifle more worldly, maybe?' The dry words were surprisingly gentle. 'I'll agree with you that Father Thomas has the innocence of a child in some ways. And if, as you say, there's someone else involved...' He paused. 'I'll take a guess that this sin of yours involves a woman. With young men it usually does. Then I grant you the Prior is unlikely to manage that very well. Too easily embarrassed. If she is gentry it is possible that he might be asked to take her confession. And if he realised you were the other party to her confession he might be very upset indeed. - Just because it is you. You do realise that don't you? That he is very fond of you?'

'We are friends,' Will sighed. The last thing he wanted was the suspicion going around that there was something untoward about his relationship with the Prior. 'That's all. But good friends and they don't always make the best confessors.'

'So I'm not a friend.'

'That's not what I... You're taunting me!'

'Well, why don't you get on with it and then we can eat. Or I can. I doubt if you're going to get much down you. Come on, make your decision.'

'You see it was Lady Amelia...'

'Lady Amelia!' At Alexander's look of profound and shocked astonishment, an inane giggle bubbled from Will.

'No, no! Her ale.'

'Ah. I've been told that her brewster has access to the local firewater. Is that what you've been drinking?'

'Not - that I was aware of. Whatever it was, I drank it like ale and I, er, drank too much for, er, wisdom.'

Alexander looked at him with a mixture of pity and rank amusement. 'I wonder you made it through your exposition as well as you did, then. Come to think of it, I wonder you didn't fall off your horse on the way back. Or - I see. You did. And somebody did some ministering to you?'

'Not quite.' His face burned. 'I, er, was a bit more... I confess. I lay with a woman.'

'Against your will.'

'Not exactly.'

Alexander's voice sharpened suddenly. 'Against hers?'

'Oh no! Anything but! - I mean... No, very much *not* against her will.'

'Well, well!' Alexander sat back, his eyes alert. 'I shall not ask who she is, but - was this fornication or adultery?'

Will was silent for a good while. Should he go that far? He had a strong suspicion that Alexander had already put the pieces of the puzzle together and made a near perfect picture. 'She is somebody else's wife. I refuse to tell you more about her. It is my sin I have come to confess, not another's.'

Will found himself staring at Alexander's hands, afraid to meet his eyes. Broken and gnarled, they were folded together while kneading each other as if the swollen knuckles were aching. They matched his ruined feet, and yet they looked strong.

'My son, I hardly think this is the first time you have lain with a woman. Is it?' Instinctively Will shook his head. 'But the others have been, shall we say, unprotected by nobility?' Will's head jerked up. 'Yes, I mean of lower class. You seem to consider this consort as more likely to be damaged. Is it just because of her social standing, I wonder? Were the others unworthy of such respect?'

'Not at all! It's because this one is married!'

'But you said, or implied that she was willing.'

'I doubt if her husband would have been!'

To that Alexander said nothing. 'And what do you expect as a penance, I wonder. My son, I suspect that your faith is thin and any penance laid on you by Holy Mother Church will mean little to you.' The arid note in the Sacristan's voice became soft, even tender, and he reached to take Will's arm and lead him out into the sunshine, no penance given.

'But, if I judge you correctly,' he went on, 'one day you will realise that life is not as easy as you think. Perhaps you are already learning. God has given you a cross of your own which will lay its penance on you whether you like it or not. It will lie across your shoulder throughout your life and I fear it will make you suffer in considerable measure. You have a conscience, Captain Forbys. For the sake of your soul and your sanity, may God keep it tender. But it means that your harshest critic will always be yourself.'

Will felt like weeping.

'I am not rejecting your plea, my son. Certainly not your confession which will remain sacrosanct. Mind you, you might be underestimating Father Thomas. He may not be as naive as you believe.'

'Maybe not. But I didn't want to offer him a conflict.'

'It does you credit. Now, go and sleep off that ale misery.'

Chapter 17 - Seeking

With heavy wooden shutters keeping the searing daylight out, a single sigh sent him to sleep. The next breath had him feeling wildly for weapons, his nerves screaming that a presence had entered the darkened room.

'Captain Forbys.' The whisper was barely recognisable, but his befuddled brain jeered. Who would draw his attention before attacking him?

'Who is it?'

'Michael. Shall I open the shutters?' He did it anyway, and Will found his eyes could tolerate the brightness after all. 'It's the middle of the afternoon, Captain.'

Camus appeared behind him, scowling. 'We need to talk.'

'Then talk.' Will heaved himself up and plunged his head once more in the bucket of water before tidying himself up.

'I couldn't wait so I took action and if you disagree there's nothing we can do about it.' Camus came no farther than the chamber door, but his face was stiff with disapproval and possibly anxiety. 'And we have news of the Bishop's messenger.' That made Will freeze, his eyes on the soldier's face at last. 'They found him in the bog and he had a wound in the back which sounds like Nicol's and Ranulf's. They fished out his horse too, drowned.'

'And his bag?'

'His bag?'

'Yes, his bag. The bag he carries the Bishop's messages in. Was that found?'

'Uh, there was no mention of it. But I've also sent my two Highlanders back up the road to Mortlach.' Seeing Will's mouth open Camus hurried on. 'One is heading as fast as he can to your parents' home to see if that missing girl is there. If not, he'll ask if your father can send out searchers.'

'And the other?'

'He's to stop at every village and ask about anybody coming back in a hurry last Friday.'

'What do you mean? From Mortlach to here? They'll all describe me.'

'I hope they do. He's to ask what time you came through on Wednesday and Thursday as well. It's who else they describe that we want. - Isn't it? Somebody coming a few hours after us maybe? Especially if that same person went up on the Wednesday.'

'There are more roads than one.'

'But only one that's logical.'

'And why would Ranulf's killer follow us here?'

'Why not? The core of the trouble seems to be here or hereabouts.'

Will's lips pinched, irritated that he had not reasoned this out for himself. Then he turned on Michael. 'Well, Brother, what are you doing here? More accusations?'

'Will! It's his brother I've just been telling you about. - It certainly isn't his fault you're so bad-tempered.' Camus's voice was cutting, but it was the bleakness of the monk's eyes which shook Will back to his senses.

'Oh... Dear God, forgive me. I'm sorry, Brother Michael. I'm so sorry. Please...'

'Captain, I came to tell you that Lek down at the kiln wants to talk to you urgently.'

'Lek? What about? - You shouldn't have left the precincts!'

'I didn't. Brother Daniel told me. Um, informed me. About two hours ago.'

Will became still once more, trying to work out how a man who could neither speak nor write managed to pass such a specific message between two others. 'I'll go down now,' he promised, sobering at last. His head still ached, but nothing like as badly as during the late morning. 'And Brother, I deeply apologise for my foul temper. My behaviour throughout today has been unforgivable.'

'May I come to the kiln?' The apology was brushed away once again.

'Uh. Do you think it wise?'

'You could fetch your sword as we leave the gate. I'd like to see how the work is going along.'

So they all trooped down, Will, Camus, Daniel and Michael and the first two did as Michael suggested and fetched their weapons before going out on to the public road. Its afternoon desolation made the exercise seem nonsense.

As they approached the yards they heard a peculiar dunting and swearing which drove Will and Daniel to run ahead of the others. It was the oaths which led them, a ripe mixture of Baltic tongues and impressively comprehensive. When they reached the glassworks they found Lek kicking like a madman at the furnace bricks with his wooden-soled boots. He looked like one of his little pagan gods elongated by surreal firelight shadows and gone berserk. Little Hus, bloated and dirty, was cowering at the farthest end of the yard, his green eyes almost totally round in distress.

It took Lek several minutes to realise that he had company, but once he did his recovery was remarkably swift. His long thin frame uncurled as he jerked his head up in tall defiance and spat one word at Will.

'*Eichen*'

Will stared. After a moment he turned and looked up at the splendid oak tree behind him, the same one against which Camus had leaned the previous night. Then he looked at the stack of logs along the inner wall of the yard. 'Oak?'

He used the same German word Lek had used but continued in Slav. 'You use oak wood in the furnace?'

Lek's temper had cooled but he expressed his opinion of it with another kick, this time at a stray log lying by the furnace, sending it spinning into the flaming mouth. Then he bent to pick up some glass which lay smashed on the ground and held out the pieces.

'Are you saying it is no good?' Will persisted, still in Slav - and realised that Daniel was nodding beside him. When he turned to look, the silent monk was watching him, not Lek, but there was no doubt that he understood what Lek was saying.

'You're not a Slav, are you? Nor a Balt?' Daniel shook his head with a touch of impatience then pointed at the wood. Concentrate on that, he was saying.

'So what kind of wood is needed?'

Lek uttered a word Will did not understand. Daniel did but had no way of translating it. Lek said something else, which sounded like 'Fargoosh.' It still meant nothing to Will. He turned to Michael and raised an eyebrow, but he could not help either. Camus was lost altogether. Then Lek gave them another word. A name. 'Theophilus.'

'Theophilus? You mean Saint Theophilus?'

Lek looked disgusted. 'Theophilus who made...' And he pointed at the glass pieces then at the furnace. Again Daniel understood. Neatly, he mimed a man writing, then pulled his hood over his head and wrote again on the air.

'Theophilus - was a monk? He wrote about glass and furnaces? In a book?' Will was bowled over by the beams from both Lek and Daniel. He had got the message at last. Suddenly he got another. Lek looked him straight in the eye for several seconds then flicked a glance at the mill next door. He was offering a trade. If Will would get him that book, Lek would give him some information he had withheld about the events last Wednesday. Was that it? He glanced at Daniel, who was again watching him, this time with an intense look of discomfort. He fully understood that he was being party to blackmail of a sort. The few words spoken were still in the simple Slav dialect Will could cope with and he sent a prayer of thanks winging that Michael in particular was not able to follow.

Then Daniel began to make a series of complex signals to Lek, at one point gesturing towards Hus who had come out of his corner. Lek frowned, then shrugged. A short, soft conversation took place between the two Slavs in a tongue which even Daniel could not understand. Persuasion? Reassurance? Whatever it was it held gentleness. At last Hus nodded and Lek turned away to move his gloved hands among a pile of broken glass. Thinking he was being dismissed Will began to turn away but a yell from Lek drew him back, to be handed several shards with more than just a single tint on them.

'Faces,' exclaimed Camus, peering forward. 'Or bits of faces.'

Will crouched and began laying the pieces flat on the ground. Some of the larger bits had crazed and two broke again as he handled them, forcing him to take greater care. They would have been much too brittle to insert into a mullioned or leaded framework. Lek bent and turned two of the shards over then stood up again to watch. As if to highlight the exercise, the sun sent a shaft of sudden light from behind a cloud. The beam held as Will sorted the pieces, about nine of them, so that they fitted together.

What they saw made Camus and Will stare at each other in astonishment. Will's own face was gazing up at them, but Will as he had looked the previous week before David's barbering, with tousled silvery hair and a rampant carmine beard. A cracked edge on one piece indicated that there was more than one layer of colour in the glass. The aspect of the face was not, in fact, directly to the front. It was turned slightly to the right, as if looking along an arm, and the eyes were filled with a terrifying concoction of alarm, rage and bewildered caution. Will looked up at Michael who was swallowing hard. They alone, alone of the visitors to the kiln, realised that at the end of the invisible arm so vividly implied was a sword, the tip of which was at Hector's throat. Whoever had painted this fractured portrait had caught the turmoil of emotions in Will so perfectly that he shivered at the uncanny sorcery.

'That's a big face,' Camus murmured, eyes still downwards and unaware of their tension. 'I can’t imagine how all these pieces were made to let them fit so well together.'

'One piece,' Lek snapped, in Slav. Then he realised that he had revealed his understanding of at least some Scots and clamped his lips tight.

'You made it all in one piece?' Lek nodded, his eyes lidding in scorn at Will's astonishment. 'It's usually three, isn't it? I mean for a window. How did it break?'

'*Eichen*.' And again Lek kicked the furnace. 'Wrong wood. Too slow.'

'This face.' Camus was still swooning over the work of art, for that was what it was, a wondrous creation. 'This is brilliant! What was it you packed for Lille, Will? A picture window?'

Will looked at Lek, beginning to understand his frustrated lashing out. To have had such a masterpiece crack because the furnace was not up to the job must be infuriating to the point of despair. Add to that his inability to produce more than four colours in this particular oven, or because of a lack of the right materials, - there was no blue here, so Will's eyes had been depicted in shades of brown and yellow

- when before them was the demonstration that Lek was capable of much, much more, and the man's sense of failure must be driving him to madness. 'No,' he murmured, 'it was no more than slabs of swathed colour, pieces for the making up of cloaks. And a full set of borders. Only those were etched on, not integral to the glass. Other glaziers had ordered only the ordinary bits and they will be putting them in position, not Lek.'

'What a waste,' Camus murmured.

Michael cleared his throat. 'This furnace was built for making pottery, not glass. It is too hot. Lek has tried to adapt it but as you see it is not successful. Or not enough.'

'How did these two glaziers come to be here?'

'I don't know. All I know is that they have been here for about five years. I - came here only when the miller and his grandchildren came and although I'm called the kiln master I know very little about the process, only what I learned from these men.'

Will glanced up at Lek, holding his eye once more. In the end the Slav shrugged, again revealing his understanding but stubbornly sticking to his Baltic tongue, his only fragment of independence. 'We were sold as slaves to a German sea-captain and he sold us again to this Priory.'

'Slaves?' Will did not dare ask if the captain in question was in the pay of his own Hansa confederates, who were not supposed to trade in human beings. He did know, however, that some Christians did not count pagans as men. They considered them animals for use and trade, as did the Livonian Knights of old who had driven them out of their lands if they clung to their old religions. Some would not be converted to Christianity even at the end of a sword. There were still Crusaders in Livonia, of course, for the Teutonic Knights had taken over where the old order left off after a severe mauling by the Pope for their cruelty. But Will also knew that the northern parts of the East Baltic lands belonged to Denmark, currently at war with the Hansa cities, and the captains hired by the League to make up its temporary navy were far from averse from milking profits wherever they could. By trading in men?

Lek was no fool, even if he were a pagan, and he watched Will coming to exactly the conclusion he intended him to. Will took a careful breath. 'I shall make enquiries about this.' He said it in Scots, wanting Daniel and Michael to hear. 'And I shall come back and tell you what I find out. I can tell you that there is no book by Theophilus in the Priory library. Brother Michael, do you know if there is a team of glaziers in the vicinity?'

'There are masons busy at Elgin Cathedral. New building seems to go on all the time there. They'll have glaziers among them.'

'I'll ask. In fact, I'd better go there right now or I'll be here in Murray forever. Camus, will you check that my horse is...'

It was as they turned to leave that they heard the jingling of metal and horses' hooves approaching along the highway from the west. Into sight rode a knight in light armour followed by two attendants wearing tunics bearing the arms of the Earl of Murray. The knight was Sir Robert de Chisholm but the men were strangers to Will. Not a challenge against Will himself, surely? No. This was too explicit. In any case, Robert was dressed as the Earl's steward. It was a message from the Earl to the Prior.

Forcing himself to relax, or at least try to, Will brushed sand over the glass picture very gently with one unobtrusive foot, rendering it unidentifiable in the dust before heading for the gateway. Again the others followed, apart from Daniel who was left gesticulating once more with Lek and Hus. This relationship was obviously well established.

At first Robert made to ride past them without giving any sign of recognition. At the last minute he slowed, his face expressionless beneath a fancy bonnet sporting a tall feather. 'In case ye're for off, Willie, the Earl wants a meeting tomorrow morning with the Bishop and the Prior, and he wants you there.'

'I canna.'

'Ye must. Disobey if ye dare, but it'll work ill against your father if ye jink it. He's in enough trouble as it is.'

'What trouble?'

'Canna pay his bills, laddie.' At that, Will realised Robert was just being provocative for the Earl had nothing whatever to do with his father's bills.

'Can you?' Even from the gateway he saw Robert flinch.

'I've a better chance o' a helping hand than he has, I'm thinking.' Ignoring the taunt so deliberately aimed at himself, Will strode off towards the North Gate keeping his anger hidden and leaving Robert to trot past him. The spatter of mud sent up by the charger's hooves was as intended as the insult.

'Please, Will. I need what is in your head. Even more, I need your wits.' Saturday morning's confidence, which the Prior had regained when the monks had reconfirmed their trust in him, was fast draining away.

'Och Thomas! If I don't leave first thing tomorrow I'll miss my fleet. They're to sail out of Aberdeen on the afternoon tide on Wednesday. As it is I'll have to ride through the night. And I won't be seeing my family,' he added plaintively.

'I - believe the soldier who has gone to your parents will be riding on to Aberdeen, um, with a request to your captain to delay by a few days.'

Will's eyes flashed. 'Oh, has he indeed. From the look on your face I needn't ask whose idea that was!'

'Forgive me, my friend.' Thomas made it sound abject, but Will had a suspicion he was not. They were standing in the Prior's chamber, which Robert had just left after delivering the Earl's message with a brevity bordering on rudeness. Beside them Brother Alexander was watching with amused curiosity, no doubt hearing the personal names the younger men were using for each other. If nothing else, the Cellarer's awareness and Thomas's acceptance of it gave Will satisfaction. 'I did insist that the meeting should be at eight tomorrow and not at ten as the Bishop demanded.

'Whose idea is this meeting anyway?'

'The Bishop's.'

'Won't this give him the visitation rights he's after?'

'No. There will be no question of his being permitted to see any of our private papers. Nor our private quarters.'

'And if he tries to insist?'

'The Earl will be here to see that he doesn't overstep the mark. Do you know him?'

'Johnnie Dunbar? Aye, we knew each other well enough when I was a bairn. He was not much more. He's the King's Justiciar in the North now, isn't he? - What about the Sheriff of Elgin? Is Sandy Watson coming as well?'

'I hope so.'

'Who asked him?'

'I did.'

'And who asked the Earl?'

'Indirectly I did.'

Will's sense of humour was returning fast. 'Indirectly?'

'When the Bishop's message came in just after you, um, went to bed, I immediately sent a kitchen boy to Lady Amelia and to Sir Robert, informing them that their

Quarrelwood lands would be discussed and did they wish to attend.'

Will grinned. 'And they went scurrying to the Earl. When all is said and done Quarrelwood is a royal benefice, if demitted on the de Chisholms through the Earl. It's only the farms below that are sublet to the Priory. Have I got that right? And the Earl would not want its profits to get into the Bishop's hands.'

'Which they would if the Bishop can establish these visitation rights. Quite.'

'Nor would the King like it, I'm thinking. Only it's the extra bit of power he wouldn't want changing hands. The Earl is the King's man but the Bishop isn't.'

Thomas was smiling himself now, his dark eyes relieved. 'You wouldn't want to miss this joust, would you, Will?'

'Smart pair, aren't you,' Alexander muttered then held his breath in case he had gone too far and offended his Prior. Thomas surprised him by rolling his eyes, which made Will laugh outright. Alexander almost did likewise before becoming practical, 'Father, what do you want in the way of provisions? If we are to feed them all, the cooks had better get started.'

'We shall feed anybody who is still here at noon. And yes, make sure there is plenty. The surplus shall be distributed locally to compensate for the lack of funeral alms-cakes last Saturday.' So many people had turned up for Nicol's service that there had been barely enough to go round and the usual funerary gifts to the poor could not be provided. As it was, even the staple bread and cheese had vanished down the throats of the congregation, leaving Priory inmates to make do later with dry oat biscuits and butter for supper and a hastily concocted vegetable stew.

As soon as the Cellarer left, Will raised the question of the two kiln workers.

'Of course they are not slaves!'

'What do you pay them?' This caught Thomas short. 'Their keep? Plus provision of their materials? What else? You should go down and see that broken masterpiece. It will astonish you. Have you any idea how they manage their work? Their sales? Or have you just accepted that their work is too specialised for the monks to participate in? Brother Michael admits he knows very little of what they do so they are virtually managing themselves, and that includes dealing with the commissions they are getting. Do you know how they get these? How they buy their materials and sell their wares? They are doing it somehow, and they're making a profit which you are getting because you are paying tithes on it to the Church. I saw the account book down in the kiln shed. And you think all that is not worth wages? Decent wages?'

'I shall investigate this, Will. It does not sound right. Perhaps - I wonder if they were bonded. That would make them serfs.'

Will snorted. 'What's the difference? They're still tied here with no hope of leaving. That means they will have no chance to develop their talents or create the fine work they are capable of producing. That can't be right either.'

Thomas looked down. 'If - we were to unbind them we would lose them. As soon as their talents were recognised they would be snapped up by one of the travelling teams of glaziers and we would have to give up glazing altogether.'

'How much glazing do you have for them here? For your own use, I mean?'

'Some. - No, to be honest, very little. By this time next year they will have finished the work that we have in hand because we do not intend to put anything other than plain glass into the last of our windows in the new Calefactory.'

'It must be driving them insane producing plain glass in a pot oven,' muttered Will. 'These are highly gifted experts. Where on earth they learned their skills I can't imagine, but they have them. Surely it is wrong to deny them the chance to use them. Remember the parable of the talents? What's more, they are already trying to improve things for themselves.'

He paused, realising that Thomas was thinking hard. 'Maybe you can help. Have you heard of Theophilus? Not the saint but a monk who has written some text book about glass.' Thomas shook his head. 'And Fargoosh? Have you heard of something like that. Something to do with trees. Or wood.'

'*Fagus*' The reply was instant. 'They must mean *fagus*. Beech.' Will's pleasure was dashed when he added, 'But there are no beech woods near here. I think it's too cold.'

'Well, you'll have to plant some if you want to keep those men.' But even as he grumbled, the seaman knew such trees would not be fit for cutting and burning for generations. 'Och, well, that settles that one.'

'We could import beech-wood, I suppose,' Thomas murmured. He was silent for a little, then he looked up. 'I shall enquire if that's possible.'

'Thank you. I'll get off to Elgin, then. It shouldn't take long because they'll either have that book or they won't.' He was opening the door before Thomas asked the question he really did not want to hear.

'Why are you so anxious to do this for them, Will?'

He examined the intricate latch for a long time before deciding to give a full and honest answer. Closing the door again he returned and told Thomas all that had happened between himself and Lek.

'This sounds like blackmail,' was the Prior's concerned answer.

'I prefer to call it trade. Believe me, the line between the two is often very fine.'

'By all means find the information Lek wants. Give him all the help you can, and I shall do likewise but... Will, are you sure you want to know what he might tell you?'

'I'm sure I don't. But I have a gut feeling that I need to know. I - won't necessarily pass on what I learn, mind you.'

Thomas did not like that either but for the moment he did not try to dissuade Will from the decision. They sat in silence for a few minutes, thinking, comfortable with each other.

'Why has the Bishop moved so suddenly, do you think?' Will mused. 'Why now? In fact I'm wondering if it has something to do with the way Brother Mark was silent throughout this morning's meeting.'

'Brother Alexander swears Mark was memorising everything he could.'

'That's what I thought. Where has he spent the rest of the day?'

'In the vestry.'

'Huh. Writing it all up, do you think?'

'He has certainly been writing furiously. I didn't interfere because I want to see what he does next.'

'Or has done? - Since the Bishop's coming.'

But the Prior shook his head. 'No. He hasn't had time. Maybe the Bishop was warned that you were to give your report this morning and that was enough to jolt him into taking precipitate action.'

'He'd have known an examination was likely anyway, after the casket arrived. I have a feeling Father Symon sent it sooner than the Bishop intended.'

'I'm sure he did.'

'How sure are you that the seal is intact?'

'It certainly looked untouched, even dust engrained.'

Will nodded and lapsed into silence again. He felt Thomas was waiting for something. An explanation for his disastrous handling of the Chapter meeting? He had decided the best way was simply not to mention it, but suddenly he found himself blurting out, 'I apologise for the sorry state I was in this morning. I didn't expect...'

Thomas's gaze fixed itself on the far corner of the ceiling but his lips twitched. 'We've all heard of Lady Amelia's doctored ale. She never drinks it herself, you know, and I doubt if she realises what is going on in her brewery.' Will blinked. It was only then that he considered the possibility. The lady had brought two jugs and poured for him from one which she had called to be replenished while she poured for herself out of the other. She had been drinking the water. 'I wonder if nobody has the courage to tell her.'

Chapter 18 – Threads Tangle

When Will emerged from the Prior's chamber, his ears caught the strains of music floating out through the church door which stood wide open to the late afternoon. Even the frenzied late wooing of the spring birds had been stilled by it. He found Justin already hovering inside the doorway tempted to listen, garden tools laid aside but hands still clothed in soil. Above them to the right, the door to the Scriptorium was also ajar, allowing James's glorious voice to soar to the ears of Daniel and Gregory above.

The lad was being trained by the Cantor, who was using a small viol and bow to illustrate the phrasing of a new French canticle for Corpus Christi. At the same time Stephen was giving James an oblique lesson in Latin, not just in pronunciation but also in its meaning and construction by asking the young novice to translate and explain the words, on the grounds that he would express the music better if he knew the context. James was lapping it up almost without realising, so eager was he to get on with the singing, and he seemed unaware of the listeners.

Justin, already Stephen's Latin pupil, recognised what his teacher was doing and exchanged a wicked grin with Will. Some minutes later, the Vestry door opened and the Sacristan headed out towards the sacramental vessel. When he noticed Will, the glower he threw at him was freezing but any hesitation, if it existed, was fractional. Ignoring him, Will lounged against the doorpost and soaked up the singing. He himself had no talent whatsoever but this gave him immense enjoyment.

Stiff-faced Mark went about his business. He unhooked the end of the long chain from the wall and carefully let it slide through the pulley on the ceiling to lower the gilded censer to within his reach. Removing the pristine linen cloth he looked inside, replenished the holy oil from a spouted canister then, after replacing the covering over the censer, pulled it up, securing the chain once more at the wall before he walked back to the Vestry. During the next few bars of music Will listened with his thoughts floating freely and his eye fell on the ghostly white and gold swinging gently above him. As he turned away, he remembered the glimpse he had caught of the vessel from the hillside the previous evening and swung back, seeing Justin's eye also following its swaying. Surely it was now higher than before? He looked at the windows and a suspicion arose in his mind, sending him on a quiet journey across the aisle and up the steps to the Scriptorium. Daniel was there alone.

'Brother, I'm just leaving for Elgin. May I ask a favour? I believe the Sacristan was memorising what was said this morning in Chapter, and that he has spent the afternoon writing it all down. I'd, um, like to know what he does with his script.'

Daniel's face was unsurprised but a faint frown gathered when Will added, 'I have a feeling that he has just passed on a message of some kind. Could you possibly watch to see if he gives anybody any papers? Maybe over the garden wall? I know it's twenty feet tall, but I noticed a fruit-picker's ladder lying behind the garden shed. And the signal would be visible only to the north if I'm right. Maybe there's somebody on the hillside on the other side of the road. My guess is that the Sacristan will try something soon. He'll either lag behind when the brothers head for the refectory or maybe immediately after the meal. He is usually the first to leave, isn't he? If I ask Prior Thomas to excuse you and arrange for your meal to be delivered here, will you watch?'

Daniel nodded. But he pointed in a sweep round the rest of the precincts.

'Yes, I know. But you can't watch everywhere and Brother Mark would be very suspicious if several people went missing from dinner to watch the rest of the walls. I'm suggesting you watch the north because the main gate is there and because the main east-west road passes that way. The odds are highest that somebody will pick up the message along there and get it away quickly. You can see the whole length of the north wall from up here. And where the walls run out you might just get a glimpse of who is on the road heading off.' Again Daniel nodded, moving his high stool up to the middle high window, which would give him the best view. The touch of mischief which glinted in his eye lent a strange attraction to his sad ugliness.

'Norbert of Caen.' That was the name of the master glazier, according to Father Symon. After meandering in a dream along the flowery springtime lanes, Will had arrived in Elgin just as the great Cathedral spewed out its last congregation of the day, a huge one which made him wonder what the celebration was. Roughly a quarter of those attending, in dapper burgher clothing, headed for the town. The rest were mainly in black but there was a spatter of brown, white and even a few Crusading tabards, all of these turning towards the various stone chanonries and deaneries, which looked to Will like small palaces. There was also a flamboyant clutch of visiting merchants, no doubt lodging at the port of Spynie.

The Bishop, who had officiated that evening, swept by, ignoring Will's tentative, 'Your Grace...' Escorted by the merchants who would no doubt dine at his table shortly, his Grace climbed aboard a wooden carriage to drive west towards his own fine fortified Spynie Palace a mile away.

All the merchants were much older than Will and far more ostentatiously robed. Will was probably richer than any of them, and consequently with considerably more power if ever he chose to use it, but that was not his style.

It was the Investigator who noticed him, probably because Will was the only individual standing still out of over two hundred folk.

'Did it not arrive?' was Father Symon's sharp greeting. 'The box?'

'Oh, yes. Father Thomas told me to thank you most sincerely. It came much sooner than he expected.'

The fat little priest said nothing, but the rueful grimace in the Bishop's direction suggested, as Thomas had suspected, that the great man had been caught on the hop by the Investigator's quick reaction. But Father Symon's position required him to take charge of all documents laid in the Cathedral's care; there was no reason why the Bishop should be consulted about any return requested by the owners. The casket had merely been sent back to its original and legal home. So, had Father Symon taken action first and then told his master? Or had there been an altercation between them with the Investigator insisting on sticking to the letter of the law and refusing to delay its return? Refusing to condone the breaching of the Priory seal?

Either would fit with his uncompromising personality.

'Was there something wrong with it?' So he had his own suspicions, had he?

'Not at all, Father. I'm here on a different trail.' He explained only that the Priory glaziers wished to consult a text book written by Theophilus.

'Norbert will know if we have one here. Come. Since his work is his life he'll be in one of two places.' He led the way back into the enormous Cathedral church where Will saw immediately that a triple window of brilliantly coloured glass had just been unveiled on the west wall, the trestles not yet removed. 'The middle lancet is being funded by the town guilds of Elgin. We have just been dedicating it. Look, you can see their patron, St Giles, Egidius that is, with his crook, and there's the child who is always with him.'

Father Symon's pride was well justified for the general workmanship was excellent. The colours blazed with life. Inside the curve of the crook hung a small, gold bell and in the background a sparkling, blue river, undoubtedly the Lossie, flowed round an exquisite, if small, representation of the Cathedral. Behind it the town with its busy streets spilled away towards the castle mound in the distance. All around St Giles crowded the artisans of the city, each and every face depicted with clarity, each individual sporting the tools of his trade and his guild badge.

The scene they represented was bustling, thriving and complex but the result, to Will's eye, was far too jumbled for artistic satisfaction. He had seen many another such picture window in many another pretentious North European city cathedral, depicting the same scramble for influence and public recognition. At the same time, he did not grudge admitting that this particular cathedral deserved its reputation as a magnificent example of canonical architecture, as fine as he had seen anywhere. At night, with all the lamps lit, it was said to be visible from far across the Firth in Dornoch or Dingwall, a great lantern in the dark, a ship of God aflame.

To the right of the guilds' window was another provided by the See of Murray itself. It was infinitely more striking. The two crosiers crossed behind the Bishop's mitred head were turned outwards, representing the worldliness of his vast and demanding Episcopal concern, his twin responsibilities to the state and the people on the one hand and the Church and its internal affairs on the other; his negotiations with folk high and low; his need to balance Caesar and God in all he did. Five other faces appeared in this design, representations of the five chaplains who had made substantial donations from their parishes, but they were placed discreetly round the edge, banished to where they would in no way diminish the overall importance of Bishop Alexander Barr himself. Here he was at the centre of the stage, clad in glowing red and purple and blue trimmed with delicate gold lace. Against the simplest of backgrounds, stone walling in neat *grisaille*, the brilliant colours shrieked a message of power and dominance. Hardly Christian, was Will's reaction.

The third window to the left was the only one to achieve a true artistic and representational balance. An outright gift from the independent Cistercians of Kinloss, (who in no way could be coerced into 'donating',) the Abbot was pictured as a shepherd, which was appropriate. The immense wealth of the Cistercians came from wool farming, but this figure was also shown as a protector of his people. There was no vaunting of personal glory here. The face of the central Abbot-like figure was not visible to the congregation as he bent to help one injured man, the head already turning away towards others in need nearby. Beyond were the woods and shores and hillsides of Murray with tiny figures at work among them, Abbey folk who, for all their diminutive size, were depicted as important in their own right however humble. The style of the glazing was also noticeably different, probably done by the Abbey's own team.

When Will's eyes wandered to another triple window farther down the west wall which was still plain glazed, Father Symon spoke dryly. 'No doubt his Grace has earmarked one of those for Pluscardyn's wealth to provide. Or all of them if he gets his way tomorrow.'

Slowly Will swung round on one heel, uncertain of the little man's meaning. 'You'll be there?' he enquired politely.

'I have not been included in his Grace's train.'

Will turned back to the Cistercian window. Outside, the setting sun shot a sudden blaze from the west which, from where Will stood, illuminated the Abbot's crosier, this time with the crook turned inwards towards the life of private prayer and holy enquiry which was his convent's primary purpose, for all its trading and farming successes. The peaceful pastoral scene sprang to life drawing the viewers in, just as the founding glaziers of old had dictated should happen in these glorious windows to God. These walls of coloured light were intended to be a means of worship as well as instruction. In this the craftsmen of the Kinloss window had succeeded, in marked contrast to the other two which almost repelled Will with their busyness and determination to dominate and flaunt. And yet, perhaps by the sheer simplicity and lack of posturing, and because of the delicacy of the etching and the kindliness of the message, Will found this creation easily the most powerful window of the three.

'I think you should come to Pluscardyn tomorrow,' he said bluntly. 'I have a feeling the case of Nicol's murder will come up and you were one of the main witnesses to the lad's injury. Add to that the murder of Father Ranulf out at Mortlach, - and I know that he's a chaplain of this Cathedral...'

'But there's no link surely?' Father Symon's voice became sharp.

'Death was delivered by an identical blow. As, it appears, to Hugo de May.'

'What!' The priest's face grew grey. 'When?'

'In the early hours of last Thursday. Probably.'

'But - why has it taken so long...?'

'At first he appeared to have stumbled into a bog but we weren't sure of that. I arranged for the soldiers from Balvenie Castle to dredge for him and I heard only today that he had been found. I thought they'd have sent to the Bishop as well.'

But then he realised that was unlikely. The soldiers were obeying him, Will, as their own chief's son and beyond that they had no responsibility. Had Ranulf been alive they would have informed him, but that was all. In his grumpiness, James Forbys might have warned them against even that.

'They found Hugo and his horse in the bog. There was no sign of his courier's bag. I don't know if that has any significance or not. But in the circumstances, may I invite you on behalf of the Prior of Pluscardyn to attend tomorrow?'

The Investigator frowned furiously.

'Unless, of course, you've been commanded not to come by the Bishop. Prior Thomas would not wish to see you compromised.'

'I'll be there,' Father Symon growled. 'Ten is it?'

'Eight.'

For some reason that cleared the little man's brow. 'Now, this book on glass. Norbert isn't here, so he will be in the glass workshops. Follow me.'

With a last look over his shoulder at the beautiful Kinloss window, Will followed Father Symon out of the church and along a maze of passages, some covered, some open, all of them now empty, then out through a portal in the inner wall surrounding the central, hallowed core of the Cathedral. More fast walking took them towards one of the massive main gates in the much more substantial outer wall. Just inside were the general workshops, used by the teams of craftsmen who were constantly involved in building, rebuilding, remodelling and repairing. As with Lek and Hus, these labourers and artisans ate and slept where they worked, some with their families who were often specialists in their own right, including some of the women, even more so in the wake of the death toll inflicted by the Pest. They created a village within the Cathedral precinct although outside the sanctified complex.

'Norbert has a team of eight, two mullion masons, a lead came-maker, four glaziers and a goldsmith.'

Will stopped dead in astonishment. 'Goldsmith?'

Father Symon shrugged. 'I'm no geometrician, but I understand that the design of fancy coloured windows is closely akin to the design of filigree settings for jewels. Something to do with the space for light compared to the weight the stone has to carry. So they tell me. Norbert is by no means the only glazier to include a goldsmith in his team as a designer.'

Norbert, when found, flatly denied all knowledge of Theophilus. Too flatly. He then went on to question why anybody would want the book and Will's suspicions increased.

'I'm a merchant. I have an interested customer. - He just wants to look, before ordering a copy for himself, I suppose.'

'A glazier?' This sharp query confirmed that professional jealousy and protectionism was involved.

'An interested scholar,' Will said slowly, thinking of himself now, but also of Thomas, or even Brother Gregory to justify the lie. Something told him there was such a book in Elgin, or in one of its houses, but Norbert was never going to allow him to lay hands on it. What was even more certain was that if Norbert discovered about the skills of Lek and Hus, they would be poached overnight from Pluscardyn. Will's neck tingled. Fine though the Cathedral windows were, - and he knew they, like the magnificent building itself, were the match of any he had seen in the great Baltic cities, - not one of the faces in any of them, even in the older thirteenth century masterpieces which were of very high quality indeed, could match the genius of his own shattered visage now scattered over the Pluscardyn kiln yard.

Never mind. The biggest and best library in the north belonged to Kinloss Abbey, and he had already thought of another urgent reason for going there.

It was well after one in the morning when he returned to Pluscardyn, weary and saddle sore, fully expecting to have his knocking ignored at least until two when the monks rose. When the gate swung open it was a relief, until he saw Brother Alexander's furious face.

'You go too far, Captain! You really do take too much advantage of our hospitality. Far too much.' He sniffed hard.

'I haven't drunk a drop!' Will objected. 'I didn't have time to stop in Elgin for a pie so I haven't even had supper.'

'And you won't till another comes around, coming in at this hour and expecting... Where have you been?'

'Elgin Cathedral then Kinloss Abbey. At the first I spoke with the Bishop's Investigator and at the second with Abbot Richard.' He chanced a grin at the candle Alexander was jabbing in his face like a weapon. 'It took me an hour of hard talking with him in his nightcap but I managed to persuade him to join us for the Bishop's enquiry tomorrow. Uh, today.'

He heard Alexander draw a quick breath, then the candle lowered enough to let him see the Cellarer's surprise melt into complicity.

'Did you now? I hope the Prior approves.'

'Don't you think he will?'

'We-ell, an independent Church witness with that much clout should help redress the balance against the Bishop, I suppose. But you'll be little use to us tomorrow if you're dead on your feet. - I've left your supper by your bed, though you don't deserve it.'

'I know,' Will said, his humility at least half genuine. 'I am most grateful.'

'Then you get off to bed. I'll tell the Prior that the Abbot is coming.'

'And Father Symon. Since the Bishop had excluded him, could you tell Father Thomas that I requested the attendance of Father Symon on his behalf - and that I have a gut feeling that the murders are going to come up.'

'Why?'

'I don't know. I just feel it. Oh, and they knew nothing in Elgin about Hugo de May till I mentioned it tonight - I mean last night.' He glanced at the sky.

'Ah, so the Bishop is not going to be very happy tomorrow. I warn you, Captain, that's likely to make him very dangerous.'

Will nodded and was about to turn away when Alexander produced a key. At the same moment Will produced a question. 'Why are you up at this hour?'

'Because Brother Daniel is waiting for you up in the Scriptorium. He had to let me lock him in so as not to alert the Sacristan. Get him out of there, will you, and lock up again before Mark rises. Daniel wouldn't budge for me when I went up to see why there was a candle still burning. I don't know what information he has for you but if Mark finds him waiting up he's just about bright enough to smell a rat.'

'Smell he's been rumbled!' Will set off at a run but a hissed warning made him slow down enough to lay his big feet quietly on the ground.

Up in the Scriptorium Daniel was sound asleep on his stool, his black head on his arm and his brushes by his elbow. Will was less than ten feet from him when he shot to his feet, dark eyes wild with alarm. It took several seconds for him to return to the placid air of the room from whatever evil place his dreams inhabited. Then he frowned at Will, frowned at the sky which was already beginning to lighten, shook his head and took a deep breath before pointing at several little figures scratched on a floured wax tablet on the table.

'Ah, so I was right. I don't suppose you could identify who collected the papers? You did!' He peered at the last delicate character Daniel pointed out. 'Well now. Isn't that interesting! - Sh! Snuff that candle!' Their hands met as they both moved to do so. A slight sound had spun up from the church below and they guessed that the Sacristan had already arrived to light the single permitted floor candle before the altar in preparation for the first service of the day. They were now trapped in the Scriptorium.

This far north in late May, it was just light enough by then for Daniel to see Will shrug against a brightening window. The priest laid a hand on his arm to guide him towards a truckle bed he slid from beneath the work table. It had a blanket and pillow on it and served the weary merchant very well as a secretive sleeping place. He never did find out how Daniel spent the rest of the night.

Nearly five hours later, Daniel roused him once more, grinning then shaking his head as the proffered large bowl of porridge disappeared in great gulps.

'What on earth is going on?' Downstairs there was a banging and clattering in the church, accompanied by unholy chattering. Daniel waved a hand towards the casket which had come from the Cathedral. The scrolls brought back in it had been tipped on end, each tied with a green cord, and confined to one half of the space. Daniel now put the Priory's own selection of charters, these tied with red, into the other half, with a wooden bar between the two collections. Beside the box a small tray held individually numbered disks, again marked in green and red, and a list with a column of red and green numbers to the left and the date and purpose of the relevant document to the right.

As soon as Will's bowl was empty Daniel slipped it under the table along with the truckle bed then waggled several scrolls under Will's nose. Will gestured to include letters dealing with land squabbles over the years to be added to the casket, although they were long out of date and probably of no importance in the context of the Bishop's enquiry; those mentioning Quarrelwood might be, he supposed. The Valliscaulian Rule he rejected; that was relevant only to the inmates of Pluscardyn themselves. Then Daniel pointed at the casket, indicating that Will should be the one to carry it downstairs. It was the perfect excuse, the ideal means of forestalling Mark's suspicions at his appearance from the Scriptorium.

Will was startled by the change in the church interior. It looked like a market place, with people - only monks so far - bustling here and there. A long line of trestle tables had been created down the middle and the seating was being placed on either side, leaving enough space around the tables to permit anybody who was interested to scrutinise the documents which Will was now instructed to lay out, unrolled and weighted by river-washed stones at the corners and with the appropriate disk numbers appended. He hid a smile when he realised that the furious Sacristan had been designated as the man in charge of preparations. He must have understood that this open scrutiny of the documents was not going to be to the Bishop's advantage.

'This is the only space we have large enough for such a gathering,' Thomas told him when at last they could find a moment together. 'And, as you said, charters are public documents. Then let them be public. Everybody who can read can see exactly what they say and there will be no quibbling.'

Will grinned. 'Unless the Bishop has a copy of that 1345 draft which says something different from ours. Um, yours. But with the Earl and the Abbot here to learn that Father Symon sent over our box still sealed just a couple of days ago, the Bishop's hardly likely to flaunt that, is he?'

Thomas, who had been looking rather tense up till then, relaxed into an answering grin. 'We'll see. May I ask you to receive the first of our guests, Will? I believe you know the Earl and Father Gregory tells me... Er, Brother Gregory tells me that Daniel saw that his party has just ridden into the valley from the west. I understand from Daniel that Lek the glazier is anxious to speak with you as well.'

'I'll combine the two jobs, then.' And he strode off towards the North Gate. Only later did he wonder how Daniel had communicated all that.

The mill stood dejected and silent. Next door Lek's furnace glowed. As Will approached it, the ground felt so warm that he realised it had been on overnight.

'Why?' He was puzzled. Lek looked at him, cool as winter brass. 'I have found a copy of Theophilus for you,' Will added, bending a little by switching to Slav. 'There are instructions for building furnaces in it. It will arrive today from Kinloss, but you can consult it only in the Scriptorium in the Priory. - Tough! That is the Abbot's condition and we're stuck with it.' It was on the tip of his tongue to offer the services of Brother Gregory or Stephen as translator of the Latin when a jingle of horse harness reached his ears. Then a laugh which he recognised soared above the happy banter of a troop of noble merrymakers out for the day. Some of the voices were female.

Before leaving to greet them, Will held Lek's eye once more. 'What do I get in return?'

The enigmatic reply was, 'You get when ready.'

'I - might need it very soon.' But Lek would not be hurried. 'There may be an investigation into the murder this morning.' But no. Lek wanted to see that book first, Will guessed, and it was going to be impossible to persuade him to cross through a church filled with Christian observers. Will would just have to wait, and unquestionably Lek was enjoying the situation. It was probably a very long time since he had had the upper hand over a German oppressor, if ever.

Will had no option but to stifle his frustration. 'Right, I'll take you up to see it once everybody has gone. Say at two, when the monks go out to the fields? Will your whatever-it-is be ready by then? For I have to leave soon after that.'

'Should be.' It was a thin promise.

Chapter 19 – The Enquiry

A hop and a skip took Will across the road and on to the opposite bank where he swung himself up into the great oak tree just as the young leader of the cavalcade reached the kiln yard gate. It brought him to horse height and he was able to watch as the thirty or so followers of the Earl's party swept round the corner off the main highway.

The standard-bearer would have been the youngest squire of the Earl's household, perhaps twelve years old and pink with pride and nervousness. Behind him strode the same two retainers who had accompanied Sir Robert de Chisholm the day before, watching for the boy's every mistake. The Earl of Murray himself rode just behind them, his barrel chest making him look taller and bigger than Will knew him to be; he was dressed in simple clothes, much like Will himself, shirt, hose, shoes and a serviceable leather jerkin, sleeveless because of the early warmth of the day. On his heels followed a couple of his nobles then a bevy of ladies, six of them plus a little dark-haired page. Then came a boisterous bunch of children on excited ponies.

Will was instantly aware of Maura but she kept her eyes away from him, as he did from her; indeed she rode at the farthest point of the group from him that she could manoeuvre. Only once did their gaze meet, so swiftly that it was over before it began, but it was enough to startle Will. Yesterday had her eyes not been the dancing blue of her dress? Today they were grey, matching precisely, it seemed to him, her simple but exquisite silk gown which was the shade of a soft dove-wing. And today she wore her wimple as it was meant to be worn, covering every wisp of her hair, the trailing scarf then pulled harshly round her neck. She was still and withdrawn. Tight with a tension which made her pale face look severe, she moved within an aura which isolated her from the rest of the world.

The centre of attraction, as always, was the Junoesque, red-haired beauty with the laugh Will remembered so clearly, a highly infectious chuckle which somehow managed to be throaty and tinkling at the same time. Marjorie Stewart, daughter of Robert the Steward no less, was now the acting Countess of Murray, an unlikely wife for quiet Johnnie Dunbar. Or were the pair not yet married, Will wondered. He had seen her just once before when he was little more than a child. A sharp forgotten pain reminded him of the hurt he had felt that day, the day when he realised that his quiet hero had learned to love somebody else more than 'ma wee laddie' who had dogged his heels on the rare occasions when they were together; Johnnie had been so stricken by his lady love that he had forgotten Will's very existence for hours on end, which had left 'ma wee laddie's' adoration severely dented for a long time.

Now, of course, Will understood. The love affair was ill-conceived, for more reasons than one. As well as being the Regent's daughter, she had been a bairn at the time Jamie succumbed to her charms. His father was the Earl of March and Dunbar, a scion of the older Celtic claimants to the throne and his mother had been sister to John Randolph, the previous Earl of Murray who had died in 1346 without an heir, bringing the fief back into royal hands. Another sister was the famous Black Agnes who had married the dominant Douglas, another man eager to try for the kingdom, although his claim was less clear. Marjorie's father, Robert Stewart, had no wish to see either family worm their way into power through union with the daughter of the current heir to the throne, a legitimate one. In the inter-regnum the Earldom of Murray had been run by Euphemia Ross, John Randolph's widow, whom Robert had taken as his second wife fifteen years back probably to gain that scarce influence in the north. A union between Dunbar and Stewart which might undermine that was unlikely to happen, so folk had thought.

But Johnnie, in his reserved way, had captivated many more hearts than Will's and Marjorie's. He had also revealed remarkable ability in the strategies of war and politics, in both fields without causing offence. In Scotland that was as rare as rubies growing on rosebushes. With strong-willed Marjorie sailing into battle as well, it looked as if Johnnie had won his lady. The King had just been persuaded that the eagle's feather of the Earldom of Murray would fit Jamie's bonnet nicely for the time being, since he had been standing in for his aunt for a while now. The push towards that was done by others, not Johnnie himself. Will still wondered whether all that helped or hindered Robert's currently shaky power base in the North.

His predecessor had been John Randolph who had died at Neville's Cross defending David Bruce, his beloved King and friend. After a long childhood betrothal John had been married shortly before the battle to Euphemia, daughter of the powerful Celtic Earl of Ross, and when he died leaving her childless, the Randolph line died with him. - It was strange that this should happen so often, Will mused, what with the King, the Randolphs, the de Chisholms. - It was John's death which returned the Earldom to become the King's gift. It also left Euphemia as chatelaine in Murray in the interim, and its management she undertook with some skill with the help of Johnnie's late father, who was brother-in-law to Randolph. She remained the dowager Countess for a decade, keeping her own dower and also entitled to a third of the Murray estates in the long run. That made her rich in exactly the way Lady Amelia had described her own rise.

Will thought highly of Euphemia and wondered why she married again after the love match which her first union had been, so they said. To the surprise of many, her choice was Robert Stewart, whose wife had died. This brought Robert the power he hankered after in the North without having to lean on any new Earl. Although her two husbands had been co-Guardians of Scotland during David's minority in France, John and Robert, just teenagers themselves when they took on the task, had been uneasy bedfellows.

At thirty-five when she remarried, the dowager and childless Countess must then have had little hope of issue despite Robert's fecundity on both sides of the blanket. But today here she was among this very group with her own four Stewart bairns up to mischief with the rest, all of them testing the patience of their minders. Her marriage, of course, had made her the stepmother of Marjorie, her successor as Countess. Will had little doubt that it was her ladyship's gentle, patrician influence which was keeping the gathering just short of wildness, perhaps along with Johnnie's own quiet expectation of propriety.

By the time all this had filled Will's mind, several young men with portable musical instruments reached him, dressed in the height of fashion - as ridiculous in their popinjay colours and extreme styles as Will had seen in any European city. One wore a yellow velvet hat remarkably like a sloppy giant saffron pudding which kept slithering on to his shoulder, requiring it to be constantly hoisted up again like a monstrous jelly inside a bag. Another wore toe points so long that he had had to tie them together and carry them, which then obliged him to walk with short mincing steps which brought a rain of catcalls. Will stifled a snigger and examined the small troop of marching men immediately behind, sensing they were having a struggle to keep their faces straight; they were clad in embellished livery similar to the retainers at the front.

Right at the back, no doubt having tagged on at Kinloss, rode Abbot Richard himself with his regulation two retainers; one of his monks carried a large wooden book box strapped to his saddle. Will made a bet with himself that the Bishop would not stick to his allotted maximum of three men.

'My lord!'

The Earl looked right, his clear grey eyes registering no recognition. Will held his breath. Had his elevation changed Johnnie Dunbar from the person he had known? He was still the least conspicuously dressed of the entire gathering.

'My lord, the Prior has sent me to welcome you. The horses are to go into that field there.' He pointed at the enclosure behind the blacksmith's forge. 'And the, um, revellers are invited to use the paddock just outside the Priory Gate.'

A slow smile trickled over the Earl's face and his eyes lit up with just that shy pleasure and total concentration on the individual before him which attracted so many people. He could make the most lowly person feel special. His chest expanded even more as he drew breath.

'Ma wee laddie!' Then the smile wavered slightly as he took in the severity of Will's hairstyle. 'I - didna realise you were one of them here.'

'No, no! But if a novice in black offers to barber you, mak sure ye refuse!'

Johnnie laughed. Leaning over he grabbed the same thick branch supporting Will. In one slick, easy movement he heaved himself lightly out of his saddle on to the bank and handed the reins over to the man coming up behind him. Behind him his wife, or lady, had been flirting outrageously with the other noble, which Will was ready to disapprove until, just for an instant, her teasing eyes met her husband's in a flash of pure love. Most folk would have missed it, or failed to recognise it, but Will was used to something similar happening between his own parents. The tiny incident convinced him that Johnnie Dunbar was the man he always had been. Honest, reliable, wise and kind, accepting what the winds of fate blew his way and making the best of whatever it was. And maybe, beneath all the trappings and public performances forced on him, he was just as shy as ever.

Will was discomfited when he realised that the Earl was studying him with equal intensity, and probably seeing just as much. Flushing, he looked away as the ladies rode by. Lady Amelia, a tiny wiry figure on a tall mare entirely within her control, quirked a wicked eyebrow at him. Then she jerked her head at the black-haired page trotting by with particular determination, face averted. Will blinked. He recognised that grey hill pony. A moment later he also recognised the scowl and the angry blue eyes which now met his, reluctance overcome on sensing his observation.

'It's nae as bad as yours!' Francie glared at his near tonsure, seeing attack as the best defence.

Stifling amusement, Will examined the short black spikes all over her head with his cheek dropped on to his shoulder. 'At least mine doesna have a tide line. What on earth did you use?'

She blushed. 'Father Ranulf's mushroom ink.'

Will let out a bellow of laughter. 'Well, ye'll be waiting a while for the tide to go oot, ma lass!' She rode on with her nose in the air; and the lady behind her turned, knocking the breath from him for a moment. Then he leaned over in dangerous delight to smack his lips firmly on hers.

'Mother! So she came to you after all?'

His mother raised a hand to the back of his head and drew him close again for another kiss. 'Which is more than you did, my son. It seems the only way I can see you is to come to wherever you are. - I brought your boots back from Mortlach.'

'Wonderful! And father?' His eyes flitted back along the parade.

'No.' Her still fair head shook, and her eyes took in the black holes she had bequeathed him. 'He's somewhere in the Borders with the King.'

Will's smile faded. The eyes were telling him something was wrong. 'And? The girls are all right, aren't they?' She would never have left them otherwise.

'Yes. Fine. Just... Oh, later, *Villi*. We'll talk later.' She had been cut short by the Priory bell striking.

'I'm afraid we have just fifteen minutes left to get everybody inside,' he muttered to the Earl. A last hug sent his mother after the ladies and, by silent agreement, he and Johnnie climbed from their viewpoint and began striding towards the North Gate.

'So what's all this about, ma wee laddie? And what do you want of me?'

'It's - really what the Prior wants. Just a fair hearing when the Bishop arrives.'

'Ah. I'll warrant he's not here yet.' When Will's head turned towards him, the Earl gave a small smile. 'He's known to work late but sleep late. Mornings are a trial for him - and he has a habit of arriving at meetings after they've started so that he can make an entrance folk are forced to notice. But I see his Father Symon is turning in off the highway.'

Will glanced behind him. Today the Bishop's Investigator was unattended and in plain, woollen church garb, although he rode the same fine hunter he had ridden on Saturday. He also kept a good fifteen feet between himself and the Abbot in front of him. Will had a second look at the Kinloss party. Abbot Richard was on top of a mule, of all things, and at that moment he kicked hard at the beast to push his way through the melee peeling off into the paddock to begin their revels. Coming abreast of Will he gave a cool nod, another slightly warmer one to the Earl.

'My Lord Abbot, the Prior's welcome to you,' Will said. 'Brother Alexander awaits you and your companions at the gate.' Another fractional nod took the old man past them.

'Now, details,' the Earl commanded, quickening his pace towards the church as they turned in through the gate behind the Kinloss party. Will summarised the Priory's governance problems in two minutes flat, guiding the Earl as soon as they entered the church to the documents which mattered now lying on the trestles. Sir Robert was already struggling to decipher one, which probably dealt with his own land problems. Lady Amelia was scanning all of them with impressive speed, in the company of the dowager Countess Euphemia, aunt of Robert Stewart's wife, and Lady Dolinda Forbys, Will's mother, the only ladies to enter.

Most of the Earl's party intended to have fun in the sun while the discussions took place indoors, but a large group of curious burghers had already arrived by the south road from Elgin in support of Sandy Watson, their Sheriff. If Sandy was miffed at discovering that he would not be the senior civil legal authority present he managed to hide it. Their work did not overlap much but the Earl, as the King's Justiciary, was undoubtedly Sandy's superior.

'These,' the Earl tapped the same two charters Will had considered vital, 'and this 1345 letter, here, are the ones that matter.' He turned to give the Prior one of his shy smiles. 'Hm. Father Thomas, I take it that you want to chair this enquiry.'

Since that - as Johnnie undoubtedly had guessed - was exactly what Thomas wanted, what he *needed* in order to demonstrate his independence and security, he smiled broadly and bowed before turning away to guide his major guests to their seats. Their placing was highly significant. Before the Earl could follow, Will touched his arm.

'There's another problem, my Lord,' he muttered. 'I don't see this part of the enquiry leading to any problems, not with all these papers to back up the Prior's case, but there is something else. I think it might... No, I think it *should* then proceed into a murder enquiry.'

The Earl straightened his broad back and turned to look up intently at Will. When he saw the distracting eyes dilate even more than before, a phenomenon he recognised in Will, Johnnie frowned till his eyebrows slashed a line across his fine forehead. Will rushed on in a low voice, explaining the barest details, all he had time for, first about Nicol, then about Ranulf and Hugo. Just as he finished, the bell stopped ringing. Two minutes. The last of the visitors moved smartly to take their seats.

There was no sign of the Bishop.

Normally there were no seats or benches of any kind inside this church. Unless somebody was ill or infirm the monks, according to the constant testing of their Rule, stood throughout all services, or occasionally leaned against the rood screen which had now been pushed aside. With their hands hidden inside their bulky sleeves they now stood round the walls so as not to obscure the participation of the public. Nobody sat behind the altar, of course, but in front of it had been placed three armed and cushioned chairs for the comfort of the most important guests. Johnnie, Earl of Murray, would be on the east side representing temporal power while the Abbot and the Bishop on the west stood for two distinct branches of church authority. As the first arrival, Abbot Richard was already ensconced in the seat near the middle, the more comfortable.

The populace settled like fluttering, rustling leaves, each individual nudging as near to the front as he could. The three ladies were escorted to the front row. There were a couple of female burghers too, Will noticed, who were allowed the same courtesy, although they drew the line at the country women who had to remain with their men folk near the back. By the vestry door at the side three seats against the long side wall faced inwards, one, the nearest to the altar, being reserved by Brother Mark. His face was very sour and not a little apprehensive. Next to him Father Symon bubbled with a mixture of grim anxiety but avid curiosity steamed out of him. Sandy Watson, the Town representative whose sharp attention was well seasoned with wry amusement, sat on the third stool.

Johnnie, meanwhile, was digesting Will's news in abstracted silence. 'I knew about the miller's laddie,' he muttered. 'And yes, there is a case for judging that one here where it happened - under the Prior's jurisdiction. If nothing else it would underscore his authority. But the other two are a different matter, Willie. They're baith kirk men. We canna remove them from the Bishop's hands, not unless I take them over myself and turn the enquiry into a state matter. I'm - not sure that's the right way to go.'

The Prior re-joined them in time to hear this. 'I agree, my Lord. If it does come to that, it will require a deeper investigation in another court. And I believe more evidence exists than has yet been found.' He deliberately did not look at Will, but he may have sensed the anxious lurch the young merchant's heart gave for he seemed to hold his breath for a moment. 'Would it be possible - legally, I mean - to deal with just the child's death today and to set the others aside?'

After a moment's thought Johnnie did look at Will, saw a further dilation in the strange eyes which made him pause even longer.

'Yes,' he said at last, then headed straight for his chair. Thomas nodded Will towards the empty seat Mark was guarding. It was exactly eight o'clock and still the Bishop had not come.

The Prior stood where a single shaft of sunlight struck the floor. In a pool of bright serenity Thomas waited for the restlessness to subside. A minute passed and still there was a fluttering akin to grumpy hens settling for the night, particularly among the townsfolk. Thomas cleared his throat. He waited on until the last of the wrigglers looked up to investigate the paralysing of the atmosphere around them, to find themselves fixed by the Prior's cool eye.

'My sons and daughters, let us pray.'

Whatever the visitors had expected, it was not that. Father Thomas was underlining that this was a House of God; and His holy services were not to be set aside, however pressing the business or however lofty the company. They had all chosen to come here and so they would take part in the normal Priory routine, whether they liked it or not.

The simple piety had a profound effect on Will that day, especially when the monks standing around the walls began to sing their hymn for Corpus Christi, wrapping the congregation in a cloak of musical blessing. Once again Brother James captivated them with the new canticle, rehearsed to perfection as far as Will could tell. Earl Johnnie was transfixed and the Abbot on the other side sat forward, leant his elbow on his knee to concentrate on the delivery of the lovely voice.

Corpus Christi. With a jolt, Will realised that today was the First of June. He should be crossing the German Sea by now to have a realistic chance of reaching Scania to serve on time on Father Jehan's team of Treaty writers. And what about Bethoc? He must ask his mother about that as soon as they had a moment together. Biting his tongue hard he forced his attention back to the worship.

The service lasted barely twenty minutes. When the Prior began the last prayer, invoking the guidance of the Lord in their deliberations, the Bishop still had not arrived but there was a new stir just outside the door. Was it Will's imagination, or did Thomas stretch the prayer out a bit? And had he chosen deliberately to stand in that solitary sunbeam?

Whatever the answers, there he stood, uttering the benediction, with his tonsured head and folded hands illuminated in the otherwise dim church, when the door clattered open to admit Alexander Barr, the Bishop of Murray. Such was the command Thomas had already established over his audience by then that less than a handful of the bowed heads dared to lift and look. The empty chair before them had been growing in significance as the service proceeded and by now many had begun to consider it an affront. The Bishop would have been the first to recognise that, of all people, the primary church dignitary of the See ought to have been present for the worship under way.

Giving no sign of noticing the disturbance, Thomas completed his blessing, giving the Bishop a bitter minute to observe the scene; trestles down the middle of the church with the documents exposed to public scrutiny; the green threads, - to signify the Bishop's own colour, he would have realised, - indicating those from the casket lodged in the Cathedral, which he had been unable to examine before their return. By peeping sideways with his head still bowed, Will saw the great man's lips tighten into a fierce pucker as the presence of the Earl and the Abbot registered, each with influence as great as his own.

Then the Prelate's eyes, the colour of summer thunderclouds, swivelled towards the three men facing inwards from the side, the only other break in the seating pattern, and to Brother Mark standing nearby. Something told him that neither Mark nor Father Symon met those angry eyes which finally met his own. Sandy Watson was keeping his head down and praying for all he was worth. For a long moment Will read puzzlement then alarm in the Bishop's gaze before it settled, at last, on the central figure in the church. It was then that the prelate realised his mission was defeated before it had begun.

Bishop Barr had chosen to attend in his finest canonical vestments, rich with red and purple trimmed with heavy gold needlework, his biggest mistake of all. Behind him Will could glimpse a number of followers, also tripped out to impress, although because of their calling most were stuck with the fanciest black they could lay hands on, although there was the flash of a white tabard with a red cross on it. The contrast between the Bishop and the Prior was stark. Still bathed in the pool of sunshine and clad in the simplest unbleached off-white of his undyed wool gown, Thomas raised his hands in a last prayer for support during the enquiry to come, then dropped them loosely by his side.

'My Lord Bishop.' Stepping forward out of the light Thomas moved from the role of church father to host. A single courteous gesture invited the Bishop to take his seat and a stir rustled through the gathering, transforming it from compliant congregation to intensely inquisitive audience.

Will rose to catch Thomas's attention. 'Father, may I suggest His Grace be given time to see at least the major documents before we begin?'

After a moment's thought Thomas nodded. The Bishop gave Will another puzzled frown before his brisk reply. 'I have seen them before, young man. I was in the team which drew up the last adjustment to the Pluscardyn charter and remember the details well.'

Thomas's eyes met Will's for an instant. Twenty five years was a long time to remember such details. A summary, via Mark, must have been useful.

'In that case, my Lord,' Thomas again gestured towards the empty chair, 'we shall begin straight away.'

The Bishop's mouth opened. He had had every intention of taking charge, if only to stamp his own authority on this renegade house once and for all.

'Do be seated, my Lord,' the Earl interpolated smoothly.

Leaving no time for the Bishop to demur, Thomas added, 'I have asked a litigation expert to examine all the documents so that we could make a report to you. I intend that we shall hear that first, after which we would value your opinion on it'.

Tension sent a bubble of hilarity bouncing up from Will's stomach. This mad comedy was becoming more extreme by the minute. Litigation expert, indeed! Bishop Barr narrowed his eyes at the very young man with the weird coiffure before him and closed his mouth again. After glancing briefly towards the Earl and the Abbot he accepted his fate.

Having summarised it once already (while drunk) then a second time compressed into two minutes for Johnnie, Will's third explanation of the evidence was simple and clear. Mindful that everybody was going to have to live with each other after the dust settled, he made every effort to include the checks and balances which history itself might have imposed on decisions made during the one hundred and forty years of the Priory's existence. No accusations were levelled at anybody, past or present. Having the documents before him from which he could quote proved particularly useful, especially when questions were invited. It was virtually a repeat of Monday's Chapter House meeting.

But he did add one detail. 'It has occurred to me that the infestations of the Plague must also have influenced the way people made decisions in 1345. The greatest visitation had already begun. In the East and then in Europe great swathes of people were being wiped out. Whole villages. Entire communities. Survivors were left weakened and prey to further illness, or to hoodlums and criminals out to take advantage of the weakness of others. Many would have been unable to complete the work they needed to do to survive. With so many people dying and so many repeated infestations to follow, the church communities must have been left as depleted and devastated as the rest of the populace, both here and in France.'

'When were you born, young man?' the Bishop demanded suddenly, unable to contain himself any longer.

'Forty seven, Your Grace.'

'So you may not know that the worst of Scotland's ills was four years *after* that new charter was drawn up.'

'The worst infestation yes, your Grace. But there had already been waves of the pestilence for nearly ten years by the time the Valliscaulian Prior-General's representative travelled to Murray in 1345, and it was much worse in the southern lands by then than in Scotland. Do we know if the mother house in Burgundy had been weakened? Here in the north the population was particularly well protected, tucked behind the mountains as they are. But they could not expect to escape forever. I believe it was against such an eventuality that the people drawing up this charter were preparing. This community is very small and it is not permitted to rise to more than twenty souls. If it should be struck, if it should lose so many members that it could not survive without outside help, then that would be the time for it to accept the shelter of the Bishopric, perhaps until such time as it could build up its numbers again.'

'I was present at many of the discussions,' the Bishop challenged. 'That was not the way of it.'

'Were you there for all of the discussions, your Grace?' Will spoke these words with delicacy.

Once more the Bishop opened his mouth, then closed it after a flicker of a glance towards Father Symon. 'Not all, no. But I can assure you that that document you are holding right now was drawn up as a fully accredited charter, not a mere draft.'

At these words from the Bishop Will allowed his eyes to widened. He turned to look at the Prior. Throughout Will's presentation Father Thomas had been standing to one side, nominally still in charge, and now both he and Will turned to look straight at Brother Mark. It was the Bishop who had made the first mention of the word draft. Mark grew white, then red, then white again.

Will waited to see if the Bishop would say more, but he too was discomfited.

'Possibly that was the intention, your Grace,' he continued after a tense pause, 'but the document has not been ratified by the people with the final authority. Those, surely, are the King himself, the Valiscaulian Prior-General in Burgundy and the Pope, whose predecessor affirmed that the house is in Papal care, not the bishop's. Um, it's here, in this document.' He walked along the trestles until he found the relevant scroll and quoted from it. Then he turned, holding up the 1345 draft again. 'Before this can be accepted as a charter, which would undoubtedly alter the current *status quo*, then these three signatories must confirm their approval. I am not an expert in Canonical Law but such a requirement is surely the common law of the land. The signature of the local Earl and Bishop would not be enough to counter the earlier decisions of both the King and the Pope.'

He swung round on his heel and raised an enquiring eyebrow to the current Earl, whose predecessor had signed the draft. Johnnie nodded.

'There is another condition to bear in mind. By its Rule, Pluscardyn may not increase its numbers beyond twenty souls. It is the same with its sister Valliscaulian houses in Scotland, at Beauly and Ardchattan, with which they are in regular contact. If, however, numbers were severely depleted in any one of the houses, it is feasible that the others could provide help, or perhaps amalgamation might be considered. This would undoubtedly be the first line the monks would take before committing themselves to outside control, - especially the control of a body which does not adhere in full to their own Rule.

'In other words, the three Valliscaulian houses belong together. They would cling closely to each other rather than allow a single house to be taken over from outside. The See of Murray may claim to oversee Pluscardyn since it is a stone's throw from its Dioscesan seat in Elgin. A claim over Beauly might just be feasible, since Beauly has in the past been within the boundaries of the Mormaership of Murray, although the Bishop of Ross might argue against that. But Ardchatten is in Argyle, a distant region most definitely within the See of another Bishop still.'

The Bishop was again on his feet, checking various documents in spite of his earlier avowed familiarity with them. Now he walked up to Will where he stood near where the Papal scroll lay. After a long scowl into Will's steady eyes, no doubt seeing the dilating which belied the calm facial expression he struggled to maintain, His Lordship held out a hand for the 1345 draft. This he unrolled and read from top to bottom, taking his time about it. Every eye in the church was on his scarlet figure. When a townsman dared to mutter something to his neighbour he found the Prior's gaze on him instantly and there were no further interruptions.

The Bishop's eyes reached the bottom of the script, flew back to the top and scanned swiftly down again, stopping a couple of times to allow for closer thought about a specific point, finally settling on the large number of signatures at the end. Will knew that all of them were of local people, all important and one or two probably still alive and present. If necessary, those could be called on to declare the intentions at the time of signing. Will glanced at Father Symon. He had a feeling that the Investigator might also have some undeclared knowledge. Had he too been involved in the clerking behind the scenes? Perhaps at the time he had also been regarded as a rising star, like Alexander Barr himself.

Then the Bishop astonished them all. 'Well, well then.' He rolled up the scroll and handed it back to Will, his expression clearing. 'That's it. You've made your case, young man.'

For a moment Father Thomas was caught off guard. After accepting defeat so swiftly, the Bishop plodded his way back to his chair, his face showing no emotion whatever. The Prior pulled himself together.

'Thank you, my Lord Bishop.' The audience held its breath. 'May I suggest a recess before the next stage of our proceedings.'

'Next stage?' The Bishop swung round in the act of lowering himself. 'I hope you are not presuming that a murder trial comes into your remit, Father Thomas!'

'No, my Lord. But I feel obliged to open an enquiry on the first of the murders. A child was killed on property owned by the Priory of Pluscardyn and current information suggests that somebody employed by us could be implicated - although I grant that this individual was once your miller. He exchanged with our man, which you know. This crime at least we ought to examine, preferably in public. I do not presume to hold a full trial here today, but is there not a case for making a note of all the information we have gathered concerning the crime? And for checking the relevant details as soon as possible after the crime while the details are still fresh in people's memories? - It is six days already since the child died. We do not want false rumours to take hold.'

When both the Earl and the Abbot agreed that this was highly desirable, the Bishop humphed, then nodded. Again he accepted defeat with the same apparent equanimity.

'Then,' Prior Thomas announced, glancing at the angle of the sun, 'we shall retire for twenty minutes in order to remove these documents to a place of safety. Brother Gregory?' He turned to the old man and murmured, 'And we shall need a scribe.' He called to the Sacristan. 'Brother Mark, the tables will have to be cleared before the bell for Sext recalls us.'

Out of the corner of his eye Will saw his mother rise to leave with the other ladies but before he could catch her the Bishop came striding towards him.

'Young man, a word.' In the cacophony which had shattered the earlier stillness during the investigation nobody would have heard the stricture that followed. 'I don't know who you are, but in Scotland the title Your Grace is reserved for the King alone.' Will flushed, to the other man's obvious satisfaction. The Bishop had not enjoyed being stuck on a pin a few minutes earlier - and Will should have known the correct title.

'I apologise... uh, my Lord.'

'But you did your work well enough.' A glint lit the Bishop's eye as he turned away, almost as if he had managed to step back from his own routing and was enjoying the spectacle of Will's embarrassment, if with dry self-deprecation. Will began to like the man, quite against his expectations.

'Mother?' Will finally reached Dolinda outside, grasping her arm to steer her aside out of the crowd streaming towards the paddock. There all kinds of fun were under way. Earlier the merrymakers had been creating so much noise that Prior Thomas was obliged to nod at Justin to close the door against it after the Bishop's entry. 'Come over to the Guest House.'

'You mustn't worry about your father, you know. There's no danger of an English invasion just now, - as far as I know.

Just minor raiding. With Robert Stewart and his sons free again, that pot of trouble is cooling too.

'Why on earth did the King imprison them in the first place?'

'Oh, personality conflicts more than anything, my dear.' She threw her hands in the air. 'Robert and David were never the best of friends. Robert can't ever forget that he was brought up as Bruce's heir for his first decade. The arrival of David must have been very unpleasant for him, a younger uncle who was a son to the king instead of just a grandson through his mother. I doubt if he has got over it even yet. Having to cede the rule twice to David after the freedom of Regency will not have helped at all. It takes very little for such an ambitious pot to boil over and I'm very surprised it hasn't done so more often than it has.'

'So what's worrying you? What's Father up to?'

'He - is looking for a husband for Elizabeth.'

'Elizabeth!' She was the oldest of his five sisters. Five years younger than Will she was by far the most gentle and vulnerable of them all. 'But what about Sanders?' Sanders Findlatter, son of a local neighbour, was his father's right hand man at Druminnor and romance had bloomed between him and Elizabeth.

'Sanders is a very good steward.' His mother gave a twisted smile. 'And of a good enough family. But, my dear, that is not enough under the current circumstances.'

Will began to flush. 'You mean he has no money, and Father needs hard cash to pay his ransom taxes. But why sacrifice Elizabeth of all people? I thought she was his favourite? He knows she's a home girl. And he knows how shy she is and that he has lost her heart to Sanders. At least Sanders would keep her near home. The man would strip himself bare to protect her. Isn't that enough?'

‘Stop ranting, dear.’ His mother looked miserable, her pleasant face carrying new lines around her bleak, black eyes. Normally she presented a serene aspect to the world.

'And why do it this way?' Will badgered on. 'Hasn't he been over to see Francis Gordon? When Bethoc marries me she'll come with a good dowry. There's no way the Bromse House can complain if *that* goes to Father for his ransom tax, is there? Even if I can't give him the money directly from me. - He hasn't been to see Francis! Is that it?'

'Oh yes, he has. He's been over there three times.'

'Well, then. - You mean he's been turned down?' Alarm flared in Will's eyes.

'N-no. Not exactly. Just - deferred.'

'What does that mean?'

'Francis thinks Bethoc is still too young.'

'But - she's nineteen. A year older than Elizabeth.'

'Don't forget how close Francis and Bethoc are. The rump of a large family left over after the Black Death struck them. Francis knows Bethoc will have to marry one day. Perhaps he just needs to time to get used to the fact.'

'What does Bethoc say about that?' Will growled.

'Don't you know?' His mother's voice sharpened.

'Me? Why should I?'

'Haven't you spoken to her? Didn't she know that you were planning to offer your suit?'

'Of course she did! It's what we've always planned, ever since we were bairns. You know that.'

'A childhood fancy is one thing, *Villi*. An adult commitment properly planned is quite another. - Have you spoken openly to her about this marriage you propose, or have you just been making assumptions? She may be waiting for a positive clue from you about your true feelings before committing herself.'

'Good grief! Isn't an offer of marriage an indication?'

'If you haven't said anything, she may fear that your father is the one desiring this union, not you. So might Francis Gordon - and he has a high regard for what happens to his wealth.'

'Och, mother! Of course she knows!'

'So you're sure of that? You've spoken plainly to her, discussed it with her?' Seeing his mouth opening and closing like a fish, Dolinda began shaking her head. 'Then you'd better go and see her. As soon as you can. You must make your intentions plain, my son.'

And there it was, here it was, the first of June, and he was already going to be late for the Scania Peace Talks. 'Och, mother! Father Jehan's going to roast me alive.' At that moment the bell for Sext began to toll.

'Mm, he might. Isn't that a gowk?' Dolinda's unsympathetic head turned towards the Heldon Hill. 'I heard him several times on the way here. I think he's jeering at you, *Villi*.'

Will wanted to wring the bird's neck. Every rocking call it made caused him to wonder just how much of a gowk he had made of himself by becoming embroiled in all these affairs at Pluscardyn. Stupid, careless fool that he was.

'There isn't anybody else who has touched your heart is there, *Villi*?'

The question hit like a hammer blow to his belly. Fortunately he had already turned away, leaving his mother to follow him back to the church. He gave no answer, hoping she would think that he had not heard.

Nevertheless, his mother's mild words burned into him all through Sext, which the Prior again insisted on holding although he shortened the service. Had Maura touched his heart? She had been so appealing, so frantic, so eager in her persuasiveness that his resistance had melted into the morning air. He had begun by feeling deeply sorry for her, locked into a miserable predicament which was none of her making.

Certainly he pitied her. Ever since that terrible, glorious hour on the bank of the hidden stream his mind had been in a tangle. It was not the lovemaking itself which had delayed him. Such was their mutual eagerness, their shared energetic ecstasy that it was over within minutes. Nor was it the adultery which had driven him to Brother Alexander for confession. It was what followed.

Lady Amelia had been wrong. Yes, Maura had looked for a husband substitute; she had planned; even tempted; but she confessed that Will was the first man to whom she had succumbed outside marriage, and she hated herself for having done so. Will was horrified, although at no point did she lay any blame on him. That did not seem to occur to her.

But he himself did. For the imbibing to begin with, for the seducing, however well tempted, but most of all for riding away and leaving her still wracked in shuddering desolation after nearly an hour of fruitless comforting. In the end she had screamed at him, near demented, to go, to leave her alone.

Yes, certainly he had pitied her, but what value had pity in such a situation? Its influence had been fractional compared with the overwhelming urges which had soon carried them far beyond pity, impelling the pair of them to complete their atavistic, inevitable coupling, driving them into a frenzy beyond all control. Impulses from the beginning of time had surged within them, driving with the urgency of life towards the procreation it craved. She had been just as shaken as he by the tumult of emotions which engulfed them, just as overcome by the resulting completion. But, no. He could not exactly claim that it was his heart which had been involved.

Ever since, at the back of his mind he had been searching for an explanation for the desperation in the girl, the reckless abandon bordering on utter despair. One possible scenario linked it with the flash of Robert de Chisholm's name which had caught his eye in the Prior's letter to the Holy Father. It had been right at the bottom, in a single separate paragraph on its own. Had it been a request by Robert to have his childless marriage annulled? If the King could set aside his wife and file for a Papal divorce for that very reason, why not Robert?

How easily Will had succumbed to Maura - and to be honest, how enthusiastically they had operated once they had got going. Now Will at last had to wonder at his lack of constancy to Bethoc. And no, he had not been exactly specific about his marriage intentions when talking to Bethoc herself. They had just assumed, dreamed when they were apart and revelled and teased when together, just as they had always done in the innocence of childhood. But then she, too, had been reticent about expressing her private feelings, while showing her lifelong warmth and pleasure in his company which seemed as strong as ever. Yes, the pair of them had indeed just assumed a closer union at some unspecified time in the future. He was sure of it still. But maybe he ought to risk Father Jehan's fury and go and see her.

'...that this young Maister Forbys will act as your legal expert again?' Startled, he pulled himself out of his reveries to hear the Bishop's dry query. The service was over, today without the usual Mass, and the eyes of the gathering were on him once more. During the interval the Bishop had discovered Will's identity, perhaps having seen him with his mother whom he had met at least once at court.

'Yes, uh, your Honour.' Once more Father Thomas was standing in the sunbeam which the progressing hour had shifted well to the left, obliging the Prior to move a couple of yards to one side. Soon the ray would disappear altogether. How would Thomas react to that?

'Just about the boy, mind,' the Bishop hedged as Will stood up, wondering how best to tackle the questioning. 'The murder of two important churchmen must be examined by my Canonical Court.'

'I fully understand that, my Lord Bishop,' Will murmured. 'But on the surface their deaths do seem to be connected with Nicol's murder and the evidence connecting them may be pertinent. May I suggest that the scribe should take notes on all the information which we turn up, whether or not it concerns Nicol alone? We can then make a copy for your own records?'

The scribe, sitting at a little desk opposite the vestry, was Brother Stephen, the Cantor, an excellent choice. The Prior had taken care that Mark was much too busy for the job.

The Bishop gave Stephen a brisk nod and sat down. A chair had been removed because the Abbot, who considered his task completed, had gone home. The remaining chair had somehow been shuffled so that Bishop Barr was now sitting almost exactly in the centre of the church in a dominant position. Still seated on the right, Johnnie gave Will the faintest fluttering of a wink at the churchman's manoeuvring.

When Will reached the front of the gathering again, he realised that its composition had changed slightly. Lady Euphemia was absent from the front row and the seating was now in a solid block following the removal of the tables and the closing up of the central aisle. Some way back sat Robert de Chisholm and his lady, both looking pale and tense. Farther back still he saw Camus and one of his Highlanders, reminding Will of a glimpse of the other MacIntosh among his mother's small retinue; she must have met him on his search for Francie.

So both Highlanders were now back and no doubt they had passed on their information to Camus. Now, where had Camus been during the earlier enquiry? Not in the church, he felt sure. Camus now half stood, as if to readjust his sitting position but in reality to bring Will's eye on him for a quick backward lift of his head. Will dropped his chin to indicate he had noticed and turned to begin.

Even before he opened his mouth it dawned on him - at last - why so many had turned up, and there were many more ordinary folk now than there had been during the earlier session. It certainly was not to see the Prior triumph over the Bishop. An instant of revulsion made him wish to turn them all out, but then he realised that macabre curiosity was as innate in him as it would be in these people. Of course they, like he, wanted to hear what had happened to the little boy they thought of as a Devil's Child. Ghoulish as it may seem, he too wanted to find an explanation for the deaths which had followed. He too wanted answers. He felt the same inquisitiveness they were exhibiting to see inside the twisted relationships which might have caused the tragedies. He wanted to paw over the sleazy secrets, expose the dirty linen.

'My lords,' he bowed to the Bishop and the Earl, 'ladies and gentlemen. Last Wednesday morning a child died in the yard at the Pluscardyn Priory meal mill which stands on the south bank of the Lochty or Black Burn. Many of you know the child, a baby who grew in body for more than eight years but not in mind. I myself saw the child shortly before ten and he was alive and well then. At that time others were in the yard. They were the older child, Francie, who is ten years old, the miller who is their grandfather, and Brother Michael who is the kiln-master at the glassworks next door. That adjoins the mill on the landward side of the stream.'

He went on to describe what had brought him and Michael into the mill-yard, choosing the most banal words he could find to counter the stench of prurience coming from the audience. Then he went on to tell how he had come to hear from Hugo de May that Nicol had been found in the River Lossie, how his own name had been linked with the death and how he had decided to return to find out precisely what was going on, knowing full well that he had no involvement and wishing to clear his name. Since this was a public forum, he confirmed, there and then, the evidence which he could offer to do so and nobody made any move to challenge his innocence.

'By the time I left Balvenie early on Friday morning there was already a strong suspicion that the Bishop's messenger had met with trouble.' He explained why. 'I can now confirm that Hugo de May's body has been found in a bog adjoining the peat moss near Mortlach.'

He had to stop for a couple of minutes until the buzz of alarm and thrill died down.

'That news came in on Monday, but on Sunday afternoon a novice from Mortlach arrived to tell us that Father Ranulf had also been killed.' Another susurration held him up. 'In all three cases, death seems to have been caused by the inserting of a long thin blade being slid into the body from behind straight into the heart. That, I understand, would have been a very swift and perhaps painless way of... Father Thomas, where is Brother Infirmarian?' It dawned on him that he had not seen the frail old man since Sunday afternoon.

'In the infirmary. I'm afraid he has had an attack of the breathless ague to which he is prone. This one has been very severe.'

'Does that mean that he cannot give evidence?'

'Yes. He is too ill to be moved. If possible I think he should not be disturbed even in his bed.'

In the pause as Will worried towards a solution to several problems this caused, Father Symon rose to ease one of them. 'Father Thomas, I saw Nicol's body on Saturday. I can confirm what Captain Forbys says - although there had been shrinkage of the wounds since the Wednesday. But if that single stab was the cause I would agree that it might have been as swift a death as the captain believes.'

Sandy Watson also stood up as the Investigator sat down again. 'I saw it too. But there were other wounds on the bairn, all down his chest and front. It was too long after the killing for us to tell the real cause of death, but we can both attest that the Infirmarian believed it was the stab wound that did the killing, and he would have seen Nicol within an hour or so of coming out of the water. The rest of the slashing was done a whilie aifter.'

'But before he was thrown into the water surely?' the Bishop demanded.

'Must have been.' Sandy stood his ground. 'Why would anybody want to slash a body after stabbing it and drowning it? Anyway the man who pulled it out said the wounds were already there and all washed clean.'

'So when was it pulled out?' This was the Bishop again, forgetting that he was usurping Will's position until Sandy cast a questioning look at the young merchant. Will let the pause linger before nodding.

'A couple of hours after noon,' Sandy continued. 'Maybe a little more. It hadna been in the water that long, so the Infirmarian thought.'

'I confirm all of that.' Father Symon's voice was distinct, although he did not raise his eyes from his fists clasped on his knees.

'So...' The Bishop tried to interrupt again. This time the Earl cleared his throat loudly. It was enough.

'So,' Will resumed, 'the killing probably took place between ten and noon.' He swallowed hard. From the start he had wished to avoid including Francie in the enquiry, but as he progressed he was becoming less and less sure that he would succeed in this. 'It looks as if more than one person could be involved. It also looks as if this is more than just a frenzied attack made by the grandfather. Yes, the child was growing impossible to care for while the miller tried to make a living for himself and his family. Yes, the folk around him gave him little or no support in his struggle, regarding Nicol as a child of the Devil, no matter how much they were told by the men of the church that every child is a child of God. But there was no blade in the mill, or in the kiln-yard next door for that matter, which matched the first wound made on Nicol's body.

'On the other hand, there are many blades elsewhere within the Priory, and several in the blacksmith's smithy across the bridge, which might have fitted. But if the same blade was used to kill Hugo and Ranulf de May, then the killer would have had to take the blade with him after Nicol was killed. We shall not know if the wounds match until somebody who saw Nicol's can examine the other bodies.'

The Bishop interrupted him again, but this time to add information. 'Both bodies should be on their way to the Cathedral right now, Captain.'

'Thank you, my Lord. The blade may also have been the possession of the killer because whoever managed to kill three people in an identical and highly efficient fashion must be skilled at using it and have an excellent knowledge of how to kill a human being in this way. To my mind, that does suggest a soldier.' Everybody waited. 'I - have been told that Hector, the miller, was a soldier before he turned to milling after his marriage.'

'I can confirm that.' It should not have surprised Will that this came from Brother Gregory. 'A fine soldier too. But it is many years since I have seen him with a weapon in his hand. You lose such a skill very quickly if you don't practise it.'

Will nodded, thinking about his bout with Robert. Had he justification for the fear it had engendered in him? In hindsight he thought not. The terror came from the knowledge that he himself was woefully out of practice.

'A number of people saw Nicol's body on Saturday. I presume several if not all of the monks resident at Pluscardyn would have seen it when it was first brought into the church on the previous Wednesday. Again Brother Infirmarian said that he considered that none of the other wounds on the body would have killed the child. To me they did indeed seem like the slashing of despair, and we believe that we have identified the instrument which inflicted those. In the kiln next door there are many tools of different shapes and sizes and there were three trowels which had found their way into the mill-yard. One of these was found encrusted with blood and lying just inside the door. If he is willing, I wish to ask some questions of the man who found it.'

Chapter 21 – Michael's evidence

Michael de May was standing beside Brother Gregory. It was with some anxiety that Will approached him and asked quietly, 'Can you? Will you? I'm sorry I was not able to warn you that I might need your evidence.' Waxen-faced, Michael trudged after Will to the middle of the transept.

'The meal mill which serves this locality lies outside the Priory wall about two hundred yards northeast of the main gate on the other side of the fishpond, and the glass kiln is next to it. Brother Michael, you are the kiln-master. You were also the first person to discover that something terrible had happened there last Wednesday. I understand that you had returned to the Priory for the noon meal which is followed by a short service.' Michael nodded. 'You then returned to the kiln-yard around one?'

The monk nodded again, then qualified it in a voice which cracked at his first effort to speak. 'Some little time after one.'

Will took a deep breath and turned to the main audience. 'May I ask you to be understanding, ladies and gentlemen. This is very hard for Brother Michael because he is the younger brother of both Hugo and Ranulf de May, both of whom we now know have died in the last few days. Both have been murdered, apparently using the same method by which Nicol was killed, and it is just possible that he too is under threat, although as time passes I believe that is becoming less likely. He is also the uncle of the older child at the mill, the girl, Francie.'

He could see that he was telling most of the local people something they knew already. As he caught Lady Amelia's eye she nodded firmly. 'I have been told that Father Ranulf is, uh, was Francie's father. He had requested a dispensation from his vows in order to marry her mother but was refused permission by the Pope.'

'That's privileged information!' Bishop Barr leapt to his feet. Will whirled round to see fury and alarm in his face.

'Why, your Grace? Many people are aware of it. As aware that the King is appealing for an annulment to his current marriage, for instance. Marriage is required to be a public declaration by both canonical and state law, so why not a refusal of such a dispensation which would govern whether a marriage might go ahead. It can do Father Ranulf no harm now, and it might be of considerable value to his child to know that he wished to have his love of her mother acknowledged.'

'But did he?'

'He must have, if he went to the trouble of begging the Pope for permission to release him from his vows in order to marry her. I - saw him with his daughter and believe he loved her dearly.'

'You are making assumptions about the marriage dispensation.' The Bishop began to grit his teeth.

'Perhaps you can tell us what happened, your Grace?' Many of the observers must have shared Lady Amelia's suspicion that the Scottish Court of Bishops had indeed pulled rank over Alexander Barr, and Ranulf as his man suffered. The timing must have coincided with the early stages of his placement in the See of Murray. Had Barr irritated his new colleagues by being a little too bumptious, a bright cleric assuming seniority too soon? Had they taken him down a peg by grasping at the opportunity which came to hand?

'It is hardly relevant to this enquiry. Please proceed.' The Bishop was telling them nothing, yet everything they needed.

'My Lord,' Will said slowly, 'Father Ranulf's status as Francie's father may well explain why he died. It is known that Hector, the miller, blamed him for his daughter's downfall and was wildly hurt and angry about it. I suppose that ultimately, if indirectly, Ranulf was also the cause of her death the year before last. If Hector was uncertain about Francie's paternity, that might also explain the death of another possible candidate, his brother Hugo. The only other possible father, I believe.'

'I think it is much more likely that my courier was killed for the contents of his bag.' The Bishop was cooling down again, and he uttered this alternative deliberately while holding Will's eye. 'I hear it has not been trawled from the bog yet. Are they still searching?'

'I don't think so. Was he carrying anything of value, my Lord?'

'Not unless you gave him something.' Still their eyes held.

'I gave him nothing,' Will declared. 'I suppose he might have been killed in error by somebody intending to rob me. Perhaps of the book your Librarian sent with me for delivery to Father Ranulf. Any book is worth a fortune. As is my father's horse. It was after midnight and a filthy night for anybody to be travelling, easy enough to mistake one man for another.'

'So why were you out in it?' This sounded sour, although the Bishop was seating himself again.

'I wasn't,' Will pointed out, irritated by the interruption. 'I stopped at Balvenie before the storm returned.' He returned to the inquiry. 'Brother Michael? Can you tell me what you saw in the mill yard?'

'Two pools of blood.'

'Where were they?'

'One was just outside the door to the mill itself, a little to the left. The other was several strides nearer the gate, by the wall which protects the millrace. It was built to stop Nicol from falling under the wheel.'

'How big were these pools? What were they like?'

Michael shuddered, then frowned as he tried to force himself into unwanted remembrance. 'The one by the wall was smooth, untrampled. Shaped like... oh, like a bitten moon. The bitten part was slightly smudged. It - looked as if Nicol's body might have been lying against the pool. It was as if the blood had poured out of his back and his curled up body stopped it from making the full round shape.' He was using his hands as he spoke and the picture drawn by them was vivid and painful. The monk was trembling by now and his eyes began to fill with tears.

'The smudges? How plain were those?' Will probed very cautiously.

'They were slight. Very slight, I would say. As if the blood had almost dried before Nicol was pulled away.'

'And the other pool? The one by the door?'

'It was a, a mess, not a pool at all really. There were spatters on the wall and the stuff on the ground was trampled and streaked and splodged, then walked all over the place.'

'Walked? There were footmarks in the blood?'

'Oh yes. Lots of them. They'd picked up the blood and walked it all over the yard and out... It was like... a charnel house. A butchery without any carcasses.' The monk shuddered once more, weeping in earnest now. Tears ran down his pale face for all to see. Will went to him and suggested in a low voice that they stop the proceedings, but Michael shook his head fiercely then wiped his face clean with the sleeve of his habit. After a few moments he recovered, looking up at Will with a touch of defiance, challenging him to continue.

'Was there anybody else about?'

'Nobody at all.'

'What about the two workmen next door?'

'There was a batch of glass just coming up to its change of colour. They couldn't leave it. I - think they were unaware of what had happened at the mill.'

'Have you any idea where the miller was?'

'No. Hector hasn't been seen since.'

'And Francie?'

'I - saw no sign of her. She might have been at the Priory. She often goes up in the mornings to ask for a gardening job which might bring in some food to the family. She hates asking for alms as if they were destitute. Sometimes they are, of course, because the customers take all the advantage they can of their misfortune.'

This was the second reference to the prejudice which had led to the family's persecution, and this time it hit home harder. Discomfort flitting across many more faces.

'I saw her in the garden earlier,' Will confirmed, 'but she had gone back home before I left. Might she have returned to the Priory after the trouble I interrupted?'

Michael thought about that, frowning unhappily. 'I wouldn't have thought so. When her grandfather got into such a state she usually hung around to look out for Nicol. It could take Hector an hour or two to recover.'

'Is it possible that she might have seen what happened?' The two young men looked at each other, equally troubled.

'Didn't she say anything to you?' Michael blurted out, then realised that was exactly what Will did not want him to say.

Will sighed, then explained about Francie's flight, which did not appear to be common knowledge, adding, 'As yet she has said nothing about Nicol to me. Nor, I believe, has she talked to my mother, to whom she went from Mortlach. But she does know about Nicol's death. She did even then, for she was in a state of shock.'

'Does she know about her father's death?' This quiet question came from Johnnie behind him.

Will noticed his mother shake an uncertain head. 'I don't think so, my Lord. I would prefer to keep it that way for the moment.'

What Will was praying for was that nobody would speculate aloud that she had run away from either place, or both, because of what she had seen occurring. If she were found to be a witness to murder it could put her in danger of being silenced forever, whether or not the killer was present. The gossip machine would ensure that every detail of this morning's business would flash across the province like wildfire, no doubt with inaccuracies multiplying like worms in a rotten cheese. The same fear governed his silence about the Baltic glassmakers. Lek and Hus were especially vulnerable, for there was nobody within the community to defend them. Brother Daniel, their only ally, could neither speak nor write on their behalf. At least Francie had a large cadre of friends and, in theory at least, a powerful family behind her.

Will decided this was a good time to get rid of another matter.

'Brother Michael, did you see anybody at all at the mill?'

Michael's mouth opened in surprise, then he flushed and the monks around the walls seemed to stiffen. 'Yes.' Out of the corner of his eye, Will saw Robert de Chisholm's head rise slightly and move forward. 'I - I'm not sure who it was.'

'Who do you think it was?'

'Speculation is not evidence,' the Bishop growled at his back.

The Earl countermanded the objection. 'Let's hear it. We can judge it better spoken than silent and we can throw it out if need be.'

'I - I think I was wrong now.' Will waited for more and Michael admitted, 'I thought it was you,' then rushed on in agitation. 'But I know now it couldn't have been.'

At this point Camus stood up. When given a nod he explained what his Highlander had been doing and confirmed Will's movements on Wednesday, listing the various folk on the way to Balvenie who had dealings with him. With a raised hand Will stopped him short about his return to Pluscardyn later in the week. As it happened, Sandy Watson had also taken the trouble to check up with George Leslie and the Dallas publican and said so. Their combined evidence left Will clear of all charges relating to Nicol.

'What exactly led you to think I was the man you saw?' Michael looked very uncomfortable. 'Was the man tall? Did he have my colouring? How long did you have him in view? What did he do in that time?'

'Yes.' There was a long, puzzled pause after that and everybody watched Michael's eyes bulge in a strange stare. 'Tall,' he agreed eventually. 'Light of hair maybe.'

'You are sure it wasn't Hector?'

That broke the spell. 'Oh, no! This man was young and upright. Not at all like Hector. Oh, he was tall once but now he is bent and, well, in his fifties. Very old. Besides he's bald headed.'

'Captain, can I take him through the next bit?' This surprise came from Sandy Watson, who went on to describe the experiments he had done with Michael on the previous Saturday. 'So ye see, two hunner yards is a fair distance when ye've just a few seconds of a sighting, especially when it's atween trees as this was. It would have been easy to mak a mistake.'

It transpired that the man Michael had seen had been behind a wall, or perhaps behind two depending on which yard he was in. Since the mill and the kiln each had a substantial wall surrounding them for safety reasons, and each wall was approximately a yard and a half tall, all Michael could say for sure was that what he saw was a man's top quarter, from mid chest up, which would have made him around six feet tall. And he could have been standing in either the kiln-yard or the mill-yard. It was impossible to tell which from the Priory gate.

Will nodded as Sandy let his audience think it through. Then he asked several men to stand up, all of them more or less his own size, and all of them relatively fair in colouring. Camus was one. Robert de Chisholm was another. Michael shook his head at every one of them.

'What about your brother Hugo? He would fit the general description.'

Michael's shock sent a hiss of whispers round the church which Father Thomas had no hope of quelling. Will's throat tightened as he realised what had happened and he drove further. 'He would have been in Pluscardyn around the time we are speaking of. He told me that himself, and that somebody had told him when I had left. Wasn't it you? It would be natural for him to go looking for you at the kiln. If you weren't there, he might have tried at the mill where your other brother's daughter lived.' Somehow Will kept his resentment in check. 'Who would have been a more natural person for him to be looking for than you, Brother Michael?'

'It wasn't him! He would never have harmed a child,' the monk gabbled. 'And it wasn't...'

'Wasn't who?'

Michael swallowed till he came near to choking in his terror at revealing too much. 'It... wasn't what you thought. It must have been Hector. You saw the state he was in that morning. You've already told us what he was like.'

'Na, na,' the Elgin Sheriff broke in again. 'I see it now. It was your ain brother ye saw, only ye didna want to. And when one or the ither o' ye found the blood, ye thought the finger would point at Hugo so ye cooked it up between ye that Captain Forbys could carry the blame, since he wasna likely to be coming back. Or... Maybe it *was* Hugo did the killing, maybe to free the other bairn from a life's burden. Aye, surely that's it. Otherwise it seems daft that Hugo should warn the Captain to stay away, or it does till ye see the reason.'

'No! It wasn't like that!'

'But it was Hugo ye saw?'

Michael swallowed again before nodding, looking very shame faced. In spite of his perfidy Will felt sorry for him.

'We didn't know whose blood it was then. It - could have been Francie's. It could even have been Hector's. All we knew was that there was a kiln trowel plastered with sticky blood lying by the doorway.' His voice was dropping in pitch and fading as he turned towards Will. 'I didn't intend you harm, Captain Forbys. Truly I didn't. It was just that I couldn't think of another way to protect... Hugo.'

Poor Michael. He was smaller, weaker and plainer than either of his brothers, and nothing like as bright. And he was a sorry liar to boot. The whole gathering had realised by now that it was not Hugo that Michael was protecting. Will decided that this nettle needed grasping.

'Let's get this straight, Brother Michael. Whatever Francie's involvement is, she certainly isn't the killer. She would have neither the strength nor the knowledge to strike killing blows on grown men, for it is looking likely that whoever killed Nicol also killed both Hugo and Ranulf. Besides, she was right beside me at the time when Hugo was killed and there were thirty odd soldiers all around us to vouch for that.'

From behind him snaked, 'That's assuming the same person killed all three, Master Enquirer. There is still a case to be made for that.' The Bishop was reminding him that he was following every twist in the argument. 'I suspect you wish to keep the child, Francie, out of this but I doubt if that is possible.' The rich voice was reasonable, even tinged with sympathy. 'If she has information to give, then we do need to persuade it out of her.'

Will pivoted round on one heel, gazing at the Bishop's calm face. There was no guile in it that he could see, just concern. In the end he sighed. 'Yes, your Grace. Er, my Lord. Mother, can you fetch her, please?'

Dolinda Forbys rose, her eyes as black as coals just like her son's. As the door opened a distant whoop snaked in, followed by a chorus of laughter. Brother Alexander glanced at the large hourglass by the vestry door then limped out after the Lady of Forbys. It was time to distribute the portions of food to the poor. But with Brother Mark rooted to the floor there would be no summoning bell today.

Chapter 22 – Francie's view

The Lady Euphemia must have been waiting nearby with Francie because Dolinda returned almost immediately, escorting them into the gloom. Will marvelled that the silence the audience was maintaining. The uneasy stillness of the church was barely ruffled by the brush of breathing and minor movement. In deference to Father Thomas's wishes, nobody bothered now to mutter even a speculation. Everybody seemed anxious to emulate the quietude of the men of the convent who had stood round the walls throughout the morning with barely a fidget.

Even Brother Gregory, the oldest monk present, did no more than sway now and then as he allowed his weight to settle first on one foot then the other. It was young David from Mortlach who found it a trial, his tiny wriggles fetching an occasional sympathetic glance from the Prior. He himself had stood as if carved from marble from the neck down, his hands hidden deep in the folds of his scapular, but with face alert and dark eyes on whoever was speaking. The Bishop was another matter, judging from the continual rustlings coming from behind Will.

Dolinda closed the door behind her. By clipping off the merry rumpus outside, the repose within was emphasised. Yet there must have been more folk inside than out.

Francie's eyes flew to Will's seeking reassurance. Overawed by the crowd she faltered, then swallowed and straightened her back. Responding to the touch of Euphemia's fingers on her shoulder she stepped forward and again Will was reminded of a little soldier as she marched down the church aisle towards him, head held high.

Something in the air suggested less than total support for the child. Was it the taint of the Devil's Bairn? Or the suicide mother? Could Hector's Celtic roots explain it? Or his apparent guilt of the crimes being discussed? Or did the watchers suspect Francie was guilty? She was the obvious candidate for one part of the tragedy, as even the least informed of them might realise. The ink black hair and its tideline did not help any.

'Don't be afraid,' Will murmured to her when she reached the transept. Even the low tone he used would have reached the nearer listeners, so quiet was the church. 'Just answer my questions. That's all.' It was the only warning he could give her. She held his gaze while Euphemia was seated, a place hastily being made available for her Ladyship. As the Steward's wife she was, after all, the second lady of the land, perhaps more elevated still, given the divorced status of the Queen herself.

'Now, Francie, have you spoken to anybody about last Wednesday?'

She shook her head, her face bloodless under the weird, black spikes.

'But you know Nicol is dead, don't you?' She nodded. 'And that your grandfather has disappeared?' She nodded again. Will did not want to give her complete freedom to describe what she knew, fearing that something she had seen would be admitted, putting her in danger from the murderer. But how could he control what she said while eliciting the information they needed?

'Shall we start at the beginning? You and I met earlier that morning in the Priory Garden when you were weeding.' She flushed, remembering what he had been doing. 'Then half an hour later we - met again at the mill. I have already told them what happened then. Now, when I left, did you go back up to the Priory to finish your job or did you stay to look after Nicol?'

'I stayed for a wee whilie.' She went on frankly, 'You see, Grandfather can be gie slow to calm down after - being upset. But then Nicol curled up and went to sleep.'

Will frowned. 'Where?'

'At the bottom o' the wall where it was warm and sunny. He usually sleeps a long while after he's been frightened, so...' A look of anguish crumpled her face. 'I shouldna have left him...'

'But you did? You went back to finish the gardening job?' She nodded. Will paused to think. 'Can you remember any of the service bells ringing while you were busy?'

'Aye. I'd still a bit to do when the Sext bell went.'

'So noon?'

'The bell rang as I left and... Then I went across the paddock to pat the pony.' She shot a guilty glance at Father Thomas but did not apologise for anything, the patting or the subsequent purloining. In any case the noon bell cleared her. It was likely that Nicol was already dead by then. If Michael's description of the undisturbed pool of blood was correct, of blood having dried before Nicol had been moved, it tended to confirm Brother Infirmarian's first impression that some time had elapsed between the first, killing blow and the slashing of the little body.

Will decided to take a risk.

'How long did you stay with the pony?'

She shrugged. 'Ten minutes. Maybe more.'

'Then what?' He breathed in, hoping he had not made a wrong assumption.

'I - got to the road beside the big oak tree.' Again she threw a look at the Prior, this time a mixture of shame and defiance. He gave no inkling of his reactions as he watched her. 'There's a wee hole in the hedge that I get through but...'

Her eyes fixed once more on Will's and grew wider and she swallowed hard, then swallowed again. She was approaching the abyss she had no wish to face, but which might have the greatest relevance of all to their enquiry.

'But?' Will spoke very gently.

'I - dinna want to tell!' Her voice rang shrill, and a spasm of excitement rippled through the audience. When the scrape of a chair came from behind, Will whirled round, his eyes furious in their challenge. The Bishop immediately leaned back again, his eyes narrowing, but his mouth remained shut. Will turned back to Francie and waited to see if she would continue without prompting. She stared at him for a long, long time. At one point tears came, but went unshed.

'You got to the oak tree,' Will murmured, 'and pushed through the hole in...'

'No, I didna.' Almost without realising, she had begun again. 'I stopped because I heard a funny noise. It was... a queer kind of grunting.' She stopped once more.

'So what did you do? Look through the hole? Stay behind the tree, or the hedge, till you could work out what was happening?' She nodded, but was still stuck.

'What was the noise?' She shook her head, unable to speak. 'What was making it? Or who?' Still she shook, her whole body now joining in the trembling. Hating himself, Will pressed on, as gently as he knew how. 'Was it Nicol?'

'No, no!' Again he had surprised her into words. 'It was...'

This time the tears did spill, just a couple which trickled down the pale face. After a moment's pathetic wiping she whispered, 'It was my grandfather. D'ye think he's dead an' all now?'

Will's hand went to his beard for comfort, found it shorn, then compromised by covering his mouth for a moment. It hid the quivering. 'I - think he probably is, Francie. I'm - sorry.'

However inadequate, the words seemed to release some of her tension and the tears dried up. 'Then,' she took a deep breath and everything burst out of her. 'It was Grandfather who killed Nicol. I saw him. He - was kneeling beside Nicol and slashing at him and - and crying. Every time he...' She raised her hand and imitated very plainly what she had witnessed, slashing through the air and grunting as each imaginary blow landed. 'Dozens of times,' she wept, 'dozens and dozens.' Now she was sobbing beyond control. It was Dolinda who came and held her, patting and rocking the child during the minutes of grief; perhaps relief from terror also came. As she began to recover, Dolinda wiped the pathetic face with the tail of her wimple.

Justin slipped out after a signal from Gregory and returned with a pitcher of water. Dolinda let her drink until the after-sobs began to settle then washed her face with what was left. And all the time the watchers watched and the listeners thought.

After midday, she had said. And slashing. But everybody else knew by now that it was not the slashing which had killed Nicol. He had been dead for a good many minutes by then, a quarter of an hour before the slashing, possibly more, according to Brother Infirmarian's estimate on first seeing the body. That viewing was only a few hours after death, after all, and the wounds would have been fresh, if washed clean by river water.

Hector, as a former soldier, must have known the boy was dead, so why this vicious, despairing attack? Could it be that he feared Francie had killed her brother? That she had reached the end of her tether, as he himself had so often come near to doing, and was he trying to take what he believed to be her guilt upon himself?

But it could not have been Francie either, unless she was a consummate liar and actress. Her story rang true - and perhaps it could be corroborated.

'Go back to the noon bell, Francie.' Will restarted his questioning only after he felt she had recovered sufficiently. 'Did you see the beggars gathering?'

She nodded, a little puzzled, then came out with something surprising. 'It was Brother Infirmarian that day. It's usually Brother Gregory or Brother Alexander.'

Startled, Will darted an enquiring frown at the Prior whose eyebrows rose. Then Justin exclaimed, 'That's right! And I was helping him that day. - And now I remember seeing Francie leaving the garden as we began dishing up.'

Gratified by hearing far more than he had expected, Will turned back to the child. 'Francie, I wish I could stop now, but I have to ask one or two very particular questions about the yard. You said you saw your grandfather kneeling. Where exactly was he?'

'By the door of the mill.'

'And where was Nicol?'

She swallowed but refused to give way again. 'Sort of half across his knee and half on the ground.'

'But you said... Hm. Show me.' She knelt on her right knee, the other raised with her left arm held up it as if cradling a child. It left her right hand free to wield the imaginary trowel. This time she did not strike, just held the hand in the air and looked up anxiously at Will. It was so graphic that all those who saw - only those in the nearest rows, although the rest craned and shoved hoping to catch a glimpse of her on the floor - caught their breaths in horror.

'Yes. I see.' He nodded at her to stand up again. 'How far away was that from where you had left Nicol sleeping?'

'Ach, yards! Well, maybe three. More than two anyway.'

'You said your grandfather was slashing. What with?'

'A trowel.'

'What trowel?'

'One of the old ones Lek gave us.'

'What for?'

'Grandfather uses them to pick out any pebbles that get between the grindstone and the workings. There have been an awful lot of them this while back.'

Will frowned. 'More than usual? Where do they come from?'

'Och, folk put them into the sacks tae bump the weight o' the corn. They ken fine they'll get away wi' it because Grandfather winna complain. Because of Nicol...' she tailed off, remembering the ghastly change in their fortunes which had been poor enough to start with.

The quality of the silence changed and chilled. This was yet another clear reference to the way the miller and his family had been victimised, and Will sensed that people were watching the Prior's reaction, which was making some of them very uncomfortable indeed.

'The trowels were grand for the job,' Francie added, missing the interplay.

'Describe them.'

Again she used her hands. 'Straight on one side and slanting on the other. See? The point was nice and...' She gagged as the implication of her own words hit her.

'So what happened next?' Will hurried on. Her face had gone grey.

'I... Grandfather... Och, Nicol was dead, you see.' Her voice threatened to rise almost to a squeak, but she punched her fists down at her sides to force herself back into control. 'He was a' still and, and… He looked dead. I could see he was dead so there was nae point in crying up help. So I waited. I - stayed where I was till Grandfather... He laid Nicol down and stood looking at him for a long time and -

then he walked through the blood and came straight for me! For a minute I thought... Then he just walked oot the gate and went down tae the burn and began to wash the blood off. He looked straight at me but never even saw me.'

The tears had begun again and Dolinda tensed ready to leave her seat, but Will caught her eye and shook his head slightly. This weeping was different, more composed, he sensed. He was right, for Francie mastered it and continued, hardly aware of the audience now.

'A' the time, he was making this terrible gruntin'. It wasna loud, just, oh, like a howl inside a whisper. Then he started walkin' up the burn.'

'Up? You mean beside it?'

'No, in it. Paddlin'. He fell ower twice that I saw but he just got up and went on - and on and on until he disappeared. And then...' She began to shudder again. This time Will's eyes appealed to his mother and she returned to put an arm around the child.

'Francie,' he asked, very slowly and softly, ' just one more question. Was it you who took Nicol to the River Lossie? Was it you who put him in?' Shivering once more she lifted her head and gave a firm, defiant nod. 'You took your pony to help carry him?'

'Aye. I put Nicol into the water just where my mother is. She'd have wanted that.' The sudden strength and confidence in her voice surprised many, and the content shocked them all. 'It was only right,' she insisted. 'She was the best one to have him then. She'd have looked after him. - And they shouldna have ta'en him out and buried him in the ground like that.' Now there was a rising rage in her which in turn horrified the listeners Her shrill voice rose even more. 'Now he'll never get to her. How's she going to find him now? They should've been together and... She's waited in the water all this time for nothing! Just for *nothing*!'

Dear God! If the softest of downy feathers had come rocking and twirling out of the sky at that moment, every person present would surely have heard it land. The child had no inkling of her mother's ignominious burial in the forest. Worse still, her water fancies were likely to stir up no end of trouble for her. The Christian community would react with disgust while those who still had leanings towards the old religions would be experiencing sharp fear at the forbidden paganism the child was suggesting.

Pain punched Will, causing such a wave of emotion to overwhelm him that he had to turn away from her, his own face contorting. Instinct made him turn towards the altar rather than expose his weakness to the watching crowd, but it was many seconds before he was able to master himself and face Francie again. It was Thomas who filled the breach.

'My child, it is only Nicol's body which we have buried and that has been laid in holy ground. Do you not know that our bodies are but caskets for holding our souls while we are on earth. When we die, our soul leaves it behind and returns to God. Like Nicol's has done.'

'And my mother's?'

'Yes.' Will spoke swiftly, his voice loud and firm, knowing none of the churchmen would ever dare. Amelia's death had been suicide, to them the greatest affront to God that was possible. Not even to give the child the comfort she craved would they have spoken. Her question had been so pointed that now he wondered if she did indeed have some notion of her mother's fate, and wanted to hear it denied. It was still to Will she was looking. 'Thank you for telling us everything, Francie. You have been very brave.'

Dolinda was turning her away when the Bishop stirred again. This time he was not to be baulked.

'Francie, why did you run away after, hum, putting your brother in the river?'

'I didna want to be with my grandfather any more,' she answered simply. 'Not after - that.'

'Why did you follow Captain Forbys?' She shrugged. 'Could you not have gone to your mother's family? To the de Chisholms, say, or to Lady Amelia?'

Francie gazed at the Bishop wide-eyed. During several seconds of agony, Will feared the gentleman was in for a very pert answer. After a deep breath she shrugged again and muttered something along the lines of Robert not wanting the likes of her around. 'Anyway, if my grandfather came back they're the first places he'd go looking for me. After the monks anyway.'

'Were you afraid...?'

'My Lord Bishop,' Will protested, his voice thick, ‘of course she'd be afraid. She was a witness to the, mm, miller's slashing of his grandson.'

'But that was not...'

'We do not yet know what happened immediately prior to what Francie saw. We may never know, especially as Brother Michael, the most likely witness, neither saw nor heard anything at that time.'

'What about the workmen at the mill?'

'I'm told there are none. Nobody would work there,' he added coldly.

'Well, at the glassworks.'

Will frowned, in annoyance at himself for failing to clear this point rather than in puzzlement, but he turned to Brother Michael. His response was immediate.

'I can explain. They were working with four vats of base liquid glass at the time, my Lord Bishop. The kiln was roaring hot and they couldn't turn away from it because the glass melds were coming up to the moment when they would change colour. When that happens, the men have to pull out all the embers from underneath the vats in order to cool down the glass in a hurry. It's always a scramble at that time. Dangerous too, as well as noisy. They'd have had no idea what was happening next door. Not for two or maybe three hours.'

The Bishop pursed his lips then sighed. 'Well, well then. But why follow the captain, Francie?'

The shrug was slightly bewildered. 'He'd protected me once already. And I didn't think my grandfather would think to look for me there.'

'But weren't you bonded to the Priory?'

'What's bonded?'

In spite of everything Will smiled at that. Every man, of course, had to have a master; every woman and child too. His own, when in Scotland, was nominally his father. Elsewhere his merchant status gave an exemption of sorts, but he was still most definitely answerable to the Danzig City Council and alongside them to the Hansa dignitaries. Like Father Jehan, who refused to leave him be today. Now this little free spirit was challenging the entire system with her innocence.

'She wanted to be my squire.' He held the Bishop's eye and kept his face and voice free of all judgment. The Bishop took a deep breath, raised one eyebrow and, mercifully, left it alone.

'And why did you run away from Mortlach, child?' Will knew his own eyes turned black at that, and held his own breath until Francie rambled, 'Same reason. Captain Forbys had to go back to Pluscardyn because your messenger was lost and I couldn't be sure he wouldna say where I was if folk asked.'

'But you went to his home at Druminnor Castle where he had arranged for you to go. Might he not have told that too?'

Francie looked at her feet. 'I wasna necessarily going to go there. I - was going to see if I could find a nunnery somewhere but...'

'But?' The Bishop's eyebrows were reaching for his scarlet cap. This was a character the like of which he had never met. 'But what?'

Francie looked along her shoulder at Will. 'He said he had five sisters and...' She chewed her tongue for several seconds before blurting out, 'I've never had sisters. I've never even had friends. Not proper young friends. Not really. Just Nicol and he didna count because he couldna even speak.'

Again the tide of pity threatened to choke Will but he shoved it back down his throat, biting hard on his tongue, and put an abrupt end to the Bishop's interference.

'When did you leave Mortlach?'

'Ten minutes aifter you did. I waited for yer horse to go by, then went the opposite way.'

In other words, long before Ranulf died. 'Then let's leave it at that.' A glare at the Bishop on his left then another, more of a look of desperation to Dolinda on his right, finished the questioning. 'Look after her, mother,' he pleaded softly.

With Lek and Hus disposed of as witnesses and, as far as the rest of the gathering knew, unreachable behind their screen of incomprehension, that left just the two novices from Mortlach to question. Cormac had come unasked along with the Bishop, anxious to meet up with David again. Strictly speaking their evidence was immaterial to Nicol's death, but the Bishop was willing to accept it on the same grounds as the entire enquiry was held, to crystallise what people had seen and heard as soon as possible after the events before subsequent happenings blurred the accuracy of them.

'I'll take this part of the investigation, Captain,' the Bishop announced, banishing Will to stand on one side by the Prior.

The sunbeam had gone. 'Since I have already questioned the boy who came to Elgin, I can take this one through the same information and we'll see if there are any discrepancies.' He raised an eyebrow at Father Symon who held his eye, then nodded. Obviously his Investigator had been present during the first questioning and would be able to confirm the details were correct or otherwise.

In the event, David acquitted himself very well, comfortable that he had told the truth on Sunday afternoon to the best of his ability. Will had a notion that he might have had a more kindly reception than the other lad, who now sat nervously at the end of the second row beside the two Crusaders. It was right at the end that the only misconception came to light, when the Bishop had finished his quizzing and asked if anybody had any further questions.

The Earl made his first contribution. 'Didn't any of you think to ask in the village of Mortlach if anybody had seen a stranger go through?'

'But nobody did! Er, my Lord.' David was surprised. 'Go through, I mean. It was from the east that whoever it was who did it must have come.'

'The east? But I thought you were looking out for the soldiers coming from Balvenie? That's to the west.'

'Aye. And that's why we were on that hillock. We could see over the village to the sweep of the road beyond it for quite a long way. But Father Ranulf had his back to that view when he began chasing us indoors.'

'You mean you were stacking these hurdles to the east of the village? On the other side of it from the peat bog?'

'Yes, my Lord. Anyway, if anybody had come through the village we would have heard them ourselves, for we were working with the door open and the road went right past it.'

'I see. So you are saying that whoever killed Father Ranulf came from the east and went back that way afterwards. Is that right?'

David nodded, and so did the other novice, both seeming certain.

'And none of you four boys saw or heard anything? No horse? No cry for help?'

Solemnly they shook their heads.

'Was anything stolen? Would you know?'

'Yes, we'd know. There's nothing to steal except the books and they're there still.'

It was while the Prior was closing the proceedings and offering refreshments to everybody that Camus stood up and scowled at Will. He was too late, for the Bishop had begun his stately procession towards the door, sailing between them and picking up a tail of followers who blocked their line of sight. Robert escorted his wife out, leaving Lady Amelia to find her own way along with Lady Euphemia. A small knot of men remained with the Prior watching the unruly exit of the crowd, now chattering and cawing like scandalised rooks.

Brother Alexander limped up bemoaning the numbers he would have to feed, which prompted Will to murmur, 'Let's hope for some loaves and fishes.'

'There's no need to blaspheme.' This came from Father Symon, but he was challenged by the taller Crusader, enormously tall even beside Will, but raddled and wrinkled by hardship and a hotter sun than ever shone in Scotland.

'He is correct.' Even the voice was arid. 'In the Holy Land they remember that this miracle came on the day after Passover. During the night before, they had feasted then set off into the desert, carrying their leftovers. Or the rich did, ready for an open air picnic. The poor had nothing, and it was the poor who followed Jesus out of town. The miracle was persuading the rich to share the food with the poor. Don't you think?'

The harsh voice was devoid of pity for either party in the story and the man looked as if all the juices in him had been sucked out long ago, leaving little more than a covering of skin on a sharply outlined cadaver. With his homily delivered he strode for the door. The Earl's face struggled to remain straight and it was while Will was trying to avoid meeting his eye that he noticed a third Crusader at the tail of the Bishop's train, this one, he realised with a shock, sporting a black cross on his white surplice. A Teutonic Knight, then, who had done his Crusading in eastern Europe. He turned and found Brother Daniel standing behind him, his half closed eyes fixed on the man's receding back. He was sweating with terror.

Letting the rest move away, Will remained beside Daniel, masking his state from the observation of others until they were alone. Ignoring the convention that a priest should not be touched, he laid unobtrusive fingers around Daniel's wrist, holding tightly until calm returned. A relative calm only. It would never be complete, Will realised. Holding Daniel's gaze, he was suddenly filled with revulsion by the inhumanity which some men were prepared to commit on others, especially in the name of God.

When he had recovered, Daniel raised his other hand, touched Will lightly on one cheek, shook his head slightly then made the sign of the cross between them with his free hand. Only then did Will remove his grip from the trembling arm.

He sighed. Then he tried to divert the man from his nightmare. 'I have a message for you. The Abbot has given permission for you to copy two sections from the book of Theophilus.' A blaze of delight filled the lugubrious face, then a look of uncertainty trickled after it when Will added,

'But Lek must consult his bit here. Neither the book nor the transcription must leave the Scriptorium. Oh, I shouldn't worry. I am sure Lek can read. And read Latin at that, though heaven knows how that came about. And I'm equally certain the Theophilus will get him into the church when nothing else on earth will. You'll see! But come and eat.'

Daniel smiled, then shook his head sadly. It was only then that Will realised, with a flush, that Daniel could not eat properly, that he was served softer foods when there was a deal of chewing required. It was Daniel's turn to touch him, a gentle, forgiving brush of the hand on Will's sleeve before turning him towards the doorway to join the cacophony outside, while he himself headed for the sanctuary of the Scriptorium.

Chapter 23 – Robert's Dilemma

Outside the day was clouding over, but there was nothing wintry about the gathering. To the relief of many, the Bishop had taken himself off with most of his followers including the three Crusaders. Otherwise town, country and castle had come to visit the Priory that day and were making the most of it. It was a very rare opportunity. Brother Alexander had excelled himself with stacks of pies and pasties, breads, biscuits, cheeses, roasted roots and smallcakes piled on the rank of trestle tables now erected inside the paddock. Earl Johnnie, heedful of the reminder of miracles, was ensuring that the plentiful supplies brought in his own train were added to the common kitty but agreed with the Prior that all ale should be well watered, if only to maintain a modicum of propriety among the wilder spirits.

Father Thomas had earlier given permission for several games to be set up in the wide sweep of level road by the North Gateway and provided bowls and skittles, which the younger novices were allowed to use on fine Sundays. A pole for ringing with horseshoes of various sizes had been hammered into one corner of the paddock and various rope or ball games were being played in another, mainly by local children. After the tension of the double enquiry, the funfair atmosphere felt unreal to Will. His mother was trying to persuade Francie to eat and drink, the Ladies Amelia and Euphemia were deep in earnest conversation and Camus and his Highlanders were hovering near the meat pasties.

Yes, Camus. As Will approached, the young soldier-soon-to-be-priest turned angry eyes on him.

'I'm sorry, Camus. I realised you wanted to tell me something but it was too involved. I was too committed to stop.'

'You didn't think it might be relevant?'

Will frowned. 'Is it?'

'It's certainly relevant to the Mortlach deaths. And wasn't it you who wanted to tie them up with Nicol's murder? Or were you more anxious to make Hector the scapegoat?'

My, but the lad was angry. 'Scapegoat? I wasn't pointing a finger at anybody. Today was just a matter of getting people's memories down on paper before they began to muddle things up. The trial comes later under somebody with authority.'

'And my evidence doesn't count?'

'Of course it counts. It's just that... Look, give me ten minutes, then we'll find somewhere to talk.' He had seen Robert de Chisholm sitting alone on the inner side of the bank where the old oak tree grew. Camus followed his gaze, calming a little.

'And that's the one you need to watch out for,' he warned.

'Why?' Will's nerves tightened.

'Because he was up at Auchdoun Castle on Thursday. A betrothal hunt, or some such. Went up on Wednesday with the rest of his family and seven retainers - leaving shortly after midday. They went up Speyside which is why it took a while for Seumas to find out, but de Chisholm came back on his own through Knockando on Friday. In a big hurry, barely two hours after you.'

Will digested that in silence. Auchdoun Castle was less than four miles beyond Mortlach. And there had been that horse in the blacksmith's field, thrashed to bits when hunting the man had said, and carrying traces of clay on its belly. A blue clay hardly seen in the Laich, so the stonemason had told him, but which Will had seen for himself up at

Mortlach, heaped by the villagers into a solid ridge between the peat moss and the treacherous bog behind it. Thinking about it now, it was that very ridge of clay, built up by the peat diggers to dry out their workings, which had probably created the bog in the first place by preventing the water from draining away.

'For what it's worth,' Camus added, 'Seumas placed you in all the places you said you were on both Wednesday and Friday. They're all laughing at the difference in your hair going up and coming down which made you very noticeable,' he added dryly, his customary good humour beginning to return. 'But Will, you can't sit on this information.'

'What d'you mean, sit on it?'

'You gave a pretty clear impression in there that Hector was the man who did it.'

'No!'

'But yes. Somebody with the strength, you said. Somebody with the skill and the knowledge of where to strike for a swift, clean kill. If you didn't say it outright, you implied it was Hector for you made it plain he had been a soldier, and a good one. You even let Father Gregory praise him as a bonny fighter. And Heaven knows he would have believed he had reason enough to kill the two men up at Mortlach, if he thought they had befouled his daughter. Oh, all right. Maybe the child's death does lie at his door, if he struck out earlier in despair. None of it's forgivable, mind, whoever did it. But you can't stick the blame on Hector just because you think he's dead already. It could still leave the real murderer in business and that could be - messy. Especially if he hasn't finished.'

Pensive and worried, Will said slowly, 'It's all true, what I said in the church. But that doesn't mean Hector is the killer. Just that he could be. We know now that he did slash at Nicol.'

'After the bairn was dead. Francie said Nicol was stiff and still and Michael said that the blood in the first pool was already very sticky. And your Brother Infirmarian said last Sunday that he thought there could be as much as an hour between the killing and the slashing.'

'Or as little as fifteen minutes. I wonder how he knows? For what it's worth, the Sheriff agrees with him after hearing what Francie said. But Hector could still have made the first blow as well, with Francie turning up when his regret set in.'

'I've more information that...'

'Sh.' Will pursed his lips seeing Lady Euphemia approach.

'Ah, *Capitaine*,' she said in French, 'your mother tells me that you are urgently needed in Norway.'

'Yes, your Ladyship. Well, in Scania.' He bowed, answering in the same language.

'Perhaps I can help. You will know that my brother, the Earl of Ross, has several galleys. He has always found plenty of uses for them, especially on the west coast, but this afternoon he is sending one to collect me from Finderyn to take me to Dingwall. Would you care to make use of it?'

Embarrassed, Will bowed again. 'That's most kind of you, your Ladyship. But what would you do?'

'Stay with Amelia, of course. Did you not know that she was my *maitresse*?' She laughed, watching him work out the relative ages. Lady Amelia, now in her eighties, would indeed have made a most suitable instructress for the highborn girl thirty years her junior. A very fine job of it she had made, since her pupil had been chosen as bride by two of Scotland's regents in turn, the second being the king elect. 'You have a choice, *mon capitaine*. Either take the small birlinn which is on its way. If this weather holds it might get you to Aberdeen late tomorrow in time to sail with your own fleet on the evening tide. Or we can arrange for a great galley - if there is one on this coast, of course - to take you all the way to Scania, or at least to Hamburg. You could ride across land to Lubeck and then cross by sea to Scania. Either would be a deal faster than your merchant fleet - and should get you there in time to escape Father Jehan's ire.'

'You must surely know him!'

She laughed again, gently. 'I know him. And I think you fear him more than he deserves. But we all have an interest in establishing peace, *n'est ce pas*?' He began to realise how formidable this gentle lady was. It left him with a plummeting heart, however, knowing that a visit to Bethoc was fading fast. Somehow he would have to find time to write a very persuasive letter to the lass.

'I - thank your Ladyship. I shall be glad to accept, according to what is available. And if the Earl of Ross is willing.' Somehow he knew he would be.

She laughed again, perfectly aware of his thinking. 'Then why don't you go and cheer Robert up.' She took him by the arm and turned him away from Camus. Will cast the bowing soldier a look of apology, mouthed, 'Later,' and complied with her Ladyship's wishes.

Robert was sitting on the bank head down, hands between his knees hanging like wet kerchiefs from wrists resting on his thighs. If Lek had wanted a personification of dejection, here it was. Or was it misery? Perhaps despair, guilt even. The Lady Euphemia gave Will a worried frown and left him to it; Robert, of course, had once been one of her own tenants when she had been the Countess of Murray, or rather his father had. Will was still working out the possible implications of the new evidence and had no wish to rush towards comforting the man.

Suddenly Robert raised his head and stared over the field towards Francie. 'Remind me nae to go to Mortlach for a *coiffure*. I canna say which o' ye is worse.'

'They'll baith grow oot soon enough.' Will sat down on the bank leaving a good two feet between them. 'I - came to offer a proposition.' Robert's back snapped straight. 'I, um, need somebody wi' land to spare.'

'Land!' Whatever Robert had expected it was not that. Will was not sure what to expect either. If not entirely unbidden, a weird idea was arriving ill formed from a distant recess in his churning brain.

'I want some trees grown.'

'Trees?' Robert's face crumpled in confusion.

'Aye, beech trees?'

'Beech trees?' The repetition was becoming stupid.

'They're bonnie trees with a cool hard wood and...'

'I ken what beech trees are. I've seen them grow in a sheltered spot doon in Galloway but they'll nivver grow through a winter up here.'

'I'm sure they will, ye know. I've seen great stands o' them far east in the Baltic lands and their winters are far worse than ever you get here.'

'What d'ye want beech trees for? They'll be nae use for fifty years or more.'

'Glass. It's, uh, a long project I'm planning.' Robert looked utterly sceptical and Will could not blame him. Had he gone completely mad? As he began to explain, he knew he was trying to convince himself as well as the bewildered man before him. 'You see, it's only beechwood which makes the very best fritted glass for high quality, coloured church windows. First of all it burns at the right speed over a day and a night for the making of the first glass mix. Then the clean ashes left over can be collected to make the next base batch while the first mixture goes on to another kiln to be annealed and painted, - or is it the other way round?' The information was straight out of Theophilus. He was thankful that he had been allowed a quick read of the appropriate chapters at Kinloss Abbey late the night before. Robert's scorn was beginning to waver in the face of this scant superior knowledge.

'And you want me to grow beech trees for this?' But not won over yet. 'While those goats in the kiln-yard twiddle their fingers for two generations, ye think?'

'Och, they're not...' Will caught back his defence of Lek and Hus. In spite of the description Michael had given of their exclusive attention to their glassmaking, any murderer might still fear that they had information to tell and wish to silence them. 'They're an unhappy pair, I grant you,' he temporised slowly, 'but with the right materials they might produce good enough work.'

'They're sodomists,' Robert growled. 'Didn't ye know? I wonder the monks tolerate them, I really do!'

It took Will several seconds to close his mouth. When he thought about it, there had indeed been the occasional sign. The sympathetic gentleness between the Balts. The soft laughter. But it was not his concern, then or now. It had nothing to do with their craftsmanship. The Prior considered that good enough to offer their work for sale. 'Father Thomas is already considering buying in mature beech wood to raise the standard of their work.' That was not quite true, but Will was determined to make it so as soon as he could pin the Prior into a quiet corner. Right then he could see Thomas talking with Johnnie and Princess Marjorie, who was providing them with barely stifled amusement of some kind.

'Where on earth would... Ah, you'll be providing the wood from the Baltic. Aye, aye, a merchant nivver sleeps, eh? And is that where you'd bring the young trees from? For the planting? How much would it cost? What would I have to pay? And the Earl would have to approve and all, mind, since it's his land in the end. - Na, na, Willie, ye're dreaming. My debts are fit to drown me already. There's no way I can join in such a flighty venture.'

'I'd be paying you, man.' That stopped Robert dead. Having said it, Will now found himself in uncharted waters. 'I see it this way.' He now had to make it up as he went on. 'Out by Rassie the other day, I rode past a few stumpy old oaks. I imagine they were all that was left after you'd sold the good stuff off. You're in charge o' that land, aren't you? The ridge that runs along the back of Alves as far as the Abbey's land? There's another stretch nearer Elgin in much the same sorry state, between Quarrelwood and the Pluscardyn farms. If you clear those areas and prepare them for planting, I'll pay you a retainer. The trees will be mine, but you'll be paid for their care as they grow. Interested?'

By now Robert was frowning ferociously, giving it serious thought at last. For the moment Will refused to consider the reactions of the other parties whose support would be vital to making this project work. Thomas might be amenable; after all the bulk of the profits from the glass would be his, or his successors'. Johnnie he was not so sure about. The Earl was shrewd and much more worldly, but he might still be persuaded that this could be the best use available for the scrub land. It was not much good for agriculture. The third party, unfortunately, would have to be the House of Bromse, and Robert picked up quickly on that.

'I thought you hadna any permission to spend?'

'I don't personally. This is Bromse business and I'd be their agent. Just look at it from their point of view, Robert. In the short term, they'll have a contract to bring the beech wood here for decades. In return they'll take away the stained glassware and sell it to churches and town halls throughout Europe, once they learn of the quality they'll be buying. They'll also ship you the young trees.'

'But the time tae plant is...'

'Aye, I know, March is the best month for planting, and I know the Baltic winna be free of ice to get them here in time for this March coming, but maybe the first lot can come from France. For now ye can get some nurse trees in, a few birks maybe, and rowan and alder. Or hazels would give ye an extra crop. Willows even, for the withies. Ye could plant the first lot of beeches in the most sheltered spots and I'd have the hardier ones here by the next season. If they were bagged and kept damp ye could maybe plant a bit later?'

'This is a huge thing! Na, na, I canna see our masters taking it on.'

'I don't see why not.' Will was beginning to believe in it himself by now. 'They sometimes do commit to long term projects, especially if they think Holy Mother Church will be interested, as I'm sure She will be.'

'This long term? If ye canna convince them ye'll end up as poor as me,' Robert growled.

'How poor is that?' It was out before he thought. In an effort to deflect the rudeness Will blurted out something far worse. 'Poor enough to divorce your wife so ye can marry money?'

'How in the Divvel did you...?' Robert shot to his feet, his face thunderous. A moment behind, Will was him furious with himself.

'I didna! Och, I'm sorry. But - the Prior asked me to witness a signing and… I didna see the content o' the letter, Robert, but your name jumped out at me from the last line. There was only one reason I could come up wi' for you to be mentioned in a letter to the Pope.'

Robert stood glaring at him, stone stiff with an emotion Will could not easily identify. After a long silence he said, very carefully, 'I love my wife, Willie Forbes. I love her. And I'll nae stand here and let ye miscall that. Nae now, nae ever. D'ye hear?'

Will swallowed hard, feeling a flush rise from the base of his neck. It was his own guilt which had driven the taunt out of him. He tried another tack.

'I suppose you'd have had to repay her dowry if ye sent her back.'

'She's from the Isles so it was all - things. Armour, dishes and the like. Nae money so it's all still there.'

'Couldn't you sell it?'

'Ach, it's all old-fashioned stuff. Besides, who's got cash to buy things like that nowadays wi' another call from John o Gaunt for a ransom payment.' After Robert's approach to the Prior about obtaining a marriage annulment, at any rate. When he learned of it, had he tried to prevent the letter from reaching the Pope? Had Will, who had carried the letter away from Pluscardyn, been intended to die instead of Hugo de May? Or had Robert believed that Hugo had been the bearer of it? But surely Robert would not be so desperate to recall the missive that he would have sunk to murder? All he had to do, if any dispensation did come through from the Pope, was to ignore it. Or marry Maura again. - Unless... Unless she had known nothing about Robert's action, and he wanted to keep the knowledge from her for fear of the hurt it would cause. And yet, there had been the desolation in her last Monday morning... No, she knew. Will felt sure of it.

'Would... Could Lady Amelia not help?'

Robert wiped his hands down to cover his face and sat down again with a blind bump. 'She has helped. After Nicol's funeral she told me she'd pay the ransom dues. Just like that. Nae pay back wanted. I canna ask for any more for my father and grandfather's dues.' He looked up to glare at Will's suspicious expression. 'I see the auld witch has been tellin tales so no. I didna kill Nicol tae rid us o' the burden o him, if that's what you're wondering. And Francie was wrong in there. I wouldna mind having her in the house at all. She's a bairn wi spunk.'

Will sat down again himself and stared at his boots, retrieved from his mother's groom. The silence became so thick that Robert finally burst out from behind his fingers, 'And she'd be safe enough wi' us.'

After a moment Will murmured, 'I suppose she would have to be.' The next bit was unkind, but it had to be expressed, if only to protect her. 'If anything happened to her you'd be the first suspect, wouldn't you, and smack in line for blame over the other deaths. Folk would think you really were killing them all for Francie's inheritance.'

Robert heaved a sigh and uncovered his face before saying quietly, 'D'ye think I hadna realised that, Willie? Ye didna have to put the ghastly thought into words.' After a pause he added, 'And it is Francie's fortune, nae mine. Although I gather I'd hae the use o it as long as I made sure there was a good dower set aside for her.' He found a twisted smile from somewhere. 'My formidable great-aunt must consider me an improvement on previous generations at any rate, if she trusts me that far.'

They sat in silence, neither paying much attention to the crowds across the field. The bells for None rang out, nine tolls, then nine more, and the monks disappeared from the field. It prompted Earl Johnnie to signal his trumpeter to blow for packing up while the Priory kitchen staff dragooned a bunch of local workers into helping clear the trestles and the debris of food. The parable's five baskets were left over and again this was distributed at the gate where the beggars had congregated, for once more in curiosity than hunger.

At last Will muttered the question which had been annoying him all the way through. 'I can't help feeling that things would be clearer if we knew who Nicol's father was.' The look he got was most peculiar.

'Ye mean ye don't know?' Robert shook his head. 'Then ye didna ask very far.'

'Just the Prior.'

'Aye, well, I suppose he would be discreet. Ye're the only one who doesna know so I'll tell ye and maybe ye'll understand it all. Nicol's father was Hector.'

'But Hector's his...' Hector! Will felt sick. Little wonder there had been so little sympathy for the man.

'Aye, Hector. Ye should know that Amelia, that's my cousin I mean, got to be very like Isabella as she grew to womanhood. After she'd let her faither down wi' Francie Hector took to drinking the strong stuff. Before that he'd never touched it, so I'm told. But when he was far gone he'd be convinced that Isabella had come back tae him. So now ye know.' Robert shrugged.

'She - ran away to Rassie, didn't she?'

'Aunt Amelia was in the Gowrie at that time, well away from here. - But my cousin came back again, this time wi' Nicol as well. I'm thinkin' Hector started drinking again about the time she - made for the river, though it took time to realise… the way he was. I'm dam' sure my aunt was beginning to fear for Francie as well and that's why she made her will the way she did, - just as soon as *my* father was dead. Otherwise he'd have found a way to suck up the lot and Francie would never have seen a groat and still be stuck wi' Hector and wi' Nicol growing bigger and more difficult to handle by the day. I'm tellin' ye this in confidence, Willie, but I think it's for the best, what has happened, horrible as it is.'

Will closed his eyes. It was still murder. Not just one murder. In a way Nicol's could be described as a mercy killing, if Hector had done it out of compassion for Francie, But three? The other two killings were of citizens of great worth to their fellow men. Neither the Bishop nor the Earl in his capacity as Justiciary would or could leave those unchallenged.

'So - you're saying it was Hector?'

'Didn't you say that in there?' Robert jerked his head towards the church.

'No, I didn't.' With a touch of exasperation he repeated what he had said to Camus, but now that he knew forced incest was involved, he had far fewer qualms about leaving the man to carry the guilt. He stood up. 'Ye'll excuse me. I've a letter to write and folk to see. If you're interested in my proposition let me know afore I leave, will ye, and I'll work out some figures for ye to decide on.'

'I'm interested. I have to be. What sort of sum were you thinking o'?'

Will had no idea just then. 'I - I'll let ye know when I've spoken to the Earl and the Prior. It'll depend on how much they'll help. Ye couldna meet me down at Finderyn at five, could ye?'

'I'll be there. But ye should know this, maister investigator. *I* didna kill Nicol - just in case that's what ye're thinking.'

'I'm not judging anyone, Robert. I was invited tae ask the questions, that's all. Till five, then.'

Camus had hovered by the gate throughout Will's spell under the oak tree. As soon as he left Robert, he was accosted.

'It must be serious.' Will did not feel as light-hearted as he sounded. Robert had not, after all, denied any involvement in the deaths of Ranulf and Hugo.

'I went to the blacksmith's this morning...'

'I noticed you were missing.'

'Will you listen! The nearest smith was busy so he sent me to another, Robert de Chisholm's. Yes, I thought that would get your attention. Well, while the work was being done I happened to lean against his bench and on it was a sword still hot from the forge. A bonnie thing it was, light and decorative. It would have fitted the hole in that cheese to perfection but for the spoon on the end.'

They looked at each other. 'Describe the hilt.'

'An Irish design, all twisted lines interlocking round the handle. I think they call the black design on it *niello.*'

'And you think the spoon had just been put on?'

'That's the bit that was hottest. And if you don't pass on that information, I shall.'

'I'm on my way to speak to the Earl right now. He'll be sitting in the judgment chair anyway so he'll need to know.'

'Not the Bishop? The Mortlach priest was his sub-Prior, wasn't he, and the other man was his messenger?'

'The Earl will still be involved as the King's Sheriff in the north. But Camus, I'm grateful for all your help. It's far more than I had any right to expect and I thank the good Lord that you were available when I needed you. - And I wish you well in France when you get there.'

The young man smiled, beginning to relax. His eyes were resting on the Priory buildings. 'Maybe the Lord meant us to meet so that I would be brought to this place. There's a particular kind of peace here, isn't there?'

'Hm. When I'm not around.' He was sharply aware of the turmoil he had brought into the lives of the monks and regretted it. 'I think they'll be glad to see the back of me.'

Camus's smile broadened. 'Very probably.'

Chapter 24 - Too Little Time

'Now, this tree-planting plan of yours. Written on your thumb nail with a pin, was it?' Will had been right about Johnnie's acumen.

'More or less.'

'Why?' Ah, the question he had no wish to face up to.

'The Prior is keen to build the three different kilns in the Abbot's book that are needed for the very best glass. Theophilus gives all the instructions. The details are precise and the glassmaker should have no trouble following them.'

'Ma wee laddie,' Johnnie said very softly, 'ye haven't answered my question.'

'He's also given me an order for Baltic beech wood, but those ashes are to be employed only for making the actual glass. In the meantime they'll use ordinary wood for firing the furnaces. - And no, I haven't answered ye, my Lord.'

A flicker of distaste flitted across the Earl's face. 'I haven't time to decide now. I'll think it through while I ride home and send you my answer before you leave Finderyn. Five, is it? That'll give us three hours or so. It'll give you time to reconsider the wisdom o' this.' Whatever had annoyed him, that last piece of advice was added with a ring of concern. 'Get it wrong, Will, and you could find yourself a disenfranchised trader without the backing o' your City Guild, from what I hear.'

'They'll have ample opportunity to give their approval or otherwise before the final agreement, my Lord. - You don't think I'm trying to cheat, do you?'

Again a flash of displeasure had twitched Johnnie's lips. 'No, but I thought you of all people wouldna feel the need to butter me up.' When he saw Will's blank expression he shook himself and gave a twisted grin. 'Och, I'm sorry, laddie. All day it's been My Lord this and My Lord that and I'm sick to death o' it.'

'I was only giving you your due! I - wasna sure how you'd wish to be addressed nowadays and I'd no wish to shame you afore others.'

'Where are the others now? Och, ignore my grumps. I've been at it too hard these last weeks. And I'm growing just as worried as you about this damned murder case. Am I right in thinking that you've more information than came out this morning? - Uh, I can see it in your face, laddie.'

'Ach, I don't know what to do for the best, Johnnie. If I tell you, you're duty bound to take it forward which could have unwanted repercussions. I could tell the Prior, or one of his priests, and they would be under the same obligation, and if I do it under the seal of confession I lay an unreasonable burden on them. I darena challenge the individual, or maybe it's individuals, concerned for fear of what they might do next out of fear. Or out of some other motive I haven't worked out yet. There are at least five people who are vulnerable because of the information they can give, and two, possibly three at risk of getting in the murderer's way for other reasons. - I see all that doesna do much for your peace o' mind.'

'And this daft scheme wi' the trees? What has it to do with the case?'

'I - suppose I'm trying to... provide protection. Hang a net around the good and the bad so that any risk of further killing is minimised.'

Johnnie looked at him as if he were mad, and indeed Will himself was beginning to wonder the same. After a long pause the Earl said, 'Well, see ye dinna strangle anybody with your net, yourself included. Till five, then.' He turned away, looking weary and worried.

Will's next stop was the glass yard. Lek had indicated that he needed time to make something and the furnace fire was still crackling as he entered the gateway. Not roaring, though, so it was the later stage of glass-making that was under way. He caught a glimpse of Hus slithering into their dwelling hut on hearing footsteps, his face glazed with terror, and Will wondered if the odd little man had been as shocked as Daniel at seeing a Teutonic Crusader in the Bishop's train. Lek looked exhausted when he ducked out into the cool fresh air.

'Been up all night?'

'We have. Making this for you.' He picked up two trowels, one in each hand, and headed back towards the kiln, reaching into one of the holes in the side. For the first time Will saw how the tools were used. 'I wouldn't usually lift it out when it's so hot, but this won't be for anybody else's use. It will probably break.'

'I can spare another hour.'

Lek shook his head, concentrating on sliding the trowels in from the sides beneath a piece of painted glass until the sloping sides came together to make a solid lifting platform. The glass lay on a softening bed of ash and lime on a metal plate over the flames. 'Needs overnight to cool but nivver mind.' Lek's Scots speech suddenly excellent, he turned round slowly, hovering with his burden before bringing it nearer to the door. 'I've never seen her before. But I saw her today among the crowd.'

'I thought you said you'd worked all night?'

'Oh, it wasn't me who painted her. I'm only the glassmaker.'

'You mean... Hus is the artist!' So that was what held the two together, a creator and a manufacturer each in need of the other's skill. Or that as well. And it had been Hus who had seen something last Wednesday. 'Brother Michael was convinced you were both far too busy in the kiln.'

'Sometimes it gets so hot that we have to step outside for a breath of cool air and a drink. Anyway,' the Balt sneered, 'we see more than they know. Like this lady here. Look at her. Do you know her?'

Will leant over to peer at the glass. It was the biggest shock of the day. There in the glass was another exquisite likeness, very small, peculiar in colouring and with bumps and bubbles marring its use for anything but identification, but the representation was unmistakable. Maura. Her expression was not unlike that of Monday morning on the hillside, a wildness born of despair cut through with an almost insane determination to do everything within her power to counteract whatever tragedy was about to befall. Above all Hus had captured, in spite of the strange colour, her ethereal beauty, the pale, alabaster-like skin against jet black hair. Beneath the surface, the intense, fragile spirit was on the brink of splintering. Or had the spirit already fractured at the moment when Hus saw her?

Shocked, Will put a hand over his eyes. Conscious of Lek's curiosity and scorn, he kept it there while he thought. Then his head went up. 'Hus is too small to see over the wall.'

A sharp new respect widened Lek's eyes. With slow care he carried the glass image to a bench of sand and laid it down, trowels still beneath. Then he headed towards the wall between the two yards and bent down to about a foot below the top. There a hole opened right through the stonework and, when Will ducked to look, he realised it would have been possible for Hus to see where Nicol had been lying against the far wall, and to see anybody who had gone near the child.

'There's more.' Taking two more trowels, Lek removed another image from the furnace. Robert de Chisholm, this time, looking frantic and frightened, as if struggling to keep his wits about him. His presence in the yard did not surprise Will, but he was reassessing the reasons for it. 'I've seen him around plenty times,' Lek added. 'And I knew the third to be Francie's other uncle. He came quite often.' Concentrating on getting the third image safely to the cooling sand tray, Lek had no need to check Will's dismay. 'He came twice that morning.'

'Twice! You mean the Bishop's messenger? Hugo de May?' He swore quietly, a seaman's crude curse without realising it. Hugo's image looked far more contained, frowning, controlled, but with a turmoil of less easily defined emotions still hinted at beneath. The artistry was near to magical.

'I need to know the timings,' Will muttered. 'Is it possible? Will you ask him?'

Lek gritted his teeth at that and his nostrils flared in doubt. Then he grimaced and turned away, signalling to Will to stay where he was. He was not to follow. The low moan within the kiln fire masked any specific words exchanged, but the tones of the voices suggested that a great deal of persuading was going on, gentle but insistent, even anxious, against a strong, frightened resistance. As he waited, Will was drawn to the kiln. On entering the building which housed it, he was struck in the face by a wall of dry heat. More used to the chill of ocean winds, he soon sweltered and his leather jerkin began to prickle his skin through his shirt. Little wonder they had to seek relief outside now and then.

The furnace construction was rough but sturdy, and he realised there was one more piece of glass in the oven, larger than the others, its picture still annealing above the furnace hole. Annealing? Was that what Theophilus had said? As the others had been, it was laid on a metal plate but cushioned against cracking with extreme heat by a soft bed of ashes and lime. Lek must have spent the entire night at work. First he would have made the original mixture, melding, and fretting the sand and ash and lime; the cylinders of glass would have had to be blown, then cut and laid flat until cool enough for Hus to illustrate before firing began again. There would have been no rest at all for either of them.

Will ducked out for a few moments of coolness then went back to peer at the last picture. Even as he watched, the colours were slowly changing, but it looked as if this would be a face in *grisaille*, shades of soft, creamy grey, and it was round. As his brain absorbed the details, he gasped, partly in sheer delight at the perfection of the picture, partly overcome by a tearing grief. Nicol had been regenerated, an angel of shocking beauty but utterly devoid of any expression whatever in the eyes or face. That emptiness was such a piercing contrast to the wealth of human cognizance in the other pieces that Will found himself weeping.

Those sudden, spontaneous tears were probably his passport to the last pieces of the puzzle. Outside, Lek had just ushered an unwilling Hus towards him. Immediately, they realised that he had seen the roundel, watched him wipe his tears with his sleeve, gesture towards the kiln in a helpless sort of way and raise his palms towards the sky for a moment as he turned to Hus, overcome with admiration. The little man stopped shaking, stopped resisting Lek's urging and gazed, frowning, at Will's face before nodding, just once. He looked like a wide-eyed baby sparrow hovering in uncertainty, just about to take fright. The care with which Lek took his hand away from his arm was revealing, too.

'The timing. Who came first?' Will asked hoarsely. With Lek interpreting, Hus told them that Maura came first. From the Priory bells, he thought it was just after eleven. He had seen her come into the mill yard, catching just one glimpse of her face as she leant over Nicol before her blue dress obscured the child from Hus's view. The dress had swished and trembled, turned and glided away and Hus had returned to the kiln without waiting to see if Nicol had wakened.

He thought she had gone back to the road. A few minutes later, from the door of the kiln, he had seen - this time from the middle of the yard without the need to use the spy-hole - a horse and a flash of blue high on the same hill path which Camus and Will had taken a few nights before. Heading back to Quarrelwood? She would have doubled back to the northeast once over the ridge.

Within minutes of seeing her up there, he had heard hooves and a man entered the yard. Back behind his spyhole, Hus had watched as this visitor, too, had bent over the child, then knelt for a minute or so on both knees, as if praying. This time there was no dress to obscure his vision, just two booted feet when the man stood up, and between them he had a glimpse of Nicol, lying still asleep, or so he had thought, as still and beautiful as a marble carving. Yes, he was exactly where Francie had left him sleeping. Or... Maybe a foot or two farther away from the far wall. Perhaps he had wriggled forward in his sleep. No, the spyhole limited his view from seeing any blood. And yes, he was lying on his right side, facing Hus with his head on his arm.

'How long was there between the two visitors? Can he give an estimation?'

Ten minutes, maybe fifteen. Then there came a third visitor, again wearing riding boots. No, not sea boots. They all looked at Will's footwear with the heavily oiled patina required to resist seawater. These riding boots had just ordinary waxing which did not darken the leather. Both pairs had been dusty. Both had been on large feet. And both had knelt for long moments by the sleeping Nicol. Hus had seen the faces as they rose to leave. There they were on the glass creations. But...

Here Hus became agitated. He could not remember which had come first. They had been no more than minutes apart; at the time he had no inkling that there would be any need for him to remember the details afterwards. A pictorial record had lodged instantly in his memory, but the timings were vague. They were merely folk coming and going in the yard next door. He had known about the fracas which Will had interrupted earlier in the morning. - Had he not created Will's image as it was at that time? - But he had had no expectation that trouble might swirl out of it.

'Is it possible they could have come together? Perhaps one coming in then sending the other to see what he had found?'

Hus listened, thought hard, shook his head. One had come from the north, off the main road running under the hill. The other had turned in from the southern, more minor road and gone away the same way. It was unlikely that they would have met.

'Did he see any weapons?'

Hugo had certainly carried a business-like sword and the expected dirk had been stuck into one boot. Yes, a normal man's defensive sword. As far as he saw, neither had been drawn, but his line of vision through the gap was restricted. And yes, the other man and the woman had indeed carried a weapon, but it had looked like the same one.

'The same one! Can you describe it?'

For answer, Lek turned away to the kiln again, this time to search among broken debris as he had done when looking for Will's image, eventually coming up with three pieces of painted glass which he held out on his open palm, already fitted together. Maura's sporting sword. Its hilt of Celtic *niello* work was unmistakable. It matched Camus's description of the weapon lying warm from the Quarrelwood forge. It matched Will's memory of the spooned tool hovering under his nose on Monday morning, with its slender blade just right for fitting the hole left in the sleeping child, but for the spooning of the tip; and with the point of its twin hidden in the leather scabbard hanging by her side.

'You're sure they carried the same one?'

'Or two that looked the same. He's certain about that.' But no, Hus could not remember whether it was the second or the third visitor which had carried the lighter sword. Not that it mattered. It could only have been Robert carrying it.

Will turned away, sick at heart. He also recognised that none of this made it easier to decide what he should do now, how he ought to react, who to tell. Something told him that Hus would flatly refuse to give evidence in any open court. If coerced, he might go mad with hysteria. Even Lek, a far more phlegmatic character, might jib at it. Will suspected Lek was much more worldly and cultured than he pretended to be. Daniel might be able to persuade him, but the evidence would still be second hand and therefore less convincing. Besides, given that these two were considered both pagans and sodomites with no benign feelings for the world in general and the local folk in particular, their evidence might not be believed anyway.

He walked up and down the yard for a few minutes struggling with the decision making. They both watched him intently. Coming back to them he prevaricated. 'Let me thank you for all your work. I think you understand that this is dangerous evidence and that you should keep it well hidden for now. I don't mean that you should destroy it, but keep it away from any chance of anybody else seeing it. Is that possible?'

Lek grimaced.

'Suppose I ask the Prior to send up a lockable box with Daniel? - There's no need for suspicion. The Prior has shown considerable trust in you already. I hope he will agree to buy in a reasonable quantity of beech wood for your use. He is also talking about providing the means for building all three of the furnaces which Theophilus describes - although I think he has something smaller in mind. What's more, when Daniel has copied the section you need, as the Abbot agreed he could, you are to have full access to it whenever you wish. Uh, in the Scriptorium only, though. They all insist that neither the book nor any transcribed part of it should leave the Priory.'

'Knowledge is power. I know,' Lec muttered sourly, torn between delight and misgiving. 'Especially if you are the only one holding on to it. How can we be sure that once the new kilns are built we won't be turned out .'

'With your gifts! Don't be daft. It's more a question of you being poached by other glass teams as soon as the quality of your work becomes known. Then the Prior's investment in you will vanish into thin air. I won't swear to it, but I think he is considering releasing you from whatever bondage you consider yourselves under. In fact he was surprised that you considered yourselves bound to the Priory. No, maybe he does expect some commitment, but he certainly objects to considering you slaves.'

Lek stared, then turned and gave a rapid translation to Hus, who looked equally sceptical.

'Father Thomas is - likely to offer you a contract,' Will added. 'If I were you I wouldn't turn it down in a hurry. Look, I - know that you face, um, particular, er, social, difficulties hereabouts, but things might change a little for the better now. You could always try adding one or two requirements of your own in the contract. Do a bit of bargaining. I'd offer my services if I'd been staying longer, but you might find that the Earl of Murray is an ally.'

Lek translated that too, and little Hus began to shiver, then fled back to his hut. 'And what do you want in return for all this good fortune,' Lek growled, disbelief so ingrained that he was hanging on to it.

'Just keep those images safe. Fix them together somehow so that they remain recognisable, then pad them and pack them into a box along with written details of the circumstances, and the times they were seen in the mill yard. And if you insist on keeping up pretences, dictate it to Brother Daniel - Oh, no. You can't, can you? He can only copy.'

'Very well, I admit I can write.'

'And account. I saw your order book the other day. You were using a system of two cross-checking entries per item which is so modern that I have seen it only once before, in an Italian document. And I suspect you understand Latin, my friend Lek, for you used the Latin word for beech when I didn't understand you. Father Thomas recognised it immediately. By the way, this might be to your advantage. It turns out that he is passionate about trees and loves the forest here. Before he became Prior he had been studying their culture, so there is another link between you. Now, I must go. May God be with you.'

Whether you believe in Him or not, but he added that to himself as he headed for the gate. Almost the only way Lek could have gained the education which was becoming increasingly evident was through Mother Church. Will did not dare to speculate on the details of that, or its tragic outcome.

'Oh, and seal the box. Tell Father Thomas to open it only if something happens to either of you.' He paused. 'Or to Francie. Other than that tell him nothing about its contents.

Will you do that?' Then he added, 'Show them to Brother Daniel. He'll look out for you.'

Back at the Priory the flattened paddock was empty, guests, monks and beggars dispersed. Will packed his gear and arranged for James to have his horse ready in half an hour's time. His next step was to ask the whereabouts of Brother Michael. He found him praying in the same chapel where Nicol had been laid to rest before burial. The young monk heard his footsteps and looked up, unsurprised.

'Is it possible, Brother Michael, that your brother Hugo could have killed Nicol?'

'Of course not! He would never murder anybody!' Indignation brought him to his feet.

'Not even for Francie's sake? Not even if he realised that that was the only way he was going to get Francie away from her grandfather and the impending danger he imposed? Never in a thousand years would she have left her brother uncared for, and while others might have taken her in, nobody wanted a Devil's Bairn, did they?'

'I - don't know what you mean.'

Will was very angry by now. 'Francie is growing up fast and I am told she is uncannily like her mother. Like her grandmother, too. I have also been told that recently Hector has gone back to drinking the firewater he'd been drowning himself in when he turned his amorous attentions on Amelia. - Which fathered Nicol on her.'

'You - shouldn't listen to gossip.' The riposte was half-hearted.

'What did Hugo and Ranulf do when Amelia killed herself, Brother Michael? When she was buried unshriven in an unknown grave? Did they just accept it all without a murmur? Did you?'

'I - hardly knew her. I was in Dunfermline Abbey.' Then he burst out, 'But I would have been here with them if I had known.' Suddenly he, too, was angry. 'What do you think they did! They came back to Elgin, of course. They were furious with Hector to the point of murder themselves, both of them, and they were none too pleased with the decisions of the Bishop either.'

'Not the Prior?'

'He was off in France, and it wasn't Father Gregory's fault. Anyway the family was at the Bishop's Mill at the time. It was only afterwards, when Francie became hysterical every time my brothers tried to persuade her to leave Nicol, that Hector was brought here and I was installed next door. And... and I let them all down,' he whispered in an agony of guilt. 'How can God ever forgive me?'

Will watched him wipe his hands down over his face, struggling for control. The action made him look very young and vulnerable, although he was probably a couple of years older than Will.

'Why didn't you tell me that Hugo had been up at the mill twice last Wednesday morning?' The question was sharp because he did not like being lied to, especially a second time after the first lie had been uncovered, in public too.

'Twice?' Michael's expression was blank.

'Once shortly before two, yes. You have admitted that, as he did. But what about the visit about two and a half hours earlier?'

'Earlier?'

'You must have been at the kiln then.' As he watched the blood flee from Michael's face he began to wonder if it was Hus who had lied, or been mistaken.

'But... how could he have been? He had been chasing all over the countryside looking for you. You said so yourself. You said he told you so.'

Will held his breath. So he had. 'That's what he said,' he pondered. He thought through Hugo's movements, murmuring them aloud as Michael listened in growing horror. He had gone to Finderyn first, then back to Pluscardyn when there was no sign of Will at the harbour. Only after talking with Michael around two had he gone back to find where Will had turned off to the south. 'He might already have been at Finderyn that morning,' he added, 'and realised that I wasn't coming when the tide turned without my fleet preparing to leave.'

They looked at each other, realising that none of his movements conflicted with Hugo being at Pluscardyn at the time Hus had said. 'Are you sure?' Michael whispered. 'I - can only think that he came while I was helping in the kiln to give one of the others a break. Perhaps - they can tell you.' He must have realised where the information came from. 'All I can say is that I did not see Hugo then.'

After a long pause, Will asked the question which neither of them wished to address. 'I'm sorry, Brother Michael, but – under the threatening circumstances I have described, do you still think it impossible that Hugo could have killed Nicol?'

Michael dropped his head to his twisting hands, watched them grow still and the knuckles bulge white. 'Not - impossible.' Then he flung up his head. 'But very, very unlikely. If he did, it would not have been in anger, and it would have been as - compassionate as possible.'

'The killing blow was compassionate,' Will pointed out softly. 'A single blow straight into the heart while the child was asleep.' It gave him an irrational comfort. 'Thank you for being frank. But I agree it's unlikely that Hugo was the killer. By the following morning he was dead himself, wasn't he. And Ranulf the very next day with what seems like an identical blow.'

'What is to happen to Francie now? We can’t be sure it was Hector.'

'No, we can't. I have talked with the de Chisholm family and my mother and now I ask your permission as her uncle. Are you willing to let her be fostered for a while at my own home? My mother’s? She would be safe there, I promise you. She would grow up away from places which hold ugly memories for her – among other girls too.'

'Somebody will have to tell her that her father is dead, and Hugo.'

'She already knows about Hugo.'

'But - you think she had left Mortlach before Ranulf was killed?'

'I'm fairly certain of that. Will you agree to let my mother or perhaps Lady Amelia do the telling? I'm sure everybody will help to keep her in touch with you. - If that is what you wish.'

'Of course. She is the only relative I have and - I am very fond of her. But she may not want to remember my betrayal.'

'I very much doubt that the thought of betrayal has entered her head.'

Chapter 25 - Decisions

He left Michael to his prayers and climbed up to the Scriptorium. Daniel's face was glowing as he studied the diagrams Theophilus Presbyter had drawn over two and a half centuries earlier. Gregory had been reading it to him, translating from another section of the book, not on glass but on recipes for pigments for painting on paper, his own craft.

'Brother Infirmarian would like to see you before you go, Captain,' Gregory informed him. 'I'll take you down.' He showed no disapproval when Daniel and Will clasped four-handed in a firm farewell. 'And there is a box in the Sacristy which Daniel can give to Lek.' Both monks had kept their curiosity hidden at his request, but Will was acutely aware of it.

Once alone with the Sub-Prior, Will dared to ask a painful question. 'Father Gregory, was it you who decided where Francie's mother was buried? She died while Father Thomas was away in France, didn't she?'

'She did.' The old man needed no help on the hazardous steps down into the church, secure in his own domain.

'Do you believe she killed herself? That she intended to die?'

The old man stopped to cross himself. 'There was no doubt.'

'And? I know she was buried in a forest. The nearest forest to where she died would surely be the Royal Forest of Pluscardyn. Somebody must have decided where. And somebody must have taken her body there and buried it.' When Gregory remained silent, he flung out, 'Is that not where Hector will be found? My guess is that he'll be there with his daughter. Hanging from a branch, maybe. Or with his own knife in his heart or across his throat.'

Gregory's eyes fluttered and closed. 'Do you imagine I have not thought of this, my son?' It was almost an admission that he did know more.

'And you intend to leave him there to rot?'

'What else do you expect? He - believed in the spirits of the forest things. I have no doubt that he wanted to return to them, to return to his daughter if he could. If there was any Christian belief left in him after all he did, perhaps he would look on... on whatever he has now done as a kind of atonement.'

'Would it change your view if I told you that he did not kill Nicol?'

Gregory stopped, one foot inside the church door, one outside, his half-blind eyes searching Will's face with a doubt he no longer tried to conceal. 'Are you sure of that?'

'Between ourselves, yes, I'm sure.' The old man sighed, almost shuddering with the depth of it. 'Father,' Will added softly, 'I believe he went with you to bury Amelia. That he was the one who dug his daughter's grave, and that you were compassionate enough to allow him to choose the spot. If you are right, if he has rejected the Christian faith in the way it must seem to him that Christianity is rejecting him, he will have returned to the old ways he knew. They bury a suicide at a point where the lands of three lairds meet, don't they? Even the Christians have taken over that habit. The Church has made of it a punishment, saying that no landlord wishes to accept them because of their sin in rejecting the life given by God, that mankind regards them as outcast for what they have done. But the old faith says exactly the opposite, doesn't it? That it gives the departed soul a triple chance of reaching their heaven, their Land of Eternal Youth, their Tir nan Og.'

Gregory's eyes closed again and agony lined his face making it older than Will had yet seen. 'Please, my son, do not blame me for following the ways in which I believe, even if you may doubt.'

'Blame is the last thing I wish to heap on you, Father! But - I think I know now where to find Hector. And I think he went there in grief for all that had happened, not guilt although that must be there too. I believe he went straight from the mill yard on Wednesday. He had nothing to do with the death of either Hugo or Ranulf.'

'If you think you know where to go, why not - let it be known.' The old eyes reopened, alert once more, and calming.

'Is that what you wish?' Will asked the question anxiously.

'I - think it may be what the Lord wishes. He has told you where, has He not?' A moment later he added, 'And look out for little Francie, Captain. You will, won't you?'

It had not occurred to Will to wonder who was looking after Brother Infirmarian in his sickbed. The Infirmary stood detached from the rest of the buildings, with an adjoining chamber specifically for mixing physicks, and its own small kitchen and chapel. In the sickroom a fire was burning and the sole patient lay near a bright window but not in direct sunlight. Even since Sunday the flesh seemed to have melted from his old bones and Will felt a jolt in his chest, realising that he may not live much longer. Brother Gregory patted his friend's hand, said farewell to Will and left. It was only then that another figure stirred behind Will, a monk he had never seen before.

'Brother Sebastiano,' whispered the old man, his voice almost gone. Will stood up as the guardian bowed then went about his business. A silent anchorite, then, still more strict than the rest, renouncing the companionship even of his fellow monks. Here, apart from the sick whom he tended, he had found a hermitage away from the world. 'His study is the use of plants in medicine.'

Will remained fifteen minutes with Brother Infirmarian before seeking out the Prior who was thinning the June apple crop in the orchard. He outlined what had happened since Thomas left the paddock for his prayers. 'I - think I should keep to myself the details of the evidence the glassworkers gave me. For the moment. Do you mind? I shall tell the Earl everything, though, and that you are keeping the box safe.' He went on to assure him that Lek and Hus were likely to remain loyal to the Priory even, he hoped, to the extent of signing a contract to that effect.

Thomas was surprised enough about that for Will to wonder if he did not, after all, know of the rumour Robert had passed on. Or was he ignoring the suspicion of sodomy out of compassion, or considering it unproven out of convenience? Heaven knew, there was nowhere else in Christendom where the two Slavs could find a home while under such a suspicion.

'I shall miss you, my friend.'

'And I shall miss you, Thomas. But I can't help feeling that you are also sorely missing the peace I've managed to shatter so badly.' They laughed together and parted amid gentle promises of correspondence and future meetings. Brother Stephen appeared at the last moment with Justin in tow, the Cantor wishing him God Speed in rank disobedience of his vow of silence, which everybody else was ignoring today. Even Brother Alexander was at the gate, long faced and pessimistic. When James would have hung around after his own expressions of gratitude, the Cellarer gave him short shrift, not wanting a witness to the last farewell.

'Well, Captain, you're off again.'

'I am, Father, and taking my conscience with me,' he added solemnly.

'Still no penance, then? No, you're not the kind to change your view just because of a touch of adversity. I'll grant you that. But the Lord will be travelling with you every step of the way, whatever you may think. At least be aware of the possibility, young man. And may He keep your conscience alive and kicking.'

'With spurs on?' Will kept his face straight for long enough for Alexander's glare to melt into amused self-mockery. Then they, too, laughed together. 'But Father, to be serious, I - would not discount the possibility. One day I might return to ask for that penance.'

'I'll look forward to that!' The voice was dry, but the gnarled hand on his arm and the eyes on his face were benign, and it gave him a deep pleasure. What a difference a week could make.

As he rode off, he marvelled at the fine quality of these men who had renounced the outside world and its rewards in order to gather together in the demanding peace of Saint Andrew's Vale. He himself had still not decided what to do about the information the glassmakers had given him, one item giving him particular pain.

At Finderyn a clutch of folk were hanging around waiting for him. He was late again, for it was already nearer six than five, but a longship is independent of the tide, unlike a sailing vessel. The ship bobbing beside them, however, was too small for the open ocean, having only three pairs of oars.

The Lady Euphemia was standing on the pier talking to a tall, hirsute man older than herself. Her brother, Earl Walter of Ross, Will realised with surprise. Normally he did not travel beyond his own lands these days, or not into wider

Scotland because of his affront at the King over the latter's high-handedness in marrying off the Earl's daughter to a crony without the Earl's agreement. With them stood Johnnie, Earl of Murray and, hovering to one side, Robert de Chisholm. Farther along the shoreline he saw, to his surprise, his mother and Francie deep in conversation. Beyond them, wandering alone and gazing at the blue hills across the Firth, was Maura. The wind was blowing her hair across her face, weaving it like wisps of strangling seaweed.

'I have a great birnlinn in Inverness,' Walter Ross announced in French, the Gaelic lilt in it much stronger than Euphemia's. 'For the sake of the peace they are trying to fix in Scania, I offer it to you willingly, but I cannot get it here before tomorrow morning. Is it to be Hamburg or Aberdeen?'

All four men turned and looked northeast. They could smell the change of air coming out of the German Sea. The steady, gentle south-westerly which had been stroking them during the last few hours was gone. 'Temperature's dropped,' Will grunted. 'I'll stick to Aberdeen, if you can get me there by Friday afternoon.'

With the decision made the bearded Earl nodded, turned on his heel, bowed to Johnnie and escorted his sister to his craft. Within minutes they were well out to sea, the oarsmen pulling with a precision which had the land folk watching in admiration. They would be home on the other side long before dusk. If only life could be handled with the same smooth expertise.

'Ye'll bide the night then, Will? Your mother will be glad of time with ye.' This was Johnnie.

'Aye - and I've just remembered. Can ye let me have parchment and ink? I've a letter to write.' Both of them were conscious of Robert's hovering, waiting to be noticed. It took all Will's self-control to remain casual as he asked, 'Well, Robert? Have ye decided?'

'I have, if his Lordship is willing.'

Johnnie looked at each of them in turn then looked again before giving a single nod. 'But I'll be keeping an eye on the whole thing. I want full reports from both of you at every step. - Ah, Mistress Dolinda. Aye, he'll bide wi' us the night and is off for Aiberdeen in the morning.' As he led her to her horse, Will turned to Robert again, naming a price for the first stage of the wood clearing. Glad of anything, Robert was surprised that it was as much as stated and was quick to do the deal. The paperwork would be exchanged as soon as possible and the moneys paid by the end of October to enable the land preparation to get under way during the winter. And the King's dues to be paid.

Wary of further contact with Will, Robert took himself off across the sands towards Maura, by now a lonely figure far along the beach. The sum Will had offered, after a clandestine word here and there, would cover a fair proportion of the de Chisholm debts. He hoped it would leave Robert less likely to yearn after Lady Amelia's riches, or to wish to filch them from Francie in turn.

He intended to have a word with the old lady in any case. For her own safety and the child's, he would ask if the wording of her will might be adjusted, and be known to have been changed? It should state a different guardian, or a second or joint one, for Francie and her inheritance, when she received it, the Prior perhaps. Robert had too much to gain from such a trust and Michael's control was weak, shut off as he was from the world in which Francie would have to live. Robert could still have the management of her affairs and could benefit from a certain proportion of it. Then he wondered if these ideas might come better from his mother, who had already done business with the old lady and whose advice might already be trusted. She had far more tact than himself and the last thing he wished was for Lady Amelia to be offended.

He was already wondering if Amelia was too shrewd to miss his manipulations when a small hand slipped into his.

'Aye.' He looked down at the direct gaze before letting his eyes linger on the spikes of black hair. 'Was that really necessary? The walnut ink? It'll tak ye weeks to get rid o' it.'

The gaze wavered and she swallowed. 'Maybe.' As he turned her towards her pony she asked, 'Can I come wi you?'

'To Scania? No lassie, I'm sorry. I'll be up to me ears in papers from morning till night, and anyway the Hansa merchants don't allow women into their houses and Faktories. - I thought you wanted to join my sisters?'

'I do, but it's second best.' He hefted her up into her saddle. 'I like your mother,' she added. 'She's nice. Very nice.'

'Mind you behave there. She's also very strict and will expect you to try hard at the lessons she's bound to give you.' From the sudden grin he got, he realised that was not going to be a problem.

All the way to Jamie's Darnaway hunting lodge her pony dogged his so that there was no chance to talk private details with Johnnie or his mother. Her ears would have heard everything. He could not even ask his mother if Francie had been told about Ranulf's death.

The lodge itself was a crowded castle in a noisy, boisterous bustle which Will suspected was its normality, a sharp contrast to the silence and serenity of the Priory. Again, wherever he went, except to the garderobe which was a great deal less salubrious than those at Pluscardyn, Francie was again on his heels. A couple of times he exchanged an anxious glance with his mother over her clinging and finally resolved to take the child away and talk to her. There was certainly no privacy to be had inside this place.

'Come on. Earl Johnnie tells me there's a heronry on the riverside. Want to see it?' Delighted to have him to herself, Francie came, and they wandered down through gigantic oaks to the wide meadow by the banks of the Finderyn River. Nobody followed. Taking the only chance he would probably have he was opening his mouth to explain her history when she spoke herself.

'I canna go wi' ye, but you could be my godfather.' Her eyes were wide and blue, blue as the evening sky. He stared at her.

'D'ye know, that's quite a good idea.'

'Aye, I know. Even if ye werena here, folk would know ye'd still be lookin' out for me. You're important. They widna do me ill wi' you to answer to. They'd know you'd come after them if they did.'

He was still staring. 'Do ye ill? Why would anybody do ye ill?'

'They did Nicol ill, didn't they?' She was looking uncertain.

'You - seemed to think it was your Grandfather who killed Nicol. Have ye changed your mind on that?'

'He couldna have killed my Uncle Hugo.'

'Agreed.'

'But somebody did. I heard the Balvenie Highlanders saying his body had been found wi' a hole in the back like the bairn's.' Memory hit him like a bolt in the forehead. Of course. The child could understand Gaelic and Seumas and his fellow had been hanging around the Priory gates today where she would have overheard their talk. 'They said bairn. And... and they said the priest and all.' Her hand was back in his, this time dragging on it with a tense reluctance to face the truth. But already she half knew what he had brought her here to tell her.

'Oh Francie... Oh, lassie. Ye've heard more than ye were meant to. But aye, I was just about to tell you that it wasna your grandfather who killed Nicol, whatever else he did.'

'He was likely just... so... fed up that it had all gone so bad,' she decided. The quick comprehension of it knocked Will's composure just as much as the resignation which was already setting in. 'And when Hugo got lost in the bog... Ach, I think they meant me to think he was my father but I knew it was really Father Ranulf, only he couldna be a proper father because he was a priest. Just the same way Michael canna look after me now.'

At that moment a big, lumbering bird heaved itself out of the reeds on the other side of the river. As they watched it tuck its long neck into a snake for flying, Will searched for some way of giving the child comfort. She appeared to know, or guess, almost all of the story. Yet, in spite of her uncomfortably adult sangfroid, he knew that underneath she was as vulnerable and disorientated as any child would be. Why else was she within an inch of him all the time?

Into the sweet air she dropped the final question. 'Did he kill Father Ranulf and all?'

He? 'Father Ranulf is dead, yes.'

'How? When?'

'Friday morning. Maybe a couple of hours after I left Mortlach - and after you left.'

'But you thought I did it!' Her voice rose in scandalised affront, sending up another heron from the marsh edge. 'And did they think I'd done it to Nicol? Is that what my grandfather thocht?'

'No, of course not!' Oh, if only he could believe that. But Francie needed to.

'They all wanted me to go and stay with Robert and Maura after my mother - died. But nobody else would look after Nicol, so I wouldna go. I wouldna ever leave him. I loved him. He was my brother. Why would I go and kill him now?'

'Exactly. There would've been no sense in it.' She was making such a good enough job of convincing herself that he kept quiet.

'That was when we went to Pluscardyn, and Michael came back from Dunfermline Abbey to... to be near us. - He's very gentle, my Uncle Michael.' Had he been too gentle? Unable to cope with Hector's failings, unable to reprimand, too unworldly to comprehend the depth of the miller's despair? It was a pity that Hugo, a much stronger character, and secular in his calling, had not been persuaded to take over the children in some way.

Hugo's position in all this was an increasing puzzle. Now Will wondered if Hugo himself had realised that Francie's position at the mill was becoming dangerous to a point that was beyond Michael's ability to manage. Could he, then, have decided to cut the tie which bound her to her grandfather? The killing had been compassionate, or as compassionate as had been possible. Nobody could deny that. But he could not possibly have killed Ranulf because he was already dead. And why did they die? No. That idea was a wisp of thistle.

'What's going to happen to me?' Francie's head was laid on his chest. He reached an arm around her and stroked the hair off her brow, giving her comfort as he had done in the hall of sleeping soldiers at Balvenie.

'You are going to grow up to be a happy, well-educated lady with lots of friends all over Scotland.'

'Will I be safe?'

'I'll make sure you are. You know, Francie, I think you always were. I don't think that anybody wanted to do you any harm at all.'

He did not dare ask who she thought might wish her ill, but he was fairly certain she had cast Robert as the villain who had killed Nicol. Probably she added Ranulf to Robert's tally, convinced that her father was the most likely person to persist in any investigation, especially if Francie insisted on one, as everybody would expect of her. Most other folk would let Nicol's sad death slide away into oblivion, seeing it as a mercy. But again it left Hugo's death unexplained.

That was cleared up later in the evening. Most of the retainers' bairns were off home to bed, thoroughly wound up by the unexpected excitement of the day. Quite a few older folk had also turned in, distinctly the worse for wear from the carousing which had continued after the party had returned from Pluscardyn. Will sat in a corner to write his letter to Bethoc, still with Francie curled up beside him. It proved a bigger challenge than he had anticipated. After discarding far too many false starts for the Earl to be pleased at the waste of material, Francie started asking questions.

'Write her a poem, then. Would that do?'

He grinned down at her. 'That's another good idea!' It took him over an hour but in the end he composed an ode for Bethoc which he hoped would let her know exactly how he felt, then sealed it up and delivered it to his mother whom he found in Princess Marjorie's chamber.

'There have been visitors, Willie. I think you should speak to the Earl. Francie, dear, you should be in bed.'

Johnnie was just retiring to his solar when Will caught him, then noticed young David from Mortlach was with him.

'I thought you went back with the Bishop.'

'Aye, but Father Symon sent me with a message for the Earl, and for you if you were still here. He says to tell you the bodies of Father Ranulf and Hugo de May have reached Elgin. He says that Father Ranulf's wound is just like the bairn's one but that the messenger's is not quite the same. And the Almoner says that the messenger had money in his bag that he was to deliver to Father Ranulf and that it looks as if the money and the bag have gone missing.'

'A lot of money?'

'I think so. It was for buying stone setts for repairing the kirk at Mortlach.' Little wonder Hugo had not wished to hang around at Balvenie, then, with the place full of acquisitive Highlanders. 'And there were other wounds on Hugo as well, he says, probably dirk wounds. He'd put up a struggle, so maybe the other folk were cut about too.'

'Give him our thanks, David.' So that explained Hugo's death, but not his two visits to the mill yard.

The other visitor was Michael. Hus had remembered something, or corrected something. Although the men who had come into the mill yard had approached from different directions, both had gone off the same way, to the north. And he thought one of them rode a horse with a loose shoe. It seemed irrelevant, but Will knew that was a rash assumption in such an investigation.

'Which one?'

'He thinks it was the man who came in from the south.'

'Hugo?'

'I don't remember any loose shoe on his horse. He wouldn't have set off across country without seeing to it.'

'Then there is our answer about how he filled in the time between the two visits. He went to the blacksmith. Which would he have used?'

'Probably the Priory smith across the bridge. - No.' Michael frowned as he thought. 'No, maybe he was too busy that day. He'd begun to repair a set of cogs for the mill which had been twisted by some idiot putting stones... Well.' He shrugged in sudden embarrassment. 'If the smith was in the middle of that job he wouldn't want to leave off. He'd have sent Hugo to his brother at Quarrelwood.'

'Carrying his bag,' Will murmured softly. Johnnie, who had already been given the initial messages, was watching him, not Michael. 'Well, we know from Daniel's drawing that the Priory smith was the go-between for Brother Mark and the Bishop, probably for a comfortable fee. I wonder if those two men realised that Hugo was carrying money? I wonder if either of them, or both, maybe, joined Robert de Chisholm's party in their trip up to Auchindoun?'

'The Quarrelwood man certainly,' Johnnie interrupted. 'Any hunting party needs a smith around because somebody always loses a shoe off his horse.'

'Hm. That could explain the blue clay on the horse's belly.' He explained about the hard-run animal in the smithy field. 'There were two sets of horse tracks either side of Hugo's animal, so either the smith took his brother, or he found another helper. The Bishop might try looking for his money near Pluscardyn, eh?'

'A crime quite separate from the killing of Nicol and Ranulf,' Johnnie concluded. Turning to the two young Dominicans, he offered them food and a bed for the night. It was too late to set out again. 'Right then, ma wee laddie,' he jerked his head to Will, 'we'll just have a run round the house before we turn in.'

For a bit of privacy, he meant. There were still far too many folk bumbling around in spite of the late hour. Oh, for the stillness of Pluscardyn, yearned Will.

Chapter 26 – Endgame

'So, who did it? And what do we do about it?' The Earl was brisk, which was nothing like what Will felt. Once more, he had said nothing about Maura. Her presence in the yard would be uncovered only if the box of glass pictures was opened, or if Lek told somebody else about Hus seeing her there. Will was fairly sure he would not.

When Will remained silent, Johnnie went on. 'Hector? I think not. Or if he did kill Nicol, he didn't kill Ranulf, for there is no sign of him going anywhere after Francie saw him leave the yard.'

'I think he'll be found where the lands of Pluscardyn, Kinloss and your own estates meet. Or what's left of him.'

That made the Earl draw in his breath. 'Aye, ye might be right. I'll see to it in the morning.' After a pause he continued, striding ahead of his guest through the untidy kitchen garden towards the stables. 'That leaves us with Robert and Hugo. It could have been Hugo, you know. There was something steely in him. Pragmatic, if you like. If he saw no other way to free Francie, and if he truly believed her to be in danger of the corruption her mother suffered, I believe he could have taken action.'

'But that action? He was a servant of the Church, after all.'

'That doesn't make him short on feelings or failings. Willie, all I'm saying is that he could have killed Nicol. For Francie's sake.'

Could have. Was Johnnie suggesting they let that idea take root in other people's minds, even if they themselves felt it was incorrect? Hugo was dead, after all, and no longer accountable. The same was true of Hector. It left the death of Ranulf unexplained, however, and the Bishop was never going to turn a blind eye to the murder of his own Sub-Prior. It also left two other possible killers, both in the right place at the right time, both with access to the probable murder weapon.

'Robert de Chisholm, now,' Johnnie muttered. 'Do you think it can be proved against him? He was there in the yard. He was up just four miles from Mortlach. He had the right kind of blade, you say. But if it now has a spoon on it I reckon his blacksmith is never going to admit to doctoring it. Or if he does, he'll swear blind that he did it months ago.'

'Especially if he has something to do with what happened to Hugo. He won't want any finger pointed at him for any reason, in case other questions are asked.'

'And the glassmaker's word alone puts Robert in the yard? He might not be believed.'

'I canna see him testify either.'

'So you've done your best to tie Robert up in this tangle of beech trees and commitments. - Ye're daft, ma wee laddie,' the Earl murmured, 'but I think I see what you're at. But mind this. I am the King's Justiciary in the north here. It's my job to uphold the law. That's why I'm here.'

A few moments passed before Will asked, 'Not to administer justice?'

'Not that old chestnut, Willie, please. – Come on round here. I want to look in on the dogs for tomorrow's hunt. - No, no, laddie. If I were to let Robert off the hook, I'm certain the Bishop wouldn't, if he had the information to convict. Barr's freedom to buck canonical law is even less than mine with a civil case. - Unless...' Johnnie swung round and peered at Will in the growing gloom. Nearing midnight, the summer colour was leaching out of the world around them. 'Ye havena told me everything, have ye?'

Will said nothing.

'You think maybe it wasna Robert?' When silence was still his answer the Earl, sounding unsurprised, sighed. 'That doesna leave many to choose from, laddie. In fact only one I can think o'.'

'Robert tells me he loves his wife,' was all Will would say.

'Enough to kill to keep her? Or to kill a second time to take the blame she holds for the first, if they're linked? I think Francie was right. Ranulf would not have left Nicol's murder to lie un-investigated and in the end the killer would have been discovered. He had to die, if only to prevent that. Why do you think the Bishop will be any less determined to find the killer of his own priest?'

'He might not look in the same direction. After all, who was to know whether Hugo had the money in his bag at that time, or whether it had already been passed...'

'Hugo never got there, ye said.'

'We - don't know that. But it could be that Ranulf was guessing who the thieves were, and when he saw them ride into the village he sent the laddies in to their books so that he could challenge them in private. If it were the smiths, they would come from Auchindoun, wouldn't they? From the east as the laddies said?'

The Earl gave a bark of laughter. 'I'll gie ye this, Will, ye're inventive! It's almost plausible. You might yet pull the net over the Bishop's eyes.'

'I winna be here.' This sounded thoroughly sour.

'Uh! You expect me to do the job? Ye've a nerve, ma wee laddie, more than ye used to have.'

'I'm not asking anything of you, my Lord. I've far more respect for you than that. Just...'

'Judicious silence at the right moments, eh?' Johnnie picked up on it all; the wish to protect the unnamed individual, though the name now hovered between them, and the likely reasons for the deeds done; the lordly title, used in resentment. 'I asked ye something earlier, Willie, when ye spoke first about the trees. Ye didna answer. Why?' After a long pause he added, 'It's a risky business, being involved with another man's wife.'

'You're making assumptions. I've a lassie o' my own, as you know fine.'

'Aye, I saw the waste o' my paper,' came the dry retort. ‘Ye might at least hae re-used it in yer practising.’

It was only after they had checked the dogs, patting and spoiling them before returning to the castle, that Johnnie gave a verdict of a sort. 'Well, well, I canna do much until the Bishop makes his move. And I canna make promises, Willie. But think on this. I've no wish to lose a good steward. From what I've seen him achieve even since March, he's ten times better than his father ever was. It's just a pity he has nae bairns to follow on.'

And there he said it all. They both knew it. That was the motivation for Robert's move towards divorce, in the hope of finding a second wife who was not barren. Next day in Earl Walter’s tossing birlinn, Will wrestled with the problem all the way to Aberdeen, hating the conclusions he came up with and fighting their validity.

On the day the letter to the Pope was dispatched, Robert would finally have been forced to tell Maura about it. From the northwest she was, so Robert had said. That meant she came of Celtic folk. A cast-off wife would go home insulted, possibly degraded in the eyes of her family. The only alternative was a nunnery and Will's instinct told him that she would quickly wither under such restrictions. She was a wild spirit, used to riding the hills and walking the shores. Besides, she may well have nursed the same vein of distrust in the Roman church which Hector had displayed. Maybe, too, she had a superstitious fear of the Devil's bairn which Amelia had birthed; that, he sensed, was why Nicol was not welcomed at Quarrelwood, even for Francie's sake.

So what had happened last Wednesday morning? An explosion of rage? Hysteria? A numb realisation, at any rate, that Nicol was still the sticking point and a move to eradicate it. Him. From their Celtic design, the sporting swords were part of her dowry; her personal possessions whose use was very likely familiar to her, for she had been wearing them, and also wore fighting gloves on Monday morning. She was there for the purpose of using them, practicing as if accustomed to them.

And so last Wednesday she had taken the one which still had its point intact, had ridden to the mill and had stabbed the sleeping child. What then? Had Robert discovered her on her way back? Perhaps realising she was missing as the party prepared to head up the Spey Valley, he had gone out to look for her, had sensed even then that she had headed for Pluscardyn. Yes, he loved his wife, but he may also have realised that she was unstable, at least on that day. What would he have done?

Whether or not he had met her coming back and got the truth out of her, he had gone to the mill to check on - Nicol? Or Francie? The contents of Lady Amelia's will was already known to both husband and wife. Perhaps he feared that Maura would kill Francie, or had killed her, in the hope that Robert as the only other surviving relative would inherit Amelia's fortune. If that happened, the need for money would be less urgent and the marriage might be saved, for there was no doubt that wealth in a new wife in Scotland as it was then was as critical as child-bearing ability.

No doubt, too, it was Robert who had the sword spooned as soon as it could be done surreptitiously. Before that, however, he must have left Nicol in the yard hoping that

Hector would carry the blame, having seen him around. He and Maura had then continued with their plans, gone to Auchindoun for their hunting party and... And what?

One of them must have killed Ranulf. Not the thieves who had murdered Hugo the previous day, Will was certain. Why on earth would they have come back to the village so near where that murder and theft had taken place? Robert at least would have known that Ranulf would search for the truth over Nicol's death, if only to pacify Francie. Had he killed to stop that happening? But surely he would never have used the same tool which had been used on Nicol. It was far too close a linking of two crimes and, whatever else Robert was, he wasn't stupid. But he might have voiced his worry over Ranulf to Maura.

Was that it? While Robert was out hunting, with others who would no doubt vouch for his presence all day on Thursday, Maura must have slipped away and headed for Mortlach carrying the light sword. By that time Hugo was dead, and Will and Francie had arrived and told Ranulf about Nicol's murder, neither of which Maura could have known in advance. Ranulf was not stupid either. Yes, his first assumption was that Hector was responsible, but as soon as he sensed Will's doubt he had looked at other alternatives. His biggest mistake had been sending his novices indoors when he saw Maura on the road. He alone had been facing east from which she approached. Perhaps he had wanted to speak with her, ask questions, even soothe her, without inquisitive ears around.

Perhaps it was the voicing of the very suspicions she feared that drove Maura to strike again. This blow was identical to the last. Whether or not the stabbing of Nicol was a lucky strike or done with enough previous knowledge to ensure a quick kill, she was skilled enough in her swordsmanship to repeat the exact process.

It could have been Robert, of course, but honesty made Will think not. The evidence of the Auchdoun huntsmen could settle that question. At any rate Robert had ridden back home just an hour or so after Will on the Friday, leaving the rest of the party , including Maura, to a more leisurely journey back down the Spey through Rothes and Elgin. Did Robert know what had happened to Ranulf? If not why was he so keen to get back? To silence Will? But no. It was to find out the reactions to Nicol's death, of course. It must have been a shock to him when he heard that the child's body had been fished out of the river, but he had learned that before coming into supper with the Prior and had come to terms with it. Will's comment about Nicol being skewered had been accepted with no more than a pause. If Will had mentioned the slashing, that would surely have made Robert panic.

By the time he had boarded his personal vessel in Aberdeen Will had accepted Maura's guilt. Robert, he thought, might have been an accessory, but he felt it more likely that he was left with the role of covering up, legally just as culpable.

'Ye'll be late for your clerking business in Stralsund,' Geordie Buchan growled, his bald bowl of a head glowing. 'Father Jehan winna be happy. Where the divvel have ye been?'

'To Hell and back.' That was so fervent that Geordie bit back the sarcasms he had nursed for days.

'Weel, at least ye found a king's vessel to get ye this far, so we'll nae complain, eh? Are you captaining this beastie or am I?'

'You are.' That told Geordie just how upset Will was. 'Carry on. Ye ken as well as I do there's a storm coming up. And I need to think.'

There was one last question which Will had to address, and he was half way across the German Sea before he could force himself to do so. Why was he so anxious to protect Maura from the rigours of the law? Reassessment of the facts convinced him anew that she was, beyond doubt, Nicol's murderer. She was by far the most likely killer of Ranulf too. She deserved to face punishment, however hysterical and unstable her actions, whatever her motives, whatever the circumstances which may have driven her to take the actions she did.

But wriggle as he might, Will had to face up to one more fact. She might also be carrying his child. By condemning one he would be condemning the other. Was this, then, to be his penance, to live with the spurs of his conscience pricking him daily?

'Aye, Brother Alexander, how right you were,' he whispered to the torturing storm. 'What a mess I've made of it all. Now I've no choice but to live with it, whatever the consequences.'

HISTORICAL NOTES

A Riddle:- *Nine mills were built on the River Lossie as it flowed past the royal burgh of Elgin. One belonged to the Valliscaulian monks at Pluscarden Priory and by royal decree they were allowed to build it on the east bank because of the way the current flowed. The river marked the boundary between Priory land on the west and Elgin Town Lands on the east, so this mill stood on the town land although it belonged to the monks. To complicate matters the monks hired a miller who was a bondsman of the Bishop. When the tithes and taxes were collected as usual at New Year (25th March) – who would get the money?*

This historical confusion is indicative of the problems leading to the rivalry between the Bishop and the Prior in this book. One hundred and fifty years earlier the then king, Alexander II of Scotland, wiped out the last of the constantly rebelling Northern royal faction. Following his grandfather's example when David I established Kinloss Abbey, a Cistercian house, in 1150, Alexander granted permission in the 1230s to the Dominicans to build a cathedral in Elgin and to the Valliscaulians from Champagne in Burgundy, France to found Pluscarden Priory just four miles away. The latter he kept in his own hands because the land was in part a royal hunting forest. To this day there are occasional echoes of the legal confusion King Alexander deliberately created in Moray.

Alexander also removed the local Celtic magnates, sending them elsewhere in Scotland, (those who survived). Replacing them with outsiders, mainly Normans and Flemings, he gave them land and responsibilities but with their acres parcelled into small lots scattered everywhere.

These were interspersed with similar pockets of liturgical land, ensuring that neighbours would not be overfriendly with each other. It was a jigsaw of small holdings within a rich area, a maze of scattered church benefices interspersed with minor estates, each with its own tower or demesne. A stronghold of a different political colour arose every few miles along all the roads, each keeping an eye on its neighbours and never quite trusting them, rendering all of them too busy defending their own property to band together as a threat to the crown.

Pluscarden Priory was burned in 1390, probably in May, two decades after this story and it is likely that documents were destroyed. As a result it is not certain what the internal decoration was like, although the Valliscaulian Order was Spartan and private in its habits. The building plan was based on that of the mother church in France and the original outline was certainly very similar to what is seen today, a building of stark beauty contrasting with the Gothic glory of Elgin Cathedral, now a ruin. Elgin Cathedral and a considerable number of other major church establishments were deliberately sacked and fired very soon after the fire at Pluscarden and it is not known whether it was part of the same desecration by 'wild highland caterans'. Surviving material, whether from the damaged houses or from elsewhere, provide names, events and many small legal cases, leaving a vivid picture of the pre-fire buildings and the life they supported. Most are in Latin but many were translated in more recent centuries, mainly by Presbyterian ministers who were amateur historians - which means that care must be taken over the interpretation of some elements in the English versions.

Bishop Bar (Barr/Bur/Burr – all spellings appear) is well-documented as a historical character at the forefront of Scottish history for decades. There is brief documentary mention of Thomas Fullonis, the Prior, with suggestions that a Father Gregory may have been a former Prior. In later decades there was a Douglas prior, the post which my fictional Brother Mark, also a Douglas, hankered after, by which time the Valliscaulian Order had given way to the Benedictines.

Today, after centuries of abandonment, Pluscarden is now a thriving Benedictine Abbey, the only working monastery left in Scotland. While still a prince of the Church, it is no longer the case that the Abbot sits in Parliament. It is a place of peace and beauty and welcomes visitors from around the world. And it sells honey from its own bees.

A last thought, the book borrowed from Abbot Richard of Kinloss still exists. Look for 'On Diverse Arts', written by Theophilus, a monk and practising craftsman around 1122, available and useful even today in translation from the Latin. And the cover of this book represents the colour of the fragile stained glass the glassmakers in the story are trying to produce. A fragment of glass this colour was found at the site of the Priory kiln chosen for this tale. There is no solid proof that mediaeval Pluscarden produced church glass, although it did in recent times, but fiction writers can surely claim licence to make assumptions.

The Amber Curse

Book 2 - A Will Forbys (Villi Vorbus) Enquiry

Chapter 1 A Ship in Sight

The old man dropped his head into his hands to shut out the light of yet another unrewarding dawn. Waiting was excruciating, especially when he did not know exactly what to expect, or why it was not arriving. How often he prayed that when he died he would go straight to Hell rather than spend time in Limbo. He did so now as the warm waxy beads of his rosary slipped between his fingers.

Several minutes later, light footsteps tripped down the stairs and a tentative knock drove him to shake off his despair and adjust the ledgers before him. The amber comforters were whipped out of sight.

'Come.'

A boy of about nine crept round the door. Some of his tallow hair stood on end in a cockscomb, leaving the rest a matted yellow felt ball.

'Just out of bed, Grif? Again?'

'No, Papa Zach! - Well, yes.' The child blushed and straightened his smock while the clerk raised an amused eyebrow. 'But we've sighted a ship! I thought you'd want to know.'

Zachariah tensed. 'We?' He struggled for calm. 'Where is it?'

'In the bay. Approaching along the spit from the east.'

'Ah. - How could you possibly see a ship so far away?'

The child blushed again, although the boys could see a long way from their sixth storey bunkroom at the top of the trading house. 'Well, it wasn't us actually. It's market day, you see.' Grif looked anxious. He had gone out without permission.

'I know.' In spite of his distress Zach suppressed an urge to laugh at the child's aching similarity to a flustered chicken. 'As does everybody else. So?'

'But some farmers have come in. They saw the ship in the moonlight. It was before the mist came down at dawn. On its own, not a convoy. They're telling everybody! It's not pirates, they said. They'd never seen this one before but it's flying the Danzig banner, they said, so it must be one of ours.'

Fingers of apprehension clutched at the old man's throat.

'Mustn't it?' the boy persisted. 'It must be Villi Vorbus's new ship that he got made in Bergen. It's what you've been waiting for, haven't you?' It dawned on Grif that the old man was upset, and now that upset him. 'Isn't it, Papa Zach?' he whispered. Grif reached out and brushed the old man's hand with his fingers, as if a human touch would help Zach to recover. Then his anxiety surged back. 'But they won't be able to get into harbour, will they? Not even if it is one of ours. All Hallows Day is past. Won't the chains be put across the mouth of the river by now? Won't the flares and bells be back in the sheds for the winter? They won't know where the safe channel is!'

'Yes, they will,' Zach soothed, turning his hand up to clasp Grif's. 'I'm sure that Villi, - who is Heer Vorbus to you, my lad, - will have Geordie Buchan on board and

Geordie is the best pilot in the whole of the Baltic. And Villi's not so bad himself, when he's paying attention.'

'But the sandbanks keep changing. You said so yesterday.'

'And they'll have lead lines on board for plumbing them. Don't worry. I spoke to Heer Kluk the harbourmaster and he agreed to leave everything where it is until the end of the week. There's no sign of icing up yet.'

Grif shivered. 'Just as well. Fancy getting stuck in ice out on the sea. They'd either have to stay there all winter or try walking over the sea to the land and you'd never know which bits are thick and which aren't. They've left things very late.'

'Yes,' the old man murmured. 'They have, haven't they? And so have you, you rascal. You should be at your lessons. Oh, very well, you may tell Brother Simon that you had to deliver a message to me and that I request him not to punish you. This time. If you sleep late tomorrow, you might find yourself with an extra beating from me as well.'

Little Grif had just enough sense to hide his grin of disbelief until the door was closed.

Printed in Great Britain
by Amazon

32495808R00215